PSYCHIATRIST, DISTURBED

A NOVEL

JOHN R. LION

Paperback ISBN: 978-1-09836-655-1
ebook ISBN: 978-1-09836-656-8

SINGULARITY PRESS

Printed in the United States of America

I thank Joseph Cowen, Carolyn Everly, Barbara and Mort Kesler, Jennifer Kraus, and Bill Reid for early readings of this manuscript. My late wife, Jill, was a constant source of warmth and encouragement. Arlene Falke edited the work and rendered much support.

The hospital and its characters are fictitious.

Prologue

"So, Vanderpol asked me," which is worse for a child, to be neglected or to be abused?"

I hadn't the slightest idea. Unfortunately, I knew a lot about the former, but had only heard about abuse from patients. I pondered the question. "Both," I ended up responding.

"Of course, of course, but which creates more damage?"

"Psychological damage? Physical?"

"Both can stunt growth," Vanderpol stated. "But I'd pick neglect."

'Neglect.' The word made my pulse quicken. I searched Vanderpol's face for an explanation.

"Neglect is pernicious. You're alone. Robbed of human contact, you withdraw. We humans need another to survive. The brain must have some connection. My theory is that the brain grows if it has someone to talk with. Otherwise, it shrivels."

"I had a hamster as a kid," I said. "It lived by itself in a cage with one of those activity wheels it could run on. It survived. It seemed content."

"I'll bet you played with it, let it out of its cage, petted it. You fed it. You didn't ignore it. Now, let's say we have a football coach who fiercely demands high performance from his players. He makes them practice day and night. Yells at them, even threatens them. Or maybe a scientist who insists that his graduate student works intensely for long hours and repeat the same experiment over and over again, almost to the point of cruelty. And the student on whom he inflicts this hardship goes on to become famous. Is that abuse or is it character building? How about a nasty military sergeant in boot camp who bullies—"

"I wouldn't call these things abuse," I interrupted. "Abuse hurts. Rape. Beatings, shoved a dark closet. Tortured."

"Even then, there's interaction."

"Dr. Vanderpol," I exclaimed. "Next you'll be telling me that abuse is therapeutic."

"Time for lunch," Vanderpol suddenly announced as he looked at the clock. "We'll have to continue this discussion."

These weren't discussions. Vanderpol, I was learning, had a need to spout forth provocation like a geyser as he graciously ushered me into the alien world I had chosen.

Chapter 1

I remember my 7th birthday very clearly. My mother gave me a cupcake with butterscotch frosting into which she had inserted a lit white candle. I blew it out with one puff and she clapped. She didn't hug me. When I looked at her face, I saw but the slightest smile, as if forced. She told me the cupcake was from the diner where she worked, and it was a customer favorite. It was my last memory of her. I never ate another cupcake.

Several days later, she disappeared from my life. No, disappeared from my life is a euphemism that spares me pain. The truth is, she committed suicide. I had sensed, to the degree that a young child could, that she was unhappy in her marriage to my father. Her unhappiness washed over onto me, and manifested itself in her withdrawal from both of us.

It wasn't until years later that I was able to look back on a profound experience during my junior high school years that left an indelible mark.

The local zoo was hosting a 'Meet the Animal' program and I was lucky enough to be selected to participate. I was assigned to the elephant exhibit and worked with the elephant keepers to help with the chores. Each elephant had a specific handler and I was assigned to a gangly and unshaven man named Hugo. He wore a Yale jacket and a Red Sox cap.

"Did you go to Yale?" I asked him.

"Barely made it out of high school," he grunted. "Been working here at the zoo for years. My education, you might say."

Hugo was devoted to the beasts which towered over him. He would stroke the elephants' trunks and they would return the affection with a rumbling that you could not only hear but feel. Hugo favored one animal named Betsy who had a one-year- old daughter, Ramona. The pair were inseparable. Betsy was a caring mother, always caressing Ramona and never letting her out of sight. But Betsy became ill and stopped eating. As she weakened, she could no longer stand proudly and succumbed to lying on the ground, helpless. Her trunk became curled and inert. Ramona was distraught. Her plaintiff cries could be heard throughout the zoo. As the veterinarian ministered to Betsy with injections and fluids, Hugo tried desperately to arouse some reaction from her. After the vet left, he would offer her peanuts, her favorite treat, but she became unresponsive. More consultants were brought in, yet Betsy became more and more lifeless and ultimately died. Hugo stroked her cold, thick body and sobbed openly when a tractor came to haul her away.

I watched all this with both reverence and confusion. I had seen people worship their dogs and cats, but never an elephant. It seemed so hugely bizarre and unnatural to me. I had a dim sense, though, that Hugo had been as much a healer to Betsy as any of the medical staff who had come and gone with their medications. He had been able to give her comfort.

Ramona was now without a mother. Hugo became her caretaker. He spent hours touching and singing to the orphan. Ramona sought him out constantly and followed him about for reassurance. She even tried to climb onto Hugo's lap, wrapping her little trunk around him. Once, when Ramona had digestive difficulties, Hugo stayed with her the whole time, even sleeping with her in her stall and massaging her side. When she recovered, Hugo smiled with joy and sang aloud with delight.

As Ramona grew bigger, Hugo started to introduce her to the rest of the herd. He knew she needed to be with her own kind to thrive. This took much patience as Ramona often balked at joining the other elephants, preferring to be with Hugo. I was curious and perplexed by Hugo's persistence, but he pointed out to me that his early connection to Ramona was a crucial element for her early survival, but now she needed more.

"You really like the elephants," I said.

"You think it's strange?"

"A little," I said. "Ramona seems to like you a lot."

"More than that. She needed to attach to me." Hugo explained that it was important because her mother had died and she was too young to be alone.

"You gotta connect. You gotta connect with someone even if it isn't your mother so your brain can grow, like it's been fertilized." Hugo intertwined the fingers of his hand. "Ramona's become attached to me. Her mother's gone so I take her place. It's called bonding."

'Bonding' was a new word for me. The closest thing that entered my mind was the assembly of my model airplanes where I used to glue balsa wood pieces together. I described the process to Hugo.

"Nah," Hugo said. "Bonding is a mental thing, a connection. You want to be with someone and that person wants to be with you."

"Love, I ventured?" I knew as little about love as I did about bonding.

"A strong feeling," Hugo said. "A closeness. Like what happens between mother and child."

Mother and child, the topic made me apprehensive. In time, I began to wonder if I had ever experienced this bonding thing with my mother. I didn't recall climbing onto her lap or being cherished by her. My father was a presence at home but any display of warmth from him was very measured. I wondered, as children sometimes do, if I had been adopted. Or did I look like an elephant when I was born, malformed and ugly, a revulsion to my mother? Then I heard about a classmate whose mother had suffered a stroke and couldn't move her body and I wondered if my mother had experienced some type of paralytic disease of her arms that made her unable to hug me. I often felt an absence, a void, that I couldn't describe, like a hunger not satisfied by food. It made me work harder in school and then in college, trying to gain the approval of my teachers and professors.

A decade after my mother's suicide, I thought about becoming a physician. I actually remember the exact moment that I committed to the career. I had been to a band concert at school and watched as my classmates reunited with their parents after their performances. Right in front of me, a young girl who had just played the violin ran up to her mother and was hugged so tightly. I remember being stirred by the mother's pride and joy over her daughter's accomplishment.

"You did wonderfully," the mother said with exuberance.

I watched in awe and jealousy. I could feel the warmth radiating between them. Hugo, the elephant handler, swam into my mind. Then, somehow, I had the thought that if I were like Richard Chamberlain in Dr. Kildare or Vince Edwards as Dr. Ben Casey from the television shows, I could become a hero and champion the sick and heal those who were alone. Medicine would become my calling and salvation. I reveled in the idea and set about to make it happen. In high school, I took biology and chemistry and in college, the requisite pre-med classes. My work was all consuming and left me little time for any social life. While my classmates enjoyed dating and fraternizing, I was so focused on my studies that I had little time for anything else. I didn't go to any parties or dances. My determination allowed me to gain entrance to Harvard, where, I labored day and night and gained acceptance to Yale School of Medicine.

At the beginning of my second year in medical school, I met Susan. She was in many of my classes and we spent countless hours studying together. She was petite, attractive, and had curly brown hair that was always falling in her eyes. Susan loved to laugh and have fun. We went to the movies, the theater, and out to dinner. She even took me dancing, a first for me. Susan came from a large family in upstate New York. She had two sisters and three brothers and was always on the phone with one of them. I didn't understand what they had to talk about, but talk they did. Susan led me around from one thing to another and I followed, sometimes happily, sometimes uncomfortably. It seemed natural that when she suggested marriage, I would acquiesce.

The intimacy of marriage was difficult for me. Susan would kiss me ardently when I came in the door, but the mere touching of our lips evoked a mild aversion, as if I wanted to escape. In time, Susan began to sense the social withdrawal which enveloped me like a protective blanket. We were celebrating our first anniversary at a fancy café and I ordered champagne. The drink made me drowsy and I began yawning.

"Ben," she began.

I hastily apologized.

"Are you bored with me?"

"No, no, no."

"You should be holding my hand," she said. "We should be talking about how we met and how we love one another. The past. The future."

I nodded. My heart started racing. I didn't know what to say.

"I can't reach you," she said sadly. Then her face hardened. "You disappear. You go underground."

"No, I don't," I argued, but she was right. I did withdraw from her.

"My birthday's tomorrow, Ben. Did you remember that?"

"Tomorrow? I thought it was---"

"I don't think this is working," she declared as she pushed the hair out of her eyes. I could see tears.

"I'll try harder." I pleaded.

"Perhaps. I'm not optimistic. I don't know," she sighed.

We separated a few months later and then divorced. I was both saddened and relieved by our breakup. I spoke to my father about it but he had little sympathy on the subject. He was sitting in our barren kitchen with a pile of briefs on the counter. This is where I always found him.

"Men and women don't always get along," he summarized. "How's your studying going?"

"Maybe I should speak to someone about my marriage," I ventured.

"Best keep one's private thoughts to oneself," he replied.

I again plunged into my work. I excelled at pre-clinical studies and embraced the clinical rotations with gusto. The less emotions that were involved, the better. In medical school, I treated diabetics, intubated patients with lung disease, looked into the sore throats of children, and even helped take out an inflamed appendix. It wasn't until I saw a young woman in the emergency room that there awakened within me a desire to study the mind.

The girl had tried to overdose after her boyfriend left her. I sat at her bedside and asked why she wished to die.

"Nothing to live for," she told me.

"But you have parents, a family and a dog. They all need you." I again thought of Hugo and his baby Ramona.

"I wanted him," she said mournfully. "I love him."

"And if you can't have him, death is the only alternative?" I probed.

"Death is always at the front door," she said. I was rattled by her words. She had opened the wound to my mother's fatal overdose and I had not the slightest idea how to repair what both she and I were suffering. I only knew that just as my fellow residents embraced surgery or orthopedics or internal medicine, I was going to specialize in psychiatry.

"A shrink," one of my fellow interns exclaimed. "But you're so good with your hands. You've got all these talents. Shrinks deal with things they can't see or touch. It's all soft stuff." He shook his head disapprovingly, but I wasn't deterred.

My mind was racing and I was thinking differently. Perhaps I could learn and understand more about suicide and maybe come to understand my mother's death.

For my advanced training, I chose one of the well known mental hospitals, Sandstone. I would spend the next three years studying depression and schizophrenia and the use of the relatively few drugs available to treat these diseases. However, I was not prepared to be so immersed into the world of troubled souls. At Sandstone, I came upon patients who desperately hunted for idealized mothers, or searched for mothers who never existed. I saw their anguish and watched them scramble for small moments of peace and well-being. Some were caught in vicious cycles of moodiness. One minute they were up and the next down. Only when they were euphoric did they feel precious, or even loved. I saw folks who either drank to forget or drank to try and find a blissful state of union with an unseen force. The continuous beseeching of both men and women evoked within me a hollowness and I wondered if I would survive the insatiability of my chosen profession.

I found myself drawn to a fellow trainee who was searching high and low for his missing mother. Looking back, I can see that we fused over a shared injury. A deep scar connected us. We were both motherless. But my relationship with him would turn out to be a dreadful, dreadful mistake.

Chapter 2

Sandstone was a stately private mental asylum built in the early 1900's and located an hour northwest of New Haven, outside the city of Hartford. It was built by a wealthy textile manufacturer whose wife suffered from repeated bouts of melancholia. In time, the single facility mushroomed into a conglomerate of buildings with greenhouses and a working farm. The hospital initially attracted patients from the East Coast and then, from other parts of the country. Eminent psychiatrists worked at Sandstone and published seminal articles about schizophrenia and depression. In time, prominent patients from around the world came to Sandstone with the desperate hope for a cure. James Hewitt, the famous British actor, entered the hospital with depression and was cured with daily psychotherapy. Mildred Conway astonished millions of concert fans by revealing that she had tried suicide. After years of psychotherapy, she improved enough to write a book about her illness. T.R. Bonnworth, the moon-walking astronaut, grappled with alcoholism and finally reached a state of durable abstinence for which he credited Sandstone.

I was assigned to Manning House, a three-story brick mansion with tall chimneys at each end. In front, wide curved granite steps were flanked on either end by ornate wrought iron railings. Inside, the entrance hallway was made of thick oak beams. The patients' rooms were spacious with high ceilings and tall multi-paned windows. As attractive as their rooms were, however, outside each window was iron grating to prevent the patients from considering escape, as if the illnesses of their minds were not enough to imprison them.

On my first day at Sandstone, I met the man assigned to me as my instructor, Dr. Jack Vanderpol. He was in his mid-forties, tall and lean, with a chiseled face. He always wore a freshly pressed pair of khaki pants and a crisp blue blazer. He was showing me around that first morning when he was abruptly called to attend a meeting with Dr. Gordon Mueller, the medical director of the hospital. Dr. Vanderpol served under Dr. Mueller and disliked him immensely.

"His Excellency wishes to see me," he rolled his eyes. "You'll meet him at noon. Be prepared. He lives and breathes Sandstone. I heard he's upset about the census here. We're not at maximum capacity and His Excellency wants the place filled, brimming with patients like the diners at the finest restaurant. He wants Sandstone to always have a waiting list so he can feel important turning people away. His goal is to have Sandstone be the most noted mental hospital in the world."

I dutifully smiled at Vanderpool's irreverence, but underneath I was anxious about my first day.

"The first day here is always a little disconcerting." Vanderpol recognized. "Wander around on your own and introduce yourself to the patients." With that he left me to my own accord.

I picked up a chart from the rack in the nursing station. It belonged to Grace Cardigan. Mrs. Cardigan had been at Sandstone for about a year and suffered from severe bipolar illness. She was a middle-aged woman with large and woeful eyes, sunken cheeks, and grayish hair. Heavy glasses dangled from her neck, as did an intricate gold pendant. Mrs. Cardigan's moods alternated between rare bouts of mania and frequent episodes of depression. I knocked on her door, entered her room, and immediately encountered a crisis. Mrs. Cardigan had scratched her wrists and arms with a simple safety pin that had escaped confiscation by the nursing staff. Blood seeped out of her cuts and onto the white bed sheets. A nurse passing by saw what was happening, rushed into the room and demanded that she relinquish her weapon. Mrs. Cardigan did, then held up her arms so that they could be bandaged. She casually asked if the cuts needed suturing, as if they were the result of a mishap and not a deliberate act.

"Doctor?" the nurse looked over at me. "What do you think?"

Mrs. Cardigan's arms were littered with horizontal and vertical battle scars. Some were red and healing and others had become puckered with age. They represented years of self-abuse. As an intern at Yale New Haven Hospital, I'd sutured up patients involved in major car accidents, neighborhood knifings, animal bites, and I'd closed operative wounds, so I surely knew how to intervene. But this was the prestigious Sandstone and I wasn't aware of protocol. Should I summon an ambulance and send Grace to a local emergency room? Psychiatrists were certainly physicians, but did they suture up the incisions on these lofty patients or was there an esteemed surgeon on call who would come and make any needed repairs? In any event, the scratches and cuts were quite superficial and suturing wasn't needed. Of course, had she punctured some millimeters deeper she might have hit a major vessel and then blood would gush out and the situation would be dire.

"She's OK," I said, thinking that she was far from OK. Any wrist cutter wasn't OK.

"Thank you, Doctor. We'll bandage her up and then you can come back and talk with her," the nurse said tersely.

I understood that formality ruled at Sandstone so I stepped out of the room and perused volumes in the bookcases of the day room. Many were dog-eared crime novels which I came to learn patients enjoyed reading, as if they could solve the mysteries of their own lives as easily as the protagonists of the stories did. From the corner of the day room, I could see the nurse wrapping up Mrs. Cardigan's arm. I went back to talk with her.

"Mrs. Cardigan," I began.

"Grace, please. Call me Grace."

"Grace. These cuts. How long have you been cutting yourself?" As I asked the question, I noticed the scar on her neck.

"Some have healed as you can see," she revealed, offering her arm for me to look at as if we were friends chatting over coffee. "Some are healing. It takes months to heal, so you can do the calculations, doctor. It's like the inside rings on a tree that's been cut down," she smiled at me.

"Years."

"Oh yes, surely. You're new here. You'll get to see lots of cutters like myself. We ought to have a support group. A club, perhaps. 'Cutters Club?' I imagine you're about to ask me why I do it. Why I cut myself? It's the very slowest form of suicide. I imagine you'll learn all about suicide."

I took a step backward. I had a fleeting desire to divulge that I already knew about suicide, that I had personally witnessed my mother's first attempt a year before she actually succeeded.

"You have a strange look on your face," Grace now observed. "You'll get used to suicide. It's very common here at Sandstone."

Chapter 3

It was noon and time for all the new residents to meet with Dr. Mueller. I was one of six new trainees and we all solemnly gathered around a massive oval table in the conference room of the Administration Building. Dr. Mueller was a tall, white-haired man, impeccably dressed in a black-vested suit which he wore summer and winter. He welcomed us as if we were being inducted into an exalted society of privileged rank. He gave us his overview of Sandstone, making sure to tell us how highly regarded the hospital was by the rest of the medical world. He did not leave out the fact that he was the psychiatrist-in-chief of Sandstone and a professor on the Yale faculty. He next proceeded to tell us how precious all the patients were.

"Each patient is here because life has overwhelmed him or her," Mueller intoned. "This hospital represents both their failures and their salvation. We are privileged to be a part of the healing process. I take a dim view of any humor made of those who reside here," he admonished. "We have an illustrious heritage." He gestured to the walls on which hung faded portraits of long-nosed, former medical directors, all of them looking quite grim and exhausted from the efforts of curing mental illness. Brass name plates identified them as the old superintendents of what was then called The Sandstone Asylum.

"There is even a patient here who was once treated by Freud," Mueller said, "though I doubt he remembers very much about it since he is in the Alzheimer's unit." Mueller remained stone-faced while a few of us dared to smile at the irony.

Mueller spouted ground rules with tactical precision. Each new admission to the hospital was an emergency, and everything we were doing was to be halted in order to attend to our new case. We were each given pagers with the firm injunctive to respond to any call within moments. Jackets and ties were mandatory, Mueller stated, looking critically at one of the residents who was wearing an open neck shirt. Morning rounds were essential.

"Now, then," Mueller said. "Why don't we go around the room introducing ourselves."

A man named Dr. Zigmund Harrington, a few years older than I, spoke first. He had gone to medical school in Mexico City and then moved to Paris to study neurology at the Sorbonne. He had published important papers on brain chemistry, had earned a second doctorate in biochemistry, and had been awarded a grant from the French Academy of Science. He was allowed to transfer the grant monies to the research laboratory at Sandstone.

"I wanted to study psychiatry," he explained, "because my father had been manic-depressive. Of course, in those days, there were no specific drugs to treat the disease, and my father yo-yo'd up and down," Dr. Harrington drew a sinewave in the air with his finger. "He bought and sold real estate in Washington D.C. like baseball cards. It was very difficult living with him." The group nodded in sympathy.

My turn was next. I had figured we might have to give little accounts of ourselves and I'd rehearsed what I would say. I was worried about how I would handle my mother's suicide.

"I'm Dr. Ben Soloway," I began. "I grew up in Boston. My father was originally from Germany and trained as a physicist, but when he came to this country he decided to go to law school and he became a patent attorney, so I grew up in a house filled with zany inventors. There were men who built flying contraptions and perpetual motion machines and battery powered meat grinders and ionic generators that made particles travel faster than the speed of light. All these folks were quite mad, so that's why I picked psychiatry as a profession." The other residents chuckled.

"I went to college at Harvard and then medical school at Yale. Then I worked at Norwich State Hospital east of here," I motioned to the window. "There are thousands of patients in that facility and I made a television documentary about the grim lives they led. The film won a prize and I guess that's how I got picked to come here to Sandstone." I sat back in my chair, finished and relieved that I hadn't mentioned my mother. I was afraid of what the others would think of me. I was anxious that they would somehow view me as a flawed human being, the way I often saw myself.

Everyone in the room was illustrious in one way or another. My fellow residents included a novelist, a Ph.D. in English literature, a surgeon, and even a man who'd been a bush pilot in Alaska. We had led lives of exemplary ambition. Why else would we have been selected for the renowned training post at Sandstone?

"Well, then," Mueller rubbed his hands together. "We seem to have a very distinguished group. I am very pleased. And," he added solemnly, "I wish you luck in your future endeavors. You'll be spending three years here in preparation for your entry into the world at large where you will practice the specialty of psychiatry. The specialty is a unique calling." he said reverently.

The group filed out. Some of us wandered down to the canteen and I ended up sitting next to Dr. Harrington, the guy who had been singled out for his lack of dress code.

"Ben," I said extending my arm. "Ziggy," he responded. "Mueller acts as though he should be in the priesthood."

"A touch overbearing," I concurred.

"Neckties," Ziggy changed the subject. "I hate them. You like neckties?" Ziggy studied my face with his large blue eyes. He was poorly shaven and had a growth of stubble on his chin.

"I have a collection of hundreds of neckties," I said. "Maybe close to a thousand, all inherited from my father who loved neckties. Narrow ones, string ties, plump ones, those very wide ones. All the colors of the spectrum with an emphasis on red. German physicists love red and black. Red is positive, black is negative."

"In Paris, we never wore them," Ziggy said. "I guess I'll get used to it. Maybe you can lend me some from your collection." Ziggy fingered the frayed collar of his shirt. He wore a light grey linen blazer and poorly pressed slacks. I looked down at his feet and saw sandals. I didn't think sandals were going to be appropriate at Sandstone.

"So, your father was very ill," I said.

"He got shock treatments. Electroconvulsive treatments. ECT, lots of ECT. They blitzed him completely and utterly. I suppose they could have decapitated him," he said sarcastically. "Would have saved a lot of money. I wonder how much ECT they do here?" Ziggy was pointing to an aerial map of the hospital which revealed the slate roofs of the mansions and halls that comprised Sandstone. You could see the very large expanse of the property. Winding and forested roads converged on a large meadow which at one time, according to photos, had been a working farm, but was now covered with grasses and red and yellow summer flowers. Across the street from the residences was Lake Jehovah which stretched out for two miles. At the shoreline you could just make out the ripples from the resident ducks swimming in it. The lake belonged to Sandstone and at times I would see patients alone or patients with their therapists walking on the dirt pathways around it. We came to call it 'Theralake.'

"A luscious piece of property," Ziggy commented. "And here's the old apple orchard. Right here, see it? I heard there was a suicide there about four months ago. A man hanged himself from one of the trees. Very prominent man. One of Mueller's patients."

"Really? How do you know that?"

"I know a nurse from here," Ziggy answered.

"And she told you about it? Isn't that a private matter?"

"Can't keep death a secret," Ziggy said.

"I would think it's up to Dr. Mueller to talk about," I countered. "Maybe he still will."

"Mueller? Does he sound like the type of man who hangs out his laundry? I doubt he'll talk about it. Anyway, I should go and meet my new boss. I'll be seeing you around."

I returned to Manning House and saw Dr. Vanderpol in the nursing station, looking over charts. Vanderpol had trained as a psychoanalyst, but behaved like a basketball coach, cheering on patients to get better. Vanderpol liked to race cars and he drove a blue Dodge Charger with an oversized engine. He would park the car provocatively in front of the Manning House iron gate rather than in the assigned parking spaces adjacent to the front granite steps. Dr. Mueller had sent him several memos about this transgression but Vanderpol persisted in his disobedience. Vanderpol's sense of irreverence, humor, and compassion made my stay at Sandstone bearable. It became a ritual to assemble in his small office after morning rounds, have coffee, and talk about the patients.

"Big news. Grace has decided to divorce her dreadful husband," Vanderpol declared. "This calls for a shot of celebration." Vanderpol pulled out a bottle of cognac from the lower drawer of his desk. He poured a token amount into each of our coffee cups. "Perhaps we can halt her antidepressants now," he suggested. "She won't need them when he's out of her life. You've observed all those scars on her arms, right? Even the ones on her neck, right near her jugular? The textbooks say that depression is genetic and biochemical, but I can tell you a bad relationship will also cause depression and make you want to do yourself in. Her husband owns all the supermarkets in New Hampshire and flies down here once a month in his private plane to see Grace. We dread his visits. We dread them more than Grace does. Before the husband has even left the grounds of the hospital, Grace is bleeding with another fresh cut."

"You really want to stop her meds?"

"No," Vanderpol conceded. "She'll need them once she leaves him. When you exit madness, you encounter depression, which she is beginning to display. Plus, what we'll have now is a fight over the large fortune. Grace has a long hike in the bleak desert ahead of her. Nice woman," he nodded. "Likeable. She has an older sister who lives in San Francisco. I think she's come once to visit Grace, but I didn't get a chance to meet her."

I spent time with Grace. She related her history to me.

"Well, I had my first mental breakdown at Smith College and my second at Julliard and my third while playing violin with the New York Philharmonic. I managed to survive them all. I was a pretty good musician. Someday I'll play for you," she said without enthusiasm.

"I would enjoy that."

"My mother's hero was the great Russian violinist Jascha Heifetz. She always wanted me to play as well as he did but who could compete with Heifetz? I certainly wasn't up to his standards. My mother was disappointed," Grace complained.

One day, I overheard her play. Vibrant notes penetrated the plaster walls of Manning House. I was amazed by her talent.

"Genius and madness," Vanderpol commented about the emanating sounds. "The worse she feels, the better she performs. Can you think of a crueler equation? I don't think so." Grace was playing a Hungarian gypsy melody as loud and as fast as she could. It was supposed to be a spirited tune but there was still a mournful quality about the music and it evoked sadness. I shook my head as if to dispel it.

"Yes," Vanderpol watched me. "It certainly doesn't conjure up joy. I think that a lot of the great music in the world was composed by sad people."

Besides Grace, I was initially assigned a strikingly pretty, early teenage girl who suffered from anorexia nervosa. She would secretly vomit what little she ate and when the staff once gave her privileges to go off hospital grounds, she purchased laxatives to rid herself of even more weight. Anorexia had a 30% fatality rate, so she was then kept a prisoner on the ward. Nevertheless, she succeeded in plummeting down to 74 pounds, at which time she was carted off to the hospital downtown. When she returned, I met with her for the first time. Sunshine was the name her parents had given her and she hated it. And them as well.

"You can't keep me here forever," she scowled at me.

"Forever's a long time," I said. "You could perish."

"My body's my own," she asserted. I could see the clavicles in her shoulders and the shrunken concavity of her cheeks. How her spindly legs supported her was beyond me. I had never seen as severe a case of anorexia as hers. It was my job to learn how to treat patients such as Sunshine. I hadn't the vaguest idea how to begin.

"And I want my mirror back," she demanded.

"Let me check on that," I replied, and she stomped out into the hallway.

Later, I recounted this to Vanderpol.

"No mirror," Vanderpol instructed. "They just look into it and see fat. It's like the reflection you get back by looking into one of those distorted mirrors at the carnival fun house."

"Can't they just go to the bathroom and look in the mirror there?" I asked.

"We time how long she can stay in there. But you're right, they can see themselves in any polished surface. Mirror freaks find their images everywhere. Remember the Greek myth about Narcissus? He found his image in a reflecting pool, fell in love with it, and then drowned when he tried to embrace it. Well, our patients are the opposite. They hate what they see in the mirror. They see themselves as too fat. The mirror is the enemy."

"Sunshine, I can't let you have a mirror," I said to her as gently as I could, and explained why we reached this decision. In subsequent therapy sessions, I tried to talk to her about her bad self-image. I felt it stemmed from how much her parents had ignored her when she was growing up and how much they favored her older sister, now a married attorney in Colorado.

"The hell with all of you," she disavowed any introspection. "I'll tell my mother that you're mistreating me. Abusing me."

Mistreating, I thought to myself. Here was a young woman who repudiated food, made herself vomit, and wolfed down laxative tablets, all in the service of weighing as little as she could to punish herself and her frantically worried parents. Yet I admired

22

her pathologic defiance and somehow sensed her inner desolation. As angry as she made me, I felt sorry for her. One dreary Monday morning when I sat down with her, I asked about her mother.

"What mother?" she barked at me. "You mean Mildred?" She was standing by the window looking out at the grey clouds.

"That's what you call her?"

"That's her name," she replied sullenly, turning around and crossing her arms to face me.

"How does she react to being called 'Mildred'?"

"What do you think? She doesn't like it." She glared at me.

"How long have you called her 'Mildred'?"

Sunshine's eyes narrowed. "You're full of questions," she accused.

"I'm afraid that's my job here," I said.

"When she was in the hospital, she had a big sign over her bed with her name on it so from then on I called her by her name."

"A hospital? Why was she in a hospital?" I asked

"Cancer." Sunshine shrugged and turned toward the window with her back to me again. It started to rain.

"Cancer? What kind?"

"I don't know. How much longer do I have to stay in this Godforsaken place?" she asked, trying to avoid the painful questions. Now I was very curious but feared that if I pushed her on the subject of cancer, she would get angry and shut down. I would lose what little momentum I had gained by getting her to talk to me.

"When your weight gets stabilized and you stop trying to harm yourself," I answered her last question.

"I'm not suicidal," she declared.

"Not directly, no." I agreed. "But your starvation is dangerous. You know that, Sunshine," I said.

"You can't make me eat." She turned towards me, her face taut.

"Sunshine, I can't make you do anything, really. You're the one in control."

"Suppose I don't eat. Suppose I become like one of those Holocaust survivors." I'd seen photos of those emaciated prisoners and I winced inwardly,

"I'm warning you."

"If it gets to that point, Sunshine, I can keep you here against your will," I said firmly. "I hope it doesn't come to that. I'd like you to get well." A sense of pity now entered my mind and softened the annoyance I had felt earlier. This evolution signaled some level of warmth which I couldn't define. Perhaps it had to do with her desperation.

"I'll escape," Sunshine predicted. And, in fact, one Sunday morning, when few staff were about, she followed through on her threat and snuck out. On the main road, she hitched a ride to her home. It was not lost on me that it was home she escaped to, the place where her evil mother was.

I expressed dismay to Vanderpol when her mother brought her back. We were in the break room. Vanderpol had walked in while I was making a fresh pot of coffee. A nurse had brought in a box of donuts but they had been devoured by the patients and only one was left. That one donut I looked upon as my lunch.

"Par for the course with these kids," he commented, shaking his head. "They run circles around us. You have to admire their determination and strength, as scrawny as they look. You want the last donut?"

"It's yours," I offered.

"No, Ben. You take it. You look hungrier."

"What do you make of the Mildred thing?" I asked him. "That's what she calls her mother who evidently had some form of cancer."

He shrugged as if it was an everyday occurrence. "Kids call their parents by their first name to escape the feeling of domination," he stopped to take a sip of coffee as he mulled over my question. "Perhaps the same dynamic holds true for Sunshine. Here she is, suddenly faced with the possibility of her mother dying and to avoid the fear of loss, she neutralizes the pain by calling her 'Mildred.' By doing this, she has managed to impersonalize the whole mother-daughter relationship. Something like that," he concluded. "You may have hit on something important, Ben."

"Purely by accident," I minimized

"I doubt that. Try not to ascribe things you discover about patients to random forces," Vanderpol stated as he picked up Sunshine's file from the table. "Something made you inquire about Sunshine's mother. You were responding to something Sunshine said or some unconscious event of your own. Probing the mind is difficult. You have to develop an awareness about it, a sense of intuition. What you ask a patient often reflects your own inner workings," Vanderpol pointed to his forehead. He looked directly at me, "We need to learn more about her mother."

I looked away from Vanderpol and gazed out the window. I was suddenly anxious.

"I've met her, actually," he continued, "when Sunshine was first admitted. I'd describe her as a stern woman. A physician. A radiologist. Peers at x-rays all day. She sees the insides of everything except the mind. Divorced, as I recall. I didn't much like her. She cries every time she comes to visit Sunshine. The father's called me from Okinawa in Japan. He's a Colonel in the Marines. He didn't grasp the nature of anorexia. He chiefly wanted to know how soon Sunshine could be discharged. Mother asks the same thing."

"Sunshine sure doesn't seem to like her mother," I said.

"One's relationship with a mother is a complicated thing. When you evaluate patients, spend some time on the early inter-actions with their mothers. You'll see how it sets the stage and regulates moods and thinking." Of course, an image of my mother flashed before me and a chill ran through my body. How was her suicide going to influence my future life? Already, my marriage had failed. Was I in store for more casualties? I must have looked ashen because Vanderpol was staring at me.

"I've hit a nerve," he gently remarked. He took a step backward.

"Nothing serious," I tried to deflect.

"If you say so. I won't delve," he said acknowledging my dis-comfort. "The stuff we see and treat rattles our cages, too. In time you may wish to engage in your own therapy," he encouraged, step-ping into a professional demeanor.

"Something to consider," I said, somewhat shaken, trying to put an end to this conversation. I quickly gathered my things, poured a fresh cup of coffee, and hastened out of the room, indicating I had patient notes to write up.

Ziggy and I met a few times and developed an early friendship. I told him about Sunshine. We were sitting in the canteen. Patients and staff came in and out. As I watched them, it was often difficult to tell the difference. Psychiatric patients weren't short of breath or didn't limp like other sick patients. All their turmoils were cloistered inside, invisible. They looked like everybody else.

"At least you're treating disease," Ziggy was expostulating. "My unit is full of buxom young women who've lost their way and dropped out of high school or college. Booze, pot, too much money."

"Keep your voice down," I said to him.

"What they all need is a good you-know-what." I was momentarily appalled by his statement, but was quickly learning that Ziggy was given to irreverence.

"We've' just arrived, Ziggy. Give it some time."

"Time," Ziggy gloomily contemplated. "Time for lunch," he brightened up. "Let's get away from this place. I know a great delicatessen."

"We'll need to eat quickly to make it back for the noon lecture."

"If you say so," Ziggy said.

I drove my old faded green Plymouth. Ziggy discoursed as we made our way down the road. It was more of a monologue, actually. He described the hardship of working day and night at his mentor's laboratory at the Sorbonne. At the same time, he took issue with America.

"I forgot what America is like," he complained. "Everyone here is staid and aloof. No passion. People dress like puppets. Food is utterly bland. White bread. Greasy donuts. Greasy cheeseburgers. American pastries, dreadful. Butter is taken out of everything."

"So why did you come back?" I inquired.

Ziggy ignored my question and carried on with his complaints. "I went to the local department store the other day. One of those malls. Full of people scooping up oversized boxes of everything and stumbling out to their station wagons with children trailing behind. Unbelievable materialism," he said, rolling his eyes.

"Unlike the famous austerity of the French," I countered sarcastically. We were passing the Clancy cemetery. It was filled with large crypts and ornate statues.

"I read that this place is filled with famous people," Ziggy motioned outside. "Dead ones. Look at the size of some of the tombs. Impressive. Would you like to be buried in one of these mausoleums? I think I would. A grand finale," he said,

"I don't think I'm ready to consider my grave site yet."

"I grew up in a house like these," Ziggy said, pointing to some opulent homes high on the bluffs above the next street. "In Georgetown. Washington DC. A big brick house with seven bedrooms and a porch that encircled the whole structure. Built in the 1700's. One of my father's better purchases," he bragged.

The delicatessen, named The Black Swan, turned out to be on a main street near Norwich. We managed to grab a corner booth with some privacy from other patrons.

Ziggy ordered a liverwurst sandwich and a glass of dark beer.

"Egg salad," he looked over at my plate. "Only an American would eat homogenized egg salad."

"Perhaps I shouldn't eat with you," I complained, getting weary of his critical opinions. "Why did you leave France?" I asked once more.

"I left Paris to become a professor," Ziggy said. "I was an instructor at the Sorbonne, but to become a professor is pretty much impossible overseas unless someone in your family was one and you published ten thousand papers. I wonder how the cheesecake is here," he abruptly changed the subject. "Shall we share a piece?" But Ziggy ate the whole portion himself, and drank a second beer. We paid our bill and I drove back to the hospital.

"How did you learn about this place?" I asked him on the way back. "It's quite good."

"Ah. It's a long story. I'll tell you sometime." I didn't press him on the point.

Ziggy studied the sky. "It's a gorgeous day," he remarked. "You sure you don't want to skip the lecture and go for a walk somewhere?"

"I want to hear the lecture," I replied. "It's titled 'The Disabled Physician.'" I was thinking that the talk might in some way apply to me, the survivor of a suicide.

"Drugs and alcohol," Ziggy said disdainfully.

Lectures, referred to as Grand Rounds, were held on Wednesdays at noon. Invited speakers held forth for an hour discussing their specialty field, following which were questions the audience could ask. Leading off the summer series was G.T. Walsh, M.D., head of the local Physician Quality Assurance Committee. The Committee was comprised of various specialists in medicine, and policed the questionable behavior of clinicians brought to their attention. The committee also oversaw physician's assistants and allied health practitioners which included radiographers, radiation therapists, nuclear medicine technologists, and respiratory therapists. Walsh's focus that day was on physicians and he presented a statistical summary. Last year, no fewer than forty physicians had been reprimanded or had their licenses suspended or revoked for mainly overprescribing drugs, fraudulent billing practices, or various acts of negligence. Addiction was common.

Walsh told some astonishing stories. In one case, a surgeon left a patient on the operating room table in order to make a bank deposit and then merrily returned to finish the procedure. Another ten had been temporarily suspended for various boundary violations. One anesthesiologist fondled a patient in the examining room. One had sex in the office and another had gone to a local motel with the patient. A surgeon who performed a breast augmentation on a woman fell in love with the results and with her as well. There was a sickening anecdote about a pediatrician who had caressed a little boy's genitals. Several psychiatrists had romances with patients and it was upsetting to hear that they were overrepresented among those who were deviant.

I was dismayed by the scope of offenses that Walsh described. Was I that naïve as to think that physicians were a hallowed group? True, there had been a medical student in my class who became a heroin user and eventually was ousted from school, but I saw him as an isolated case. In those days, there wasn't much publicity about bad doctors. Everything about them was hushed up. I couldn't understand why a doctor, who had spent years and years in training, would throw away his career with such bad judgment? The real question seemed to be for what was the doctor really searching? It had to be something so primal that it obscured all sense of the present and the future. A quest for intimacy? Some kind of bonding defect?

At the conclusion of the lecture, someone in the audience asked why all these transgressions seemed to occur within the medical profession.

"Perhaps you are in a better position to answer this question," Walsh passed off the query to Mueller. "Gordon?"

Mueller rose, nodded augustly to Walsh, and took the podium. He paused for effect.

"A most important lecture, George. Vital. Vital and sobering. Particularly sobering for all of us, I'm sure. The medical profession is a difficult one. It attempts to heal the sick but often overlooks illness in its own ranks. 'Physician heal thyself.' But we have large gaps in our vision. Our blind spots can be overwhelming. We form intimacies with patients but often lack personal intimacy with anyone else. We prescribe drugs to alleviate their anxiety and depression, but. some of us are prone to these emotions as well and so, too, seek the consolation of these very drugs. Patients clamor for solace and comfort, but we shield ourselves from realizing that we, ourselves, have the same needs. All of us," Mueller intently scanned the audience, "can succumb to crossing thresholds we ought not to cross. First, we allow a patient to stay late into the session, then we see the patient off hours, then we lend him or her a sweater because the room is cold and then we share a meal with the patient and thus down the insidiously treacherous path we wander." Mueller started pacing in front of the podium. "Vigilance!" Mueller raised his finger in the air. "Constant vigilance protects us from our own reckless acts. Vigilance," Mueller repeated and clasped his hands together. He could have been describing the dangers of Communism or possibly the Bubonic Plague the way he was ardently appealing to his audience.

"But I am speaking too much," Mueller suddenly caught himself and stopped, "George?"

"Well stated, Gordon," Walsh unctuously offered. "We are all vulnerable. Now then, I'm sure that there are more questions."

Hands in the audience flew up. What screening should be done? Why were men guiltier of violations than women? What were the ages of the doctors? Were they married? Were they psychiatrically ill? Walsh fielded the answers.

"We've time for one last question," Walsh pointed to the back row. Ziggy rose from his seat.

"You haven't said anything about the role of the patient," Ziggy said rather loudly. "Aren't some patients blameworthy in these matters? The model you're presenting is that the patient is utterly innocent and the doctor is the evil villain. Is this an accurate clinical picture? Can there not be evil patients who coerce and exploit and even seduce doctors?"

People swiveled towards Ziggy and whispered to one another. Walsh seemed stunned. Mueller craned his neck to regard Ziggy.

"A provocative statement," Walsh finally said in reply. "May I opine that it is exactly that kind of thinking that gets a person in trouble. A patient is ill, the doctor is not. Illness confers susceptibility.

You would no more make such a statement in the financial world where a fiduciary responsibility is the guiding ethic. Therefore---"

"I would," Ziggy interrupted. "Morality is bilateral. Victims in any aspect of life must accept some responsibility for their actions. Even those who invest money in the financial world must do their homework before choosing an advisor."

"I would suggest that this dialogue be continued another time," Mueller said curtly as he tapped the face of his watch. "We're out of time. Thank you all for coming. And our deepest gratitude to you, Dr. Walsh, for a most sobering lecture." He shook Walsh's hand and escorted him out of the hall with some haste.

"Are you drunk?" I said to Ziggy. "Jesus, man."

"Righteous bastard, that guy is. Delights in persecuting practitioners. A doctor who's weeding out the misfit. Purity and goodness."

"Ziggy! The cases he presented were hardly purity and goodness."

"I'm sure he'd say they're the tip of the iceberg."

"Jesus, Ziggy."

Ziggy had reseated himself and gazed up at me. There was a crooked smile on his face but his eyes seemed swollen and slightly bloodshot. He ran fingers through his blond hair in a gesture of superiority.

"Authority figures. Not your thing," I ventured.

"I hate zealousness."

"Get yourself a cup of coffee," I said to him and headed over to Manning House. Vanderpol was already there. He'd also attended the lecture.

"I imagine His Excellency wasn't too pleased with that doctor's comment," he quipped as he lit one of his Cuban cigars. "He'll likely be called in for a little friendly chat. Mueller's been known to evict misbehavers, though it's early in the game. You have to buy into the holiness of this place. It's not friendly to subversives. What's his name again? I came in late."

"Ziggy. Sigmund Harrington."

"Dr. Harrington has a small point but it's probably best said in private. Take our friend Sunshine. All her little escapades drive everyone around her crazy. She's very manipulative. A sufferer and a perpetrator all in one. By the way, check on Grace," Vanderpol instructed. "She's a touch hypomanic and unusually upbeat. She is using the phone a lot and sleeping very little. A breakthrough of joy and craziness," Vanderpol let loose with a plume of exhaled smoke. "Manic-depressive illness. The 'elevator disease' is what we call it, up and down."

"How can she move so quickly from depression to mania?" I asked, perplexed. "She just finished cutting her wrists and arms and now she's on a high."

"She has what we call a rapid switch form of the illness. She can go from depression to mania within 24 hours. It's pretty rare. Most folks move slowly from one state to another."

I murmured that it was all baffling.

"Most of this stuff is baffling," Vanderpol replied. "We understand little of it. Cause and effect are hard to pin down. The mind goes in many directions at the same time. You'll get used to it," he nodded reassuringly.

"Should we use more medication?"

"Your decision, Ben," Vanderpol said. "Might help." Vanderpol gave me wide latitude in treatment. I lucked out having him as my attending. I had heard from other residents that their bosses ran the show, instructing them on the dose of a drug or a privilege level.

Vanderpol was more hands-off and encouraged me to think for myself. I appreciated his confidence in me.

One night, I was dozing in the on-call room reserved for the resident who covered the hospital during the evening shift. It was around midnight. A patient named Sanchez Remo Esposito was being admitted. Esposito was a famous symphony composer whose music had been compared with that of Beethoven. Esposito was a raving manic, disheveled, intoxicated, and spoke with a stream of consciousness that defied interruption. He informed me that he needed to immediately contact conductors Erich Leinsdorf of the Boston Symphony Orchestra and Leonard Bernstein of the New York Philharmonic.

"I've an important new symphony I want them to perform," he told me. "It surpasses all symphonies ever written. Also, call George Szell in Cleveland."

"Mr. Esposito," I challenged, but he interrupted me.

"Right away," he barked. "Immediately, you hear?" He was very menacing.

"In a moment," I tried to counter his intimidation. "I need to find out why you're here. What happened to bring you into the hospital?" I tried to gather some semblance of a history.

"This can all wait," he snapped at me. "It's imperative that I speak with these men immediately. Never mind, I'll have my secretary call them. Where is your telephone? I have her number here, right here. Kindly bring me a phone this second, young man. What is your name? I lost my glasses. Soloway. Whoever you are, Mr. Soloway, if you wish to practice medicine ever again, you'll bring me a telephone. Instantly," he banged his fist on the examining table. "You hear me? Call asshole Mueller and tell him I'm here, go head and call him. Have you heard any of my symphonies, Doctor? I hope you have, though doctors generally don't appreciate fine music, too busy taking out people's appendixes. Appendices, I should say."

I stepped out of the room and called Vanderpol about the matter of phone privileges. For very ill patients, we often forbade this link to the poisonous world that had precipitated their entry to Sandstone.

Vanderpol was at home watching a rerun of a NASCAR race.

"Hendrix is ahead," he told me, "Car 31, though I don't think that means a lot to you. What's up?"

"Sanchez Esposito wants to talk to the heads of the symphonies in Boston and New York and Cleveland."

"Ah, he's back. He uses us as a pit stop like these racers I'm watching. Never properly takes his medication. I assume he's high?"

"Grandiose."

"That he is anyway. That's his normal baseline state," he commented cynically "All these playrights and writers and musicians are the same way. I used to keep a list of them. So, why do you care if he calls these people?"

"It's inappropriate. And there's the privacy issue."

"Esposito, entitled as he is, doesn't care one whit about privacy. He typically announces publicly when he's going to be hospitalized. The press loves it."

"So, it's OK?"

"Up to you. I can see it both ways. 'No' means you're the boss. Then again, sometimes saying no is much more work than saying yes. You'll work it out. Do what you think is best."

I ended up giving Esposito the phone. He snarled instructions to his secretary.

"I'm going to give you an injection," I told Esposito. "It's to relax you.

"The hell you are," he yelled. "Get Mueller in here."

"I'm in charge," I said with some trepidation. Two nurses held him back and I stuck a needle in his thick shoulder muscle. With the drug aboard, he was asleep within minutes. At that moment, Leonard Bernstein actually called him back.

"Is Sanchez all right?" he asked with concern.

I was amazed. "I think he will be," I managed to say.

"The poor man. So ill. So gifted and so ill. Please convey my sympathy to him. We hear he has a new composition which all of us are eager to hear." Fifteen minutes later, Erich Leinsdorf was on the phone inquiring about Esposito.

"He is a gifted man, Sanchez is. Please tell him that I hope he recovers quickly."

I assured him that I would, wondering what motive Esposito would have to regain his sanity if illness worked this well for him. With time, I became less intimidated by distinguished patients who tried to manipulate their illness to stay special. But I wondered about Esposito. There was surely something drastically wrong with him. How had he developed his amazing narcissism? What must have happened to him early in his life to make him capable of becoming so exalted? I pictured the specialness lying dormant inside his mind, ready to uncoil and spring out whenever the flimsy checkpoints in his brain faltered. In a way, I was envious of his pathology, wishing I, too, could feel so impenetrably confident.

When I told Ziggy about my encounter with Esposito, he hardly responded.

"Sorry, having a bad day. We had a little sexual escapade on the hall last night. Thomas was found in bed with Dorothy. Dorothy's underage so we had to call the parents. That is, I had to call them and they were not pleased. How could this happen, they asked me.

People think a hospital protects you from everything. Germs and diseases. Slippery floors and falls. Indigestion and food poisoning. Sex. Suicide. Anyway, they're calling Mueller to complain. One of the girls on the unit is pregnant and she's psychotic. We've had two runaways. One new admission, a girl who loves razor blades. Don't you have a cutter on your unit? My attending insisted that a pelvic be done on my patient so the internist came and did it. She hides blades in her crotch. Can you believe it? This place is like a zoo with wild animals. I'm setting up my lab. I'm glad I have my research." Ziggy worked on a hall in which most of the patients were adolescents and their escapades truly unsettled him.

"I need to get away from these crazies" he added.

"The quiet comfort of test tubes," I remarked. "Peering through the microscope to see what's really there."

"I doubt there's any science to what we do here," Ziggy asserted.

"And you thought the specialty would be brimming with things that could be measured?"

"I don't know what I thought. Something," Ziggy summarized. "What am I supposed to do with these patients of mine?"

"Is this a serious question, Ziggy?"

"These patients all have something biochemically wrong with their brains," he answered.

"That's your answer?"

"Talking has its limitations."

Ziggy's nihilism stumped me. I intuitively knew enough about psychiatry to comprehend that the repair of lost souls was an amorphous undertaking and Vanderpol had alluded to it. If Ziggy believed otherwise, he was in the wrong profession.

"Why exactly are you here at Sandstone, Ziggy?" I asked.

"To get my certificate of training as a psychiatrist. So I can get grant monies for my research."

"That's it?" I asked incredulously.

"Mostly."

"You aren't interested in learning anything about human behavior?"

"Yeah, that too," he said quite unconvincingly.

"Are you interested in mental illness, Ziggy?"

"Mental illness interests me. Patients with mental illness, I don't know. Maybe a little."

I shook my head. I didn't know if Ziggy was simply being provocative or if he truly felt what he said.

Days later, I visited Ziggy. He lived in a rooming house in a working class neighborhood not too far from The Black Swan, our newest haunt. He rented two rooms and a kitchen. On the living room walls hung many black and white images of axons and synapses and dendrites and neurofibrillary tangles often seen in Alzheimer's disease. Magnified by the electron microscope, the photographs looked like bacteria or viruses trying to get a foothold on a petri dish or in someone's brain. Spidery branches reached out foreboding of disease.

"They're a little creepy," I said.

"They're beautiful," he took issue with me. "Protein structure at the molecular level. Perfectly lovely. I wish I had color images, they're even more spectacular. This is what illness is all about. Illness is a molecular imbalance."

"Disease is what people get," I countered. "People."

"People with deranged chemistry."

"Maybe you'll change your mind," I sighed. I looked around the room for personal touches. "No pictures of old girl friends?" I asked Ziggy. "Relatives? Parents? A dog?"

"In boxes," Ziggy said. "In storage. A lot of stuff is still in storage." Just then I noticed a small framed image of a man in a suit.

"Your father?"

"Father, such that he was able to take care of me, given all his preoccupation with work."

"And your mother?"

"Ah. My mother. My mother left the house when I was ten years old. She'd had enough of my father. Disappeared. My father hired detectives but to no avail. My belief, and I'm sure you think it's delusional, is that my mother married Mueller."

"Mueller? Our Mueller? Jesus, Ziggy, what's your evidence?"

"I'll show you a picture. Wait a minute." He disappeared into the bedroom and brought forth a small photograph in a gilded frame. "See the resemblance?" He pointed out her face to me. "See the nose. Look at my nose."

I did as he asked and glanced at his face but saw no obvious similarity. But the photo made me think. When was the last time I looked at photos of my own mother? Had I even kept any?

"She's Mueller's wife," Ziggy was saying.

"Ziggy, this photo of your mother isn't evidence of anything," I said. "Why are you showing it to me? It doesn't make sense."

"It does. Wait until you see her. Then you'll know. She's married to Mueller," he repeated.

"So here you are at Sandstone. Why wouldn't your own mother look you up after all these years, particularly now that you're so close by?"

"Guilt," Ziggy replied angrily. "Simple guilt. She abandoned me and now she's guilty as hell for having done so."

"Don't you want to see her?"

"I'm not sure."

"This is quite some story," I said. "Is this really why you're here at Sandstone?"

"Actually, I came to Sandstone a week early, thinking for some reason that I'd get a glimpse of her but I didn't. I ended up driving around and around for hours and that's how I found the Black Swam."

"You really don't want to see her?"

"Perhaps." Ziggy poured me a small amount of Scotch and a larger quantity for himself. He sat on a dilapidated leather armchair. "So, what's your life story?" he asked.

My story. I hesitated. Part of me wanted to reveal it to him, but there was something about Ziggy that I didn't quite trust. Perhaps it was his lack of respect for Sandstone and Mueller. I envisioned him easily violating any confidence that I might reveal.

"An unhappy marriage between my parents," I ended up saying.

Ziggy abruptly switched topics. "By the way, did I tell you I saw Mueller today. He was at a staffing. Kind of gave me a frosty reception, probably because of that comment I made about patients being culpable. How old do you think he is? Sixty, I'm guessing. Married twice. His present wife, whom I suspect is my mother, is a journalist. No kids, except me, if you believe my theory. Two Bernese Mountain dogs, you know, those gigantic animals that carry the kegs around their necks and constantly drool."

"How do you know all this, Ziggy?"

"An interview in a magazine. I forget which one. He's Canadian. Studied at McGill, then UCLA. Mueller wrote a book about childhood depression. Several books. His wife—my mother—won a Pulitzer Prize for some articles she wrote about child abuse for the Washington Post. Mueller was a chairman at Columbia before he came to Yale. I have one of his books." Ziggy rummaged through a pile of newspapers and handed me the volume. DEPRESSION: MYTH AND REALITY was the title. I skimmed the forward. Mueller gave thanks to the National Institute of Mental Health where he had spent a year and from whom he had later been given grants. He also thanked various scientists and editors, and his wife. I imagined that the title of his book was one which surely appealed to the faculty professors who endorsed his promotion and directorship of Sandstone. Yale had a tradition of seeking hard data to temper soft subjects, particularly when it came to psychiatry.

"You've read his book?"

"Not for me," he waved his hand in the air.

"No? Isn't this part of your research?"

"I skimmed it. He doesn't know what he's talking about. His knowledge of brain biochemistry is at the level of a high school kid. A stupid book," Ziggy said as he refilled his glass. Ziggy drank generously though I hadn't as yet seen him very drunk. He also smoked pot and offered some to me. I declined and asked him where he got it.

"These days? At the hospital," he replied.

"Sandstone?"

"Sure."

"Our hospital?" I was incredulous.

"Don't look so surprised," he said. "Wherever there are adolescents, there's pot."

"On the unit you work on?"

"The kids sell it to each other. We confiscate it but they get more. There's a stash of it on the unit in the nursing station. It's right in one of the lockers."

"And you help yourself to it? Ziggy, that's horrific!"

"I've obviously disclosed too much to you already." Ziggy drained his glass. "Enough. Suppertime." And that was the end of the revelation.

We ate at a low-grade Chinese place. For dinner, Ziggy ordered two bowls of Hot and Sour Soup into which he heaped several spoonfuls of rice. I diddled with the day's special, Egg Foo Yung. I was preoccupied by Ziggy's purloining of hospital marijuana.

"You shouldn't take that stuff," I finally said out loud.

"You mean I shouldn't smoke pot?"

"You know what I'm referring to."

"Sanctimonious, aren't we, Ben."

"Bullshit," I retorted.

"I obviously don't smoke it in front of them," Ziggy exclaimed indignantly and emptied the second bowl of soup, "I'm not a fool," he said defensively. "I don't think I want to talk about this anymore," Ziggy crunched open his fortune cookie. 'Great happiness will enter your life,' it proclaimed. Little did I know the fallacy of the prophecy.

"Seems doubtful," Ziggy commented. "Unless I win the Nobel prize."

"Mine says that fortune awaits me," I read out loud.

"Did you ever get a negative fortune?" Ziggy asked. "Something that says you will encounter great misery? A seizure, perhaps, or a sudden stroke? Leprosy?" He grinned cynically.

"No one would come back to the restaurant," I said. "Who would manufacture such misfortune cookies?"

"A sadist. Or some regressed schizophrenic. A sicko. Someone who wants to play a prank on the public. There are such people, you know," he smirked. "They like to make others suffer." I pondered this conversation and wondered whether Ziggy's comment was an oblique reference to Mueller or to Mueller's wife, who, Ziggy had declared, was his mother.

"Let's go," Ziggy got up from the booth we were in. I drove him to his lodgings. Neither of us spoke. He had told me too much.

After I dropped him off, I continued to the hospital A new admission had arrived. His name was Ted Henderson and he was psychotic. He was the son of the owner of the Chicago Cubs baseball team and he was very ill with auditory hallucinations. As soon as he had been checked in, he personalized his hospital room and tacked up a voluptuous image of the movie star Gina Lollobrigida and posters of the Beatles and of Elvis Presley. He unpacked books about airplanes and fighter pilots and put them on a desk. The otherwise empty room became stuffed with the trappings of a teenager.

"You must want to learn to fly," I commented to engage in conversation.

"I've flown already," he informed me. "My uncle owns a stunt plane and he let me fly it for a few minutes."

"Must have been exciting."

"Yeah," he said with weak enthusiasm. He was preoccupied. I asked him about hearing voices.

"Sometimes."

"You've heard them today?" I asked.

"A little." Ted surveyed the corners of the room.

"No one is watching," I reassured him.

Ted got up and covered a small crack in the lower wall with a book.

"You're safe here," I promised him.

Ted inspected the ceiling and studied the central light fixture.

"What are they, these voices?" I probed.

"Just voices."

"What do they say?"

"Stuff."

"Who are they?"

Ted shrugged.

"Men? Women?"

"Both."

"They laugh at you?" I ventured.

"Sometimes, yeah."

"About what? Why are they laughing?" I delved deeper. He shrugged once more.

"They want to hurt you?"

He shook his head.

This ordeal of interviewing him was exasperating. I had read that paranoid schizophrenic patients could be highly secretive and not divulge the contents of their disease. It was as if they erected lead shields around themselves to avoid being harmed. I didn't want to threaten Ted so I stopped the interview, said goodbye, and went to the nursing station to prescribe some Thorazine. Of course, there was always the recurring problem of getting a wary patient to take the medication in the first place. What had Mary Poppins sung in the movie I'd seen? 'Just a spoonful of sugar makes the medicine go down.' It surely wasn't that simple with psychiatric patients.

Night came and I went home. In contrast to Ziggy, I lived on the third floor in a modern apartment building. I didn't know my neighbors and had no great desire to meet them. The rooms I had were quite empty. I had no pictures on the walls and many of my belongings were still in boxes. On impulse, I opened a carton labelled 'diplomas.' At the bottom I found a wrinkled and faded menu from the diner where my mother had worked. I unfurled it. The specials of the day were chicken fricassee and navy bean soup, for 75 cents each. I pictured my mother in a white smock. I sat in front of my tiny television but I didn't turn it on, I was lost in thought. I reviewed the day's events but ended up thinking about my ex-wife. At Christmas time last year, she had sent me a card with a photograph of her new husband and their young son. All of them were smiling at the camera, wishing me a happy holiday. In the background was a twinkling Christmas tree. Susan had loved Christmas and the pageantry of the season. My parents had never celebrated Christmas, my father proclaiming that it was sentimental foolishness. I once asked my mother if she liked Christmas.

"I do whatever your father thinks best," she'd replied. "Too much emphasis on buying presents. A waste of money."

And so I had no interest in the festivities that Susan found thrilling. It was one of the many differences that emerged between us. She liked sex while I was indifferent to it. She liked fancy meals while I was content with simple fare. She dressed well and I shopped at second-hand stores and purchased the plainest of pants and shirts. All in all, I decided, she was three dimensional while I occupied only two dimensions.

I heated up a can of spaghetti, read about depression, and went to sleep.

Chapter 4

Every day, I met with Sunshine for an hour. Most of our sessions consisted of evasive maneuverings on her part. She hated this and that, her body, her parents, her past, her future. I would emerge from therapy exhausted by her anarchism and amazed that so much psychic energy could be devoted to the mechanics of anger. After seeing her, I would head for the snack shop for a restorative cup of coffee.

"Heavy fortifications betray underlying vulnerabilities," Vanderpol expostulated during a meeting in his office. "You've got to find a crack in Sunshine's armor. It may take a while until you get there. Until she trusts you. Remember, you're an evil parent. We've talked about her mother. Her father being a Marine tells you something."

"I'm not a Marine," I protested. "I'm not her mother."

"We're someone to everyone," Vanderpol avowed. "Whenever we wander into the force field of another patient, we become the person they're doing battle with. If that doesn't happen, something's wrong. It means they've stopped caring. They've given up." Vanderpol nodded and extracted a cigar from his blazer pocket and sniffed it. From his jacket he next withdrew a chrome lighter, then as quickly repocketed the device.

"Cutting back. Trying to cut back, I should say. One cigar every four hours." He loosened his tie and leafed through a folder on his desk. "How's Grace?" he asked.

"Her mood is pretty normal. Neither high nor low." I had seen her earlier in the day. She'd been sitting in a chair reading the newspaper and smiled at me as I'd entered the room.

"Her husband's lawyer called me," Vanderpol related. "He wants to depose Grace. What do you think?"

"He'll probably be quite aggressive," I said. "I'm not sure what it will do to Grace. Can it wait a bit longer until she's sturdier? Her mood's only been stable for a week. We need more time."

"More time," Vanderpol echoed. "Yes, we'll give it more time but with Grace's condition she may never have a robust period of stability. I heard that in Scandinavia they're using lithium to treat manic-depressive illness. It isn't available yet in this country because there is no profit to be had by the pharmaceutical industry. Lithium is just a simple salt. Maybe someday we'll get it. In the meantime, we have to treat the highs and treat the lows and hope that Grace doesn't do herself in."

'Do herself in,' I thought with a flash of alarm. I recalled Ziggy telling me about a hanging.

"Tell me more about the suicide here a while back," I asked.

"Indeed. A depressed biology professor from Stanford University hanged himself. In the apple orchard. It was in broad day-light, right in the middle of the day, no less. Not a soul saw him do it. Fashioned a noose with his belt which they had let him have, and he did the deed. We held a special conference which Mueller reluc-tantly attended and where he tried his best to justify the treatment that had been rendered to the man. They'd known he was suicidal and restricted him to the hall for months. Eventually, the patient complained and they gave him ground privilege. That's when he did it. Some suicides can't be prevented, no matter what the hell you do. We're not a prison, and even in prison, inmates kill themselves. If you look at the research, you'll see that Sandstone suicides aren't that different from prison suicides. For sure, the folks who come here are special, and their agonies often represent upper class strivings. This biology professor was accused of plagiarizing some paragraphs in his textbook and he was under investigation."

"I heard Mueller cut down the apple tree's branches."

"He cut the whole damn tree down," Vanderpol said. "He punished the tree. The tree caused the suicide. Apple trees can be very dangerous."

I grimaced. The irony was not lost on me.

* * *

Ziggy called me later that night.

"I've been thinking," he announced. "And I think you're right. I won't repeat the offense."

I told him I was relieved.

But at the next morning rounds, the subject of the stolen marijuana came up.

Every work day morning, the medical staff met for rounds in Thurston Hall, an amphitheater which had seating for 50 people. The meeting had been ritualized by Richard Mellingsworth, a psychoanalyst who developed the theory that psychiatric hospitals were a small community and that the inhabitants of that community needed to share information and interact regularly. Thus, every behavior was everybody's business, a rather strange contradiction to the otherwise sanctified privacy of psychotherapy.

"Good morning," Dr. Mueller boomed from a podium at the foot of the assembly. "Let us begin with new admissions."

One of the residents gave a brief synopsis of the patient he had admitted the previous day. She was a 51-ear-old woman who had become addicted to the pain medication she'd received from a doctor who had taken out her gall bladder.

She's on a detox regimen," the resident related. "We'll withdraw her slowly over the next week or ten days. Then we'll see what emerges. She's had depressions before."

Staff nodded as this information was relayed.

"Other comments?" Mueller asked. "Dr. Hightower?" Mueller acknowledged a hand raised in the air.

"Two girls cut their wrists last evening," Dr. Hightower said. "Nothing serious, but it seems to be something of an epidemic. We've restricted the girls to the unit."

"Thank you, Dr. Hightower." Hightower was a matronly woman who had been working at Sandstone for at least a decade. She was the attending at Crawford Hall, the ward to which Ziggy was assigned. Ziggy didn't like her and proclaimed her to be too pious.

A short-statured man with white hair spoke up. His name was Walter Olesker. He was from Ohio and had worked at the Cleveland Clinic. He specialized in the treatment of psychotic illnesses and schizophrenia. Rumor had it that he had cured a member of the Rolling Stones who had taken hallucinogens and become psychotic.

"Michelle Adams is still AWOL," he said. "Her parents haven't heard from her. They've hired a private detective. One of our girls says that Michelle has an old boyfriend in Alexandria, Virginia, she might be there. We're trying to find his name. She's without her medication."

Dr. Olesker," Mueller oozed, "we've a new crop of residents here who may not be familiar with the case. Perhaps you could summarize it for us briefly." Mueller had the eerie ability to know almost all the clinical faculty by name. It was part of his eternal scrutiny of the hospital.

"Surely. Michelle was admitted a half year ago after an overdose. She's a volatile girl given to rages and she hears voices. She hit a teacher at school. That's what got her here. Her grandfather is Senator Blaine from Washington State. He comes to see her regularly, and after each visit, we get a batch of letters from his office complaining about our treatment. Not enough therapy, too much therapy, not enough freedom, too much freedom, bad food, too little exercise, the wrong medications." Olesker took a pause to emphasize the vexation of dealing with a powerful figure and admitted, "We'd rather he didn't come, but he's paying for her care. Now with her missing, we are dealing with irate blame and exaggerated complaints. He insists she should have been in a locked unit, but because he complained so much when she was cooped up all the time we'd been giving her ground privileges for the past month. I fully expect him to yank her out of here. He's now talking about McLean Hospital in Boston."

"If anyone here gets any inquiries from family or from the press, the calls should be routed to my office," Mueller said crisply. "Now then," Mueller lowered his voice, "there's a new matter that's come up. Some confiscated marijuana has gone missing. Disappeared. This is a most serious matter, we typically turn over illicit medications or drugs or paraphernalia to the police, but before we could do so, the supply was gone. We've had to report the loss to the police and the police have notified the federal authorities. They are now conducting an investigation." Mueller began pacing. "I don't need to tell you the sensitive nature of this event. We've no idea where the marijuana went or who might have been involved but I am inviting anybody here who has information to come to my office and speak with me. This will be held in the strictest confidence. I can tell you, however, that the theft seems to have occurred on Crawford Hall."

"We are very distressed about this," Dr. Hightower said.

Silence descended on the crowd. My gaze cautiously swiveled towards Ziggy who was staring straight at Mueller. I began to feel anxious and perspired as if I was a co-conspirator.

"The drugs were under lock and key, I take it?" someone asked.

"Of course. We don't have a central bank vault, obviously, but we do take reasonable precautions. Key control is a vital part of hospital security. Officer Flannery, do you wish to say something about all this?"

Flannery was head of the internal security at Sandstone. I hadn't noticed him sitting a few rows down from me. He was a portly man in a blue uniform and he rose with effort from his seat.

"Perhaps it's best if you come down here and address us," Mueller said haughtily.

Flannery descended the stairs slowly and walked clumsily to the podium. Mueller stood aside.

"Key control is a big issue in a hospital this size," he began. "Because we have locked units for some patients who are impulsive escape risks, we try and limit the number of keys that are available. Even so, areas can be breached. We've had folks jimmy doors and even get duplicate keys made at a local hardware store but we've had no major thefts from any of the pharmacy cabinets on the halls. Access to the cabinets is pretty tight."

"Is it known which patient or patients brought in the mari-juana?" a voice called out.

"Sometimes we know, but not always. Kids get stuff and share it. Visitors can be a problem. This is a big facility to monitor."

"You have suspects?" someone in the audience asked.

"The inquiry has just begun," Mueller interceded. "Suspicions are premature."

"No suspect or suspects," the officer echoed.

"What happens if law enforcement wishes to interview any of our patients?" one of the residents inquired.

Mueller authoritatively raised his hand. "In theory, we must accede to any interviews the authorities would wish unless there is a compelling clinical reason not to. Once again, I ask that you refer all such issues to me. No one must speak to any member of the police without contacting my office first. In the case of the minors under our care, notifying parents will obviously be a concern. Now then, are there any other questions?"

There were none, and the group disbanded with more noise than usual as they turned to their colleagues to discuss the unsettling news. When I next looked over to where Ziggy had been, he had disappeared. I made my way outside and saw him walking down the path to the canteen. I rushed to catch up with him.

"Ziggy," I blocked his way.

"Ziggy what?" he halted. "What? Never mind. I know. You think I took all the stash they had on the hall? That's what you think?" His mouth was curled in anger. "Pompous Mueller. Federal investigation my ass. The only thing he cares about is the reputation of his precious hospital. I'll bet you he called the Feds himself," he spat in disgust.

"Ziggy, you yourself told me you took the marijuana."

"I said I took some, not all of it. A pinch is what I took. I'm not stupid, Ben! I'll bet others availed themselves of the stuff."

"Ziggy," was all I could say.

"What do you want me to do, Ben? Huh? What exactly do you want me to do? You want me to go to the Father and confess to having taken a hit? That'll do wonders for my career, won't it. Defrocked, de-licensed, arrested, jailed. Nice, real nice. That's what you want me to do? I made a mistake, that's clear. A stupid mari-juana mistake!" he argued. "Is that freaking possible in your mind, Ben, that people make errors? You've never made one, right?" he challenged. "I'm convinced you're the Yale wunderkind who sailed through life on glass-smooth seas. What exactly do you want me to do?" Ziggy stood stock still, glowering at me.

A group of giggling girls passed by. An unshaven man with Einstein-like white hair shuffled in front of us.

I was at a loss for words. I had no idea what I wanted Ziggy to do. I had no idea how to resolve the problem, as if it were my problem to resolve.

"I've got to see my cases," Ziggy stepped past me defiantly. "You go have an ice cream cone and wrestle with the solution to my problem while I go back to work." He marched away and up the hill towards Crawford Hall.

I considered asking Vanderpol for his advice, but feared that he would start probing as to why I had even formed a friendship with Ziggy. I began to ask myself the same question. Surely, some of the other trainees were more sober and dedicated. There was another psychiatrist at Manning House who'd gotten his doctorate in literature from Princeton and had taught for years before attending medical school. He devoured psychological literature and was always reading the classical papers by Freud and Adler and Jung. I had lunch with him several times and we discussed books. He was certainly a pleasant man, but I nonetheless preferred the rebellious-ness of Ziggy for reasons I didn't really understand.

To shake off my uncertainty, I returned to my caseload. My first patient that afternoon was Sunshine, and I girded myself for the onslaught, a cup of coffee in hand.

"For those patients who drain you dry," Vanderpol had coun-seled me, "you want to be sure to have eaten and have a beverage you can nurture during the session. Just make sure they can't throw it at you."

"I don't feel like talking," Sunshine glared at me.

"You rarely do," I nodded, but I ignored her comment. "Tell me about your parents."

"I have no parents," she shot back at me.

"We all do, Sunshine."

"So?"

"I know your mother's a doctor. What was she like as you were growing up?"

"I never saw her. She was too busy doctoring."

"And your father?"

"He was never home. He was always sent for duty in other parts of the world. Why is all this important?" she asked. "It seems like a waste of time."

"A waste of time?" I shook my head in disagreement.

"Totally."

I was silent for a moment, trying to think of a reply to these obstructive salvos of hers. I'd been sitting in a chair but got up and paced. "You know, Sunshine, you can defy me as much as you want but I'll still be your doctor. You're very ill, Sunshine. Someone has to set you straight and I'm that someone. I really would like to help you, if you'll let me. And, even if you see me as evil, I'll still try to make you well. I think you're a very lonely person, Sunshine. Your folks may have been too busy with their careers to care about you. Is that correct? You came second or third. Your sister was first. You weren't. Am I correct? It must have been very difficult for you."

"This is all bullshit," Sunshine mumbled. She was playing with a gold Rolex wristwatch her mother had given her for her recent birthday. She unhinged the clasp and transferred it to her other arm but it didn't fit and fell from her wrist. She got up from where she was sitting and stepped on the watch. I heard the crystal break as she ground it into the floor.

"Sunshine. Sunshine. What purpose did this serve?" I pointed to the floor.

"It's all bullshit," she repeated angrily.

I was gathering up the courage to more directly confront her. "So, I have a theory. My theory is that part of you wanted to become sick so it would bring your parents around. But now you feel even more unwanted than before. Now you're the mental patient at the Sandstone House of Nuts. And me?" I pointed to my chest. "Me? I'm the parent in your head. Your mother. Correct? Look at me, Sunshine. Look up at me, please."

A tear ran down her cheek and onto her chin. She quickly wiped it away with her fingertips. It was the first time I'd seen Sunshine cry, the smallest door to her soul.

I related the session to Vanderpol during supervision.

"You massaged out some fluid from her tear duct," he smiled at me. "An important little teardrop, though. You'll probably have to pay for obtaining it. But you're correct. A person has to be first to someone. Usually, it's the mother but it could be the father or an aunt or grandparent. Unless we feel we're a treasure to someone, we never catch up in life. We run at a deficit, much like a vitamin deficiency. In any event, you've made Sunshine vulnerable. Well done. Expect a wire brushing at your next encounter with her." I recoiled at the wire-brush analogy. But the phrase 'treasure to someone' gave me greater pause. I realized that a part of me was like Sunshine with a sense of being cast off. I wondered if I would I ever recover. I visualized baby elephant Ramona emitting sounds of distress.

"It does get better," Vanderpol noticed my demeanor change, and tried to reassure me about Sunshine. "But remember what I said about people being fortified. It's one of the more intriguing parts of our profession. No one's what they seem and the real person is often not even discernible to the self. It's like the mind and the brain don't recognize one another. Sometimes they're at war. It's amazing, though sometimes I have to admit that it gets tiring, all this quest to find the truth." Vanderpol loved to talk and vocalize his thoughts. His diatribes often revealed gems of insights which I found uplifting.

"By the way," he reminded me, "please go see Grace. She's high."

Grace was in her room playing the violin frantically, with lost notes and erratic cadence. She threw the instrument on the bed as I approached.

"I can't talk to you now," she proceeded to tell me. "I'm too busy as you can see." There were papers lying all over the room, on the bed, the floor, the dressing table, all crumpled in haphazard piles. "I'm almost out of paper," Grace complained, slamming the carriage on her typewriter. "What time does that stationery store in Willowbrook Corner close, do you know? I need more paper. Be careful," she warned as I stepped further inside her room. "Don't move that pile over there, I may need to refer to it. My husband's stupid lawyer should be disbarred, the bastard. Bastard! I'm writing a letter to the New Hampshire Bar Association to complain of his ethics. Do you know what he wrote me? Can you guess?" I took a few steps around the papers and leaned against the doorway, listening. Grace's face was flushed and there was spittle at the corners of her mouth. "He told me that my claim against my stupid husband is frivolous. Can you imagine that?" She didn't wait for a response and rambled on, wildly looking around. "Where is it, his letter. Wait, I have it here. No, it must be over there. You're standing right next to it, doctor," she exclaimed, pointing "that one right there, right by your foot."

"Grace," I bent down and flattened the sheet of paper.

"Is it from his lawyer?"

"No, it's one of your drafts to the Bar Association."

"It needs some more work. It's best you leave now, doctor."

"Grace."

"Thank you for coming."

"Grace, you're high. Manic."

"I'm annoyed," she snarled, "With you doctors we're either depressed or manic. Everything's sickness, there's nothing in between. Please leave now," she said adamantly.

"Grace," I said, but it was fruitless. Her speech was like hot lava pouring out of a volcano.

In the nursing station, I wrote orders and increased her drug dosage. Afterwards, I left the hospital and drove over to Ziggy's place, still concerned about his using hospital marijuana. He answered the door with a spoon and container of yogurt in hand.

"Ah," he exclaimed. "Dr. Morality. I'm surprised you deign to be in my corrupt presence." Then a thought occurred to him, "Or did Mueller send you?"

"On my own, Ziggy," I assured.

"Yes? Well come on in. You want some yogurt?" I followed him into the kitchen. "I'm writing up a new case. The owner of a fancy restaurant downtown. In his spare time, he trains attack dogs and he fell in love with this German Shepherd. The two of them were inseparable until the dog bit him one day. Turned out that the dog had a brain tumor and had to be put to sleep. The patient is completely wasted by it. Feels betrayed by the dog even though he knows better. Misses the beast. He has photos of himself cuddling the dog, just like a man and his lover. He actually thought of suicide. Very strange, but at least it's not one of those young women on my hall who are forever slicing themselves." At this point, I noticed a pile of plastic-wrapped shirts on the table, and two boxes of shoes. Dangling over a kitchen chair were several neckties. Ziggy observed me.

"I've reformed," he quipped. "I've finally adopted the Sandstone uniform. New shirts and shoes. Going to give away my sandals. Well, maybe not give them away, just store them. Now I need some new sport jackets. Mueller will approve, though he'd probably like it better if I wore somber suits. These neckties are pretty jazzy," he dangled one before me. It was dark red with bright yellow sunflowers. He held it against his chest. "With a blue shirt? What do you think?"

"A big move," I complimented him.

"Thank you. You see? Rehabilitation is possible. How about a drink? I brought this with me from Paris when I came here. Twenty-five-year-old Calvados. French. We drank it all the time when I trained."

"A sip."

Ziggy completely ignored my request and poured us each a third of a tumbler.

"Look. I found this picture." Ziggy handed me a frayed photograph of a handsome white Labrador retriever staring directly at the photographer.

"Quite striking," I said.

"He is. He was," Ziggy gulped a mouthful of the liquor. "Unfortunately, my father shot him."

"Shot him? I don't understand," I stared at Ziggy.

"Shot him. Shot him. Bang. Dead," Ziggy snarled at me. "He was pissed at me because I hadn't done my homework and I stayed out late so he took his trusted Army .45 and shot him. It was the same gun he pointed at my mother. Do you know why he pointed it at my mother? Can you guess. No, you can't guess. He was pissed that she bought a bunch of green bananas. She liked green bananas, he liked ripe bananas and so he accused her of disrespecting him. I was a witness to it, and afterwards, I wanted to kill him. I used to fantasize using his own gun to do him in but he kept the thing locked up and kept the key with him at all times. Shortly after that, my mother left. She left this time for good." Ziggy's face was now contorted with fury. "She'd left before and returned, but not this time. She disappeared that night for good. Gone. Vanished completely. I was 10 years old at the time, and I never saw her again. He didn't either. He hired detectives but nothing came of it. She vanished into the ethers, just like that," Ziggy emphasized, snapping his fingers. He poured the rest of the liquor into his glass and pounded the cork into the empty bottle. His hands shook.

"Let me have some," I motioned, not wanting him to become drunk. I poured half the amount from his glass into mine.

"Never left a note for me," Ziggy went on. "My father went to the police and filed a missing person report and they actually interviewed him. They probably suspected him since the police had been called to the house before because of arguments they'd had. I often wondered if he had killed her. I suppose he could have. He could have killed any of us. He was a madman. A bipolar madman. Wonderful stuff, this Calvados. So here I am, Ben, a shrink trying to make sense of the world. I suppose I should go into forensics and work with homicidal maniacs so I can understand my father. My dog was named Fonzi," Ziggy murmured as he stumbled over to a chaise lounge and threw himself down on it, his hands behind his head. "I suppose your family was a 'Leave it to Beaver' variety compared to mine. Nice and sane. I take it your father didn't have a .45 semi-automatic to maintain order in the home."

"No." I was distressed by the sudden outburst of painful childhood memories being thrown at me from left field.

"No," Ziggy repeated and finished his drink.

I had a mental image of our living room with my father sitting in his red vinyl rocking chair, patiently listening to a client's account of a new invention that would improve man's plight on the planet. And all the while, my mother dutifully went to work at the diner in Watertown, Massachesetts. He always showed me these inventions that people brought to him. I remember once asking if he showed them to my mother.

"Your mother's not interested in my work," he'd replied, irritated. I was quite young and was slowly realizing the large estrangement between my parents.

"About my mother," Ziggy started up again. 'There was this professor in Paris who had trained at Sandstone, and he talked about having dinner with Mueller and his wife. He showed me a photograph he'd taken of them at the restaurant. I was startled. It was very strange because Mueller's wife resembled that old framed picture I have of my mother. The one I showed you. She looked older than she does in my photo but there's a resemblance. So, what's the probability of it happening? One in ten million? A hundred million? I hate to think of any mother of mine marrying Mueller. Jesus! What kind of woman would marry Mueller?" Ziggy's speech was getting thick. He rubbed his eyes and yawned.

"I may take a nap now," he said.

"That's quite a theory you have, Ziggy," I said, but Ziggy was now snoring. He'd fallen sound asleep.

I cleared the table, thinking that a man seriously looking for his mother would surely find her somewhere in the world. The idea that Ziggy's mother had ended up with Mueller seemed bizarre. If she had, wouldn't she reach out to the son she hadn't seen in 20 years? Especially if she knew her son was a doctor employed by her new husband. The whole scenario seemed fanciful. I scooped up the glasses from the table, put them in the sink, and placed the empty Calvados bottle in the trash bin. It was then that I noticed the torn remnant of a gummed label on the bottle that said 'Frazier Park Discount Liquors.' That liquor store was in a shopping center a short drive away from Sandstone. Hadn't Ziggy just declared that he'd imported the liquor from Paris? I was confused. I got in my car and took off.

I drove aimlessly through the countryside. Ziggy preoccupied me. What did I care about how much he drank or his use of marijuana? His actions seemed to cross a serious professional boundary. And this story he'd just related about the father killing his dog to discipline him for not doing homework and the story of his threatening the mother over bananas. Were these accounts to be believed?

I came upon a local shopping center and pulled into the parking lot. I stopped the car in front of a small cinema. Film posters depicted future attractions. One caught my eye. It was for the classic movie Casablanca, starring Ingrid Bergmann and Humphrey Bogart. I remembered the film. It was one of my favorites. The image from the poster showed Bergman looking lovingly at Bogart but in the film, she'd left him twice, the second time at Bogart's urging. It wasn't that uncommon. Women left men all the time and men left women. These were central themes in all literature, films, and opera My mother had left my father, but he had left her first by ignoring her. And the way I saw it, she got even by killing herself. I stared at the poster, transfixed.

Chapter 5

That night I was on call at the hospital. A few patients needed sleeping pills, one had a skin rash that I couldn't identify but seemed innocuous, and someone on Lascomb Hall had punched a wall with his fist and was now complaining about the pain in his hand. I sent him downtown to the hospital for an x-ray. A female patient on Ziggy's unit had superficially scratched herself with the prongs of a barrette, so I headed over to the hall. There was a rather voluptuous young blond sitting in the nursing station and cheerfully joking with staff as I entered. Melody was her name. I led her into one of the interview rooms.

"Let's see your cut," I instructed. She peeled off the single bandage on her wrist. The cut was small and bled only slightly but her arm had multiple slices, some were healing and others were jagged scars, just like those on Grace's arm.

"You must have been upset," I commented.

"I thought Dr. Ziggy was on call," she replied.

"He's your doctor?"

"He's cute," she giggled. "Whenever I cut myself, he inspects the cut and strokes my arm, and it feels better. He has strong hands."

"And did you cut yourself tonight expecting him to come?" I asked, alarmed.

"Sort of."

"Sort of what? Why did you cut yourself, Melody?"

"I felt bad."

"About what?"

"Just bad."

"Depressed?"

"Sort of."

This questioning led me nowhere, except to again confirm the maddening phenomena of patients who cut their wrists in response to loss, disappointment, the need to punish themselves, or the simple need for attention. But this time I wondered about Melody's statement regarding Ziggy. Was this just a simple infatuation these young girls had with their male caretakers or was there more to it? After Ziggy's angry reaction to the marijuana incident, I decided to refrain from another encounter with him. I instructed the nurse to rebandage Melody's cut and I gladly left the building.

In the course of my training some years earlier, I had attended a rather gruesome lecture by a professor of psychiatry from the University of Pennsylvania who had written a book on self-mutilation. He showed slides of more innocent disfigurements such as piercing and tattooing or the carving of initials on the skin. Then he revealed a whole world that existed about which I knew nothing. There was an underground world of sadomasochism where men and women wore testicle or nipple clamps and encouraged others to whip them. Horrific slides depicted men and women who had set themselves on fire or plucked out their eyes or even castrated themselves during bursts of psychotic guilt. The audience squirmed with discomfort.

"Now, what I haven't talked about at all is another realm of self-imposed injury from drug and alcohol abuse," the professor told us. "Or states of anorexia or obesity. I call these conditions the self-mutilation of internal organs but this is the subject for another talk," he mercifully concluded. We clapped politely and left the lecture hall, chastened by all the self- maiming we had seen and heard described.

I recounted the lecture to Ziggy.

"It's all biochemical," he responded. "There's something missing or overabundant in the brain that makes people want to feel pain. We'll eventually find what's wrong and supplement the missing substance or administer a drug to fix it. There are lots of illnesses that are the result of deficiencies. Scurvy, for example."

"You actually think self-mutilation is like scurvy?" I was appalled. "Just give them some lemons?"

"That's right."

"So, you think every mental condition represents something missing in the brain. Or there's too much of something?"

"Right."

"The dismay you have about your mother abandoning you and taking up with Mueller is also a biochemical aberration?" I challenged his theory.

Ziggy didn't answer, but his face became a degree paler and he dismissed me, saying that he had patients to see.

The next morning rounds yielded a surprise. Mueller seemed more animated. The group came to order.

"I am delighted to have some gratifying news to report," he boomed. "The drugs that we thought were missing have been accounted for and I am happy to report that the case is closed. There will be no further investigation. But," he dutifully cautioned us, his finger once more in the air, "we must be very vigilant about this drug matter. Drugs are a fact of life now in our society, and some of our younger patients will continue to be drawn towards abusing them, whether they are here or on the street. The risk, obviously, is higher among those who have privileges outside the hospital or go home on weekends or go to work or school during the day and then return to Sandstone. I've initiated a surveillance task force to this effect, and we will begin to formulate a policy concerning the searching of patients who go in and out of our campus. Dr. Cassidy is the logical person to spearhead this project, and I've asked him to say a few words. Dr. Cassidy? A few brief words before we adjourn?"

"Howdy and good morning to y'all," Cassidy boomed, grinning widely. Cassidy was the antithesis of Mueller. Tall and rangy, he wore a western style suit with a string tie. He also occasionally sported a cowboy hat and riding boots. Cassidy was the former Louisiana Commissioner of Mental Health and he had published some early papers on the use of methadone in the treatment of opiate addictions.

"Now, y'all have a problem," he drawled. "Many folks comin' here these days have drug problems. Hallucinogens, weed, even opium stuff. Young people, mostly. So, we're gonna have to do more searches than we used to and that'll rub folks the wrong way and it'll put a lot more burden on nursin' staff. Been talkin' with legal about maybe havin' a new admission policy form that people sign when they come here. Anyhow, we'll be keepin' y'all posted 'bout all this," he paused to gather his next thought "Should mention that our new methadone program's gettin' off the ground soon and we'll keep you posted 'bout that also."

I could see the scorn on Mueller's face as Cassidy talked with his southern twang and informality. A flurry of hands went up with people concerned about the invasion of privacy, the physical limits of body searches, the possible penalties for the finding of contraband and how the public might react to the idea of a drug maintenance program that flew in the face of Sandstone's hallowed tradition of talk therapy.

"I think we've explored this enough for one day. Thank you, Dr. Cassidy," Mueller brought the subject to a halt. It was known that Mueller took a dim view of men and women whose illness was principally characterized by a lack of will power. On the other hand, Sandstone could ill afford to lose these patients to the private rehabilitation centers that catered to Hollywood figures and limelighters in need of drying out. Cassidy had been lured to Sandstone to precisely address this problem. The most recent such patient admitted to Sandstone was Sofia Barbarosa, the gorgeous movie actress who drank too much and seemed to specialize offstage in taking overdoses whenever lovers tired of her egotism. Publicity about her impending arrival at Sandstone sparked a gratifying flood of referrals. Sofia, herself, viewed Sandstone as yet another opportunity for self-promotion.

"My agent wants to issue a press release about my visit here," Sophia told me. She wore a low-cut dress, expensive jewelry and very high heeled shoes. "What do you think, doctor? He says that people admire movie stars like me who have human—human—"

"Vulnerabilities," I finished for her.

"Yes, that's it. What do you think, doctor? You think it's a good idea? I wish I could have a drink." She twirled the flashy gold bracelets on her arm.

"Why don't you wait a bit before you issue a release. Let's start your therapy first. You've only just arrived."

"If you say so, doctor," she said with disappointment. I didn't envy the forthcoming treatment effort by the physician to whom she would be assigned. I was glad I was only responsible for the admission workup.

After seeing Ms. Barbarosa, I searched for Ziggy, wanting to question him about the drug supply that had rematerialized. I found him at the library in the basement of the administration building reading a journal article on attachment theory.

"What's up?" he quipped.

"You weren't at the morning meeting," I said. "You missed Mueller's announcement that the missing drugs have been returned. The marijuana. Nothing's missing anymore."

"That so? That's what Mueller reported?" Ziggy regarded me with an innocent face.

"How did that happen," I whispered to Ziggy, noticing the librarian.

"How did what happen?"

"You know exactly what I'm talking about, Ziggy."

"I'm reading something very interesting," Ziggy ignored my curiosity. "It's about attachment theory. The famous British psychiatrist, Bowlby. Did you know that Bowlby came from an aristocratic family that believed parents should spend no more than two hours a day with their children so as not to spoil them? Bowlby was raised by a nanny. Later on, when he was a psychiatrist during the war and the bombings took place in London, over a million children were shipped out to the countryside. Many of them ended up in orphanages. Many didn't thrive. Some died. Bowlby didn't buy into the belief that there was an epidemic disease spreading across the country. He believed the children suffered and even died because they weren't properly nurtured. Did you know all this?"

I changed the subject abruptly. "You returned the marijuana, Ziggy. How did you do it?"

Ziggy ignored me and went on with his lecture.

"They were given food and water, but not hugged or held. If the infant doesn't form a bond and attach to the caretaker, he becomes a casualty. That was the beginning of attachment theory. There's a morbidity and mortality associated with failed attachment." Ziggy's chair made a large screeching sound as he pushed it back on the hardwood floor and stood erect. "Shall we get some coffee?"

"Coffee? Answer my question about the marijuana," I demanded, dismissing the subject of attachment which clearly hit close to home.

"Listen, Ben," Ziggy stood stock still in the middle of the room and hissed at me. His eyes drilled into mine. "The event is over, OK? It's over and done with."

"Just like that."

"Exactly."

"Exactly," I murmured, unconvinced.

"Tell me what Mueller said," Ziggy now asked.

"Mueller. You barely know the man but for some reason you've decided he's your nemesis. Well, for the future, he is putting some kind of search policy into effect. It involves searching new patients and those returning to the hospital."

"Really. Well, that's what assholes do. They make stupid policies. Will we now be searched as well? Or are doctors exempt? Maybe they'll x-ray everyone who comes through the front door. Or even better, strip searches. Now that would be enticing. Where shall we go for coffee?"

"I'll pass on coffee," I said.

"You're pissed."

"Perhaps." But I was thinking about Bowlby and I wondered if I was like one of the English children who had been sent into a barren orphanage.

"I don't think I was properly nurtured," Ziggy suddenly declared.

I gaped at him. Ziggy had never shown much curiosity about the workings of his own mind. My God, I thought. Was it really possible that Ziggy and I suffered from the same malady? Plagued by the same void? Motherlessness?

"Yeah, well something's sure wrong with you," I answered, turning around and hastily stomping out, unnerved.

It so happened that the next week's speaker was Dr. Francine Chase, a child psychiatrist from Tulane University who spoke on the very subject of childhood attachment. She showed movies. In one film, a child showed no interest in either his mother or father, preferring to play with a toy water pistol. In a contrasting movie clip, a child clung desperately to his mother, except the woman wasn't his mother at all, it was an utter stranger. In a third movie clip, a child was separated from his mother and he cried so pitifully that we onlookers audibly moaned in sympathy. When the mother reappeared, the child was ecstatic and we actually clapped in relief.

"Now, we have here three kinds of attachment," Dr. Chase explained. "In the first, there are elements of autism where the child attaches to no one. In the second example, we see a child who is entirely indiscriminate and attaches to anyone. The third is something that many of us experience as we raise children and occasionally leave them, but we always return to them. Our absences take some getting used to on their part, and eventually our children tolerate our leaving them because they have formed a durable sense of attachment. Now, let me show you some experiments with Rhesus monkeys at the University of Wisconsin's primate labs. This important work is being done by Dr. Harry Harlow. Here are some film clips."

In the films she now showed, the infant monkeys were separated from their mothers. Their reactions were even more disturbing than those involving humans. Harlow had constructed wire frames of mother monkeys with rudimentary heads and eyes. One frame was bare but had milk available. A second frame was covered with terry cloth and had no milk. The infants preferred the terry cloth monkeys, and went to the wire cloth frame only for the milk. Lacking their real mother, most of the animals seemed completely wasted by these experiments. They rocked back and forth and howled with inconsolable grief and anger. If the researcher was attempting to show the importance of early mother-child attachment, he had succeeded only too well. Anxiety descended on me. I suddenly felt acutely forlorn. I had a strong impulse to wrench myself out of my seat and flee the lecture.

"Aren't you bothered by the animal experiments?" a listener asked. "Can these animals ever recover?"

"I get this question all the time," Dr. Chase answered. "It's interesting. We seem to react more to the monkeys than to humans in an analogous situation. The pathos we feel for the animals seems to exceed the anguish we show for the kids similarly deprived. I don't know why that's so. But no, the wounded animals don't recover and Dr. Harlow is having trouble with the animal rights people."

"And do humans who have the equivalent of wire mothers ever recover?" another person asked.

The auditorium went silent. Dr. Chase struggled with an answer.

"Some do and some don't," she said quietly. 'Of course, we don't have enough data yet."

"But do you really need data?" Ziggy called out. I turned to see him seated in the back of the amphitheater seats, as usual.

Ziggy's comment effectively ended the lecture. People filed out, sobered by what they had seen. Ziggy was outside the lecture hall, smoking and pacing.

"A horrible lecture," he said to me. "Atrocious."

I was seized by the thought that I had experienced a variation of a wire-cloth mother. Could I turn out to be as desolate as the monkey? Thus far I was managing reasonably well but who knew what the future might bring. All these insecurities were piling up. I needed to talk to someone about my emotions.

"These awful pictures of kids and monkeys," Ziggy was saying. "Sadistic research is what it is. Experimenters like that should be banned."

"I agree. I could hardly bear to watch."

"I hope the animal rights people shut him down," Ziggy said. "I hope his grants get canceled. I hope he becomes an experimental subject some day and is tortured the same way. Tortured to extinction. To death." Ziggy's facial muscles were contorted with anger. I fled to Manning Hall, seeking refuge in my patients who, for all intents and purposes, were as disturbed as some of the animals I'd just seen.

* * *

Diagnostic conferences were held 30 days after each patient was admitted, and then reevaluated after another 60 days. To these meetings came all staff who had contact with the patient. This included the attending psychiatrist, the resident assigned to the case, nursing personnel, any relevant social worker and the psychologist who might have administered IQ or personality tests. There was also an invited discussant who was a senior clinician from either the hospital or community or from the psychiatric service at Yale. Mathew Cole McAllister was the name of the expert chosen to weigh in on my patient, Sunshine. McAlister was a psychoanalyst. Psychoanalysts were revered in those days, and many acted as if they possessed the sacred key to the contents of man's unconscious. In their world, there were no random events. All of man's behaviors, awake and asleep with dreams, reflected the drives and conflicts of the mind. Vanderpol subscribed to psychoanalytic theory, but was not orthodox about it.

"Most of what we think and do is determined by unseen forces," I would hear him say. "Our job is to make the patient aware of these forces so they can steer the car better."

I presented the case of Sunshine, the course of her illness, her parents, her sister, childhood, school, friends, as much information as I'd gleaned from my weeks of contact with her.

"You've obviously studied this young woman very thoroughly," McAllister complimented me. "Tell me more about the mother."

"She is terrifically worried about Sunshine. The nurses tell me that she cries when she leaves her."

"And have you observed how she cries?" McAlister questioned.

"How? No. She cries after she leaves Sunshine's room. Sunshine doesn't accompany her to the front door."

"Crying takes many forms," McAllister extracted a pipe from his jacket pocket. "There's soft weeping, loud wailing and also moaning and sobbing. More important is how a person deals with their tears. Does he or she suppress them immediately or let them flow? Does the person make an immediate attempt to wipe away the tear? Is the crying cathartic? Do they feel relief after they weep? Many people, both men and women, are embarrassed to cry. Some want to cry but can't. Others go to movie theaters in order to safely cry. Others won't go see a sad movie because they're afraid they'll cry" McAlister paused for a moment and lit his pipe. "Some of my patients angrily grab fistfuls of Kleenex when they cry, and others refuse a single Kleenex and still others ignore the box of tissues sitting on the table next to them and prefer to use their own handkerchief."

"So," he continued, "is the mother crying because she genuinely loves her child and feels sorry for her, or is she crying because of guilt or because Sunshine rejects her so much?"

I'd never considered the complexities of crying. Crying. When was the last time I myself cried? At my mother's death? My father had censured my weeping. "Be strong," he had commanded. He himself had not shed a tear. I recalled weeping at my father's death when he was obviously not there to stop me.

I forced myself to return to the matter of Sunshine and her mother.

"Is there affection between them?" McAllister asked me.

"Not much," I said.

"You've met the mother?" McAllister inquired.

"I have," Vanderpol spoke up for the first time.

"And you, Dr. Soloway?"

"No," I said, alarmed.

"Ah. You should," McAlister said gently. "You'll have to explore the matter more," he said. I was sure he noticed my reddened face.

"And try and determine the interaction between the mother and Sunshine. It's crucial. The mother child bond is everything. The life-sustaining oxygen of affection, if you'll forgive my being melodramatic." McAlister lit his pipe and the sweet fragrance of flavored tobacco filled the room. "If affection turns out to be lacking, determine how far back it goes."

"How far back?" I didn't understand.

"To the beginning," McAlister nodded.

"You mean when Sunshine was born?"

"Long before. Her mother's mother. Parental behaviors can be inherited just like facial features are inherited. Sunshine's grandmother may have been unable to show affection and passed that down to Sunshine's mother. Then, ultimately, Sunshine becomes the one who suffers. If affection is an issue in this case, it may help Sunshine to see that its absence goes back a generation or even more. It may help Sunshine to be more forgiving of her mother. Some cultures are stoic, like the Scandinavians who hold back on the expression of emotions, while other cultures, like Latin Americans, exhibit a more exaggerated display of feelings. It's most intriguing," McAllister said, smiling.

"Now. About your patient's problem with her mouth."

I stared at him.

"The anorexia. I know it's an eating disorder but it's more than that. It involves the mouth, no? The mouth," McAllister pointed to the pipe in his mouth. "If you think about it, everything we do involves the mouth. Eating and drinking, smoking, chewing gum, speaking, kissing, the mouth is a hollow tube that runs through man's body and exits the anus. The mouth is the entry portal to human functions. A baby's existence depends on the mouth. Sunshine's repudiation of food and solace reflects early life experiences."

McAllister's psychoanalytic interpretation of Sunshine's disease took me aback. In time, I came to learn how the psychoanalysts conceived of illness in symbolic terms. Asthma could represent anger that could not otherwise be directly expressed. People with excessive rage developed ulcers or colitis. In what came to be called psychosomatic disease, the malfunction of the body reflected hidden emotions. "You have a lot to explore," McAllister summarized. "I don't envy the task you have ahead."

The case conference ended and I felt most inadequate. At home that evening, while forking sardines out of a can, I fretted over the consultation with McAllister. I must have looked like a fool to him. My omission of not meeting Sunshine's mother and not seeing the interaction between the two was huge. How could I have overlooked this? The time had clearly come for me to delve into the subject of my own mother. I needed someone to talk to. It was long overdue.

I had the momentary urge to phone Vanderpol and ask him to recommend a psychotherapist. Then I had second thoughts. Did I want him to know that I was seeking therapy even though he himself had urged me to consider it? I paced the apartment. Here I was, learning to become a psychiatrist and I was ashamed of the fact that I myself needed psychiatric help. I could barely open the phone book to begin looking for therapists. Then I remembered I had read some informative publications about anxiety which was authored by a Joyce Templeton, M.D. Her office was actually not that far away from where I lived. I located her in the phone book and pinned her phone number to the small bulletin board in the kitchen next to the phone. It glared at me and I found myself dialing the number.

"My name is Ben Soloway," I said into her answering machine. "I'm a psychiatrist in training at Sandstone Hospital and I would like to meet with you to discuss therapy." How would this Dr. Templeton interpret my message? I started to analyze myself. Would she hear me as earnest or needy or did I come across as anxious or depressed? Well, then, what difference did it make how she heard me? The more important issue was whether she could help me unravel myself, not how I appeared. Clearly, I was still fraught with concern about my appearance and worth to others. I frowned and looked for my jar of instant coffee. I put in three teaspoons for extra strength.

Chapter 6

Dr. Joyce Templeton had two chairs in her consultation room. One was a typical college-alumnus hard-backed wooden seat, and the other was an overstuffed armchair which I chose and promptly sank into. My position forced me to gaze upwards at her. Dr. Templeton had grey hair, a thin mouth, and a prominent and deeply slanted nose. She seemed to wear no makeup at all and she wore wire rim eyeglasses. At one time she might have been attractive, but she now looked aged and tired. Her frame was small and she was a bit gaunt, perhaps from the cigarettes she chain smoked. Still, her smile was a warm one, and she welcomed me to her office.

"So. Here you are, an emerging psychiatrist."

"Somedays it seems as if the process will take forever," I said.

"Indeed. You are liking it so far?"

"Very much."

"You have difficult patients?"

"A few."

"And the rest are easy?" she grinned broadly.

"No, no, they're all difficult," I admitted.

"The specialty is a demanding one. Hospitalized patients are particularly arduous. Many systems have failed them. They may recover but they never forget their in-patient stay. I've found that some patients, strangely, look back on it as a time of consolation. Others are terrified of the experience. Who is your attending?" she inquired.

"Jack Vanderpol."

"Dr. Vanderpol's a fine clinician. One of the finest, in my view."

"I'm learning a lot from him."

"Good. Now perhaps you could tell me how you came about picking me as your therapist," she asked.

"Convenience," I heard myself say, immediately regretting the silly reply. "I live close by."

"Beyond convenience," she smiled again.

"I've read the papers you've written."

"So, I have credibility. Credibility is useful. But I'm guessing there's more to your choice in selecting me?"

Templeton's question startled me. I really had not consciously thought about my deeper and obvious choice of her as a woman. I squirmed in the seat. She regarded me closely.

"I'm taking a wild guess that what you want to talk about has to do with a woman," she said. "Am I right?"

"My mother," I mumbled.

"Important," she said.

"How do we begin?" I hesitantly asked.

"You dig in," she said. "Any place is good to start."

"It's a long start."

"I'm sure. But are we in any hurry?" Dr. Templeton asked.

I shook my head.

77

"I assume your conflicts have been going on for a long time, no? It is hard to start treatment. Most people are initially scared of revealing themselves. We humans are such utterly private people. Psychiatrists, particularly," she added.

* * *

Ziggy came over to my apartment later that day. He accepted a beer and then went over to the window.

"What's this?" Ziggy regarded a handsome old Questar telescope my father had bought me. The brass was tarnished after many years of disuse, and dust covered the alignment mechanisms. It sat on a small tabletop tripod. I'd recently unpacked it.

"Can you see the rings of Saturn?" Ziggy asked, fingering the instrument.

"And the moons of Jupiter."

"You have a telescope and I have a microscope," he said. "Which is better, do you suppose? To look outside or inside?"

"Our careers seem to be predicated on looking inside. Well, to be more precise, we look at different things. You look inside the cell and inside the chemicals of the cell."

"And you?"

"I think I have more curiosity about the whole organism, including myself." Against my better judgment, I described my beginning session with Dr. Templeton. I was disappointed, Ziggy wasn't interested at all about the matter.

"I'm going to pass on therapy right now," Ziggy said. "I can't see the benefit of it. I'm not symptomatic. I'm not depressed or anxious, so why would I need to see a shrink?"

"To be a better shrink? To learn about yourself?" I countered.

"How is getting shrunk going to make you a better shrink?" he quizzed. "You don't undergo dissection to be a better pathologist. You don't submit to having a heart valve replaced in order to be a better cardiac surgeon."

"It's different."

"Different how?" Ziggy disputed.

"Self-knowledge, then" I contested.

"Bah," he dismissed. "Simple self-indulgence." We argued as we always did without any closure.

I saw Ziggy the next day in the canteen. He was sitting at a table with the young blond girl whom I recognized as a patient on his unit. I had seen her when I was on-call. She was laughing at something he was telling her. He motioned me to his table.

"I was telling Melody about the time I talked my way out of a speeding ticket by telling the policeman that I was a doctor on the way to the hospital to deliver a baby. This was in France. The cop ended up leading the way with his siren blaring, He didn't know it was a psychiatric hospital!" Both Ziggy and Melody erupted in laughter. My solemn appearance made them stop.

"What's wrong," Ziggy said.

"Nothing. I'll meet you outside," I said, and abruptly exited, troubled by what I had just witnessed. Ziggy caught up with me on the path around the Administration Building.

"What the hell," Ziggy exclaimed. "What was all that about?"

"What are you doing with her," I challenged him. "What the hell are you telling her jokes for? She's a sick cookie. She is a patient, for God's sake. I saw her when I was on call. She had cut her wrist. What the hell are you laughing about with her?"

"What are you talking about? What are you, some kind of moral censor?"

"It's a boundary thing, Ziggy."

"A boundary thing? What the hell? I'm sitting in the open in the canteen with a patient. It's not her bedroom. A boundary thing? Really, you are sick, man."

"It's inappropriate," I declared.

"For you, Mr. Saint. For you maybe it's inappropriate because anything that smacks of fun or joy is inappropriate. For you there's evil everywhere, in every marijuana joint, in every glass of booze. I'm guessing in anything sexual, too, though I purposely haven't asked you about your sex life but I can only imagine you're puritanical about women also." He was getting more menacing as he spoke. "You know what's wrong with that girl, that Melody?" Ziggy jerked his thumb in the direction of the canteen. "You know what the hell is wrong with her? What's wrong with her is that her father is a minister and her mother is a social worker, and she was never allowed to even think about masturbating. She was raised in a straitjacket," he said with contempt. "Her God damn favorite color is white. Cleanliness. Goodness." A spray of saliva erupted from Ziggy's mouth. I found his diatribe almost blasphemous.

"The patient's a raving case of self-destruction," I shot back at Ziggy. "I read her chart. She's overdosed God knows how many times, she gets drunk, and she's broken all the windows in her room at home. To cover up all her cuts, she wears only long sleeves, Ziggy, all of which I'm sure you have observed. And there's the cut on her neck."

"Did you tell her to take off her blouse so you could see it?" Ziggy retorted.

"You oughten to be socializing with her."

"Gentlemen!" a voice barked at us. Vanderpol materialized. I hadn't seen him approaching. We both instantly became mute.

"You guys need to go indoors," Vanderpol said, coming closer. "Finish your argument somewhere private."

"I guess you could hear us," I said dumbly.

"Security should be coming any moment," Vanderpol said. "Someone thought you were patients involved in a fight and called them." In the distance, I could see two blue and white security cars briskly winding their way towards us.

"Why don't you both get out of here and I'll tell them everything is under control. "

"I'm sorry," I said, embarrassed.

"Beat it now," Vanderpol instructed.

We went our separate ways. When I looked back, I could make out Vanderpol talking with the officers. Ziggy had disappeared. I made my way back to my unit and went into the small library located next to the nursing station. Vanderpol entered a few minutes later.

"A little diagnostic quibble?" he said to me. "Or something weightier."

"Both."

"Sounded heavy duty to me."

"I criticized Ziggy for sitting in the canteen with one of the patients from his unit."

"Just sitting?"

"Laughing together. He was telling her a joke."

"What kind of joke?"

I repeated what Ziggy had told the girl. I told him I thought it was inappropriate. "Sometimes I think he doesn't appreciate the illnesses of his patients. He thinks they're just spoiled girls."

"Which girl was he with?" Vanderpol asked.

"Melody."

"Melody. I've heard about her. She's quite distressed." Vanderpol lit his cigar and lowered himself onto a couch.

"Ziggy shouldn't be flirting," I said.

"Yes, you're probably right." Vanderpol concurred. "But the patients on that unit are very seductive. They fall in love with their doctors. That's the special peril of working on that unit. Falling in love. Working there creates more problems for doctors than any other unit. Hopefully, your Dr. Ziggy will learn in time," Vanderpol said, looking perturbed. "If he doesn't, things will become awkward. I guess I should ask you what you see in him? He seems somewhat provocative."

"I'm drawn to his rebelliousness," I said truthfully. "I've been so very obedient all my life." Then I blurted out the story of his mother. "He has this crazy belief that Mueller's wife is actually his mother. His mother left the family years ago."

Vanderpol rolled his eyes. "Oh my. Is he serious about this belief?"

"Yes."

"That's quite a story. How does he come to that conclusion?"

"He's tracked her down somehow."

"He has evidence?" Vanderpol raised his eyebrows.

"Evidently, from what he tells me."

"Does Mueller know any of this?"

"I don't know."

"Ben, this sounds like a man you ought to stay away from."

"I'll try. I've spoken to him about therapy."

"And?"

"Nothing. No interest."

"Not a good sign." Vanderpol said.

"I'll try some more."

"In this business you have to know when you need help. If not, you're susceptible to all the illnesses you treat. All these patients," Vanderpol gestured towards the main hallway, "are infectious. Sandstone is a hot box packed with viral diseases. Hand washing doesn't work. Antibiotics are worthless. We can go mad. Some of us do." Vanderpol looked me in the eye. "As regards the patients, it's OK to get therapeutically involved with them but keep a little distance for yourself. Have a full life. Play a musical instrument. Mountain climb. Drive fast cars." He grinned at me. "Did I already mention therapy to you?"

"You did," I said. I wasn't ready to reveal the fact that I had begun treatment. As I left Manning House, I thought that despite Vanderpol's warning about Ziggy, it wouldn't be that easy for me to part company with him, for reasons I didn't understand.

* * *

I looked in on Grace. She was calmer and listening to the radio while reading the classified ads in the New Haven Register.

"Anything interesting?" I asked.

"Not really," she said looking up.

"A car? A dog?"

"Actually, an apartment."

"Really, Grace? An apartment? For yourself?"

"Yes. I doubt I'm ready, though. Just a thought."

"You were high a few days ago. Your moods are still very erratic but it's good that you're thinking of an apartment." I was pleased that she was contemplating a future for herself.

"Someday they'll have something for my moods," she said hopefully.

"Someday. Something to stabilize moods."

"Then I'll be normal, yes?"

"Yes, Grace."

"Something in the brain must control moods, isn't that so?"

"I'm sure."

"Will we find it?"

"I think so." I thought of Ziggy. I pictured a laboratory full of Ziggies, all dressed in protective gowns, standing at benches while beakers and flasks bubbled with important fluids. We at Sandstone on the other hand, wore ordinary jackets and suits with no pretense of being scientists.

Chapter 7

At morning rounds, an announcement was made regarding the discharge of three recovered patients. All of them had been hospitalized for at least a year. Mueller always took pride in these matters, as if he himself had effected the cure.

"We've had a gratifying number of remissions so far this year," he proclaimed. "The Board of the hospital is very pleased with our numbers. Of the 100 patients admitted since the first of the year, almost 87% have been helped by our interventions. Sandstone stands in its own class I'm pleased to say." Mueller seemed to expect a congratulatory clapping of hands but no applause was forthcoming. As to his statistics, no one disputed his claims.

"Well then," he composed himself. "Is there any new business?"

"There's a new admission coming," the on-call resident stated. "He is from the Wainscott family in Chicago. The family wanted to air transport him from the family summer home in Martha's Vineyard. They asked me if a seaplane could land on Lake Jehova but we insisted upon a more conventional arrival. He's 19. Two members of the family will arrive with him. Well, they're not really family member, they're hired staff to escort him around here and sort of chaperone him. Umm," the resident cleared his throat, "it's a tricky case. The boy's been repeatedly arrested for drunken behavior and the court apparently agreed to another round of treatment if he attended Sandstone. He's said to be quite entitled. Largely raised by his father," the resident added. "Mother was alcoholic and died of liver cancer."

"Chaperones?" someone asked. "We've never had patients with chaperones here."

"That is correct," Mueller quipped. "This will be a bit of an experiment. The boy has been at Chestnut Lodge without much improvement. We hope we can help him here. I've spoken with his former therapist who emphasized the need the boy has for external controls." Mueller relished taking on the failures from other facilities with the tacit message that Sandstone could do better.

"The case is a delicate one, of course. Marvin Wainscott, as some of you may know, is our ambassador to Great Britain. As for any sense of entitlement his son has, we must treat him as we treat all the other patients and avoid giving him unearned privileges."

Within a few days, Marvin Wainscott, Jr. arrived. His escorts turned out to be blazer-clad and muscle-bound young men who followed him around the hospital campus, correcting him for every single indiscretion in which he engaged. I happened to be in the canteen one day when Marvin wandered in and ordered an ice cream cone.

"I want a goddamn big cone," he barked at the volunteer behind the counter. "Not like the pissy little one you gave me last time."

The two escorts swung into action. Approaching each side of him, they gently squeezed him by the arms.

"Try being polite," one of them growled.

"Get your hands off me," Marvin said through gritted teeth.

"Polite," the other young man emphasized. "Hold the ice cream cone, please," he instructed the girl behind the counter.

"God damn please," Marvin said to the woman holding the empty cone.

"No cone for you, Marvin."

"Hey, I said 'please.'" Marvin tried to worm his way free from his escorts' tight grip.

"Try again," the escort told him.

"Forget it," Marvin said, turning around and stomping out, almost knocking over an elderly patient. I wondered much about Marvin's rages and from where they emanated. Did he emerge from the womb screaming and yelling uncontrollably? Had there been a soothing presence in his early life? Within a few weeks, Marvin was declared as 'difficult to treat.' The escorts were dismissed and he was transferred to Lascomb Hall for very disturbed patients where he was medicated against his will. The announcement was made at morning rounds.

"I imagine that His Excellency was not happy about the transfer," Vanderpol said as we made our way to Manning House. "Mueller likes patients to behave."

"What medication can they possibly give him to make him become polite and well behaved?"

"They'll load him up with Thorazine and numb him down. That'll work for a bit until he refuses the drug. I suspect there's more to this than him just being impolite. He has a history of having conned people. His father, for one. I hear he took the Ambassador's credit card and charged thousands of dollars' worth of clothes and stereo equipment. He seems to have little or no conscience. Officially, his diagnosis would be a personality disorder. The question always is whether the patient is mad or bad. We get these bad boys here from time to time and we don't do particularly well with them. Not that reform schools do any better. Have you ever visited a prison?"

"A prison?" I said naively.

"A jail. A lockup. A penitentiary. A detention center. Call it what you will. Something with bars or barbed wire fences. The dark side of the moon," Vanderpol regarded me. "Would you like to accompany me sometime? I do some consults at Leona."

"Maybe," I said cautiously.

"Sandstone is a sanitized version of reality. Another chunk of the world resides in prisons. Mueller has never wanted anything to do with Leona or any of the other evil forensic facilities around the state. But the fact of the matter is that people commit crimes and some of them are mentally ill." We rounded the corner of Manning House and Vanderpol stopped to light his cigar. I was getting fond of the aroma.

"Anyway, how are the rest of your folks coming along? Grace? Sunshine? Ted?"

"They're tough cases," I sighed. "Tough cases. Particularly Grace with her moodiness. I suppose it's good that a bad mood is cancelled out by her elevated mood so we have something to be thankful for."

When we arrived at Vanderpol's office, he opened the window and breathed in the early autumn air. "People pay terrible prices for their ups and downs," he declared. "Try not to glamourize mood-iness. I know it makes writers write and musicians compose and all that stuff but these folks exhaust themselves and their families, not to mention their bank accounts. Sometimes it's all for nothing because they still hang themselves in the end. That's what happened to Virginia Woolf."

"Virginia Woolf drowned herself," I differed.

"Hanged," Vanderpol said.

"Drowned. Drowned." I repeated adamantly. "In the river near her home. She put rocks in the pockets of her coat." I knew what I was talking about because my mother had once tried to drown herself the same way. I became a little agitated and I think my hands started to tremble. Vanderpol noticed.

"Hit a nerve again, eh?"

"Yes." I could feel myself burning inside with shame.

"You want to talk about it?"

"Another time," I replied, mortified by my reaction in the presence of Vanderpol.

"Try not to wait, Ben. You have to have a clear mind to work this stuff."

"I've begun," I fidgeted nervously. "Therapy."

"Good," Vanderpol said. "Very good."

"I wish there were some healthy people to treat," I said.

"If there were, they probably wouldn't need treatment," he laughed. "Sure, occasionally we get someone in that isn't very ill. But remember, this is a funny farm. Anyway, Ben, it's important you get out of here occasionally and associate with normal people. Speaking of which, sometime I'll take you to the track. Lots of noise and smoke. It's a lot of fun."

I couldn't for the life of me see how racing automobiles could possibly be enjoyable. Knowing little about it, it seemed like a reckless and dangerous sport. I said so to Vanderpol.

"You're probably right," he said. "Do you consider yourself risk adversive?"

"If you mean walking on the railroad tracks while the train is coming, yes. I don't think I ever dove into any body of water where

I couldn't see the bottom." Oh, I chirped, "Once I gambled at a slot machine."

"You won?"

"Lost. Five dollars," I grinned.

"Ah, Ben, you're going to have to take chances in this profession. You'll have to confront patients who become angry with you. You'll have to tolerate suicidality. You'll have to let patients go home for a weekend even if they're not 100% ready."

Vanderpol consulted his watch. "I think group therapy starts soon. You never know what the group will want to talk about. I ran it earlier in the week and the patients talked about how mean the doctors were. The satanic doctors gave them no freedom. We ruled their lives, and so forth. I got beat up badly."

"I suppose it'll continue today, then," I said morosely.

"Try not to take it personally," Vanderpol said. "Remember that the patients need to blame someone for their plight. We're the easiest target. The challenge is to see if you can swivel their resentment or anger towards the more vital people in their lives. The ones who have really disappointed them."

Group therapy with all the patients at Manning House took place three times a week. I was anticipating a frontal attack of the type Vanderpol had mentioned but a slightly different theme took place. One of the patients began to cry about how long her depression was lasting and how hopeless she felt about her life. Others tried to comfort her but at the same time, there were patients who had been at Manning for many months and despaired over ever reentering their former worlds.

"My family has forgotten me," a woman said woefully.

"Mine also," an older man lamented.

"Mine just wants to get rid of me," another said.

At first, I had tried very hard to resolve these agonies by invoking the curative powers of medication and psychotherapy. As time went on, I came to see that the comments made reflected deeper losses of love and affection that had existed long before their entry into Sandstone. The yearnings of the group members exhausted me and I was glad when the hour was over.

That afternoon, I wandered into the nursing station, pulled out my patients' charts and read the nursing notes. Grace hadn't eaten her meals. This could be a sign of mania or depression. Manic patients often had so much energy that they forgot to eat. In depression, their appetites evaporated. Sunshine, though, had eaten three chocolate cookies. Such was the nature of my chosen profession that the intake of cookies was the tiniest therapeutic triumph.

Grace was at the beauty salon. Instead, I found Sunshine listening to the popular folk group Peter, Paul, and Mary. She looked like a scarecrow even after months of therapy. Her extremities still were like sticks.

"If I had a hammer," Sunshine mimicked the music, "I'd smash all the presents my parents have given me." She looked up when I entered. "One time, a few years ago, my mother gave me a fancy Raleigh bicycle that she had specially painted blue, because blue is my favorite color. Anyway, the first time I rode it, I smashed it up and that was the end of it. There's some other stuff around the house that I'd like to smash."

"Besides your watch?"

"My mother has a precious vase she bought in Japan. I bet it would splinter into a million pieces. I saw her hug the vase. Not me. The vase."

"Oh, Sunshine," I shook my head in dismay. "You have all this anger inside you. And it shows up in your unwillingness to eat. Speaking of which, you still look very thin."

"I've gained weight. It's from eating three chocolate cookies yesterday, I'm sure."

"Sunshine, you're as thin as a rail."

"Well, I can't exactly check how I look, can I, seeing as you took away my mirror."

"You can see your own skin and bones."

"You can't make me eat."

"As I've said, Sunshine. We can't make you do anything."

"That's right."

"Right." We stood there, glowering at one another. "Your mother has come to visit?"

"She tried. I didn't want to see her and I told her not to come."

"I guess she wasn't pleased to hear that."

"Not much about me pleases her"

"So that leaves you with a choice of dedicating your life to please the unpleasable parents or dedicating your life to pleasing yourself. Right?"

"I can do whatever I want. Is our session over?" Sunshine now asked.

"Your call. Shall we stop?"

"Yes," she asserted. "I'm going for a walk." Exiting her room, I noted that she didn't slam the door on me as she usually did.

I stayed late that evening to use the library and read about psychopaths, those predatory and conscienceless members of society who conned others and had no remorse for what they did. I had a momentary and disconcerting thought that Ziggy might be in that category because he had so cavalierly taken, and evidently replaced, the marijuana. He seemed to have had no emotion or guilt about it. But the more I read, the less compelling the concept of psychopathy became as applied to Ziggy. Taking marijuana didn't create the diagnosis. Ziggy had distinct achievements to his name. He had been a scientist, he was a physician, he was studying to be a specialist. The stakes were too high for him to be a smoke-and-mirror man. Simply neurotic was what he was, I concluded. He was a man obsessed with the defection of his mother. A psychopath wouldn't care about his mother.

On the way home that evening, I stopped at Fergies, an ice cream parlor a few miles away from Sandstone. I ordered a double fudge sundae and took it to the window which faced a corner of the Pine Mountain Country Club. It was quiet outside as I gazed through the window. Most folks were home with their families. The street was dimly lit but as I looked closer across the way, I saw a young man and woman sauntering arm in arm up the main road of the club. Ziggy? It looked like the outline of Ziggy but I wasn't sure. The girl was blond, that much I could ascertain in the dark. Ziggy with Melody? It was impossible. I stood up and watched them disappear. No, it couldn't be. What on earth would he be doing at the venerable Country Club? Ziggy didn't play golf. He wasn't a club member. I must be mistaken. Intrigued, I found myself abandoning my ice cream, leaving Fergies, and crossing the street to the entrance of the club grounds. Nobody was in sight. I walked further, then began sprinting. The main clubhouse with its columned entrance was up ahead on a small promontory. Fancy cars lined the graveled, circular driveway. Inside, I could hear the commotion of people and the fast beat of Lester Lanin music. I entered the main foyer and saw tables with cardboard nameplates for the guests. In a festooned ballroom, I saw swirling couples dancing to the big band sound of 'Tea for Two.' I started searching for Ziggy amidst the large group.

"Can I help you?" a uniformed man spoke out from behind a desk.

"No," I said, startled.

"Delivering something?" he asked politely.

"No."

"Picking up somebody?" he quizzed more harshly.

"I was following a couple I just saw," I said.

The man stood up, now, more sentient.

"You mind if I ask you what your business is here?" he came towards me.

"I'm a doctor from Sandstone Hospital up the street." I pointed outside. "I saw a couple and thought it might be one of our patients who shouldn't be here."

"The loony bin place?"

"Hospital," I corrected him.

"What, one of the inmates escaped?"

"She was with a man."

"Yeah? Most of the girls here are. How would I know if she's a patient or not?"

I bypassed his question. "Can anyone just walk in here?" I asked. "To this dance?"

"People have cards," the guard said. "Everybody's got an invitation."

"Everyone?"

"Yeah. Some of the bigwigs don't but everybody else does. Why? You figure she'd crash the party? I've been here all night. What's the name of this inmate?"

"She's a patient. I can't reveal her name."

"She's escaped and you can't reveal her name?"

"No. Blond, she's blond. Attractive. About 20 years old."

The guard scrutinized my face for some seconds. I started perspiring.

"Mind if I ask you, Mister, if you got some kinda thing for this girl? Maybe that's why you're here?"

I stepped backward in recoil.

"Maybe you should leave?" he suggested.

Though phrased as a question, it was clearly an order so I said goodnight and went back down the hill. Looking back, I could see him watching me. Inside Fergies, my ice cream still sat in the glass bowl, now fully melted. I stared at it for the longest time, my head crammed with question. Did Ziggy write privileges allowing her to go off campus? It seemed most unlikely.

The next day, I called one of the nursing staff on Ziggy's unit and asked whether one of their female patients had gone missing the evening before.

"I don't think so. Do you want me to check?"

"No," I said, suddenly realizing that this was none of my concern. I was playing a foolish detective game and ought to mind my own business. If Ziggy transgressed, it would soon enough be found out.

My inappropriate interest in Ziggy's behavior became a subject for discussion when I saw Dr. Templeton a week later. I ought to have been talking about my mother but I latched onto Ziggy instead. She patiently listened to my ranting for a while before speaking.

"So, is the issue here why you like him? Or is the issue why his behavior disturbs you so much?"

"Both."

"So, you feel responsible for him?" she inquired, lighting the first cigarette of the session.

"I didn't think I did. But I guess I do."

"In your mind, is he a sibling?"

"I have no siblings."

"Yes, now I recall. But did you ever wish for a sibling?" she asked.

This visit I had chosen the hard-backed chair in Templeton's office. I was at eye level with her and stared back at her, puzzled.

"You seem surprised by my question."

"I don't ever recall wishing for a sibling," I said perplexed.

"No? Many single children do. It's often a burden being the only child. Everything is shifted and placed on that child when there are no others on which to spread the responsibilities. Not to worry, we will probe this matter further another time. For now, please continue telling me about your mother," Templeton prompted. "It may shed light on the problem with your Ziggy."

"My mother," I exhaled slowly. "My mother. Sometimes I don't think I had a mother. She was very aloof. She seemed to take no pleasure in me. She had very little education and she worked at a local diner as a waitress. My father was a patent attorney, but reserved and not affectionate. I never understood their marriage. There seemed to be no joy in it. He tolerated my mother and drove her to work every day and picked her up every evening, but that seemed to be the extent of their interaction. I never knew if they loved one another. My father had all sorts of businesses and clients from all over but my mother took no interest in his work. I would occasionally ride my bike over to the diner and sit on the stool at the counter and watch her wait on customers. She fetched their coffee, recited the daily specials, carried over steaming plates of food, cut sandwiches in half with a long-handled knife to which she had fastened a red ribbon, handed them their bills and took their money. Sometimes, I was jealous of the attention she paid to strangers during the day, only to have her return home at night to watch television quiz shows and basically ignore me. She never inquired about my day or school work. My father oversaw that. I seemed to be—" I stopped for a moment as I tried to swallow the lump in my throat. Dr. Templeton, nodded, waiting for me to continue.

"Like an orphan," I admitted.

"She is still alive?" Templeton asked.

"No. Nor my father."

"What did they die of?"

"My father suffered from dementia but pneumonia took him in the end."

"Ah, an awful disease. What was his name?"

"Herman."

"And your mother?"

I lapsed into silence, not wishing to answer. I felt my eyes tear up.

"Something painful," she said.

"Delores," I whispered. "Delores was her name and she did herself in," I mumbled.

"Oh my," Templeton exclaimed, looking startled. "Suicide?"

"An overdose. After a fight with my father. She'd tried before." It was hard to talk and momentarily hard to put sentences together.

"A previous overdose?"

"No. She tried to drown herself."

"You were with her when she tried?"

"Yes. I was nearby when she overdosed as well."

"How old were you?"

"When she died, I was seven."

Templeton took a deep breath and exhaled. "I obviously had no idea about all these events. You've been through a terrible tragedy. Several tragedies. You've spoken to someone about your mother?"

"No one," I said looking away. "I had no one. No therapist. No one."

"You kept it to yourself. All these years?"

"Yes."

"Like a treasured memory," Templeton said. "Except that it is a nightmare. Something you don't want to get rid of. Because of the pain involved?"

"Pain," I repeated. Was it pure pain? Or some kind of guilt? Or an inability to confide in anyone?

"We have much to talk about. It will be difficult for you," she said with understanding.

"I will do it," I said with as much confidence as I could muster in that moment.

Templeton arose from her chair to signal the end of the hour. "Good," she said to me, nodding, with a somber look on her face. "See you next week? Will this time work for you weekly?"

"Yes," I replied without consulting my schedule. I would make it work.

Outside, in the dazzlingly sunny street with cars honking all around me, I hunted for a bench where I could sit down for a few minutes and compose my thoughts. I took a deep breath and exhaled. Was I that terrified of confronting my mother's suicide? It would be overwhelming once I began talking. I realized I was afraid of being disabled by sorrow, unable to work, unable to even exist. I shivered. I got up and started walking. I kept walking and walking trying to disperse the anxiety welling up inside. I must have covered five miles because the heat from the sun had subsided and my panic was receding. I returned to my car, put my memories to the side and drove back to the hospital. It began to rain. I decided to see Ted. I went to his room but he wasn't there and I found him sitting on some steps at the back of the building. Now there was a thunderstorm in progress and Ted was soaking wet. He wore earphones and he had his hands over them as well. I couldn't tell whether he had been crying or whether his face was wet from the rain.

"Ted," I said to him. "Come inside."

He made no attempt to move. Had he heard me?

"Ted," I repeated, and moved in front of him. "Ted."

He waved me away.

"Take off those earphones," I raised my voice. He didn't respond. I hesitated about what to do next. Should I get the staff to surround him? It could lead to a physical confrontation if they tried to intervene. Instead, I just sat down next to his hunched form and did nothing. Lightning flashed and the clouds rumbled. We were drenched. Finally, after 15 minutes, I gently reached over and lifted off the earphones. He didn't oppose me.

"Voices," I said. He nodded.

"What are they telling you to do, Ted?"

"Hang."

"Yourself? Hang yourself?"

"I won't"

"How do you resist?"

"I just do."

"How?"

"The 23rd psalm."

"That cancels out the voices?"

"Yeh." Just then, a tremendous crack of thunder occurred. A lightning bolt descended into the woods before us. Ted jumped up and moved towards the doorway. The rain intensified and the howling of the wind was fearsome. Ted rushed through the doorway and ran to his room, leaving a trail of puddles on the floor. I followed him. A nurse appeared.

"The Lord is my Shepherd," I started reciting. I saw Ted's lips move and join me with the rest of the prayer. He then started to undress.

"What happened?" the nurse asked.

"We got caught in the rain."

"Ted shouldn't be outside," she rebuked.

Ted was suffering enough and he surely didn't need any criticism from staff.

"And you're soaked, Dr. Soloway. Look at you."

"Leave us," I said to the nurse.

Ted had stripped down to his underwear. I got him a towel from the bathroom. He got dry clothes from his dresser and plunked onto the bed.

"I thought the rain would wash away the voices," he explained.

"You hear them right now?"

"Gone."

"Good."

"They'll be back."

"When they return, you have to seek out one of us to talk to, Ted. Do you know why the voices tell you to hang yourself?"

"I stole a candy bar once."

"Death for a candy bar, Ted?"

Ted looked at me pitifully. "Thank you," he said.

"For what?"

"For sitting next to me outside."

"Ted," I gulped. I started shivering from being wet and cold.

"You need to change," Ted said to me.

"Yes. I'll increase your medication some more." I stood up.

In the hallway, I ran into Vanderpol and told him what had happened.

"He's a very dangerous case," Vanderpol said.

I concurred, placing him on close observations so someone would be nearby at all times.

Chapter 8

Each month, we celebrated the birthdays of patients currently residing at Manning Hall. Many were chronically ill schizophrenics whose trust funds allowed them permanent housing at Sandstone. Some, like Grace, had recurrent mood disorders and came in and out of the facility with regularity. This particular month's birthday party was given for Miles Haggerty. Miles had been at Sandstone for six years.

He was turning 60. Back then, 60 was close to being old. Much of his existence consisted of staring at a book or magazines. Or, he looked blankly at television. He often laughed out loud at nothing we could discern, and on other occasions he appeared terrified of voices we could not hear. Miles had been ill most of his life with a diagnosis of chronic undifferentiated schizophrenia, the cruelest form of illness characterized by largely untreatable delusions and hallucinations. These were accompanied by a regressed state of functioning, similar to someone with Alzheimer's Disease. But despite Miles's regressed status, he was assigned to a psychiatrist who came in regularly to sit with him and attempt a conversation, but the effort was unilateral. Miles' family resided in Tennessee. His children rarely came to see him but they sent photographs of events going on in their own lives in an attempt to keep in touch. Only, it seemed to do the opposite and widen the tragic gulf between all parties. Of course, Miles was unaware of his exclusions from the family outings and celebrations

The staff had placed six lit candles on a chocolate cake and they carried it into his room, singing. Miles was asleep in a rocking chair, a fine wool blanket draped over him. One of the nurses tried to wake him. As the candles began to burn down, one of the male aides gently pulled him by both arms into a more upright position. Miles gazed at the cake with absolute vacancy in his eyes, quite unresponsive to the pleas of everyone. One by one, the candles burned down and were blown out by staff. Pieces of cake were silently passed around on paper plates. The care and compassion the staff tried to accomplish had fallen flat. It was a sad, pathetic scene. People quietly left the room, patting Miles on the shoulder.

I thumbed through his voluminous charts. There were three of them, like the complex memoirs of a famous adventurer, except that Miles's life was heartbreakingly eclipsed by an illness that defied understanding. Initially, he had experienced delusions and hallucinations, but time had dulled the passions of derangement. Now, he largely existed in a world of autistic withdrawal. He had received several courses of electroshock treatments without any relief.

"Dementia," I said to Vanderpol in the nursing station. He was writing orders and looked up.

"He has impaired memory for sure," he agreed. "He's always disoriented. We could test him but I'm already sure his cognition is minimal."

"We should document his dementia. Work him up. Radiologically."

Vanderpol shook his head. "Pneumoencephalograms are painful," he said. "Injecting air into the spinal cord so it gets to the brain is dicey. And what do you expect to find?"

"Atrophy," I said. "Shrinkage of the brain."

"Something remedial?" Vanderpol challenged me. "Something we can fix?"

"I'd doubt it."

"Something operable, then? Something we can remove?"

"Probably not," I conceded. "In the end, my own father developed a dementia. When I visited him, he stared right through me. He didn't know an apple from an orange."

Vanderpol put down his pen and closed the prescription book. "Sounds awful. How long did he have it?"

"Four years."

"So, you know a lot about dementia, then?"

"I read every book I could find. I had him seen by every specialist. Every test was done. To no avail."

"I'm sorry," Vanderpol said. "From what you've told me, he was a man of the mind."

'A man of the mind,' I thought. Well, he did have a fine mind at one time but it lacked the capacity for affection.

"We really should work Miles up. It's the right thing to do," I pressed on.

Vanderpol sighed. "If you really want to work him up, you'll need to contact Miles' family. They want to be informed about everything we do and why we do it. They still harbor a lot of guilt for not taking him to a psychiatrist sooner, not that it would have made any difference. So now they want a say in everything we do, even at this late stage in Miles's life. Be prepared for a lot of questions. They are bound to ask you what difference it will make with what you find. Do you know how you will answer the questions?"

What Vanderpol was really asking and pointing out to me was that if the findings objectively concluded Miles was suffering from dementia, Sandstone had reached the limitations of any intervention. And that meant, possibly, moving Miles to a nursing home.

"I predict they'll fight you," Vanderpol said, "even if you show them an x-ray of his brain. They won't give up easily. And I predict something else, they'll call Mueller. So be prepared for a call from His Excellency. This isn't just a patient you're dealing with. It's a whole interlocking system of family and patient and political pathologies. Mueller won't like losing a patient to any Frost Palace."

I had never heard of the term.

"Pre-cold storage," Vanderpol explained. "Our code for a nursing home, the stop before the morgue."

As Vanderpol had forecast, Miles's daughter was appalled at the suggestion of a brain workup.

"He cannot tolerate any kind of neurosurgery, if that's what you're thinking," she protested. "What, precisely, is there to be gained? I'm very upset by the idea."

"He may have a dementia," I finally said to her.

"No doubt. And you seek to prove it. To what avail?"

I wasn't experienced enough, despite Vanderpol's warning, to understand that change of any kind could be unbearable for a family who had finally attained some kind of equilibrium in coping with chronic illness. Miles was content at Sandstone and the family didn't mind paying a small fortune to have him out of their way. Here I was, covertly suggesting a nursing home with all its vicissitudes of compromised care. He most likely would die much more quickly in new and strange surroundings.

"I hope you will discuss this more fully with your staff," the daughter said coldly and with authority. "To be frank with you, I am most disturbed by your suggestion."

Miles's family was intimidating, but no more than Mueller. Within a day of my forging ahead with the consult request, Mueller's secretary called me in to see him.

I had never set foot in his domain. His office was large, with floor-to-ceiling windows and heavy crimson drapes pulled to the side. Deep blue carpeting covered the floor. On one wall hung photographs of famous psychoanalysts, including Freud. On an adjacent wall were aerial photographs and frayed blue architects' renderings of floor plans and buildings. A third wall was lined with shelves filled with books so neatly ordered and stacked that it was apparent no one ever read them. Mueller sat behind a majestic mahogany desk with ornate clubbed feet. Behind him, on each side of the window, hung a museum worth of diplomas and commendations from various societies and foundations. Plaques of appreciation alternated with gold engraved inscriptions enclosed in glass. They demonstrated his esteemed prominence in his field.

"Now then," Mueller wasted no words. "I imagine you know what all this is about. Miles Haggerty. I am given to understand that you are challenging the status quo in his case. The family has informed me, with great alarm, that you are suggesting another neurological assessment. He's had several. I trust you are aware of that, yes?" I nodded my head slightly. Mueller continued, not waiting for an answer. "Yes. Dementia seems to be the issue in your mind?"

"It is," I agreed.

"Indeed. Over on that wall is a picture of Eugen Bleuler. You see him? Second from the left. A remarkable man. In 1899, he was referring to schizophrenia as 'Dementia Praecox.' I'm sure you know the story. He believed schizophrenia was a progressive deterioration of the brain. A simplistic theory, as we appreciate it today, but many patients with years of schizophrenic illness do burn out, as you will learn the longer you stay here, if you do not know it already. It may well be then, that Mr. Haggerty has some degree of brain deterioration. The question is, how assiduous to be in the matter, is it not? Mr. Haggerty has suffered much in his life." Mueller pushed himself forward on the large empty surface of the desk, palms down, staring at me as if to reinforce his point.

He had not offered me a chair since I arrived and I remained standing.

"Perhaps it might be best to let matters be?" Mueller cautiously phrased it as a question. "To spare the family more grief."

I'd not personally met the man before me and so could never have appreciated how obnoxious he was. "I'll think about it, Dr. Mueller," I said diplomatically.

"I'm confident that you will make the correct decision," he forced a crooked smile.

But I didn't think about it long, nor did I obey Mueller. I sent Miles down to see a high-powered professor of neurology at University Hospital and a few days later received a report suggesting a pneumoencephalogram.

I accompanied Miles to get the test, as I had accompanied my own father when he had gone to the hospital for the same procedure. Lying on a table, I watched fluid drained from the spinal column and oxygen injected in its place. Miles moaned with pain as the table was tilted to force air into his brain. I could barely listen to him, the suffering seemed unbearable and a part of me wanted to stop the procedure.

The radiologist retrieved the film, pushed it up onto the view box, and snapped on the light.

"Here we go," he said, almost proudly pointing to the image of Miles's brain. Miles's ventricles were enlarged, and all the sulci and gyri looked like shrunken islands and inlets swollen with flood water, except the water was air. Brain shrinkage leaped out at me, as it had when I had looked at my father's images. In a normal person, the surface area of the brain would have been fuller and allowed more neurons to be packed into the cortex. I was engulfed in melancholy. What had I really wanted to prove with Miles's case? I stared at the x-ray. There was more absence than substance.

"A whole lot of nothing," the radiologist whistled. He was already dictating results as I left the room.

"Sometimes modern science doesn't do us any favors," Vanderpol commented when I summarized the ordeal upon returning to Sandstone. "You must be pleased with yourself, Ben."

Was I really pleased with myself for defying my superiors with what I had done? The one gratifying thing that came out of my efforts was that a psychiatrist would stop seeing Miles and stop billing the family for visits from which Miles got no benefit whatsoever. But I still had doubts as to why I was so compelled to prove the obvious, against all advice. Where, exactly, did my iconoclasm come from, I asked myself. I'd wanted to be triumphant and acknowledged by my peers for my brilliance, that much I had to admit. Still, what was it all for?

"I should have taken your advice and left things alone," I finally confessed to Vanderpol.

"Well, you confirmed a diagnosis," Vanderpol said. "You confronted what no one cared to confront. No one will be happy with you but they aren't necessarily happy with the objective truth." Vanderpol paused for a moment. "You know, you're a bit of an idealist," Vanderpol looked at me. "You're aware of this, Ben?"

My cheeks reddened.

"In a generally good way," Vanderpol added. "But not every diagnosis we make needs to be confirmed at the molecular level."

This statement brought to mind the philosophy of Ziggy, whom I hadn't seen in a few weeks.

"In this profession, we act on hunches and wisps of emotions and a spoonful of mind readings," Vanderpol continued.

I thought about Dr. Mueller. He surely wasn't going to congratulate me on my diagnosis. I said as much to Vanderpol.

"No, he certainly won't be happy for you, or happy, period. He rarely is. Some people simply aren't happy. You'll learn that. They're not depressed, just unhappy beings. Things went wrong early. Antidepressants won't work. Shock treatments do nothing. Talking, maybe."

"Mueller's got a lot of power," I stated.

"Of that he has convinced himself," Vanderpol countered. "You see the dynamics? First you have to believe yourself that you're powerful and then you have to be feared so that no one challenges you. Your difficult friend Ziggy hates Mueller, does he not?"

"He does."

"Mueller cultivates fear and dislike. He is very good at it."

"I don't suppose the Muellers of the world end up committing suicide," I glumly observed.

"They drive others to suicide," Vanderpol pointed out. "People try and kill them but they don't kill themselves, no. They're enviably immune from self-destruction." Vanderpol laid a plump cigar on the counter. With a small pocketknife, he neatly cut it in half. "I'm trying to wean myself," he explained. "But it's a bit of a game because I'll smoke the other half after I finish the first half. I should be throwing it away but I can't bring myself to do it. These are such good cigars. Do you have any advice for me, doctor?" he jested.

I shook my head.

"No? OK." As a good mentor, Vanderpol happily gave me advice on how to handle my next encounter with Mueller. "Get ready for another onslaught," he prophesized. "Just politely listen to him. Don't try and defend your position. Be sure to thank him, no matter what he says."

"Patronization," I said.

"Absolutely," Vanderpol said.

But Mueller never called and I assumed that he found out the results of the test from the family, whom I did notify. Miles's daughter wept at the news, as if she had just learned about his illness. I crossed paths with Mueller some weeks later as I was coming down the road to Manning House. He looked the other way and we walked past each other without a word.

When I got back to my office, there was a note on my desk from Vanderpol telling me we would be visiting Leona prison in the morning

Chapter 9

We took Route 5 after the morning commuter traffic was subsiding and when we hit a relatively uncrowded portion of the road, Vanderpol abruptly floored the accelerator of the Hemi-powered Charger. The machine lunged forward and the speedometer needle jerked to 100 miles per hour. The windows were wide open, and the roar of air and engine noise flooded the passenger compartment. I cinched my seat belt tighter.

"Ever drive this fast before?" Vanderpol called out to me, grinning.

"No," I yelled back at him. "Could you please slow down?"

"That's what my first wife always said to me," he shouted back, still grinning.

I didn't know what to say. I knew almost nothing of Vanderpol's life and had been too inhibited to ever ask.

"My second wife also," he hollered. "She hated speed. You have to like speed. Have you ever been married?"

"Yes." It was not lost on me that we were exchanging intimacies in the midst of roaring speed, both of us fixated on the highway ahead.

"Still married?"

"No." I hoped Vanderpol wasn't going to ask me about my marriage. It was something I only wanted to talk about with Templeton.

"Two wives sound like a lot," I said after a long pause.

"I wouldn't recommend it. Actually, there were three, but I don't think the first counted. We were children, she and I." Vanderpol swerved around some cars. "Gets expensive, all that alimony." A bus loomed up ahead and Vanderpol edged toward the left lane and whirled past it. Then there were a clump of cars and Vanderpol was forced to abruptly slow down.

"Thank you," I said, grateful for the diminished speed.

"You like roller coasters? I'm guessing you don't," Vanderpol looked over at me. The color had drained from my face.

The question evoked a memory of my father taking me on a roller coaster ride at Nantasket Amusement Park. He'd had a client who'd invented a magnetic safety device to be used on railed vehicles. I'd been a child and had been terrified by the lurching ride.

"That's right. No roller coasters for me," I said.

"No black diamond ski trails, then," Vanderpol took the exit at a reasonable speed. Signs for the prison loomed ahead. "It's OK. You seem like a fine doc," he said," even if you don't like speed and risk." His compliment had a reassuring effect on me. I often wondered what he thought of me and my diagnoses and treatment efforts. The patients themselves were not exactly fountains of gratitude for my efforts.

"We're going to see a guy named Ray McCarthy. Goes by the name of Buzzy. Buzzy killed his wife. Pretty gruesome. Hit her in the head with an ax, then chopped her up. Severed her head from her body, lopped off her ears, her tongue, a lot of mutilation," Vanderpol stated impassively "The rule of thumb in these cases is that the more gruesome the murder and the mutilation, the greater the chance is that the patient may have been psychotic. You should look at the autopsy photographs. Grab my briefcase from the back seat. They're inside."

I hauled over a thin leather attaché. Within a manila folder were a dozen color 8 X 10 images of a viciously dissected body. On the autopsy table was a fragmented skull. Fingers were amputated from one hand. Grotesque lacerations covered the torso.

"My God!" I gasped. I really wasn't expecting such sickening images.

"It isn't easy to do all that damage," Vanderpol commented. "You have to be very strong. And very angry."

"An ax, you said."

"A sharp ax," he emphasized "The pathologist mentioned that. He identified the murder weapon as a very, very sharp ax. The markings suggest it. Freshly sharpened for the act, who knows? Perhaps we'll ask him. Here we are."

Leona prison occupied a few acres of barren land with a tall, razor-ribbon fence completely surrounding it. Four corner turrets overlooked the recreation field where prisoners were congregating. The guards in the turrets carried rifles, and search lights were mounted on swivels. Vanderpol swung into the prison visitors' lot and parked far away from other cars.

"Dings," he said, locking the vehicle. "You know what a ding is?"

I shook my head.

"You're blessed. A ding is a small dent made by another car door banging against yours. I can't stand them. It's a disease, ding phobia is. You can tell who is a ding phobic in every parking lot you go to. We park far away. Some people hog two parking spaces and straddle in the middle. An untreatable condition, I might add.

Anyway," he informed me, switching back to the matter at hand, "I'm hired by the public defender to see if this man might have been insane at the time he killed his wife. Some are, but very few. Less than 1% of insanity defenses in the whole country are successful. But this guy sure butchered up his wife, so we'll see."

We walked to the entrance of the penitentiary in silence. Inside the entrance were thick glass enclosures behind which stood uniformed staff. Vanderpol went up to the counter and spoke through a microphone. He put his papers into a bin that slid open from under the counter. A surly guard inspected them and slid them back. We placed our wallets on a conveyor belt while we ourselves were scanned. Next, a grim-faced officer waved a metal detector up and down our bodies and we passed through a sally-port. Inside was a room furnished with green plastic chairs that had seen better days. The room was cramped and hot. Visitors, some with children, waited their turn to see the friends or relatives whose behaviors had landed them in this forsaken place. A soda machine's refrigeration unit loudly vibrated.

Hey! Doc!" a muffled voice called our from a doorway. "This gotta be a contact visit?"

"Yes." Vanderpol yelled.

"Take a while," the guard said.

"Contact visit means that you sit in the same room with the defendant and not behind a glass or metal partition," Vanderpol explained. "That means that it takes more time for them to find a secure room. They sort of punish you for this request by making you wait."

"Even if the visit is authorized?"

"A prison exists to isolate prisoners from the outside world. It makes no difference to the administration if God Himself authorizes the visit. They'd make Him wait as well. Here, let's share the morning paper," Vanderpol offered as he pulled the paper from his case, handing me a section.

I read about the latest sports news and got updated on local politics. The big headline was about astronauts preparing another trip to the moon. There were photographs of the landing site. Vanderpol happened to look over.

"Can you spot Sandstone?" he asked.

"Sandstone?" I frowned.

"Sure. It's a bleak, airless surface. Sort of like here."

"Dr. Vanderpol," I exclaimed, surprised at his irreverence.

Vanderpol shrugged. "Have to be able to vent occasionally."

"I take it you don't regard the hospital as a haven."

"Of course. It's both a haven and a hell, all in one. It's the moon and the sun combined. Radiant and desolate. If you stay there long enough—"

"Vanderman!" a female guard called out. She stood in a doorway. A large heavy-set woman, her uniform was adorned with badges and a two-way radio dangled from her belt, along with handcuffs and pepper spray. Vanderpol chose not to correct what she called him as we were led down the long corridors. No one spoke, but occasionally our shoes would squeak on the old well-worn vinyl floor. We went through a number of sally-ports and waited patiently for the guard to unlock and relock each secured section until we came to a small room with a single screened window. We went inside. Behind a single table sat a rather distinguished looking man, about 40 years old. He obviously had taken time with his appearance. His har was preened back very nearly and he sat with confidence, his eyes bright with watchfulness. He wore an oversized orange jumpsuit but his muscular body was still evident underneath. His general demeanor was intimidating. His hands were on his lap and he wore handcuffs.

"Press the button here when you're done," the guard said, and slammed the thick door behind us.

"Arrogant motherfuckers," McCarthy grunted. "Who the hell are you?"

Vanderpol made introductions.

"The motherfucker public defender insists that I'm crazy," McCarthy growled at us. "She's frothing at the mouth with fervor. A juicy insanity case to raise her profile so she can resign from the public defender's hellhole office and get a nice lucrative job with a private firm. She keeps asking me if I heard voices," he sneered "I guess you both will do the same. Did I hear a little voice telling me to ax my wife? Or did I think there was a plot against me? Paranoid delusional shit. She doesn't like it when I say no, no voices, no delusions. God bless the bitch, she's trying to do her job. Sexy little babe, actually. Nice legs. Anyway, I fired her. I take it you're here at the request of the new public defender." He chillingly smiled, making me recoil. "So. Ask away, doctors." McCarthy tilted his chair back and smirked at us. "You guys got ink blots to show me? Rorschachs, I believe they're called."

I was amazed at his vocabulary and obvious intellect. I had expected a heathen monster of a man.

"No ink blots," Vanderpol answered, staying very professional as he extracted photographs from his briefcase.

"Oh. Real photos," McCarthy observed with pleasure. "Much better. You'll want me to free associate to these photos. Show me a picture of a man saluting the flag and ask me what I think about it. Excellent," he clapped his hands and his handcuff's rattled. I noted well-manicured fingernails.

"These are crime photos," Vanderpol said. "But before we start, you understand that what you tell me isn't confidential? I'm hired by your attorney, but I still prepare an independent report. I'm not your psychiatrist."

"Thank you for motherfucking telling me what's blatantly obvious," McCarthy quipped.

"Fine, then. Now you've admitted killing your wife," Vanderpol stated.

"There was nothing to admit," McCarthy said. "I was the one who called the motherfucking police to tell them what I did. I was a bit too hasty about it, though. I should have finished the job."

"How so?"

"Isn't it obvious? I didn't finish taking off the fingers from her other hand. And the toes. I wish I had finished the job. It was easy enough to do. I had the right tool. I should have taken out her eyes but I didn't have the right tool for that. I needed something small and sharp. Scissors, perhaps? I should have removed her eyes. She had lovely eyes, blue ones." He stopped for a moment remembering. "I thought about removing her eyes for a long time. I don't know why I didn't. Maybe you two shrinks can tell me why. Isn't that what you do? Tell people what their real motives are? Are you interested in the ax I used? The motherfucker public defender was all hyped up over the ax. It was a plain, ordinary ax. Nothing special, I bought it at Sears. I sharpened it myself. In preparation for the deed," he chuckled and swung his feet onto the table.

I was incredulous. Hearing McCarthy speak so brazenly about his crime defied imagination. Vanderpol plowed on, seemingly impervious to McCarthy's astonishing arrogance. He laid out the first photograph.

"I'd love to have those photos as a keep-sake," he grinned. "I'd like to pin them up in my cell." McCarthy's own eyes were glowing with excitement. His face was flushed.

"Tell us about the murder," Vanderpol said.

"What do you want to know?" McCarthy challenged, pointing at the photo. "That's my motherfucker wife and I killed her and dismembered her," he matter-of-factly admitted. "She deserved it and I'm perfectly glad I did it even if I have to spend the rest of my life here, or even face the chair. I am quite pleased with my work."

Both Vanderpol and I regarded McCarthy, momentarily at a loss for words. Vanderpol recovered quickly and managed to get a life history from the man. Remarkably, he had received a master's degree in biology from the University of North Carolina and then worked as a college instructor. As to the provocation for murder, it was his wife's recurring infidelity. He had warned her, he told us, by assaulting her, and using physical force, but she nonetheless defied him and continued seeing other men. Hearing this story, I wondered what immense pathology she herself harbored to remain in the marriage and place herself at such extreme risk.

The interview ultimately came to an end. Vanderpol and I stood up.

"Are you doctors satisfied?" McCarthy asked as if we had just finished having dinner.

"Satisfied," Vanderpol repeated, taking a deep breath. "Your crime is horrific. It's beyond any comprehension, Mr. McCarthy," he said, looking at him.

"You can call me Buzzy, now that we've met."

"I hope to never see you again, Mr. McCarthy."

"My crime should be a lesson to all motherfucking unfaithful women," McCarthy warned with a snarl.

Vanderpol whirled around and pressed the buzzer.

"I do believe I've upset you," McCarthy said derisively.

Vanderpol stared at him wordlessly.

"Do you want to talk more about it?" McCarthy laughed wickedly. Just then, the guard appeared and steered us back through a maze of doors. We eventually found ourselves outside on the street. The bright sun blinded us for a moment but the fresh air felt good. We walked to the car in silence. Vanderpol unlocked the driver's door and immediately reached inside to retrieve a cigar.

"Well, then," Vanderpol took deep puffs. I could see that he, too, was shaken by the encounter. It took him a while to speak.

"Well, then," he repeated and turned to me. "Do you want to describe what you just witnessed?"

I leaned against the car, bewildered and shocked. I'd read and seen on television accounts of various murders over the years, but to have confronted someone so unremorseful was frightening. McCarthy was a slaughterer, an executioner proud of his work in the midst of a psychotic fury, except he wasn't psychotic at the moment. He was also a man with impenetrable narcissism. I expressed these things to Vanderpol.

"I'd liked to have slugged him," Vanderpol said. "But I'm sure he's stronger than I am". As Vanderpol maneuvered the car out of the parking lot, I asked what would become of McCarthy.

"He'll get life at Leona with a crime of that magnitude. Perhaps he'll end up on death row. The only thing I wonder about is whether his vanity will ever crack open. He's presently in ecstatic denial. Denial like that is hard to maintain, like keeping a fire going without enough wood. It's remotely possible that he will become suicidal in the future as the reality dawns on him. Denial takes a lot of energy." he explained to me. "Lots of fuel and sometimes the fuel runs out. Not right away, of course. Years, sometimes. Many years later."

As we got closer to Sandstone, Vanderpol asked me if I believed in evil. I replied that I did. He then asked whether I considered McCarthy sick or evil.

"Couldn't he be both?"

"Sure. Absolutely," Vanderpol stifled a yawn. It had been a long, upsetting day and he was driving a lot slower than when we had started in the morning. "Man's a flawed species," he declared. "We're heathens, all of us. Barely civilized heathens, just like McCarthy. The thinnest veneer of civility. If we're lucky, we had parents who roped in any of our crazy episodes and tamed our propensity for evil. Care to speculate about McCarthy's mother?"

"If he had one," I snarked.

"Everyone's got one somewhere. Behind a tree or under a rock. Most of the folks here or at Sandstone are on a hunt for a fantasy mother. Did you ever see the TV show 'I Remember Mama'? Peggy Wood plays a wonderful, warm, all embracing mother who was intelligent and indulgent. An unobtainable fantasy for most of us."

"Motherfucker," I recalled from the conversation. "McCarthy used that word a lot."

"The term dates back to the 1800's. It is an obvious term for incest but now it's used as an insult. It represents the disdain someone has for someone else whom he considers to be perverted. It also has a distancing effect. In prisons and jails, it's a defensive way of keeping others away from you." As had become the pattern, Vanderpol used the opportunity to explain more about the dynamics of relationships. "McCarthy killed his wife and when you delve into the past of people like that, you tend to discover they obviously did not have the best mothering experience. They seek partners and try to transform them into the mothers they never had and when they can't make the change, they become enraged. A man has to have a mother and when she's absent from his life, he'll construct one, from a wife or even a father."

The barbarism of what I'd just seen deeply upset me. "How could McCarthy have chopped up this woman the way he did?" I asked Vanderpol. "It's sickening."

"Ben, people do awful things to one another. Think of wars. Think of the Aztecs who engaged in sacrifice and cut the hearts out of living people. If you hadn't seen the photographs of McCarthy's wife, it wouldn't have hit you so hard. Granted, McCarthy is one frightening specimen."

"I hope they execute him."

"Someone else in the world will take his place, Ben."

Just then, I had the most dreadful thought. Could my mother have ever considered harming or killing my father instead of herself? I had read that death had two vectors, in and out. What determined how men and women handled their rage? "Jesus," I exclaimed out loud.

"They nailed Jesus to the cross," Vanderpol declared. "Talk about brutality."

"Why couldn't McCarthy just have left his wife," I began. "Wy couldn't she have left him?"

"You will meet people who cannot think of any way to escape a bad situation, Ben. They're stuck, trapped, immobilized. Most of us can walk away from a bad situation or try and repair the damage, but other folks can't. McCarthy could have left his wife," Vanderpol continued. "But he was paralyzed by her and needed to destroy her and himself. Obviously, assuming the wife's infidelity is true and McCarthy didn't imagine it, her behavior was lethally provocative. Almost a death wish."

We had arrived back at Sandstone. Vanderpol eased the car into the main driveway and let me off at my car. I immediately drove home and took a long hot shower, standing under the cleansing spray for a long time, trying to rinse off what I'd heard and seen.

* * *

I decided to visit Ziggy the next day.

Ziggy's research efforts were carried out in the laboratories located near the administration building. On the second floor was a wide-open space with hooded counters and sinks, on which sat complex distillation assemblies heated by several Bunsen burners. A centrifuge was noisily whirling. Ziggy, in a long white coat and plastic gloves, was pipetting aliquots of blood samples into plastic trays. A cage of mice sat next to him. The animals were in constant motion, hurling themselves over one another and peeking through the grillwork.

"I'm missing a shipment of mice from my supplier," he grumbled at me as I entered. "I'm out of mice. Completely out of mice. I've phoned the company three times and they keep promising to send a shipment but nothing's come. Damn them. I'm in the middle of a crucial part of the experiment. I borrowed some mice from a researcher down the hall but now I'm completely out." Ziggy lowered the plastic lid on the tray of blood samples and placed them in the refrigerator.

"What are you doing?"

"Measuring serotonin," he answered curtly.

"Which is?"

"Brain metabolism. Not your thing, I'm sure. You're not a brain chemistry person."

"I think you're correct," I said.

"Sure." Ziggy snapped off the centrifuge, slowed the final revolutions by hand, and began emptying vials. "A colleague and

I are giving a paper at the Federation Meetings in Chicago. Very important meetings. You want to come with me and learn how the brain works?"

"I'll pass,' I said. "Are you going to grand rounds today?" I asked him.

"What's the subject?"

"The Psychology of Spiritualism."

"You're not serious," Ziggy declared. "Does it look here like I'm studying spiritualism? Do these little test tubes contain spirits? Why would I want to attend a lecture on spiritualism? How about a lecture on magic? Or on Buddhism? Who arranges these inane lectures? I bet it's Mueller. You think someday this place will have some substantive lectures on the neurochemistry of illness? Or brain pathology? Or biological makers? Genetics, maybe? You probably have to go downtown to hear stuff like that. Evidently Sandstone is for the mind and downtown is for the brain." Ziggy's face crinkled with contempt. "Would you like to donate some of your blood for my research? Soon we'll be testing humans. You could be a first," Ziggy held up a syringe.

"See you later, Ziggy," I hastily said, moving towards the exit.

"If you come across any mice, let me know. I need mice."

I went to the lecture. The speaker discussed how prayer could heal some depressions, how a shamen could cure some diseases, and how meditation could reduce blook pressure. And stress. Ziggy would have hated all of it.

* * *

"Mice," I was saying to Dr. Templeton. I was back in her office for my weekly visit. I had chosen the overstuffed chair this time and I was talking about my mother. "She was scared to death of mice." Actually, my mother had been scared by many things for much of her life. She dreaded driving on highways, crossing the Mystic River Bridge, entering the Sumner Airport Tunnel, heights of any kind, elevators, thunderstorms and lightening, spiders, snakes, bears and other assorted wildlife. She lived a constricted existence and narrowed her world to the house and the diner. She never traveled far and never accompanied my father on his trips. My father had been a worldly man. He spoke French, Italian, and German. Many inventors from other countries consulted with him as they sought patent protection in the United States. It was difficult to understand what my father saw in my mother and what common interests they shared. They often argued. I related to Templeton the recollection I had about my parents on vacation in Acadia National Park on Mt. Desert Island, Maine. I was six years old. They found a small luncheon spot on an idyllic little cove by the ocean. My father was absolutely delighted to see lobster rolls on the menu and promptly ordered a large one for himself and one for me. My mother, however, did not share his enthusiasm and declared that she wasn't hungry.

"We're in Maine where lobsters are a specialty," he berated her.

"I will have a cheese sandwich," she professed firmly.

"You can choose a cheese sandwich at your diner," he fumed. And we ate in silence. Afterward, they went for a walk on the stony beach, but in different directions. I stayed alone and skipped rocks into the tide. Suddenly, I saw my mother walk into the waves, fully dressed. At first she was up to her ankles but then the water reached her thighs and then she was at waist height, but still upright. I didn't understand it. It was late spring and the water was icy cold. The water level reached her shoulders and she kept on marching forward. I stood there staring, confused, and when I could only see her head above the waves, I screamed.

"Mother!" I shrieked as loud as I could, terrorized.

My father turned about, uncertain as to what was happening. Then, comprehension set in and he came running, splashing towards her but she had already gone under completely. He groped around for her where she had disappeared and finally managed to grab her and drag her back towards the shore. She was heavy with all her clothes on and he lost his grip a couple of times. It was agony to watch. I was helpless. Finally, he reached the sandy shore. She lay still, gasping. I moved next to her. I remember a large wave came hurtling inward from nowhere and washed over us.

"Are you mad!" my father shrieked at her. "Are you entirely mad!" Then we both noticed that all the pockets of her dress were bulging with smooth rocks from the beach. She must have stuffed dozens of them not only into the pockets but into the front of her dress as well. We ripped open her clothing and started pulling out the stones. Piles of them began to mount besides her.

"Throw these far out into the water," my father commanded furiously. I was searching my mother's face. She was ashen. I ignored his order.

"Did you hear me? Throw the rocks into the water!" he bellowed. "Get rid of them!"

I did as I was told, reaching into her pockets and plucking out more stones. Then I froze, panicked by the whole ordeal.

"Why are you stopping?" my father said harshly. "Keep going. Don't stop!"

My mother labored to get up, but stood wobbling on her own, her hair dripping wet. My father steadied her and holding her arm for support, took her to the car. We drove back to the motel in utter silence.

The effort of telling this story to Templeton quite depleted me. I sat and stared at her.

"And how did it end?" she asked me.

"It didn't. We never spoke of it."

"Tell me about the overdose, then," Templeton encouraged, ignoring my shaky composure. "I'm sure this must be awful for you to talk about."

"The end. The end," I wavered. A bolt of anguish made me want to hurl myself out of the chair and head for the door, much the same way I had felt watching the lecture about the Harlow monkeys. My muscles stiffened. I felt wretched. The whole nightmare came flooding back again. I moved forward in preparation to stand.

Templeton saw me stiffen and shift in posture. "Are you wanting to run?" she deduced. "I can understand that. Try and continue." She opened a fresh pack of cigarettes, unfiltered Camels.

I forced myself to breath slowly. "One day, when I was seven years old, she and my father had a big fight. Up until the time she had tried to drown herself, I never realized how alienated they were from one another, but they were. They lived under the same roof but were very estranged. Then one day they had this argument. My mother had been on the phone with a friend of hers from the diner and they were somehow talking about my father. She described him as a man who made a lot of money from other people's crazy ideas. My father overhead this and confronted her. He was very angry and told her that he was a reputable attorney who represented people with important ideas. He let her know that he was held in the highest esteem by clients and colleagues alike. Then, he suddenly slapped her in the face. I can still see it in my mind. I can hear the noise of the slap on my mother's cheek." I broke off here and wiped my tears. Dr. Templeton shook her head, ever so slightly, in a gesture of sympathy. I glanced at my wrist watch and saw that we were past the hour.

"We can go over," she said kindly.

"Then she ran out of the room," I continued. "She disappeared into her bedroom and locked the door. I knocked."

"Let me be," she called out.

"Please," I begged her.

"I'll be out in a minute."

"But she wasn't out in a minute. I sat on the floor outside her room and I heard the medicine chest open and close. I heard water running. Then it was silent. Minutes passed. I became anxious. Panic-stricken, I pounded on the door. Then I ran to search for my father but I couldn't find him. So, I went back and pounded on the door some more and I even tried to break into the room but without success, I wasn't strong enough."

I paused, recalling the terror I felt at the time, sitting outside the room, not knowing what to do, helpless.

"My father eventually showed up and when he, also, couldn't open the door, he called the police. By the time the police came and broke down the door, she was dead." Tears flowed down my face. Templeton pushed a box of tissues toward me but I was so distraught I didn't even notice. I was openly sobbing now, my shoulders shaking. The effort of telling the story after being suppressed all these years was overwhelming. I couldn't stop.

"This is horrible," I moaned.

"Slowly," Templeton said. "Go slowly. Take your time."

"You've got someone else waiting outside," I reiterated. I wanted the session to end.

"He or she can wait."

"Dear God," I moaned. "I've been holding this in for so long."

"Oh," Templeton said. "Oh my. You haven't told anyone about this before?"

I shook my head.

"How enormously difficult," Templeton emphasized. "And how terribly, terribly lonely. You must have felt very alone. How very hard and difficult. It is one of the most painful things to lose a parent so young but to not be able to talk about it is even worse."

I was exhausted and simultaneously liberated to be able to finally tell my story and have someone listen to it. Templeton gave me some time to gather my thoughts before I eventually left her office and headed back to the hospital. I was still in shock and needed fresh air and I found myself on the path that wound around the perimeter of Lake Jehovah. The path cut through the woods and became quite tricky at several places. I was not paying attention when I stumbled on some tree roots and fell. When I got up, I saw that I had scratched my leg and was bleeding, but I continued walking.

I hadn't mentioned to Dr. Templeton that I had watched the police crowd around my mother's inert body. I wanted to touch her but they kept me out of the room. I wanted to scream but I didn't. I sought out my father who was talking to a police officer.

"She had tried before," I heard him say, in a matter-of-fact tone.

"To drown herself," I interjected.

"Let me speak with the officer alone," my father briskly intervened. "Go to your room, I'll meet you there." Later, he did come upstairs and sat on my bed but he didn't touch me. He told me that sometimes, awful things happened and we would now have to continue our lives without my mother. I remember him rubbing his forehead. Then he went downstairs and made a dinner which I couldn't eat. I remembered the meal. It was the leftover meat loaf that my mother had prepared a day earlier.

"Try and eat," he'd said. "We need to begin to forget what happened. Your mother's gone" he said coldly.

It took about an hour to complete the walk around the lake and I prayed that no one would see me. It was mid-afternoon when I arrived at the road across the street from the hospital and I saw Vanderpol's car whizzing up the road. He screeched to a stop and rolled down his window.

"What happened, Ben?" My clothes were covered with dirt from the fall.

"I stumbled walking around the lake. I fell. I'm OK."

Vanderpol regarded me quizzically.

"I needed to get some things off my mind."

Vanderpol nodded. "You want to talk about it?"

I shook my head.

"Does it concern a patient?"

"Oh no, not at all. Stuff from my past."

"It's private, then."

"Yes." I nodded.

"OK, Ben. I imagine I should leave you alone then."

"I'll go home and change," I said.

"Good. See you in a while." He roared off up the hill.

At home I took a hot bath. I soaked in the tub. Steam rose. Slowly, the images of my mother faded like an aircraft vapor trail in the sky.

Chapter 10

Jolene entered our lives on Labor Day weekend.

Ziggy and I had gone to the Deli to have lunch. I tried to park in the already overfilled Claron Street garage and was maneuvering into a space when I misjudged the distance and backed up into the car behind. There was the jarring sound of crumpled metal. Getting out, I saw a red Chevrolet convertible with a newly inflicted dent in the front fender and bumper. I stood there, mortified.

"Not too bad," Ziggy said, exiting the car and inspecting the damage. "They can probably hammer it out."

"It's hard to hammer out a bumper and the fender will take paint work," I pointed out.

"From a distance you can't see too much."

"Ziggy," I started to argue with him when someone came walking towards us. It turned out to be the car's owner, a young blond woman wearing jeans, a tight fitting, short sleeved tee-shirt, and high heels. She had a backpack and was carrying two bags as well.

"I just backed into your car," I exclaimed guiltily.

She came alongside me. I could smell her perfume. She put down her bags and began intently inspecting the damage, running her hand along the crushed metal.

"My father owns a body shop," she murmured. "I was a body man for a while. Body woman, I suppose, to be more accurate." She stepped backward and glanced at me. "I estimate about $200 worth of repairs. A new bumper. Right here, they'll have to yank out the dent and fill it in and blend the paint. It's non-metallic so the blend shouldn't be too difficult. I might be able to do it myself when I go home for Thanksgiving."

"Here's my insurance card and license," I thrust them out to her. "I'm really very sorry." I was impressed by her knowledge of automotive repair.

She gazed at me. She had high cheekbones, a small mouth, and tight, suntanned skin. "You want to settle this outside the insurance company?"

"I don't know."

"Your call," she smiled.

"I'd let the insurance company pay," Ziggy said. "Why have insurance if you don't use it?"

"The insurance company always wins," she turned to Ziggy. "If you use them, they use you. There's a reason the industry builds the highest buildings in all the major cities We just did a case example in class."

"Class is where?" Ziggy was quick to ask.

"University of Connecticut. UCON. The business school."

"Uh oh," Ziggy teased. "A future executive."

"I'd be glad to write you a check," I decided.

"That'd be great," she said.

"We need to sit down for this transaction," Ziggy said, motioning to the restaurant where we were headed. "Can we buy you a cup of coffee? Or a beer?"

"A glass of water is fine," she said, brushing back her hair.

Inside, Ziggy and I sat opposite Jolene. Jolene Winchester was her name. She was from Vermont and in her second graduate year of study. She was very pretty, and both of us were immediately attracted to her. She gave us equal attention, laughing at the things we said in conversation. Ziggy had two beers and became somewhat disinhibited while I found myself becoming more anxious at the emerging thought of dating her. Ziggy did most of the talking.

"Are you in any kind of relationship?" Ziggy asked while imbibing his second bottle. "Married? Engaged? Divorced?"

"Well, now," she tossed back her hair. "That's rather personal. I could ask you the same question."

"I'm not," Ziggy said. "I've not found anyone like you."

"And you?" She smiled at me.

"Divorced."

"I am pure and uncontaminated," Ziggy said with mock pride.

"OK you guys," Jolene looked at her watch as I took a blank check from my wallet. "Time to go. I guess this is an interesting way to meet new people."

I handed her the check and as she took it, she momentarily touched my arm. I found the fleeting gesture enormously arousing. As we left, confusion enveloped me. A woman. I hadn't dated a woman since my wife.

"An interesting woman," Ziggy was saying, as we walked back to the car. "Sexy."

"Yes." Thus, began the strange and rivalrous relationship between the two of us and Jolene. Within a day, Ziggy had called her for dinner, that much he confided in me. It took me much longer to get up the nerve to approach her. Ziggy and I didn't talk about Jolene at all. Was it in the service of maintaining our relationship? I wasn't sure.

Meanwhile, Dr. Templeton confronted me about my last session.

"We've unfinished business," she said. "We left off on a critical note. Your mother's suicide. I'm sure you'd rather not talk about it"

I recoiled, knowing what was coming.

"Did your mother leave a suicide note?" Templeton asked.

"No," I shook my head.

"Would you have wished her to?"

"She never said goodbye," I said dejectedly, as all the feelings from the past came rushing back.

"Many people who kill themselves don't say goodbye," Templeton said. "It seems they only want to exit their lives. No one else counts in that moment. It can often be a spur of the moment thing but built up over time. Then they suddenly act on their shattered emotions, triggered by one small incident, enough to put them over the edge. I take it you've not yet had any suicides in your work?"

"Not yet. I suppose I will," I sighed. "That's probably the worst outcome of my profession."

"Indeed," Templeton answered. "But about your mother. Did her death bring much acute sorrow or some sense of relief, or both? Sometimes suicides bring relief."

"I should have intervened," I said.

"You were a child," she pointed out "How, exactly, could you have intervened?"

I shrugged, unable to answer the question. What, really, could I have done?

"The feeling inside me is that I ought to have made her pay more attention to me," I stated. "Does that sound strange?"

"Not at all. Neglected persons think that. Sometimes they become behavior problems so that they are noticed," Templeton said, "But some parents are so preoccupied with themselves and their pathologies that there's no energy left over for others, including those to whom they gave birth."

"How can that be?" I challenged, banging on the sides of the chair.

"It just can. People are self-contained entities and they struggle to survive," she pointed to the window. "Like the birds we see flying outside. Their whole lives are focused on survival, constantly searching for food and struggling to stay away from predators. Perhaps that was the fate of your mother. Of course, it doesn't have to be yours," she concluded. "It seems that you are building a life for yourself."

I just gaped at her, trying to digest her words. There was a long pause.

"And speaking of the absence of nurturance, I would like to suggest an interpretation for your strange interest in this Ziggy friend of yours. You seem to want to be continually steering him on the right path in life. You want him to behave. To me, this suggests that part of you has become a mother to him. The mother who abandoned you is the mother you are playing out with Ziggy. In effect, you care what happens to him." Templeton lingered for a moment. "What do you think?" Templeton searched my face.

I pondered her interpretation. "It can't be," I protested.

"But it can indeed be. The mind hunts to replace what is missing. Sometimes, it takes a convoluted path. People become physicians in order to minister to others in ways they feel deficient. Good and noble things can come out of deprivation, provided we have resources to express our anger and deal with disappointment. Otherwise, there is just rage. Of course, you must be careful and be aware not to be dragged down by Ziggy's aberrant ways."

I nodded, recalling that Vanderpol had also urged caution in my friendship with Ziggy.

"So. There is much more to talk about," said Templeton, bringing the session to a close.

These sessions with Dr. Templeton evoked feelings of dread, and while a part of me appreciated that the insights would be of benefit, I still approached them with anxiety and caution. I seemed to have little control over the direction of the sessions and was surprised by what spilled out and the unexpected emotions that came up in the hour. I would emerge from treatments wearied, as if I had just worked out in some gym and lifted weights or run on the treadmill. I mentioned this to Templeton at our next meeting.

"We're talking about your mother," Templeton explained. "You've built up memories and emotions about her and we're exploring and possibly even challenging them. The mind doesn't always like to be probed. It recoils and resists. It's like exercising a body muscle that opposes your efforts. It's fatiguing. Plus," she added," we are talking about a very sad event. You are grieving. Grief that has been inside you since you were seven years old, perhaps even earlier. It is emotionally draining to let go of something that has been with you most of your life. It is work, very hard work. And, just like studying for school or training for sports, it can only be processed over time. This is long overdue, this matter of looking back, no?"

Grieving, I considered the term with dismay. Obviously, she was correct but the idea that I had been thrashing about under a shadow for the largest chunk of my life was dispiriting, as if I had wasted an epic amount of time, short changing my life. I said this to Templeton.

"But you haven't at all, have you? Here you are, an accomplished man, a physician and now a resident specializing in his profession." She looked at me to see my reaction.

"Perhaps," I said, soothed by her statement. Cigarette smoke wafted in the air.

"I've been meaning to ask you," she said bringing the topic back. "Have you been to your mother's gravesite recently?"

"No."

"Where is she buried?"

"At a cemetery near Boston. My father's grave is next to hers. It's strange. He wanted to be buried next to her," I commented.

"They had a bond," Templeton said. "They were married. But on the matter of the gravesite, perhaps you could consider going sometime?"

"Why?" I balked.

"We've been talking about your mother's death. It will help bring closure," Templeton replied.

"Sweet Jesus," I moaned. "Sweet Jesus."

"What is happening here is that you are getting in touch with loss and rage," she answered. "She was taken away from you and you were robbed of her."

"She left me," I accused.

"You are a survivor of a suicide," Templeton whispered quietly. "A suicide induces an enormous amount of confusion. You will find in your work that grieving and loss are what drives most human behavior. People spend their lives coping with various losses. They buy fancy houses and purchase expensive automobiles in their attempt to fill the void in their lives. But the acquisitions will always fall short of their mark. I'm sure you will notice this."

After the session ended, I stood in the open doorway and hesitated. Then I turned around.

"Why wasn't I enough?" I asked. "Why wasn't I important enough for my mother to live?" I had repeatedly asked this question of myself and now I said it out loud.

Templeton motioned me to come back into the room and close the door.

"Two things," she began. "First, you will learn that when patients are in the midst of abject hopelessness, nothing matters. They can only think of ending what they are stricken with, a relationship gone sour, financial ruin, loss of a loved one. And second," she said, almost berating me, "you must avoid doorway revelations. Patients say the most crucial things as they are leaving. It obviously precludes discussion as we are out of time."

"I'll do better," I said.

"Of course," she replied.

And once again, I was out on the street, reeling from the session.

Chapter 11

A week later, Sunshine's mother asked to meet with me. We sat in the library. Sunshine told me she did not wish to be present.

"I'll just start arguing with her," Sunshine said. "She'll want to know why I'm not better. She'll ask why I'm not getting more medication or if shock treatments might work. You'll see. Good luck."

Sunshine's mother came dressed in her Sunday best, a crisp suit, pearls, high heels and white gloves. She sat erect with her legs crossed. She looked me straight in the eyes, her face taut.

"Thank you for meeting with me," she said. "I'm obviously here to ask whether my daughter is making any progress." She forced a polite smile.

"Not as quickly as we would like," I replied.

"No. I don't see much change. This little caper of hers, thumbing a ride home, upset me very much. Do you know why she escaped from here? Did something happen? She could have been abducted or even killed."

I thought to myself that Sunshine was more likely to die from self-imposed starvation than anything else. "It was a risky thing to do," I agreed. "But to answer your question, no, nothing special happened here beyond her reactions to the therapy. Sometimes we touch on things that upset her."

"Such as? What exactly does the therapy consist of?" She fiddled with a large ruby ring on her finger. I was aware that in her profession as a radiologist, she was most likely to see improvements in a disease from the tiniest changes in an x-ray, the narrowing of a fracture or the shrinkage of a tumor, something tangible. How was I to explain the benefits of a talking cure?

"We talk about her body and the distortions she has about it and we talk about her need for control. We also talk about her lack of identity and her need to—"

"Does she talk about me?" Sunshine's mother interjected.

"She does."

"And are you at liberty to tell me what she says?" she asked curtly, smoothing her skirt to deflect her agitation.

"Partly. Like all adolescents, she feels her parents are overcontrolling."

"An example might help," she said.

"I've not got a good one. Kids find all kinds of faults with their parents and for the most part, the parents are quite reasonable. It's often more about the fact that the parents simply exist."

"It would be better if I didn't exist?" Her eyes moistened and I reached for a box of tissues which we were normally kept on the table in the lounge, but none was there. I got up.

"Stay," she said, almost like a command. "I have a handkerchief." She pulled one from her purse and dabbed her eyes. I recalled what Dr. McAllister had said about crying and thought that the woman before me needed to be self-sufficient. But surprisingly, she started to soften, "I don't feel I've been the best mother to Sunshine. My divorce. My career has been all consuming. It was so crucial to me, so very crucial. I lost sight of things I should have done for Sunshine. Simple things. Going to her sporting events, PTA meetings, those kind of things. I regret I didn't even attend a play she was in because I was giving a paper at a meeting on the West coast. Is it too late?" she asked me through glistening eyes. Her anguish was considerable and she covered her face with her hands. "Is it too late? Is there any chance I can still make it up?" She shifted to the edge of the chair.

"Not too late, no, not at all." I said it with conviction but I had inner doubts. I thought about the desolate monkeys I had seen. Was restitution possible? Were the structures of the mind flexible enough to allow new attachments? Or were the brain's circuits encased in cement?

"She needs time, more time," I said. The answer probably applied as much to me as Sunshine. I, too, had a long way to go in my therapy.

"This illness just runs its course, then," she took a deep breath, nodding. We talked a bit more about anorexia and then she stood up, thanked me, and left. I didn't know whether she stopped to see Sunshine or not.

I stumbled out of the meeting and sought Vanderpol.

"Repair is possible," he said. "A lot depends on how awful the deprivation is to begin with. Kids thrown into foster homes often don't recover no matter how maternal a foster parent can be. The wound is so raw and deep it becomes permanent. The brain is scarred. However, sometimes, a pet dog or cat can do the trick," he added. "It's all got to do with bonding. We are still trying to fully understand it. A few years back, we had this terrible kid here. He was a monster, an alcoholic, a real delinquent. No one could reach him. Then one day, he captures a Monarch butterfly and is transfixed by it. He spent hours studying it, taking notes and monitoring it. It was miraculous, he was fascinated and entranced by the Monarch and he began to collect more butterflies. Believe it or not, he is now a college professor specializing in butterflies. Lepidoptera, I think is the term for it. Who knows? Perhaps you'll research bonding someday, Ben. It's the secret to civilization, you know. If we don't bond, we revert to primitive animals."

A 'Hugoism,' I thought to myself. Elephants.

The season had changed and cooler weather prevailed. I had been at Sandstone for almost five months. My patients were momentarily without any crises. Grace's moods had stabilized. She was continuing to think about an apartment and independence from the hospital. When patients showed signs of improving, we sometimes allowed them to have weekend passes away from the place. I interpreted the interest in her own apartment as a good sign, that Grace was actually considering life outside the hospital, at least on a temporary basis. She would be able to use the hospital as a stepping stone and safety net, if need be.

"It's a month-to-month rental," she said excitedly

Vanderpol had a more muted response. "Be careful," he said to me. "When they leave the mother ship, they sometimes regress. They are highly protected here. They have no real-life responsibilities, like bills, cooking and cleaning. Everything is catered for them."

"But she'll return here during the week," I said, defending her request.

"She'll be on her own on Saturday and Sunday," Vanderpol differed. "But It's a big world out there and very different from life at Sandstone. Don't underestimate the impact of leaving this place."

"Should I nix the project?"

"No. Let's see what happens. As long as we keep an eye on her."

Late one night, I finally called Jolene. It took courage. It had been close to a month since the fender-bender. She answered on the first ring.

"I'm the one who hit your car," I said nervously.

"I was hoping you might eventually call. So here you are. It's past ten o'clock. Are you just getting done with work?"

"It took time to get up the nerve to call you," I said.

"Yes, quite a while. Well, here I am. I'm actually sitting naked in my front window, waiting to see if someone will look up and notice me."

"No, you're not," I said.

"I am. But so far, no one's observed me. Perhaps I'm losing my touch."

"Jolene," I gasped, shocked at her forthrightness.

"Yes?"

"I was going to ask you out."

"I see. My comment has deterred you, right?"

"A little unnerving, that's true." I mumbled.

"So, are you going to ask me out?"

"You're dating Ziggy," I stated.

"So?"

"I don't want to start a rivalry."

"Ah, a man of nobility. Well, it's your call. As I said, I'm here, sitting by the window."

"Naked, as you say."

"This bothers you, Dr. Ben?"

"A little."

"Or is it my forthrightness? I'm known to be provocative."

"I'd like to take you out," I said, "but I need to look at my schedule." What a terribly lame excuse, I thought.

"So, you didn't look at your schedule before you called me? Or you don't have your schedule in front of you? Or I've scared you off?"

I was at a loss for words. Caution descended on me. "A little," I finally muttered. "I'll check and call you back."

"Do that. Perhaps we have stuff in common. Maybe we'll get it on, as they say. You shrinks are a weird group. Very careful, so very careful. Anyway, take care."

I was roused by Jolene's voice and intimidated by her at the same time. I didn't understand. Was it her sexual inuendoes? The fact that Ziggy was dating her? Or just an unease with women that had plagued me all my life. I described the issue to Templeton.

"I freeze when I'm socially around the opposite sex," I said, describing my reaction to women.

"Freeze," Dr. Templeton pondered my choice of word. "The word 'freeze' conjures up an image of the North Pole. Thick ice and deep snow. Bleakness. Is that what you mean?"

"More like numb," I corrected.

"Numb? Or frightened?"

"Frightened." I clarified.

"So, you do have a distinct feeling," Templeton said. "And do you have some thoughts of what or why you are frightened?" I had chosen the usual soft chair and I raised myself upright from a slumped position. I really didn't know the answer to her question. I recalled that my ex-wife would repeatedly inform me that she could never tell what I was feeling. I related this to Templeton.

"Ah," Templeton exclaimed. "This becomes more complex. You are now talking about two phenomena, though they are clearly related. We have on the one hand some fear of intimacy with women, no? And on the other hand, a general difficulty expressing emotions. Am I correct?" She took a sip of water from a glass she had before her and lit her cigarette. "In any event, we were going to talk about your marriage. Perhaps you would start by telling me how you met your wife."

"While dissecting a cadaver," I said. "In medical school. In anatomy class. A rather unusual way to meet."

"Actually," Templeton quipped, "that's how many doctor couples meet, in medical school, over a dead body." She allowed herself a small grin.

"We dated for a short time and became engaged. A typical romance. Divorced after a year of marriage. The marriage was my wife's idea. It seemed exciting but then it cooled down fast. Like the relationship ran out of steam. An abrupt onset and a fast remission. Love was, then love wasn't. You know, Dr. Templeton, I can't even recall if it really was love. Was it love? I suppose it was. I thought it was. And then it wasn't anymore. God, I can't even recall it precisely. I'm not proud of it. I know I feel sick talking about it." I looked out the window for distraction. "You're going to ask me what 'sick' means, I know. Empty. Lost. How am I doing?" I slumped back into the chair and closed my eyes. "Lost," I said once more.

"She felt the same, your wife? I notice you haven't referred to her by name."

"Susan."

"Susan," Templeton repeated. "A name sharpens a memory, reduces emotional distance. And when did you first sense the dissolution of your relationship with Susan?"

"I think it was around the time of our first anniversary. I'm not sure. I guess I don't want to remember."

"No doubt painful to recall."

"Susan was a good woman. She went into pediatrics. Kids. She was good with kids. Kids loved her. I used to be jealous of the fact that kids loved her. Then one day she told me that she wanted a divorce. There was no other man, she said, it was just that she was unhappy living with me. I saw it coming but didn't know how to fix it," I rubbed my eyes, ran my fingers through my hair, upset at the recollection.

"Do you miss her?"

"Do I miss her?" I said out loud. "No, not really. I think I feel badly that the relationship failed and it was my fault and I'm a little jealous that she went on to have a better life. But do I miss her?"

"Yearn for her," Templeton clarified.

"No. Should I?"

"She's not your mother," Templeton said. "It sounds like you were never really invested in the relationship to begin with."

I considered this remark. It was true, Templeton's observation was correct.

"Did you begin dating again?"

"No."

"You're dating now?"

"I've recently met a woman and I am thinking about dating her," I shared.

"You'll have to be prudent until we understand more about women in your life."

I thought about Jolene's eroticism. "Yes," I said to Templeton. I looked around the room for diversion and my eyes fastened onto a painting hanging over Templeton's desk. I didn't recall seeing it before. "Is that new?" I asked her.

"No. It been there for years. Your vision is slowly clearing. The fog is lifting. You know it takes months for some patients to see the picture. I take it as a sign they are slowly emerging from themselves."

I looked more closely. It was an oil painting with rich dark colors in the foreground and light hues in the background. A man was wistfully looking out at the sea. His face was narrow and pensive and he held in his hand a pair of binoculars. What was he looking for? It was impossible to determine.

"Your reaction to the picture?"

"He's searching," I said. "But for what I obviously don't know."

"I imagine for the same things that you are searching for. Something that isn't there, perhaps? Something on the horizon very distant."

"My vacancy," I said, somewhat foolishly. "The vacancy within me. There should be a sign on me saying 'Vacancy, Inquire Within.' Here I am a shrink and I can barely manage to talk about myself and my past."

"I don't think you are behaving like a psychiatrist," Templeton said in consoling me. "You are feeling like a human being," she corrected. "How normal people feel."

I cleared my throat. "Is our time up," I pointed to my watch.

"Yes. And as usual, you seem quite relieved by it," Templeton nodded. "Someday you may tolerate these visits and even find them a solace."

* * *

The following Monday during our coffee break, Ziggy informed me that he no longer was dating Jolene.

146

"That was quick," I commented.

She's too demanding," he said. "Too needy."

"How is she too needy?"

"She just is."

"Very informative, Ziggy."

"She wants sex all the time," he complained.

"And that's bad?" I felt a stab of jealousy.

"And she imbibes. A lot," he emphasized "You'll see if you date her. Something's wrong with her."

"One of your chemical imbalances," I teased.

On my first date with Jolene, I took her to an amusement park about ten miles away from Sandstone. We laughed and giggled on the merry-go-round, crashed into each other with bumper cars and competed vigorously when we played ring toss. Our mood was light and frivolous.

There was a large dance hall at the park and it was the central draw of the crowd. Big bands came from afar to perform on Saturday nights and it was only when we started dancing slowly that Jolene became somber and quiet. When the band launched into a rumba and some swing music, Jolene brightened and her eyes twinkled. She happily whirled to the beat, laughing until she was out of breath. Then, once more, while dancing to a blues number, her mood became subdued. A few times her cheek brushed mine and at the end of the evening, her head was on my shoulder.

We left the park and I drove slowly through the side streets leading to her apartment. We hadn't talked about anything of substance and I knew little about her and her life. But her perfume and mere presence were enough to thrill me. I wanted badly to ask her about her dates with Ziggy. What did they do? Had she liked him? Walking her to the entrance of her apartment she held my hand and thanked me for the evening. There was no kiss, nor any mention of a wish to see me again. I drove off feeling a mixture of desire and disappointment.

A new patient awaited me in the morning. Her name was Regina Sullivan and she was the Chief of Staff to the Governor of the State and had descended into a melancholic bout upon discovery that her husband was unfaithful to her. She fidgeted in the chair, highly agitated.

"How could he do this to me," she said forlornly. "How could he betray me like this? Thirty years of marriage. Destroyed, all destroyed. He's with her right now." Tears of pain began to well up and her lips quivered. "She's a young veterinarian, the person we take our dog to," she put her arms around herself, cold with abandonment.

I began work on her grief, her husband's duplicity, her fury at him. Slowly, I uncovered a sense of worthlessness on her part. Then came vague suicidal thoughts which morphed into a more serious wish to die. Even though I had started her on an antidepressant, she was getting worse and I began to become alarmed. I had been reading about electroconvulsive therapy for depression and asked Vanderpol about it.

"Aha!" he exclaimed. "Shock treatments. You can't mention shock treatments here at Sandstone. It's undignified. It is not acceptable in the culture here. We're much too sophisticated. Shock is for the lower class. Shock is crude. His Excellency hates shock, absolutely abhors it."

"Even if it works?" I countered.

"It's looked upon in the same way you would look upon the use of a coat hanger to induce an abortion, "Vanderpol commented.

"It's never been used here?" I asked again.

"We send patients out to one of the shock mills nearby. Places where that's all they do. They do a little at Yale New Haven. Not here. If you want to learn about it, call Dr. Buchanon at the University. He does it. Or you can send the patient to Farmington Oaks. It's a private facility that does it. Shock mills do shock, and little else. No talking. Quick in and out, bzzzzzz, that's it."

"You don't like it?" I asked him.

"On the contrary. There is a group of us who are pushing to do shock here. We've written a position paper and submitted it to His Excellency. He says he's studying it. I predict that's all he'll do. Bzzzz," he joked again, his fingertips at each temple.

"Are you giving shock treatments to Dr. Mueller?" I asked facetiously.

"His skull is too thick," Vanderpol said. "Shocks won't penetrate it."

Chapter 12

At the Arnold Restaurant near Hartford, Jolene and I drank martinis. Jolene had two, which had loosened her tongue. She began talking about her upbringing in Vermont. She came from a family of nuns, and her two sisters were in a convent. Jolene had escaped from the suffocating Catholicism and entered Smith College.

"Full of prissy girls," she said. "It's up there in those sacred hills of Massachusetts in Northampton, where it snows all winter. Zero degrees. I transferred to UC Berkley as fast as I could."

"Some switch," I said.

"Some switch is right. From prissiness to debauchery. Drugs galore. But I finished. Gosh, these are wonderful martinis. I'd like a third but you're only on your first."

"Your liver must be larger than mine," I said as our antipasto arrived. Jolene dove into it with the intensity of an animal emerging from hibernation.

"Where was I?" she asked. "I'm getting pretty drunk right now."

"Berkley. You didn't tell me your major."

"Art history. What they call a gut major. Then I worked for a year for a swish art gallery in San Francisco. They sold Andy Warhols and Jackson Pollacks and all that high-priced stuff. They needed a half-dressed babe to be a secretary. An art assistant is what they called me but I was a secretary, made coffee." So," she broke off as dinner arrived and the waiter placed steaming plates before us.

"So."

"So. You are a handsome man," she studied my face.

I was flustered.

"I'm too forward. Sorry. Where was I?"

"You were an art director."

"An assistant. Acting school came next."

"You've had many careers." I was intrigued.

"Too many. Acting school. I went to acting school and then back to the east coast. Wow, this is the best sausage dish I've ever tasted. You want to try some?" She handed over a fork speared with a piece of meat. "I'd like a glass of Chianti," she signaled to the waiter who approached the table. "No, wait," she called him back. "Better make it a bottle," she grinned.

"Jolene," I cautioned.

"I finished acting school and the only acting gig I ever got was to be in a television commercial as--can you guess?" Jolene took a gulp from her glass.

"No."

"A smiling car rental agent. Hertz to be precise. I was quite good. I handed a happy couple the keys to a bright yellow automobile. But so much for my acting career, eh?" She smiled. "You'll have to help me finish this wine," Her speech, now, was somewhat slurred.

"So, how did you end up in business school?" I asked.

"Quite a circuitous route, I must admit. I got interested in the business part of art. So I quit acting and opened a gallery in Soho with a friend of mine. We sold prints and we actually made money!" she chuckled. "I also ended up giving lectures at The New School on retailing art. And, voila, I was in the business world." Somehow, Jolene had managed to eat and talk at the same time. Her plate was empty, and she had drained her wine glass as well. She pulled back her hair and looked me directly in the eyes.

"Would you like something for dessert?" I asked.

"You," she answered. "I'd like to have sex with you." She was wearing a sleeveless blue blouse buttoned to her neck, and she began to slowly unfasten the buttons, revealing the top of her large breasts.

I was mesmerized. Somehow, I managed to pay the bill and drive her to my apartment. As we entered the front door, she began to pull her clothes off, one piece at a time, leaving me a trail to follow right to the bedroom. In bed, Jolene was insatiable and as excited as I was. I was thrilled to be able to satisfy her. Exhausted, finally, we fell asleep intertwined. But in the morning, I awoke alone. Her side of the bed was empty.

Chapter 13

Each week, we attended educational lectures on diagnostic and treatment issues. We were assigned topics to read ahead of time. As I made my way to the administration auditorium that afternoon, my mind was in a turmoil. Instead of preparing for the lecture as I normally would have, I had spent the evening before in bed with Jolene. I barely knew her but she had quickly taken up residence in my head. What did she and Ziggy do? Was sex with me better than sex with Ziggy? My thoughts were totally preoccupied and in a whirl over my social life as I took a seat around the table. The other residents had already assembled. Dr. Martin Tor from Yale was speaking about Mourning and Melancholia, Freud's famous book on depression. Freud had described the role of various psychic forces, all of which Dr. Tor diagramed with arrows on the blackboard as if they were a series of football plays. Depression was anger turned inward, he explained to everyone present. I barely paid attention. Where had Jolene gone so early in the morning? Why had she left no note? I was strongly attracted to her. Was there any substance to our union?

Dr. Tor now started talking about the devastating 1942 Coconut Grove night club fire in Boston. Close to 500 people had died. It was the deadliest nightclub fire in history. Dr. Erich Lindemann, a psychiatrist from Boston had studied the survivors and families over the years, becoming an expert in the field of bereavement. He confirmed, in practice, what Freud had theorized decades earlier about normal grieving and pathological grief.

"Patients who can grieve openly are healthier than those who suppress their grief. When grief is unexpressed, it can turn into melancholia. Depression occurs."

All I could think about was Jolene heaving in orgasmic ecstasy and yearning for more sex. At the conclusion of the lecture, I fled to Manning House.

Sunshine was waiting for me at the front entrance. She wanted permission to attend her mother's 50th birthday party at the Goodwin Hotel in Hartford. It was with great effort that I brought myself back to the present to concentrate on her dilemma. We walked to her room.

"Do you want to go?" I asked. "Or are you caving to her wishes?"

"It's easier to go than not to go," she said, scowling.

"Is it?"

"I really don't want to go. But if I don't go, there'll be consequences. It will be hell."

"Hell is for the damned," I said. "Are you that bad?"

"You know what I mean," she said, resigned.

"Sunshine, she'll back down if you stand up to her," I encouraged.

"She. My mother," she said, whimpering. "She does not back down."

"Sunshine, you have to try. Stand your ground. You can do this."

"She'll be furious," she said somewhat fearfully.

"And? So what?"

The nurse knocked on the door and announced that there was an important call for me. I excused myself.

"Will I see you tonight?" I heard Jolene's sultry voice over the phone.

"Jolene? You disappeared," I responded.

"I had an early class. I left you a note."

"No, you didn't," I challenged.

"No? I was sure I did. I meant to, anyway. I was running late."

"Jolene, I'm seeing a patient right now. I'll call you back," I said in my most professional manner, in case anyone could overhear.

"Why can't you talk now?" she demanded.

"I'm in the middle of talking to a patient," I said again.

"Why can't the patient wait a few minutes?"

"She can't, Jolene."

"She? What does she look like?"

"What? She's a teenager."

"I would think you'd rather to talk to me."

"I do, just not right this moment." For a few seconds, it seemed as though I was talking to Sunshine and not Jolene.

"Fine," she clanged down the receiver. I left the nursing station, dazed.

"I called her," Sunshine walked towards me. "I told her I wasn't going to the party and she hung up on me."

"That must hurt," I said.

"Did I do the right thing?" she asked plaintively.

"Jolene," I started. "I mean Sunshine. Sunshine, you did the right thing, absolutely yes."

"Who's Jolene?" she looked askance at me.

"A friend."

"A girl friend?"

"I don't know yet," I answered honestly.

"Is she nice?"

"Sunshine, I don't think---"

"You've never been married?"

"I'm not sure this is a useful thing to discuss, Sunshine."

"I'll bet you have been," she said. "Unless you're cheating on your wife."

I paused, quite unsure how to proceed.

"I would never go out with a married man," she declared.

"Divorced," I decided to say. I took a deep breath.

"It's so difficult," she burst into tears. "Why is all of this so difficult?"

Why, indeed, I thought? Uncertainty coursed through me. I knew and didn't know the answer to Sunshine's huge question. The act of her mother hanging up on the phone had pierced Sunshine's heart just as Jolene's hanging up on me had done. I could feel the burn inside. And now there was the urgency on both our parts to call back and repair the damage.

"She has to love me," Sunshine now insisted. "I'm her daughter," she blew her nose. "I'm supposed to be loved. I need to be loved." Her lament echoed inside me.

"Listen to me, Sunshine. You can survive even if you don't get all the love you want from your mother."

"She should be here. Not me," she said vehemently.

"Perhaps."

"But she'll never be here. She wouldn't let anyone put her here. But I'm stuck here," she bowed her head mournfully, covering her face with her hands in torment.

"Only as long as you don't stick up for yourself." I told her. "And eat."

"If I stand up for myself, she'll disown me," she started to cry.

"Sunshine, that maybe true for a while. But she'll eventually come to respect you. You have to be firm and hold strong."

"You're sure?" she gazed at me intently.

"Almost 100%."

"Why not 100?"

"Because, Sunshine, I'm rarely 100% sure of anything," I replied, and she smiled weakly, but it was a smile. I felt momentarily victorious that this defiant and anorectic girl cared about what I had to say. It was the beginning of an attachment. Just then my mind flashed back to the comment Dr. Templeton had made, that someday, I would find solace in my therapy with her. Why did insight and intimacy emerge so slowly, I pondered? Did it have to do with the difficulty of clawing a pathway through the billions of neurons that formed the densest forest in our brains? Ziggy would say that the chemicals took time to soak all the neurons.

"To be continued," was all I could say to Sunshine at the end of our session.

I next spent time with Regina Sullivan. Apparently, the antidepressant had begun working and her mood was improved. Indeed, she had enough energy that she launched into a harangue concerning her husband and how she was going to sue him and take all his money and hire an investigator to take photographs of him with his girlfriend and she would send the photos to the church where he was a deacon.

"Perhaps you could defer on all these actions until your mood stabilizes," I suggested.

"Absolutely not. I am signing out of this hospital today."

"Mrs. Sullivan," I pleaded. "You've just arrived."

"I feel much better. The medication you prescribed is doing the trick. I'll continue my treatment outside. I have work to do."

"You were suicidal," I reminded her.

"Gone. Those feelings are gone."

"If you say so," I capitulated and prepared her discharge papers.

"Sometimes patients seal over," Vanderpol commented on her case. "The hospital is like a soothing blanket we used to lug around when we were little kids. You know, one of those ragged things that we couldn't sleep without."

"But she's not entirely well," I said.

"She may be back," Vanderpol said. "Right now, she has an enemy to vanquish."

Ziggy, to whom I told this story, had, of course, an entirely different reaction.

"Her metabolism got corrected by the antidepressant," he concluded. "It's all a matter of molecules."

"Absolutely," I said. "Why didn't I think of that? The molecules, of course."

"Bug off," Ziggy said.

I sought out the staff phone in the break room and tried reaching Jolene several times without success. Her unavailability made me anxious, but I needed to focus on my work and I temporarily put her out of my mind. I looked at my schedule and went to meet with Grace. She had been stable for several days and staff had actually taken her to look at an apartment but when I saw her, she was solemn and quiet, absently flicking through a magazine.

"So, Grace, do you like the apartment?"

"Oh yes," she answered flatly.

"You don't sound enthusiastic."

"Oh" she tried to brighten. "I am a little down but I imagine my mood will pass."

"Depressed, Grace?"

"Am I? If you say so," she said nonchalantly. "I've been thinking about how the furniture would fit in the apartment. I'll need to rent some furniture for the living room and bedroom, or else buy some."

"Do you enjoy shopping?"

"Oh yes," she said, still without any enthusiasm.

Later in the day, I discussed her with Vanderpol. She was on a maximum dose of antidepressant and I wondered about ECT if her mood plummeted any further.

"Wait a bit longer," he advised. "Why don't you meet with her a little more frequently. You know, you'll have to clear ECT with Mueller and you've already crossed swords with him."

"You said there was someone downtown."

"Buchanon. But there's a committee of three clinicians who have to sign off on treatments. They all have to be in agreement," Vanderpol noted.

"I could have her seen by them now." I said eagerly.

"Iconoclastic, Ben. Be patient," Vanderpol held up the palms of his hands. "Is she suicidal?"

"No."

"So we have some time".

"We have to wait until she's suicidal?" I was amazed.

"Ben, you may not like it but there are policies in place for treatments, not to mention politics as well. Remember Semmelweiss? In 1860, he told German surgeons to wash their hands before operating. People thought he was crazy but years later his findings showed a dramatic drop in fatalities. What I'm trying to say is that things take time to become mainstream. ECT is still a bit voodoo."

"I don't like seeing Grace depressed," I said.

"Sure. Of course," Vanderpol nodded slowly.

"Just sitting around. I don't like it."

"That's why I race cars. There's a pile of helplessness in this business," Vanderpol put his feet up on the desk and leaned way back in his chair to the point of almost tipping over. Then he abruptly straightened up as if to make a point.

"You need a compelling hobby," he said to me. "I've mentioned this before. Something you can turn to while waiting for these folks of ours to heal. If they heal," he added.

* * *

I finally reached Jolene late that night. She was icy cold on the phone.

"Why are you calling me?" she demanded.

"I said I'd call you back. You called me, remember."

"I've a lot of work to do," she said, detached.

"OK."

"OK. We'll speak another time."

"Christ," I exclaimed. "Just because the moment you called me at work and I couldn't speak with you that second? Is that why you're pissed?"

"You just want sex," she accused.

"You were the one who suggested sex," I retorted. "At the restaurant, I might add."

"What's the expression you shrink's use? Distortion of reality? That's what you're doing. Right now."

"Are you crazy? What reality are you talking about?"

"All you men are alike," she now blamed. "All of you."

"All of us? Does that include Ziggy?" I had broken my vow of not mentioning his name.

"Never mind him. To fix my car cost more than I thought. The bill was 250 dollars," she declared, avoiding my question. "Send me another check," she ordered.

"Are you drunk, Jolene?" I asked. "You're skipping from one subject to the next."

"No. A little, maybe." She began crying.

"What the hell is going on?"

Jolene said nothing. I ended up driving over to her apartment where we made rather desperate love. In the morning, I looked around the apartment but saw no trace of her.

* * *

"You'll join me in shooting a few rounds?" Ziggy phoned me. "There's a range not far from here. It's supposed to be near an industrial park. I'm sure we can find it. I'll bet you've never fired a gun. A handgun? Maybe, you've fired a rifle at camp when you were a kid. I doubt you ever hunted. You're not the hunting type."

"No gun of any kind," I said. "What on earth makes you want to go to a firing range?"

"I haven't used my gun in a while. I just cleaned it and I'd like to use it," he stated.

"You've a gun, Ziggy? Jesus. Why would you own a gun?"

"A .38. Regular police issue," he said proudly.

"Why a gun?" I repeated.

"Psychiatrists don't own guns? Is that what you're saying?"

"Where do you keep this gun?"

"Under my pillow," Ziggy teased.

"Seriously?"

"What difference does it possibly make where I store my gun?" Ziggy questioned.

"Have you been threatened? In the past?"

"Never. I just like guns," he claimed.

"I've never shot a gun," I said.

"Guns scare you, right?"

"I'm not sure I want to go shooting, Ziggy."

"It'll do you good. Make you feel powerful. You'll learn. I'll teach you. It's a good skill to have."

"Why? For what?"

"Marksmanship. Protection. We live in uncertain times," he said rather dramatically.

"I'll stay home, thanks anyway," I tried to end the conversation.

"I'll pick you up in ten minutes," Ziggy said and hung up before I could protest further. Just as with Jolene, I was left hanging

The shooting range was an indoor affair, wedged between two gray single-story factory sheds. Inside, a clerk stood behind the front counter where a sign stated the hourly rate. There was a large assortment of variously priced pistols and semiautomatic weapons for sale. In a separate glass display case were the rental guns. Ziggy had brought a black plastic carrier lined with foam rubber. His pistol lay inside. He handed it to the clerk for inspection.

"My friend would like a .22 single action. That one over there," he motioned to a small chrome six-shooter. "And a box of rounds. I need rounds also." Ziggy took my .22 and his gun and we went deeper into the store. There were ten alleys next to each other. Overhead, on wires, were moveable targets. We laid our pistols on the counter in front of us and donned ear protection.

"This is a very small caliber," Ziggy spoke loudly and clicked open the chamber. "Six rounds. Not much kickback. Here's how you load it." He handed the small pistol to me. "Now, you finish. Good. Now close the chamber. OK. I'll move the target up close to you, wait." He pressed a button. A motor-driven holder with a paper bulls-eye dangling from it whirled towards me. Ziggy stopped it at about 15 feet from where I was standing.

"OK. I'll show you the stance. Like this, feet apart, arms out-stretched, hands like so," he illustrated. "OK. Now, pull the hammer backwards. Ok. Now, aim for the target. Good. Ok. Pull the trigger slowly."

I did as I was told and the gun fired. The recoil distracted me but a hole appeared in the upper corner of the target.

"Use the sights," Ziggy instructed.

I shot round after round, reloading and firing. My accuracy slowly improved in the next half hour, and I began hitting closer to the bullseye. Ziggy encouraged me to move my target a little further away so more effort was required. I found the mental concentration tiring. Ziggy, meanwhile, had his target much further down the range and was demonstrating his acumen with a number of shots clustered around black center.

"We'll change the target," he said, and disappeared. When he returned, he had sheets with a human figure in black silhouette and he clipped one to each of our target holders.

"OK. Aim for the chest," he ordered with a sinister voice.

"Ziggy," I put down my gun.

"Damn it, Ben, just shoot!"

"No, I prefer the bullseye target."

"Watch," Ziggy said, and whirled the target down range. He aimed and rapidly fired six rounds through the head and neck of the figure. I watched, somewhat horrified. Ziggy reloaded and next put six rounds through the chest. His face was grim and he licked his lips in tension. "I'm using a .38," he said. "More powerful. Would you like to try it?'

"No" I said emphatically. And I meant it.

"Next time, maybe."

"At whom were you shooting?" I asked at length.

"No one in particular." He emptied the chambers.

"A burglar? An ax murderer? You seem so determined."

"Takes focus to shoot well," Ziggy replied. "Had enough? Let's leave."

"Quite an experience," I said as we got back into the car.

"Sometimes it's very cathartic. You pretend the target is someone you don't like. Could be the asshole who cut you off on the highway. An old enemy. Anyone," he chuckled as he slid out of the parking lot and onto the main thoroughfare, as if energized by the sound and smell of cordite. A chill ran down my spine. Thinking about it later, I would have expected him to identify Mueller as a possible target to shoot at, but somehow Ziggy never mentioned his name.

Back at the hospital, I saw Grace. Her mood had picked upwards and was holding. I asked again about the apartment she had recently visited.

"I think it's nice," she said to me.

"You've looked into some furniture for it, Grace?"

"Oh yes. I can rent some from a store nearby. Of course, I've got a lot of furniture of my own, but it's in New Hampshire. I hope it's still there and my evil husband hasn't carted everything away."

"Would he do that, Grace? Is he so vindictive? Would he take your belongings without your permission?"

"You don't know him," Grace frowned. "I am so looking forward to being on my own." But her tone of voice conveyed ambivalence. Initially, I had endorsed the apartment idea. Now I was uncertain as to whether the apartment was the right thing for her.

"You look a little doubtful," she observed.

"A little."

"Because I'm not jumping up and down with joy?"

"What worries you the most about being away from Sandstone?" I asked.

"Nothing, really. I've never been in a place on my own."

"Even in college?"

"Oh," she replied. "I always had a roommate."

"Is that the main issue in your mind, Grace? Being alone?"

"I think so."

"What happens when you are alone? What goes on in your mind?"

"I get heebee-geebies," she said. "But I think I can made it."

"Heebee-Geebies is what, Grace?

165

She shrugged. "Something I get when I'm by myself. Nervousness. A funny feeling of being all by myself. No one to talk to. No one to listen to me. But I still want to try the apartment." Grace raised a fist in the air.

I knew many people who hated loneliness. They ran the radio or television set all day, seeking noise and distraction. Loneliness was a first cousin to being neglected or even abandoned. Bars existed to foster companionship and assuage isolation. I often wondered which was worse, drinking alone at home or drinking in a crowded bar.

"A toss up," Vanderpol said when I asked him. "But everything that's lonely isn't bad., Leonardo DiVinci worked alone and look what he accomplished. Many people embrace solitude. I once did some consulting work for the Navy. We had to screen people for submarine duty and for Arctic weather station duty. Obviously, submarine sailors would have to tolerate very close quarters, sleeping a few inches above one another," Vanderpol illustrated the distance with his hands. "The Arctic weather folks had to endure isolation for months at a time. So it's all relative."

"About Grace," I moved the subject. I expressed my reservations to Vanderpol.

"Let's see how it plays out," he said. "She may decide against it on her own. It'll be a test of her judgement."

"Shouldn't we control her judgement?"

"There's a thin line between controlling patients and allowing them to have free will. We have to take some chances in the service of growth. What's the worst that can come of Grace trying out her apartment?"

"She'll fail and return to the hospital," I replied.

"Yes. She could view the whole thing as a failure and lapse into a depression again," Vanderpol arched his hands behind his back. "Or, she might just need support and encouragement to adjust, if she likes the place. She has to leave this hospital someday. She can't stay here forever."

"What's the longest a patient has stayed here?" I asked.

"Continuously?" Vanderpol sighed audibly. "Well of course there was Miles. He'd been here many years as you well know. But we also had a middle-aged man named Jerome who came to us after his daughter, a drug addict, overdosed and died. The father simply couldn't cope with the loss. He was very despondent and guilt ridden. Nothing we did helped. His shame and grief were too much. The staff even took him to the cemetery where the daughter was buried, to help with closure. He was inconsolable. We gave him various concoctions of medications and even ECT, but he stayed a broken man. He came and went from here for almost a decade. In the end, he killed himself, right here at Manning."

"Oh my God!. Killed himself how?"

"Talk about determined. He had saved up a lethal amount of medication which he took and then he hanged himself. He wasn't taking any chances. A dreadful case," Vanderpol shook his head dismayed.

"Did he have any other family members?"

"He had a wife but she was unable to comfort him. Poor thing. Some patients lack the ability to be comforted," Vanderpol stated. "My theory is that they're born that way. They're hatched, not born. No one's around to caress them. Missing in Action, as they say in the military.

Chapter 13

I talked more about Jolene when I next saw Templeton. She listened intently, puffing on her cigarette.

"I find her very interesting," I began. "Though I don't know much about the real her. She's a bit of an enigma."

Templeton raised her eyebrows.

"Love hasn't entered the picture yet. It's too soon. I think about her a lot."

"Be careful," Templeton said, her facial expression now sterner.

"Of what?"

"Falling in love."

I was perplexed. "Careful of falling in love?"

"Exactly. I advise against it."

I regarded her with disbelief.

"Sometimes people entering therapy fall in love. You've read Freud's statements on the subject? He stated that the cure for all neuroses was to fall in love. What he meant by that was being in love makes you immune to painful issues that you need to address. We won't be able to make much headway on the matter of your mother or your related difficulty expressing emotions. That's because you'll flee into the arms of your lover to avoid facing any uncomfortable feelings."

I sat silently for a moment, stunned. Templeton was staring at me. "Are you telling me not to become involved with anyone? I met this woman I like. I think I like her. It would be hard to stop seeing her, I mean, I'm not sure I want to stop seeing her."

"Of course," Templeton said, "I cannot stop you from seeing anyone, nor from falling in love. I am only saying that it may make our sessions less productive. Sometimes, in the past in such instances, I have suggested delaying therapy. It's something you might keep in the back of your mind. Therapy is very beneficial when there are no complications. Romantic complications are the worst. Would you like to tell me the name of this woman?"

"Jolene. Why do you ask?"

"Once again, Dr. Soloway, a name makes a person real, does it not? We discussed this when you described your wife and I asked you her name."

"You never call me by name," I found myself accusing her.

"But I just did."

"First name."

"You would like that?" Templeton looked at me inquiringly.

I nodded.

"Ah. Yes, many patients wish a friendship with first names. Yet this is a professional relationship and so there are constraints. It works best, I think, with a certain formality, as irritating as this might be. Do you call your patients by first name?"

"Actually, I do."

"In hospitals, that's often the case. Like a big family. I suppose it works, though I think I'd have trouble with it. But I imagine you call some of the doctors by last names, do you not? The senior clinicians. What do you call Dr. Vanderpol? "

"Just that. By last name," I said.

"He calls you by first name?

"Yes."

"And do you know why you call him by last name?"

I'd never thought about the matter. "Respect, I guess."

"Of course. Though you would wish a closer relationship, I imagine. Perhaps it will come. And with me?"

Did I want a closer relationship with Dr. Templeton? I wanted closeness of any kind, an intimacy, someone to love, someone to love me, a spirit, a force to guide me. I felt a small lurch inside me. "I think so," I said.

"Many patients do. But let's stick to convention. Now, getting back to your romance, I suggest you think about it as you have some decisions to make about this Jolene."

I certainly didn't want to stop my therapy and I didn't want to stop seeing Jolene. The rest of the session became a haze as I grappled with these choices. Outside of Templeton's office, I wrestled with her advice. I would be very careful, I decided. I would avoid falling in love. That would be my goal.

Back at Manning House, I now had a full complement of patients. I met with Sunshine three times weekly. She had taken a volunteer job at the canteen in preparation for a job outside the hospital. We talked endlessly about her mother. Slowly, she put on some weight and was making progress She surprised me one day and said the most astounding thing.

"I think I'd like to be a psychiatrist someday."

I hesitated in replying. For Sunshine to lapse into such a positive statement defied clear understanding. I had to tread carefully and support this new notion of hers, but without undo emphasis, lest she again put up her guard.

"An interesting thought, Sunshine. Is this something you've been thinking about for a while?"

"Why? You don't think I could become one?" My attempt at neutrality quickly failed.

"I think you could."

"But you're not sure. I can see that."

"You've got to be careful, Sunshine, that you don't project your uncertainties onto me or anyone else. You've got the smarts to become whatever you want. Have your parents expressed reservations about this idea? Your mother?"

"I haven't told anyone," she said.

"Tell me how the idea of becoming a psychiatrist came to you."

Sunshine tilted her head from side to side. "You're one," she stated.

I was delighted with the possibility that I could be a positive force in her psyche. I felt a small rush of joy.

Vanderpol saw her reaction as more precarious. "She's identified with you which is good. Now you've become an important figure. Be warned, you can just as easily become disappointing to her. Good identification is when you can tolerate the foibles of the person you admire. There's a healthy flexibility to it. Primitive identification is different, it's more rigid and fragile. You idealize the person, then you devalue the person the minute he or she isn't doing what you want. You can go from love to hate in a flash."

Love to hate. Perhaps this transmutation could happen with Jolene and my early passion with her could somehow turn ugly.

Just then Grace came in the front door. She'd just returned from the apartment she had rented for the month.

"I think I'm going to like it," she said. "It has a dishwasher and a disposal. Wall to wall carpeting."

"Very nice," I commented. It was good to see her engaged with her new adventure but it was also important to make sure she stayed grounded in reality. "Grace, you realize you'll be on your own when you're there?"

A fleeting shadow crossed her face. "Oh yes," she recovered. "It'll be such a relief to be away from that terrible man," she turned the conversation to her forthcoming divorce. "All our married life he made fun of me. Called me a psychological weakling. Now, I've finally found the courage to get out from under his fiendish clutches. With your help, of course," she added.

"Do you see a down side at all?" I tried not to burst her bubble but to help her see different perspectives.

"Should I?" she asked in earnest.

"Perhaps you'll miss the routines of the hospital while you're away."

"Oh, I doubt that, Doctor. Do you think I will? It's only for the weekend. I'm sure I'll make new friends."

"By the way, Grace, do you hear from your husband at all? Your ex-husband, I should say."

"Thank goodness, no."

"No news whatsoever?"

"Some papers to sign from his attorney. Legal things. Not from him directly, no."

"Is there ever a moment when you miss him, as bad as he was for you."

"Why no, doctor," she said. "Should I be missing him?"

"You might," I said to her.

"Oh dear," she responded. "I hope not."

The holidays were approaching. Thanksgiving was around the corner, and after that would come Christmas. Psychiatrists referred to these holidays as "Norman Rockwells" because of his famous painting of the idyllic and beaming family clustered around a perfectly roasted turkey. The painting was far removed from many of the patients' struggles about reunions with siblings and parents, and often, the holidays were very far from joyous. What were Grace's plans for the holidays? Would she be alone or sitting in the hospital watching a parade on television. Later in the day, I chatted with Vanderpol about what I sensed to be Grace's wavering attitude toward her apartment and her naïve approach to the forthcoming festive season.

"The holidays are such wonderful times," she had said to me.

"Yeah, well, you're correct to be concerned," Vanderpol agreed. "Grace was glued to her husband and even though she's split from him, remnants of the glue remain. She should be missing him a little bit, but we'll see. Some people seal over fast from broken relationships and move on. Some mourn in little bits and then there are others who never, ever, get over their loss. It's a tough time for patients here. They're all locked into highly ambivalent sentiments about their families. You mind the holidays?" he asked me.

Taking a moment to consider the question personally made me suddenly feel forlorn. The sensation took me by surprise. I nodded.

"The holiday fantasy is a divine fantasy. A big misconception. An imperfect reunion. You've got a place to go?"

"A group of the residents are getting together," I told him

"Good. Bad to be by oneself," Vanderpol commented.

I instinctively thought about Jolene. What would she be doing on Thanksgiving? I would call her tonight.

I looked in on Ted. He was still hearing voices. His parents were due to visit that afternoon. I upped the dose of his medication.

"You have feelings about their coming to see you?" I asked him.

He hastily turned away from me.

"Meaning?"

"You'll see. They always put on a show," he said.

On schedule, Ted's mother and father appeared. The father was brimming with questions.

"Why is he still hearing voices?" he demanded to know. "He's been with you for almost three weeks. What can you tell us? He can't stay in the hospital forever. Has he made any progress? Do you think military school would be good for him and something we should consider?"

"I'm opposed to military school," Ted's mother murmured. She sat erect at the very edge of her chair. "This problem of his isn't cured with discipline. He's very ill, Thomas," She looked away, distraught, reaching for a handkerchief from her pocketbook.

"Progress," Ted's father reiterated. He was the head of the American Telephone and Telegraph Company and a man used to demanding definitive answers.

"He's not been here that long," I said. "We're still observing him. Three weeks is a very short time to complete a full diagnosis."

"These voices he hears. Does he tell you why he hears them? Is the medication doing any good? Do you think it's helping? Should we have a consultant?" The questions came in rapid fire and made it impossible to hold a meaningful discussion.

"Thomas," Ted's mother chastised.

"We have to know, Virginia," the husband retorted.

I launched into my commentary about first psychotic breaks, the uncertainty of the future, the dreaded disease of schizophrenia. The mother watched me intently, her lips pressed together in worry.

"I don't understand this," the father said defensively. "It's all so alien. So very alien to me. No one in my family has mental problems."

"Does he suffer a lot?" the mother asked me quietly.

A few hours later, I saw them take their leave. I was touched to observe Ted's mother with her arm around her son's shoulder while his father followed stiffly behind. When the mother hugged Ted, it triggered an isolated memory of my own father hugging me, but under vastly different circumstances. Early one morning, he had taken me to see a demonstration by one of his clients who claimed to have invented a one-man flying machine. My father was highly skeptical, but he was devoted to those who hired him. That morning, we drove north from Boston to Acton, a sparsely populated farm town with many pastures. Arriving at one of them, we came upon a small group of cars and trucks parked near a flat field. There was also a newspaper reporter and a television crew setting up equipment. A fog hung low and there was heavy dew on the ground. In the middle of the gathering stood Mr. Noonan, my father's client. He was decked out in a close-fitting rubber suit, high topped woodsman boots, and a leather helmet. Men were beginning to buckle onto his back a plastic case out of which dangled two stovepipe-diameter tube. They oozed white foam. Mr. Noonan enthusiastically greeted my father and pumped his hand. He then proceeded to introduce my father to the crowd as his attorney. I remember that my father, sensing the possible calamity that could result from the forthcoming experiment, hastened to inform everyone that he was only a patent attorney. The propellant tanks rumbled. Mr. Noonan announced that he would be the first man in human history to fly solo into the air without the aid of an airplane. The ingredients of the propellent in the rockets were confidential, he stated, but he would be demonstrating regulated combustion with a uniquely potent thrust that would shoot him into the air and then, when controlled, would allow him to gently land.

"An ill-conceived venture," my father muttered and took me by the shoulder and steered me far away from Mr. Noonan.

A count-down ensued, and at the stroke of zero, Mr. Noonan pressed a button attached to his vest. The rockets exploded with a deafening roar and catapulted him into the air as a stream of fiery smoke shot out of the nozzles of the device strapped to his back. He rose upwards for a few hundred feet, spinning violently, then reached an apogee and began to plummet to the earth. As he neared the ground, both rockets caught fire. In an instant, Mr. Noonan became a flaming missile and dove headlong into the ground. The impact was sickening. The crowd screamed and men with fire extinguishers rushed towards the ruins. I began sobbing and my father put his arms around me as we watched the remains of the catastrophe detonate into a fireball. I recall hearing a siren far away. I remembered my father smelling of pipe tobacco, shaving emollients, and damp wool from his three-piece suit. I shared this recollection with Templeton when I next saw her.

"How old were you?" she asked.

"Nine or ten. Something like that."

"Did he hug you other times?"

"It's the only time I can remember," I said. "Hugging," I mused. "The importance of hugging."

"More than important," Templeton said. "It's vital. Without it we wither."

"How can that be?" I challenged her.

"It's the way our world works."

"There must be other worlds," I countered.

"That speculation doesn't help us here, does it? We're here to unravel your relationship in this world with your mother and father."

"Why would he take me to a place where a rocket contraption was bound to fail and end in disaster," I asked.

"Why indeed?" Templeton frowned.

"A father's job is to protect, isn't it?"

"It sounds like your father was both present and absent in your life," Templeton observed.

I thought about this after the session was over. Present and absent? What exactly did she mean? Present as a figurehead but absent as a source of hopefulness and well-being? If only parents instilled these principles and understandings from the moment of birth, perhaps the world would be a different place. My life would be different.

Chapter 14

I hadn't seen Ziggy for ten days. Usually, when I knocked on his apartment door, he answered in a matter of moments. This time, there was a delay, and I heard footsteps and murmuring inside. The door opened, revealing a hastily dressed Ziggy and a woman in the background, slipping into her shoes.

"I'd best leave," I said quickly.

"No, no, no, no, no," Ziggy countered my statement. "Absolutely not. Ben, this is Melissa. Melissa, Ben, my colleague at work." Melissa affected a lukewarm smile.

"Melissa's an astronomer," Ziggy declared.

"Stars and planets," I said, inanely.

"Sunspots, actually," Melissa said. She had on a sweatshirt, cargo pants, and untied sneakers. She had short black hair, presently unkempt, and large wire-framed glasses. It was difficult to gauge her age but she seemed older than Ziggy.

"Sunspots. Those things that keep erupting?" I asked.

"You're thinking of sun flares," Melissa corrected.

"Melissa was telling me that they disrupt communications," Ziggy said.

"That's the magnetic field," Melissa countered.

"I can never understand," Ziggy began, "how the sun keeps on shining. They say it'll shine for the next million years or something. I mean, how is that possible?'

"More like 5 billion," Melissa again corrected.

I backed away from them towards the door.

"We were just going for a drive," Ziggy said. "You can join us if you like. We're headed to the zoo. Melissa likes animals. Then we're going to have a picnic somewhere."

"I have to be back at the observatory this evening," Melissa reminded Ziggy. "I've time reserved."

"You can't see the sun at night," Ziggy hauled a six-pack out of the refrigerator.

"Correct, but right now there's a new comet I'm tracking." Melissa wiped the surface of her glasses. They were quite thick and without them, she looked softer. "It's just coming into view."

"Ziggy, why don't the two of you go without me," I said. "I've some write-ups to finish."

"You sure? It's a beautiful day."

I nodded.

"I'll see you out. I'll be right back," he said to Melissa.

Once on the street, he asked me about Jolene. "You're seeing her?"

"I am."

"Right. Be careful."

"Of?"

"Like I said, she's a man-eater," he warned.

I already had a sense of this but to hear Ziggy state it so suc-cinctly made me uneasy. Yet Ziggy's history with women didn't exactly inspire me. From what he had told me, he seemed to have had a string of unfulfilled relationships. There had been a tennis pro, an Air France flight attendant, a woman who played harp for the Orchestre National de France, and a third-year medical student from Seattle, all of them short-lived. Had he loved any of them, I once asked?

"Nope," he said, almost proudly.

"Not even a little?"

"Freud said that love was a loss of the self and an immersion into the identity of the other," Ziggy recited. "A fusion of two parties. Do I have it right?"

I was amazed to hear Ziggy quote Freud. He hardly ever cited literature, let alone Freud, or anything else that wasn't biochemical in nature.

"I ain't never fused," he continued as we walked down the block.

"Never ever? Infatuation? As a kid?"

"Maybe as a kid," he dismissed and began humming "Tea for Two." Ziggy rarely hummed or whistled and I was flabbergasted by his choice of song. In my mind, I heard Lester Lanin at the Pine Mountain Country Club playing it. What kind of coincidence could this be? It couldn't be a matter of random chance. My instincts heightened.

"How about the lovely young women on your unit?" I heard myself ask.

Ziggy stopped abruptly and faced me. "What? What did you just say?" Sternness spread on his face.

"Infatuation. The girls on your hall," I forced a smile.

"Didn't we have a little argument about my sitting with a girl in the snack bar? You gave me a lot of crap for that and now you're actually asking if I had a relationship with one of my patients? What,

I'm some kind of pervert, is that what you really think of me? Jesus Christ!" Ziggy stepped back.

"I was kidding, Ziggy, honest. I shouldn't have said what I said. I'm sorry, Ziggy."

"I don't fall in love with patients," he grumbled. "How about you, Dr. Sanctimony. Your hall is half full of women."

"Too old and too ill to be attractive," I said. "If I were on your hall, I'd have trouble not finding myself drawn to some of the girls."

"Yeah. Maybe you just would," Ziggy growled. "I don't know why I stay friends with you, Ben. I really don't." And he abruptly turned around and went in the direction of his apartment.

I sought out Vanderpol. Chopsticks in hand, he was munching Chinese food. Several opened cartons stood before him on the desk.

"Want some?" he offered. "Spare ribs, this one here's egg foo young. And pork fried rice. I ordered too much. From that new place on Trabian Road just below the hardware store. Not bad." He pushed a container towards me.

I slid onto a chair and hastily rattled off my story of what had transpired at the Country Club.

"Ah, Ben. Are you sure about what you saw? It sounds somewhat worrying. Perhaps you need some distance from your friend. If true, it's serious."

"He needs correction," I said.

"You're here to treat patients," Vanderpol gesticulated with his chopsticks, "not staff. It's difficult enough to control patients. One of the things you learn about this business of ours is that we control less than 25% of what we treat. Maybe on some days it rises to 50%. It's peanuts. We control peanuts. C'mon now, Ben, eat something. Leave Ziggy to learn from his own mistakes, though this may be a huge one."

"He could be one of those impaired physicians we heard that guy lecturing about," I argued. "Maybe he should be forced into treatment. How could he ever have gotten into this place? You'd think the admissions people would have screened him better than they did."

"You underestimate the hospital's narcissism," Vanderpol countered. "It loves published papers and the people who publish them. I understand Ziggy has written a lot about this catecholamine theory of affective diseases. That's big. They figure this man Ziggy might be on some kind of fast track to a Nobel Prize," he handed me a plate and a set of chopsticks. "That would make Sandstone even more famous, so the hospital and Mueller are going to overlook stuff as long as he writes articles and lectures and mentions in his credentials that he's from the wonderous Sandstone. Eventually, though, he may stray far enough that Mueller can't look the other way."

I spooned some fried rice onto the plate. I hadn't realized my hunger. As I ate, Vanderpol launched into one of his discourses.

"You'll soon see, all of us go into shrinkdom because we want to solve something that needs solving. Something that happened to us in our life. Some unresolved family stuff, some kind of dysfunctionality in our family. Why else choose psychiatry?" Vanderpol emptied the remainder of the rice onto his plate. "We're looking to find answers but we're also looking to establish some sense of order. Control. We think we can control patients so we can feel better," He lit his cigar now that he had finished eating. "We're all part detectives, don't you think? We're all searching for answers. We," he pointed to himself and then to me, "choose the human mind. Other people choose other stuff. Solving crimes, finding a cure for cancer, discovering a new planet in the sky, discovering a new vaccine for some illness, whatever. We're all hunting for something. Something primal. Very primal," he reiterated as he gathered together the empty

plates and plunged them deeply into a waste basket, as if to emphasize the aggressive effort it took to heal ourselves and those we were
assigned to treat.

Chapter 15

Every year, Dr. Mueller hosted a pre-Thanksgiving party at his stately home near Hartford. It was a lavish affair to which all the residents were invited. There was an endless array of hors d'oeuvres, with an open bar set up around a flamboyantly lit kidney-shaped outdoor pool. A buffet dinner was served inside with a number of small tables placed throughout the first floor receptions rooms of the house. It was an imposing gathering and the guest list included hospital staff and members of the psychiatry departments at Yale, as well as local politicians. A string quartet provided soft background music.

Ziggy and I went together. Ziggy seemed nervous about attending, stating that he hated these kinds of staged events because they were so ostentatious. But I knew that he still believed that Mueller's wife was his mother, and that he might actually see her in person. I was going to say something about it but feared that it would stimulate his anger.

"Mueller's showing off his balls," he said with derision as we drove through the tree lined streets of the town.

"They say the food is terrific. Roast beef and lobster. You'll like the bar, anyway. Brand liquors, they say."

"I wish I hadn't said I would go," Ziggy said. "A liverwurst sandwich would be fine."

Automobiles now lined the street as we entered the upscale residential neighborhood. Young men wearing red jackets were opening the doors of the cars ahead of us to let people out.

"Look at all this excess," Ziggy complained. In front of us, a man with a dark suit and a woman in an evening gown exited a black Mercedes sedan. "Actually, I think that's the dean of the medical school. I recognize him from his picture. Good looking woman. Christ, this is like Hollywood," he scorned.

"Sandstone is like Hollywood," I reminded him.

"A drink is what I need," Ziggy stated as we left my car and immediately headed to the crowded bar. He scanned the crowd. "A generous vodka martini," he said nervously when it came to his turn. The bartender handed him a large stemmed glass filled to the very brim.

Ziggy immediately took a big gulp. I accepted a beer.

"Mueller's wife is likely to be at his side, so if we want to spot her, we'll have to find Mueller," Ziggy looked around earnestly.

"We don't have to see either of them," I said. "I doubt we're his favorites right now."

"I want to see Mrs. Mueller," Ziggy insisted. "I just want to see what she looks like."

"Ziggy, perhaps you could forget about this theory of yours and just enjoy yourself here." I started to get anxious. I prayed Ziggy wasn't going to make a scene. "Let's stay away from Mueller, OK? I don't want you to antagonize the man any more than you already have or I already have."

"I just want to see him for a moment," Ziggy argued.

"No."

"I need to," he insisted.

"You don't. If you head in his direction, I'm leaving," I threatened.

"So leave, then," Ziggy hissed.

We were walking down a hallway and through a library. The living room was thronged with people, and in the center stood his nemesis, his arm around the shoulder of what I presumed to be his wife. Both were talking with animation to another couple. Mueller's wife had a wide, bright smile revealing radiant teeth. She was dressed demurely in a long, dark green dress. A silver pendant hung from her neck. She seemed to wear very little make-up. Her hair, closely coiffed, was light brown.

"Jesus," Ziggy muttered as he gazed at her. "Jesus."

"She's your mother, Ziggy? You believe that she's your mother? How do you really know? Are you going to speak with her?"

Ziggy precipitously plunged back through the crowd away from her. I hastened after him as he went to the bar and ordered a double martini which he grabbed from the bartender and drank with the intensity of a thirsty man downing water in a desert. Then he struck out in the direction of Mueller's wife again.

"No, Ziggy," I grabbed him by the shoulder. He pushed me aside. Some people nearby backed away, sensing a possible brawl. A large man in a white coat who had been standing near the bar quickly approached.

"Problem?" he asked.

"Just wanted another drink," Ziggy said, his speech beginning to thicken.

"You might want to hold off, my friend," the man said. I could now see the emblazoned red and white security crest on his coat.

"I'll take him home," I said.

"Good idea. I'll follow you out to your car." The three of us went around the side lawn of the house and out to the street. The man signaled the valet and within a moment, my car appeared. Ziggy stumbled inside. He reeked of alcohol as he flopped back against the seat and closed his eyes. He was asleep within minutes. By the time I got onto the highway, he was snoring. When we arrived at his apartment, I had difficulty extracting him from my car and I had to push him up the stairs to his apartment. Inside, he lurched into the kitchen, opened a cabinet and took out a bottle of gin. We wrestled for it and I finally got it out of his clutches but not before he had swallowed several mouthfuls. Then he staggered into bed and passed out. I left.

Amazingly, he came to work the next day, although he looked gaunt. I tried to understand the prior evening's events, but without any success at all.

"A great party," he summarized. "Though I don't recall too much. Did we eat dinner?" he grinned.

"Ziggy, you were completely smashed. You took one look at Mueller and his wife and went berserk."

"Can't stand that Mueller. I assume that was his wife."

"Did you recognize her?"

"I don't want to talk about it. Good vodka martinis," Ziggy smirked. "Did I have two or three? I forget. I appreciate you taking me home. You did drive me home, didn't you? I don't recall that either." He was completely non-plussed by his behavior.

In subsequent days, I tried again to resurrect the evening, but Ziggy persistently claimed amnesia and I gave up. Vanderpol had been at a car rally that weekend and hadn't attended the party. I told him about it.

"Is it even remotely possible?" Vanderpol asked, "the assertion about his mother?"

"I've no idea."

"There are these strange syndromes in our field. Capgrass Syndrome. It's where a patient thinks someone in his life has been replaced by an imposter, but these are very rare syndromes and I would doubt Ziggy is that ill. Why doesn't he make contact with this woman if he thinks she's his mother?"

"I've asked him that but I don't get an answer."

"Unless he's terrified of being rebuffed. That would be a double trauma, wouldn't it? Abandoned #1 and rejected #2. The mind can only take so much."

Later that week, I attended a seminar on catecholamines which Ziggy gave. He had put together a slide show of synapses and receptor sites and formulas showing the synthesis of various neurotransmitters in the brain. He spoke with surprising confidence and enthusiasm. One of the residents asked him whether the emotions of joy and despair could someday be traced to specific transmitters.

"Are you asking whether there is a unique transmitter for every emotion man experiences?" Ziggy paraphrased the question. "Well, there are an infinite number of emotions, and there can't be an infinite number of neurotransmitters. So no, the more likely chain of events is for the neurotransmitter to activate the part of the brain that stores the emotion."

"But how does the brain store emotions?" the resident persisted.

"We don't know that yet," Ziggy said. "But we will. It's coming. There's a neurophysiological basis for all man's thoughts and feelings."

"Even the soul?" a resident challenged.

"Can you define the soul?" Ziggy fired back. "If you can give me a crisp definition of it, or a location in the brain, we'll someday be able to elucidate the chemistry of it. That's the trouble with Freud. What is the id? Where is it? Where is the superego? These are all lovely constructs but that's all they are. The brain is made of chemicals," Ziggy asserted. "Ordinary proteins. Building blocks of proteins. Cells and membranes, millions of them, possibly billions. Every single cell with a special and specific function," Ziggy pushed back his chair in emphasis, both hands expansively waving in the air, almost like a cheerleader.

Residents surrounded him at the conclusion of his talk. I was edging out of the room when Ziggy turned my way.

"Enough about chemicals?" he shot at me.

"I have to see my next collection of chemicals," I answered. "A patient." The residents chuckled.

* * *

Grace's stability seemed precarious. A few days earlier she had moved into the apartment but her satisfaction with it seemed hollow. When she returned to Manning House on Monday, she was agitated and paced the floor. It was an effort to get her to stop and sit down, and even then, she knocked her knees together and writhed with distress. Her eyes were wide open with the stare of desolation.

"What's happening?" I asked her.

"Nothing," she swallowed nervously. I fetched her some water and she drank it timidly.

"You seem very anxious, Grace."

"Not really."

"Grace?"

"Maybe a little bit."

"Is it your new apartment?" I prodded gently.

She shook her head and struggled to rise.

"Just hold on," I said, gently pushing down on her arm.

"I'll be fine."

"Grace," I found myself raising my voice. "You're not fine at all."

"No?" She looked at me beseechingly.

"Something's happened."

"No."

"Your husband."

"Not really."

"You've spoken with him?"

"No. He called my sister, though."

"What about?"

"He invited my sister to Thanksgiving dinner which he always has in Rhode Island. Providence. He has it at the big fancy hotel. I can't think of its name."

"Not you? You weren't invited, were you?"

"Why should I be? We're getting divorced."

"Still, would you like to have been invited?"

"I don't know."

This painful questioning continued for some minutes, and although Grace half-heartedly denied it, I was positive that I was witnessing a longing she still had for her husband. So here we were, upholding her divorce, trying to make her independent but not properly paying attention to the fact that residual attachment remained. I realized that much more work was needed.

Over the weekend, I had picked up Jolene and we had driven to Lighthouse Point Park Beach near New Haven. I had a lot of misgivings about Jolene. The passion between the two of us was simultaneously thrilling and disquieting. Against my better judgment, I brought up the matter of her morning disappearances.

"So, where do you go, Jolene, in the morning after we've made love all night?"

"That really bothers you a lot, doesn't it?"

"Wouldn't it bother you?" I asked indignantly.

"Early morning class. We had a seminar. An investment advisor named Peter Bernstein gave a seminar on stocks and bonds." She hiked herself up on the seat of the car and tucked in her bare legs. "I wasn't rushing off to screw another guy."

"No?"

Jolene giggled and stroked my arm. The small gesture was stimulating and I took a deep breath. She moved closer and put her head on my shoulder. "Are there sand dunes at this beach?"

"I think so."

"Secluded ones?" she whispered.

"Why?"

"Guess." she switched on the car radio. It was the noon news. There were raids in Hanoi, President Johnson announced the withdrawal of 10,000 troops. She promptly searched for another station.

"We need music," she said. She found a jazz station. Duke Ellington was playing 'Sophisticated Lady.'

"A stupid song," Jolene said. "About a woman that can't get over a man and her whole life is ruined."

"It happens," I said.

"Good sex would have kept both the woman and man satisfied," she yawned and stroked the back of my neck. I could feel my heart beating quickly.

I had wanted to take the opportunity of this day trip to talk to her more about our relationship. "We can't just have sex," I began.

"You sweet man," she answered, and then kissed me on the cheek.

"No. Really."

"You seem to like it. Am I missing something?"

"I need to know more about you."

"You shrinks are all the same, you know that?"

"You've seen many?"

"Sure. I started when I was a teenager. My first shrink was a woman. I hated her. Anyway, I believe that you don't have to know the inside workings of all the people you meet. It really isn't necessary. You can be intimate with a stranger, you know."

"You mean sex?"

"Sex, that's right. It's the best form of intimacy".

"You dated Ziggy," I said. "Was that intimate?"

"You mean, did I screw him?"

"Did you?"

"Look, we're here, the two of us. Let's not dredge up the past."

"You've screwed any of the shrinks you've seen?"

"One other. Years ago."

We were at a red light and I disengaged from her to look at her face and see if she was serious.

"The light's green," she pointed.

"What other shrink?"

"When I was in rehab."

"Jesus, Jolene. You were in rehab and you had sex with your psychiatrist?"

"Only once," she qualified.

We left the highway and entered the curving streets of a small harbor. The air was salty. I had looked forward to our outing but Jolene's abrupt disclosure obliterated all such pleasurable thoughts. This woman could never be a serious part of my life. I wanted to turn around and take her home.

"I'm not sure I want to learn more about your exploits, Jolene."

"You're right, you don't have to hear about anything I've done in my romantic life, but you asked." Jolene's tight pink sweater was tucked into her skirt and she had on a wide red belt that accentuated her tiny waist and large breasts. Where was the beach, she wanted to know as she stretched up in the seat, making herself look even more desirable.

"The rehab was for what?" I finally succumbed to a question.

"You're not going to leave any of this alone, are you? OK. Here's the story. I went to this place for alcohol. Drugs, too, but mainly alcohol. It was called Farley in North Carolina. I stayed there for six months. And since you're going to ask me about the sex, it was with the psychiatrist who ran the place. He was an Italian named Guiseppi Castalone. We were attracted to each other. That's it. There's no more to tell."

I made a turn into the parking lot of the deserted beach. "There's no more to tell?" I erupted. "There's no more to tell? What the hell kind of statement is that?"

"You want the details about the sex?" she shouted back at me. "Is that it? Why did you bring me to this stupid empty beach, anyway?"

"Jesus," I kicked open the door and got out.

"Why don't you take me back home."

"Alright. Why don't?" I got back into the car.

Jolene took off the baseball cap she was wearing and shook her hair free. It cascaded around her shoulders.

"Why don't I?" I repeated. The sun was shining brightly but it was nonetheless a cold day and the gusts of wind were strong.

Why don't we go for a walk," Jolene said. "Before we return."

"Sure. A walk." We got out of the car and walked silently, side by side. Dust whirled around us and stung our eyes. Ahead, the expanse of sand shimmered and beyond it were the pounding waves. Jolene reached out and took my hand. As we headed down to the water, the wind became fierce and we leaned into one another for support.

"Turn back?" I asked. Algae, reeds and small sticks scooted by us at high velocity.

"I can take it if you can."

We pushed against the wind all the way to a wall of boulders defining the end of the beach. Nearby was a deserted snack shop and we leaned against it as a shelter from the wind.

"I want to continue the conversation, Jolene."

"I knew you would."

"I want to hear about this psychiatrist."

"He went back to Italy. To his wife and kids."

"You loved him?"

"Does it matter, Ben? We've all loved before."

"Did. You. Love. Him." I was becoming angry.

"I suppose I did."

"And you didn't think there was anything wrong with having sex with your psychiatrist?" I demanded.

"You should have been a clergyman. A holy man. There's something wrong with you, you know that? You're not normal."

"So, you're saying, normal people screw their shrinks, is that it?"

Jolene jolted off from the side of the snack shop like a racing swimmer pushing off a pool's edge. She started running back down the beach, her gait accelerated by the wind at her back. I took off after her but she outdistanced me. Her run turned into a smooth jog as she headed for the dunes beyond the lifeguard platform. I watched her dart over them and disappear into the hollows. I followed her path, but when I got to the mound of sand and beach grass, she was gone. I ran down the boardwalk to the car but she wasn't there either.

The main road was a half mile away, and the road to it was empty. I was mystified and anxious as well. My mind was racing. She'd deserted me again. Gone, disappeared, probably easily hitching a ride from anyone who saw an attractive girl in the middle of nowhere. I scanned the dunes, and then I saw her head peeping up from behind the dune ahead of me. And as quickly as she appeared, she ducked down and was gone. I ran towards her and started climbing in the sand to the top. Below me, in the recess of the sand was Jolene. She was naked and looked up at me with a leer. It was as provocative an image as I had ever seen, her hair streaming in the gusts, her nipples taut from the cold air. I descended the dune.

"This gets us nowhere," I blurted out.

"Could get us warm," she said, shivering.

"Listen," I started.

"Take off your damn clothes," she said, her teeth chattering.

"Jolene, for God's sake, it's in the open and the middle of the day."

Jolene came over to me and kissed me, her mouth open and her tongue exploring mine. I pressed her to me. And then I stripped, my erection painfully hard as I entered her and we tumbled onto the cold sand and both exploded with excitement. We lay there, panting and shivering, watching a single engine plane fly low overhead, then turn and dip even lower, closer to our position. Then it noisily flew away.

"Voyeurs," Jolene said. "That's in your bailiwick."

I got up, dizzy with ebbing desire and confusion. I plunged into my clothes. She dressed, but more slowly and seductively. We made our way back to the car. Inside, I ran the engine and turned up the heat.

"I can't believe it," I said. The windows started to fog up from our breathing.

"What exactly can't you believe?"

"What just happened."

"That we had sex."

"No. That I tried to have a conversation with you and it somehow turned into sex. I let it turn into sex." I was berating myself.

"Hot coffee. I need a hot drink, if you can find a place around here," she replied. "I don't know what you're talking about."

I turned up the defroster. "A simple conversation," I said.

"Look," Jolene turned in her seat and faced me, her voice shrill. "I think I've had it with you. You've turned a perfectly good afternoon into a psychological session. Forget the damn coffee. Take me to the nearest taxi stand if you can possibly find one or a bus stop. Just take me there. OK? I want to go home alone, OK?" Rage contorted her face. "Jesus, God, you are screwed up big time,

I don't know how you can possibly help anyone in your business. You're sick. Just drive into town. Just do it," she snarled.

"Take it easy," I said getting rattled.

"Drive!" she yelled at top volume.

I reached over to her shoulder and she swatted my hand. "For Christ sakes. Go!" she shrieked.

We reached the main road and headed back into the village. Sure enough, there was a bus stop ahead.

"Stop here," she snapped and lurched out of the car.

"We're at the end of nowhere, Jolene. You don't even know if there's a bus coming."

"Yeah, well, the end of nowhere is better than being with you," she slammed the door shut. I sat in the car for a moment, then parked and got out and approached her.

"No further," she growled at me like a threatened animal.

"Jolene."

"Go home."

"I'm sorry," I said foolishly.

"Go home."

I obeyed and drove home, distressed. When I arrived and gathered my things, I saw that Jolene had left her open backpack in the rear seat. She must have taken her wallet as it wasn't in the bag. However, there was a vial full of barbiturate capsules. There must have been close to 100 of them. I stared at them, thinking that Jolene was just as ill as any of the patients I had at Sandstone. I thought about my mother and the pills she had taken. I never knew what they were as the police confiscated them when they found her body. When I questioned my father, he declined to tell me about them.

"What's done is done," he had said "The past is the past, we mustn't dwell on it."

As I sat there in shock, looking at Jolene's stash, it dawned on me that I had wandered into a volatile relationship not unlike the one I had with Ziggy.

Chapter 16

Grace was a touch better Friday morning, enough for me to let her go to her apartment for the weekend. I had no idea, though, what prompted the improvement beyond the comfort and security of the hospital. After finishing my rounds with the other patients, I stopped at the canteen for coffee and saw Dr. Cassidy reading the New York Times. He was the psychiatrist from Texas who had talked about the new drug program at Sandstone. I introduced myself.

"Seen you around," he said good-naturedly. "You're on Jack's unit."

"Dr. Vanderpol."

"Right fine man. Straight shooter. Feet on the ground, not like some of the others 'round here," he commented "Place is swarming with 'lysts. You know what a 'lyst' is, right?

"Analysts."

"Guess I should be might more respectful. Anyway, I myself stick with addicts."

"I have a question about addiction," I began.

"That so?"

"Is sex an addiction?"

"Get that question quite a bit now, what with all the sexual permissiveness goin' on. Don't really know much 'bout it, but I'm guessin' that sure, you can get addicted to sex. Why not? You got a patient with a sex problem?" he inquired. "Pretty rare here, Sometimes I get to thinking this place is like a buzzard graveyard. Hope Mueller ain't here listening, shouldn't talk like this," he smiled. "I should refer to him properly as Doctor Mueller. Guess I don't think of the man as a doctor but that's beside the point. So, who's the patient?" he winked at me. "Or is it you, maybe?"

"Jesus, no," I said, but Cassidy was a perceptive man and clearly the matter had very much to do with me. Jolene's sex drive was having a powerful effect on me.

"Next question. Is it sex with many women or sex with just one woman?"

"One."

"Wouldn't see that as addiction, really," he pondered. "Maybe too much screwing, not enough talkin." He paused, looking at me quizzically. "With sexual addiction, you don't care anything about the relationship. And, you don't care who you have sex with as long as you can get it off. Make sense?"

It made sense, but my mind was on Jolene. I had an image of her standing at the bus stop, furious with me. Had she made it home?

"So, who wants the sex? You or the woman?" Cassidy was asking.

"It makes a difference?"

"Nah," Cassidy shook his head vigorously. "Can't say it does. I was just curious. So," he consulted a watch embedded in a turquoise bracelet on his wrist, "gonna have to attend a group meetin.' You come over to my hall one of these days? Don't get many visitors. Not very popular, my craft. My folks are simple alkies or needle freaks. Ain't got the trust funds like the ones in your unit. My theory on mental illness is pretty simple. Got a trust fund, you become depressed or schizophrenic. No fund, you guzzle and sniff. You like my theory?" Cassidy laughed, absolutely delighted with himself. I emerged from the meeting feeling incomplete. Discussion with Cassidy had not been enlightening,

* * *

"Shall we continue discussing your mother, then?" Templeton was saying to me.

"If you say so."

"I don't say so," Templeton clarified. "These sessions are yours, are they not? I'm sure you'd rather not talk about your mother but we have to at some point. The agenda is yours. In your work with patients, you'll find that they can blame you for bringing up unpleasant topics they want to avoid. Some patients shut the doors between sessions. Others burst into the room already talking about the issues at hand."

I felt momentarily chastened as Templeton lit the first cigarette of the hour.

"My mother," I took a deep breath. "My mother. The woman who worked at the diner. She couldn't wait to get up in the morning and go to work at that foolish diner," I said.

"Why do you call it foolish?"

"A life spent working at a diner? What kind of life could it have been?"

"A diner has many people, no? I imagine she could have had a very rich life there. Perhaps even richer than life with your brilliant father who was always in the world of patents. But you ask what kind of a life could it have been for your mother. What kind of life would you have wanted for her?" Templeton emphasized the word 'you'.

Phrased that way, the question stumped me. What was I complaining about? Would I have wanted her to be an opera singer? A Boston socialite? A member of the local bowling league? No, of course, the answer obviously had something to do with me.

"Perhaps," Templeton conjectured, as if she could read my mind, "the life you would have wanted for your mother had more to do with you and less to do with her."

"I competed with the diner," the notion suddenly coming to me.

"Perhaps."

Envious of a diner with chromed jukeboxes. In my mind's eye, I imagined my mother laughing with all the other waitresses and patrons, enjoying herself. Picturing it all, I was awash in dismay.

"A memory bothers you," Templeton observed.

I was thinking about a time when I was six years old and I had yelled at her and demanded that she stay home with me. She hesitated, but left nonetheless with my father. Why didn't he urge her to stay at home? We didn't need the money. But like clockwork, every morning, the two of them got into the car, she in her apron, my father in his vested attire, and at the end of every day, he would pick her up and bring her home. Sometimes I went with him. He would always wait outside the diner, at the curb, never venturing in. It was as if the place was contaminated. Or was it that he couldn't bear to see her so animated and happy, something she never displayed at home.

"What kept them married?" I asked out loud. "What on earth did they ever love about each other? Why did they marry in the first place? And have a child? Have me?" I craned my neck and studied the perforations in the ceiling tile. "I'm surprised I feel so wretched," I said. "Dear God. Here I am, a psychiatrist. I keep saying that, don't I?"

"What you feel doesn't invalidate your profession. Not at all," she reassured me. "Indeed, it gives you an insight to know how your patients feel when you explore their past with them. In fact, we're always building up walls in our mind to survive and protect ourselves from harsh realities. And then we forget what's inside and are surprised and shocked to discover it," she explained." Your relationship with this Jolene women? How are things proceeding?"

"They're not," I replied.

"Because?"

"She wants sex. I want to talk."

Templeton nodded.

"I'd like to talk. I'd like to touch her. Just hold hands with her and kiss her."

"Yes, of course, these are the normal behaviors of intimacy. They have been absent in your life and are only now coming into your awareness. Still, you will have to be careful about this Jolene. She can fool you and mesmerize you with her sexuality. So many people get fooled and seduced by sex, no?" Templeton left it as a haunting question. The hour was over. I stood up and made my way to the door.

"Sometimes I feel all alone," I said, turning around.

"Of course you do. Of course. Without affection, we are quite lost and alone. It's a palpable feeling. Some patients describe it as a suffusing ache. It's very real. It's often worse when you are with a crowd of people. We will talk more next time," she said, crushing out her cigarette in the glass ashtray on her desk.

I made my way out of the building and walked around to dissipate the tension I felt. Despite Templeton's warning, I thought about

Jolene and found myself speeding home to listen to my answering machine. Had she called? I pressed the blinking button in anticipation. Why did I even care about her? I felt a prisoner of some kind of crippling force.

Her voice erupted on the tape.

"No curiosity at all about how I got home, Ben?" her voice caustically venting accusations into the machine. "Jesus. Not even a damn phone call? You dump me at a forsaken bus stop and roar off and that's the end of it all?" Click, the message ended.

I turned around and hurled myself outside, slamming the door. Jolene. My mother. Jolene and my mother. Similarities? No, there were none. They were polar opposites. But there had to be some logic to it all, some form of psychic causality to account for my entanglement with the woman. The union of sex. Flesh. Did my therapy kindle all this? I was distraught over the loss of control of the events in my mind. Finally, I got into my car and drove to the hospital to seek out the refuge of patients to treat.

Grace was there, distraught.

"I started to cook something in my apartment," she told me. "In a pressure cooker. It's still cooking. I forgot to turn it off. I just remembered."

"Can your landlord get into your apartment?" I asked.

"I tried. He's on vacation."

"No one else? A neighbor?"

"I've not met any. No one has a key except me." Grace rubbed her eyes. "Will it catch fire? I'm afraid it could."

"Does it have a pressure valve?"

"I don't know."

"You're sure you didn't turn it off?"

"Quite sure. I wanted to get back to the hospital."

I pondered the matter. Nursing staff coverage was minimal at the hospital that day so there was no spare person to send.

"Is there a maintenance man? You know how to reach him?"

"No." Grace's helplessness was infuriating. I pondered the matter. Should I call the police or the fire department? It seemed extreme. Would going to her apartment be a boundary violation? I could take Ziggy with me.

"I'll check on it," I said reluctantly.

"Thank you ever so much. Here are my keys."

I took them, but told her that I didn't feel quite right going into her apartment and hoped I would find someone to let me in. Then I called Ziggy and he agreed to come with me. He was scowling as he got into my car.

"I have a new lab assistant and the asshole turned off the lights last night and also turned off all the electricity so my refrigerated samples are wasted. Can you believe it? Three months work down the drain. I'd like to strangle the guy. No, strangling would be too kind."

"Christ, Ziggy," I commiserated.

"Here we are, presumably flourishing physicians, going to turn off a pressure cooker. Are we at the height of our careers? Or at the bottom?" he intoned. "After we run this absurd errand, let's stop someplace so I can get drunk," he said quietly

"I would like to get dinner," I replied. "I'm hungry."

"Well, then, you can eat and watch me get drunk. I'm supposed to give a seminar at NYU and planned on presenting data from some of the experiments which the asshole just destroyed. Christ!" Ziggy punched the dashboard of the car. "Did I tell you I saw an article on Mueller the other day? In Newsweek no less.

There was an article about California making LSD legal and they interviewed Mueller, who knows squat about LSD. He proclaimed the drug as 'satanic'and said that it was one of the most dangerous mind-altering substances to ever be produced by mankind. Can you believe that crap?" he snapped.

"We're here," I cut him short, pulling up to an attractive set of garden apartments. Evergreen shrubs lined the bluestone walkway which was covered with a maroon awning. The foyer was thickly carpeted and expensive, with several sofas and upholstered chairs looking out on a veranda. A repairman was changing lightbulbs next to a bulletin board. I introduced myself and explained the situation to him.

"You want me to let you in?" he said.

"Please," I said. We made our way upstairs and he opened the door and then disappeared. I was reluctant to invade Grace's privacy and had hoped the repairman would check the stove. But with his fast getaway, I had no choice but to proceed into the apartment.

The living room was empty.

"You got the right place?" Ziggy asked. He passed me by, his footsteps echoing on the parquet flooring. In an adjacent room was a single bed with a nightstand on which stood an empty vase and a phone. There was an adjustable metal music stand but it was empty of sheet music. On the otherwise barren wall hung a small embroi-dered sign which proclaimed 'Home Sweet Home.'

"There's a face cloth, one towel, a bar of soap, and a tooth-brush in here," Ziggy called out from the bathroom. I heard the med-icine chest open and close. "Nothing," he added.

In the kitchen, as Grace had predicted, the pressure cooker steamed on a low flame. I turned it off. I was curious as to what was inside but it was too hot to open. The refrigerator held a half gallon of milk and a decaying apple. I checked the kitchen cupboards. They were all empty save for a small box of Wheaties. I stood there, surveying the barrenness.

"Is she moving in or moving out?" Ziggy asked.

"In, supposedly."

"There must be more to come, then," Ziggy said. "Let's go find a bar."

"There's something very wrong here," I said.

"Decent place, if it were furnished."

"She said she's moved in. She hasn't. It doesn't look like she ever will." I was thinking the room looked more like that of someone planning to die than planning to live.

"OK, I've earned my drink," Ziggy announced.

"You know something?" I suddenly turned on Ziggy. "I am not taking you to some damn bar to watch you get blitzed. You want to get blitzed, go get blitzed on your own. Ok?" I was getting really annoyed with him. "I'll drive you someplace where there are a bunch of bars and you can drink yourself into a stupor and take a cab home. Ok? Do you understand, Ziggy?" I picked up Grace's phone.

"Yeah, sure. Be cool. Whom are you calling?"

"The hospital. To tell the staff to place Grace on suicide observations. Let's go," I said, and we retraced our steps to the car. On the rest of the way back to Sandstone, Ziggy have me his self-proclaimed lecture on suicide.

"It's all biochemically mediated," he declared. "There's either too much of something or too little of it. We know something about the dopamines and their function. I'm sure that someday we can obliterate suicide with the right medical formula. In rats, you can raise and lower activity levels with the right drugs. In primates, you can observe social withdrawal and some of the signs of depression, and then you can administer the right medications to bring them out of it. There's some work coming out of Scandinavia showing that dopaminergic compounds can affect mood within a day. Even sunlight plays a role as it's obviously affecting melatonin production which affects sleep which affects mood. The stupid hospital in which we work is a century behind. I'm surprised they even believe in germ theory."

"Are you finished?" I asked, exasperated, coasting to a stop at the curb in front of a bar. "By the way, I've been meaning to ask you, if you think Mueller's wife is your mother, why don't you go see her?"

"It's none of your business."

"I'm sure it isn't, but I was just curious."

"Go to hell, Ben."

"Go bathe your neurons in alcohol, Ziggy," I shot back.

"See you on campus." He slammed the door and strode to the door of the tavern. I watched him enter the dimly lit interior and pictured him on the barstool, guzzling beer and brooding about his mice.

Once home, I ate canned chicken and against all better judgement, I called Jolene.

"I was thinking about you," she said.

"Yes?" I said guardedly.

"I think I don't want to see you again," she said, her speech somewhat muddled.

"You're drunk, Jolene."

"You have to see the patient to make that diagnosis, don't you?" she challenged.

"Is that some kind of invitation to come over?" I asked. "You just told me you didn't want to see me anymore."

"Both things are true," she said.

I knew what I was doing as I was doing it, but I was incapable of stopping myself. I was like a drug addict, poised with needle in hand, knowing full well that I was about to become a victim. When I rang the bell to Jolene's apartment, she opened the door, stark naked, a red bow around her waist.

"You never asked me how I got home from the beach," she sneered at me.

"No. How did you get home from the beach?"

"The police chief drove me home."

"The police chief. Why would a police chief drive you home, Jolene?"

"I'll give you a hint. Actually, you're looking at the hint," she giggled. My jealousy intensified my lust. Jolene and I ripped off my clothes and we fell on the carpet together. When our respective hungers had been extinguished, we crawled into bed and fell asleep. As usual, when I awoke, she was nowhere to be seen, but a red ribbon lay on the pillow. I leaped out of bed, sickened by my capitulation to her. I started rummaging through her apartment. On one wall hung a photograph of Jolene handing keys to a couple who were about to get into a yellow Hertz Chevrolet. I remember her talking about it on our first date. On another wall was a picture of Jolene in a bikini at the seashore. Next to it was an enlarged photo of Jolene's smiling face. The other walls were bare. Fake flowers decorated an area in the kitchen. I opened closet doors where clothes hung in an orderly fashion. I couldn't bring myself to inspect the drawers of her dresser. What did I expect to find? Love letters? I felt defeated. Obviously, as Templeton stated, I was seeking something far more transcendent than an orgasm with Jolene. In anger, I picked up a phone book and threw it against the opposite wall and watched as it bounced against a lamp which smashed onto the floor in pieces.

Stunned by my action, I sat and gaped at what I had done. Shards of pottery were everywhere. It was a mess.

Finding a broom, I swept up the pieces. Then I sat on the edge of the bed, bleak and exhausted. What would Templeton say to me if she saw me now? She would tell me that I was finally getting in touch with myself. Was I? What did it all boil down to? A man is hatched and not born, tossed out of the nest, seeking a union with someone who had yet to appear. Who would she be? Where would she be? It wouldn't be Jolene, that's for sure. Years and years ago, I had watched Ramona climb up on Hugo's lap. Hugo had a beatific smile on his face.

I fled back to the hospital. It was my haven, a sanctuary of the ill and I was among them. I wanted to see Vanderpol but he was at a staff meeting. I stopped by to see Ted. I could feel the Rolling Stones pulsating inside his room. Entering it, I witnessed Ted rocking on the bed with his hands over his ears again. His eyes were tightly closed. I strode over to the record player and turned down the volume.

"It's the voices," I said.

"Turn it back up, man," he pleaded.

"Tell me what they're saying."

"Please," he motioned to the record cabinet.

"What do they tell you, Ted. To kill yourself?"

Ted started to move past me and I stopped him. "The voices?" I insisted.

"Aliens," he said.

"Who are they? Who are these aliens?"

"People"

"Alien people?"

"Whatever."

"They're hallucinations," I said. "They're not real."

"Not real," he echoed without believing it. The mind played diabolical tricks. How had Vanderpol put it? "We're full of perverse and malevolent thoughts and when the fuses don't work right, all the electricity inside our minds bursts forth and sometimes patients die just to get rid of the torture." Just then, one of the nurses came through the doorway and asked if I could step outside and talk with her.

"We think Ted isn't taking his meds," she said to me in a low voice. "We bring them to him in a cup which we leave at his bedside and when we pick up the cup, it's empty, but housekeeping found a collection of pills in one of his shoes. About a week's supply."

I was dismayed. Here was a very ill young man who wished to escape his hallucinations and simultaneously refused a drug that could help him. It made no sense. I thanked the nurse and told her I would write the order for liquid medication to be given while someone watched him take it. I reentered the room.

"Ted," I said. "Let's go for a walk on campus."

Ted regarded me. "A walk?" He was perplexed. "It's getting dark. Why a walk?"

"A change of scene. Some fresh air."

"A walk? Where to?" He was stiff with caution.

"Around the property."

"Will we come back?"

"Sure. Absolutely." Vanderpol had told me that sometimes walking side by side with a patient, rather than a face-to-face encounter, could facilitate a better discussion. Ted reluctantly put on a jacket and we went outside. It was cold. Squirrels scampered along the limbs of the old oak trees. The sun was beginning to set. Ted was oblivious to it all and stared straight ahead.

"Ted," I began. "Have you experimented with hallucinogens in the past? Psilocybin? LSD? Those sorts of drugs?"

"A little."

"Pot."

"Some."

"Daily?"

"Sometimes. Why?"

"You've used a lot of drugs?"

"Maybe. Is it important?"

"You've had some bad trips?"

"A few. Why is this important? I think I'd like to go back to my room."

"You haven't been taking your medication, Ted."

"Can we go back?"

"In a minute. Why take all these hallucinogens and not take the medication that might help the voices go away?" I asked logically.

"I don't like the way your pills make me feel," Ted said.

"How?"

"Funny."

I didn't know how much of Ted's reaction to the medication was actually due to the various and subtle side effects, and how much was due to simple rebellion against parents and the world at large. We were passing a basketball court where a group of young patients were excitedly playing and hooting and laughing. And in contrast, here we were, casually strolling by, discussing a dire case. I waited until we were out of earshot.

"What is your mood, Ted?"

"Down"

"Down. Like depressed?"

"Yeh. Got my mother's illness," he added.

"Which is what? Depression?"

"They gave her shock treatments."

"When was this, Ted?"

"A while ago."

"How depressed was she?"

"Bad."

"Did she try to kill herself?"

'She just stayed in bed all day."

"Ted, have you ever tried to kill yourself?"

"Not really."

"Not really means what?"

"I took too many drugs."

We had rounded the corner of the Administration Building. A bus had driven up and patients were disembarking from a trip to a local mall. They swarmed around us as they set out to return to their respective halls. Ted and I threaded through them. I was thinking that I would probably never have learned about his mother's illness if I hadn't suggested a simple walk. Vital information from patients was given or withheld with such seeming randomness.

"You've got to give the Thorazine a chance, Ted. If the voices continue long enough, they could become more permanent. You have to help me stop them."

Ted halted on the path. He looked stricken. "OK," he said. The validity of his 'OK' was, however, surely uncertain.

As I left him in his room, I heard the music start back up again. I discussed his case with Vanderpol.

"Schizophrenia's awful," he said to me. "Assuming that's what he's got and not a whopping psychosis from all the stuff he's taken. Sometimes it's a chicken egg business. Does he take drugs to avoid the voices, or do the voices come from what he ingests? Anyway, when you clear up all the craziness, depression often emerges. His mother told you nothing about her illness?"

"Nothing."

"It didn't exist or it doesn't exist, right?" he said, frustrated. "Do patients with hypertension, thyroid disease or cancer hide it from their doctors? No. They ask for help. Only in our profession do patients try to hide their symptoms. Shame, stigma, whatever you want to call it."

"His alien voices," I began.

"I used to try and make sense of the voices our patients hear. What deep seated sin makes Ted persecute himself?"

"He told me he once stole a candy bar."

"Nah, hard to believe. Sex? Masturbation? Lust for his mother? It's guesswork. Take these girls who cut themselves. They'll tell you a bunch of things. Cutting makes them bleed and then they feel alive, or cutting relieves some inner tension, stuff like that. Sometimes there's a good explanation and sometimes there isn't." Vanderpol lolled his head back in the chair. "What it all comes down to is eradicating the voices. Snuff them out with drugs. And who knows how all these drugs work? You see, Ben, you've embraced the specialty of witchcraft. Isn't that what your friend Ziggy is working on? I imagine he's got a fancy vocabulary for it. 'Selective inhibition' or 'selective ablation' or selective something. He'll be able to tell us precisely.

"Assuming he makes it here," he added, looking straight at me.

* * *

214

Christmas came. 'I'm Dreaming of a White Christmas' wafted through Manning House. Some of the patients walked around the campus singing carols but without much enthusiasm. Vanderpol but his hands over his ears.

"Bing Crosby drives me crazy," he said. "All this forced merriment. The nurses love it. The patients hate it and they can't wait until it's over. The gifts, the endless gifts. You celebrate the holiday?" he asked me.

I shook my head.

"Right. It's a painful time for our patients. Thanksgiving is bad enough because it has to do with family, but Christmas is super special, religious and mystical. A virgin birth, a supreme being, a specialness that the people here strive so hard for," Vanderpol swept his hand in the air. "Have you ever thought about it, Ben? Thought about Christianity. Heaven. In Christianity, no one dies. They pass. They're all reunited in heaven. Think of it. You get to see all your loved ones again in heaven. Wouldn't you want to see your parents again in heaven?"

Vanderpol's question astonished me. Would I ever want to see my mother and father again? I hadn't ever thought about the idea. They were both dead and gone and I was left with the remnants. What purpose would it serve to see my mother again. Did I even long to see her?

"No," I concluded.

"No. I guess there's undigested stuff in your head, no?" Vanderpol commented.

"Lots."

"Ah," he said. "So we help others digest. Some brandy?" He reached into a drawer of his desk.

"What are we celebrating?"

"Our sanity." He uncorked the bottle and poured the liquor into paper cups. We drank in a silence that I was grateful for.

Chapter 17

A few days later, Vanderpol took me aside.

"You seem under the weather," he said to me. "In this business, you can't treat agony if you yourself are agonized. So, tell me about it. A relationship, I'm guessing." With a cigar in his mouth, Vanderpol talked like a gangster.

"A girl, yes."

"That'll do it, yup."

"I'm sorry it shows."

"Can it be solved? Or is it over?"

"I think it's done," I said.

"Nice girl? A longstanding gig?"

"No," I replied.

"Just lust?"

"Right."

"Well, we can get carried away by lust just as much as love."

"You think the patients can tell?"

"I imagine they can tell you're preoccupied," Vanderpol answered.

"You could tell," I declared to Vanderpol. "If you could, they can."

"Listen. When I was in analysis, my analyst's wife was dying of cancer. He told me. He told all his patients because he wanted them to know that his occasional preoccupation, or sadness wasn't their fault. He continued to treat folks. One or two left him, because they couldn't deal with it, but the rest stayed and benefitted greatly. He was an amazing man. It's OK to be preoccupied," he noted. "You just have to explain it to the patients."

"Tell them I broke up with a girl?" I was aghast.

"No, just tell them you're a bit preoccupied with a personal matter," he advised "They'll probe, of course, but you'll hold firm and eventually they won't think it's their fault that you're preoccupied. Remember, they have been ignored much of their lives. They always think it's their fault and blame themselves that they've been ignored. That's the default causality an adopted child concludes. I was given away for adoption because I was bad, that kind of thing,"

Group therapy was made up of all the patients at Manning House. There were 15 of them and we all sat around in a circle. The underlying principle of the therapy was that the group functioned as a family whose members reenacted their turmoils. I made an announcement before we began.

"If you all have noted me to be a bit distracted lately, it isn't because of any of you. It's because I am having some personal difficulties which I'm dealing with. I'm going to try very hard to focus on what we talk about today."

"What kind of difficulty are you referring to?" a woman promptly confronted me. "Doctors frequently get hooked on the various things they prescribe," another patient addressed the group. "Is that it, doctor?" she regarded me.

The woman next to her spoke up. "Marriage troubles," she quickly concluded. "Even though you don't wear a ring, I assume you're married. Either that or some other kind of relationship issue." Janet was her name. She was around 40 years old and had overdosed after her second marriage failed.

"Is it a bad thing? Are you in trouble?"

Sunshine was in the group. She stared intently at me, then silently, and with exaggeration, mouthed the name 'Jolene.' I tried to ignore her.

"Maybe it's a woman. Or possibly a man?" The group tittered.

"Maybe he's behind in his taxes," a man said to the group.

I had become a human inkblot onto which patients projected themselves. I held my ground.

"It's a relationship I'm trying to fix," I explained, "but it'll work out. In the meantime, we have work to do here."

"Physician heal thyself," one of the patients quipped.

"I think I can," I smiled at them. "Just as I think all of you can fix the things that bother you."

"My boyfriend ditched me," a patient announced, and the group immediately pivoted toward her plight and, thankfully, away from mine.

* * *

The next morning, I found Grace lying in bed, her eyes fixed on the wall, her mouth parched. She'd not eaten or taken in any fluids.

"I think I'm at the end," she whispered, her voice hoarse.

I cornered Vanderpol and pleaded the case for Grace to have ECT. He listened patiently to my description of her apartment and her condition and went to see her himself.

"Grace," he pulled the chair close to her bed. "I hear you're feeling really bad."

Grace made an effort to pull herself upright. She was malodorous from not having showered that day. Her hair was unkempt.

"We need to get you washed up," Vanderpol smiled at her. "And a little something to eat, Grace. You can't stay in bed."

"A little later," she said, and closed her eyes.

We retreated to the office. Vanderpol pulled out her chart.

"She has no fever. Her vital signs are OK. We did lab work last week and everything's normal. But you're right, she's severely depressed. All right. Work her up for ECT," he concluded.

"I did that already," I said. "I also called Buchanon. Dr. Buchanon's got a waiting list of several weeks. I suggest we use the Farmington Oaks place you mentioned."

Vanderpol frowned.

"I don't know what else to do."

Vanderpol pulled out an aluminum tube from the pocket of his blazer. "I was saving this for a special occasion," he explained, unscrewing the top and sliding out a dark cigar. "This sure isn't a special occasion. It's more of a crisis." He snipped off the end with his pocket scissors. "Have you seen Farmington Oaks? I suggest you visit the place and meet the mad director." He sniffed the length of his cigar and lit it. "Come back when you have met him and we'll talk. Fair enough?"

"Agreed," I said, and called Farmington Oaks to arrange an appointment.

* * *

Farming Oaks was located north of Sandstone. I drove along a winding country road bordered by large estates and rolling fields.

After ten miles, I came upon a small wooden sign next to a hedged lane that led to a sleekly modern, ranch house-like structure. It had an expansive lawn that featured an elaborate stone fountain. A porpoise sprayed water high into the air and it cascaded down into a pool from which sculptured mermaids peeked out. A rich ivy arbor covered a bluestone patio that jutted out from the main building. Underneath the canopy sat, what I presumed to be, various patients bundled up against the cool morning as though they were in a tuberculosis sanitarium. All had blank expressions on their faces as they puffed on their cigarettes. Several elegant, full-sized white poodles roamed the property. In the driveway were two station wagons with the letters 'F.O.' painted on their sides. Inside the front door was an elderly female receptionist to whom I announced my presence.

"Doctor will be with you shortly," she said. "Here for your treatment?"

"No, I called ahead. Just a visitor."

"A salesman?" she asked.

"No."

"Drug detail man? What company?"

"Not that either, no."

"Inspector?"

"No, no, I called ahead." I repeated. "I want to consult with the doctor about giving a patient shock treatments."

"Oh," she relented, gave me a forced smile, and returned to her typing. I sat in the small waiting room with oriental rugs and deeply cushioned chairs. On the facing wall were various photographs of pioneers in electroshock therapy. There were portraits of Ugo Cerletti and Lucio Bini, the two Italian neuropsychiatrists who had invented its usage. Next to them was an ornately framed image of Lothar Kalinowsky, who presently practiced the craft of shock treatment at Gracie Square Hospital in New York. Astonishingly, on another wall, were signed photographs of celebrities whom I didn't recognize and who had scribbled laudatory comments on their photos, such as 'Thanks for Your Help' and 'With Gratitude.' A yellow canary chirped inside a cage in the corner of the room. In an elongated tank, iridescent fish wove in and out of a complex coral maze. As I was examining them, an unusually thin man wearing a starched, white coat bounded into the room. His polished hair was preened back, exposing a wide forehead.

"Arthur Viventi," he chirped. "Medical director here. How may I assist you?" He gawked at me through thick glasses. The coat came down to his ankles. A stethoscope dangled out of a side pocket. Over a plastic protector on his front pocket were several pens and a thin flashlight.

"You've many creatures," I gestured to the fish and bird.

"Indeed, indeed, they divert the patients. Those who come here are often quite despairing," Viventi intoned with fervor. "We are their last hope. And I understand you are contemplating treatment for one of your patients?"

"A depressed woman."

"Ah, of course, of course, Doctor. I didn't catch your name."

"Ben Soloway."

"Dr. Soloway. Soloway. You're not, by chance, related to the Olympic gold medal skier Karl Soloway?"

"No." I shook my head.

"He was a patient here and did very, very well. I can say that without violating confidentiality because he spoke publicly about it and there's even a signed picture of him here somewhere. Well, then," Viventi clapped his hands together. "I am always pleased to have a visitor. And where exactly is your office, then, doctor?"

"Sandstone Hospital."

Dr. Viventi's enthusiasm dropped several octaves. "Ah yes, of course, very well-known indeed. Not much electroconvulsive treatment is carried out there, as I understand it?"

"No. Very little."

"No. Almost none. So," Viventi attempted to energize himself, "you would like a brief tour then? I am scheduled to begin a treatment shortly."

Viventi whisked me into a room that, for all the world, looked like a prison execution chamber. An adjustable lamp descended from the ceiling and illuminated a tilting surgical table from which straps dangled. Alongside stood an IV stand.

"We give all our treatments in here," Viventi explained. "Then the patients are transferred to our post-op room here," he led me to a room with multiple cots, "where they rest until the anesthesia wears off. We keep them around for a few hours after to make sure they're clear enough to go home. Some we even drive home, if needed. A door-to-door chauffeur service. We use sodium amytal and a muscle relaxant. You've seen the treatments done?"

"At Norwich State Hospital."

"An extremely busy facility," Viventi said. "Not enough doctors, if I may be candid. Here, I oversee every patient myself. Of course, I have assistants but the treatments here are very personal. We pride ourselves on it. And we treat a large array of patients. Depressives. Some schizophrenics. Sometimes we get in a manic type. Maybe an intractably psychotic patient. It varies. Sometimes we give treatments to alcoholics, it depends. Unfortunately, electroshock treatment is still regarded as a somewhat unorthodox treatment, despite the fact that it is administered throughout the world and has been for decades, with enormous benefit. A great injustice, we all feel. Someday soon it will be seen as mainstream. Later this year, Italy will host a world symposium on the subject. Last year, in London, almost a thousand clinicians attended from all parts of the world." Viventi was becoming evangelical. I asked him about the standard number of treatments for most patients.

"Perhaps a dozen to start. Sometimes more. Sometimes, folks come back for maintenance if they need it. Some patients relapse. Some need several courses of treatment." Viventi consulted his watch.

"And memory problems?"

"Of course, some problems occur, as you would expect. To some patients, such a loss is a blessing. We had a patient the other day who wanted to kill his supervisor at work. We treated him and he forgot all about it. You'll have to excuse me, Doctor. Today is our busy day. We have 11 patients scheduled. Some new ones, some returns. It always depends. Perhaps you'll be referring your patient here, then? I think you said she was depressed. We do well with that kind. Talk to Penelope on the way out, my secretary. She swears by shock treatments. Saved her life. Nice to meet you," he concluded, and sped away.

I said goodbye to the receptionist on the way out.

"They do wonderful things here, doctor," she volunteered, and proceeded to tell me that shock treatments had stopped her from attempting suicide. She had tried three times, all with pills.

"And how many treatments have you had altogether?" I inquired.

"Oh, I lost count, my memory isn't what it used to be. Quite a few. Doctor still treats me occasionally when I slip back down. Several of us here get the treatments. Sort of like a booster," she tittered. "Some very famous people have come here. Most of them don't want it known, of course. We've even had some people in show business. Last month we had a rock-and-roll singer. And a famous politician."

"I see the photographs."

"Oh, those, they're doctor's favorite patients. They've been here a few times. Is your practice nearby, doctor?"

"Sandstone Hospital."

"Oh. That's the place where they do that thing, I can never pronounce it. Psycho-something. Analyzing people. Am I right? You lie on a couch and talk about your childhood. It must take a very long time. Is that right?" she asked.

"Longer then shock treatments," I responded.

I headed back to Manning House where I related my adventure to Vanderpol.

"The good Dr. Viventi never turns anyone down. Well, has his enthusiasm tempered your desire to shock Grace?"

"No."

"Right. I didn't think it would."

"What about Dr. Mueller?"

"His Excellency," Vanderpol pondered the problem. "His Excellency. His Excellency. Here's what I think we should do. We should meet the problem head on and both go see His Excellency. I mean, he can't really refuse us, but to do this and not tell him would get you in trouble. You've already crossed swords with him diagnosing Miles's shrunken brain without his approval. I'm faculty and he can't toss me out. You're more vulnerable. Safety in numbers. I need to cast a vote here." He reached for the telephone and set up a meeting for that afternoon.

I was once again in Mueller's office with Vanderpol at my side. This time, Mueller offered me a seat.

"We've a woman on the unit who's gravely depressed," Vanderpol began without any preamble. "We need to give her ECT and Dr. Buchanon's got a long waiting list so we want to take her to Farmington Oaks."

Mueller swiveled his gaze between the two of us. "I would much prefer you use Dr. Buchanon. How long is the wait?"

"Weeks," I said.

Mueller ignored me and looked at Vanderpol. "Is that so, Dr. Vanderpol?"

"We can't wait weeks," Vanderpol declared.

"You've spoken to Buchanon yourself?"

"No."

"I see. Just young Dr. Soloway here. If this is such a critical matter, Jack, why wouldn't you call Buchanon yourself and plead the case?"

Vanderpol met Mueller's stare head on.

"Much is accomplished by direct contact, Jack, as you know," Mueller said with a waxen smile.

Vanderpol took out a cigar as if to light it, but chose against it.

"I don't think my intervening with Dr. Buchanon is going to be successful, Dr. Mueller. Coming from you, the odds may be better, I don't know. But we're dealing with a life-threatening matter here and I intend to start ECT as soon as possible. I'm here as a matter of courtesy only. I'm sure none of us wants to lose a patient when rapid and effective treatment is readily available. I don't think Dr. Buchanon's ECT machine is any better than the machine used by Dr. Viventi at Farmington Oaks. In fact, I suspect they are the exact same instrument. And, of course Dr. Soloway and I will be monitoring her treatment and progress. So, we're going to pursue the matter."

"You can be dismayingly indifferent to the reputation of this hospital, Jack." Mueller tried to regain control of the situation. "Our philosophy is to preserve the mind, not destroy it with jolts of electricity."

"On the contrary. I like it here and I want the best for our patients here. As I know you do. Thank you for meeting with us so promptly," Vanderpol stood up. Mueller remained seated as we filed out.

"Notify the sister and set up the treatments," Vanderpol instructed once we were out of earshot. "What do you imagine we'd find if we performed a pneumoencephalogram on Dr. Mueller's brain?" he grinned.

"A pathologically hypertrophied ego," I laughed. "Massively enlarged, bulging at the skull walls."

"Precisely so," Vanderpol patted me on the shoulder. "There's an apocryphal story about Mueller. They say he was making rounds once, and he came upon a patient who was about to stab herself in the neck. They say he told her he had an important meeting to attend, and if she was going to do it, to be quick about it because he was short on time. She got so angry with him that she stopped and threw the knife at him."

"I take it she missed."

"Sure," Vanderpol said. "He's got a shield around him just like the comic book heroes."

Late that evening, I told Ziggy what had transpired with Mueller.

"Asshole," he grunted. "These days the world is full of assholes. I got my mice and now I can't get an isotope I need. All these radioactive substances are tightly controlled and you have to file new papers with every company you deal with. Plus, the patients on my unit are all acting out. One of them has filed a complaint against me. Or, I should say, the parents have. They're accusing me of having met their daughter outside of the hospital. She told them I took her to a dance. Me!" Ziggy pointed a finger at himself.

"A dance?" I was holding my breath.

"Yeah."

"Where?"

"What earthly difference does it make where. She says I met her after hours."

"Does she say you seduced her?"

"No. That's the only thing missing. But it's bad enough. I think I don't want to talk about it anymore." He stopped to catch his breath. "So, you're sending your patient to get her brain buzzed. Good for you."

"Ought you to get an attorney, Ziggy?"

"An attorney?" Ziggy regarded me quizzically. "You consider it to be that serious?"

"Ziggy," I started, then stopped, confused by the issue at hand. Should I confront him about what I'd seen at the Pine Mountain Country Club? Was my perception accurate? Suppose I was wrong? He'd be furious and rightly so. But why wasn't he, himself, more concerned about the girl's accusations? If it were me, I would be panicked by her mere allegation, even if it were false. Why wasn't Ziggy more upset? It was odd. I recalled Buzzy, the murderer I'd seen with Vanderpol at the prison. Was Ziggy as indifferent or remorseless as Buzzy had been?

"When do you send your patient to the shock mill?" Ziggy abruptly asked me.

"What? As soon as I can."

"My father had shock treatments," Ziggy said.

"You mentioned that the first day we met, I remember."

"By then my mother had left him. She'd had enough of his moodiness. He had over 50 treatments. Did I tell you that? Maybe it was 75. Sometimes every other day, I remember that," he recalled somberly. "When they were through with him, his mood was stable. Flat. Pancaked. They'd buzzed him enough to make his brain wafer thin. No more moods. Of course, there was no more brain activity either. What the hell. The past is in the past. Here and now is what counts," he said bringing himself back to the present "How's Jolene?" he switched subjects suddenly. "You still see her? Or did she screw you to death like she screwed me to death. That's all she does, screw. Now she's one who needs some help. Maybe ECT."

"I want to get to know her," I said.

"You won't ever know her," he retorted. "Women like that don't give you a chance to develop any kind of relationship. Myself, I need someone to look after me and adore me. Make my meals, wash my clothes, wait for me to come home at night. A wifely mother. Two thirds mother, one third sex object and companion. No, seven-eighths mother. Never mind. You get the drift," he said rather despondently.

"Perhaps so," I said. But my mind was still on Ziggy's transgression.

* * *

I had phoned Grace's sister in San Francisco to inform her of the forthcoming ECT treatments.

"Oh dear," she said to me over the phone. "It's that serious, is it?"

"It is, yes."

"I was hoping maybe a change in diet might help her. And some fresh air. Whenever I call her, she's in her room. She seems to sit in her room all day. What exactly do these ECT treatments do?"

I, like all the other psychiatrists in the world, had no idea what exactly ECT did. "It delivers a shock to the brain and can help depression," I said, rather inanely.

"She said she was looking forward to moving into her apartment," the sister said. "But she doesn't sound like it. She's ambivalent."

"That's so," I agreed.

"Is she playing her violin, Doctor? That always makes her feel better."

"Hardly at all, a little, perhaps" I replied.

"Thank you for all you are doing," the sister suddenly said.

I certainly didn't think I was doing much. In the midst of this conversation, the thought of Jolene sprang into my mind. It was a jarring diversion. I thought about it and conjectured that it had to do with the polar opposites I was grappling with, Grace's despair and Jolene's lust.

Chapter 18

While Grace was having her first shock treatment, I was sitting in Dr. Templeton's office having my own therapy session. Templeton had a bad cough and sucked on Luden's cough drops while continuing to puff on a cigarette, now with a filter in place.

"You've a bad cold," I said, too inhibited to question the prudence of her smoking. "I hope it goes away quickly."

"Thank you," she replied, not one to be sidetracked by any discussion about her health. "You have some thoughts about our last session?"

"Upsetting," I answered.

"It seemed so, yes."

"Afterwards I went home to see if Jolene had called me. It felt so urgent at the time. There's still an urgency to my relationship."

"I'm sure you have been thinking about her. Do you see any connection between this Jolene and your mother?"

"I knew you'd ask that," I said.

"If that's so, why didn't you ask it for yourself?" Templeton challenged.

"I guess I haven't wanted to delve into it."

"Evidently. Because?"

"Because." I wrestled with the right answer. A memory seeped in. My mother had once broken her leg at work when she fell on some spilt coffee. My father took her to the hospital where the fracture was set. She came home and hobbled about the house on crutches for the next month, while she recovered. She was off from work for four weeks. She slept a good deal and watched the soaps on television. One day, I wandered into the living room where 'The Days of Our Lives' was playing. A man and woman were tearfully parting, and my mother was sobbing in sympathy as she flicked off the television. Attempting to stand on her crutches, she almost toppled over and then leaned against me for balance.

"I thought she might hold onto me and hug me," I said. "She didn't. Jolene doesn't."

"Did she hug you often, your mother?" Templeton asked me.

"Rarely. No memory comes to mind."

"Do you know why she didn't?"

"I never saw her hug anybody."

"You've wondered about that?"

"No."

"No?"

"No," I persisted.

"A child who isn't hugged much usually wonders why," Templeton declared, slitting the cellophane of a fresh orange colored box of cough drops.

"She must have had her reasons," I said.

"Her reasons are clearly upsetting you."

I felt tears forming in my eyes. I glanced at my watch. Time to leave. I arose.

"We still have a few minutes."

I now told Templeton that one of my patients was getting ECT. Simultaneously, I wondered out loud whether it could ever help me.

"Oh gracious," she exclaimed. "ECT for you? Certainly not. Is this your way of punishing yourself?"

"It just floated into my mind."

"Evidently. As you know, not all depressions can be talked out. Some are too debilitating. But I am sure we will be able to bring some resolution to your own bad feelings without any shock treatments. Stay hopeful. Things are coming along. See you next time."

'Things are coming along.' I thought. The whisper of enthusiasm from Templeton cheered me. But I felt drained that evening and fell into a deep sleep. In the dark early morning hours, I was awakened by Jolene's call.

"I'm taking a course in entertainment law in New York City," she paused. "Perhaps you'd come with me."

"Christ." I stuttered, half asleep.

"I leave at the end of the week. The course is at Columbia. At the law school. We can stay in the dormitories."

"And screw," I scoffed.

"Of course."

"Jesus, Jolene. It doesn't occur to you that I have duties here at the hospital? Your entitlement is unbelievable!" I said raising my voice.

"So, you don't want to go," she shot back.

"How can I possibly go?"

"Sign out to someone else. Isn't that what doctors do?" she said righteously.

"There's no one to sign out to, Jolene. I'm in a training program."

"Sure. Of course. See you," she said, and slammed down the receiver, her habit.

I was in the kitchen, clutching the phone tightly as if to strangle the stupidity of the conversation. Why did I even attempt to talk rationally with that woman? There was no future whatsoever with Jolene. Why care at all? Why even waste a single half-breath on dialogue with her? I got dressed and walked around the neighborhood in the dark to relieve the frustration boiling inside me, until dawn made its appearance. I headed over to the hospital cafeteria and deviated from my typically austere healthy breakfast by ordering a double omelet with bacon and buttered toast on the side, washed down by a large orange juice and three cups of coffee. I belched with the fullness of the meal, but it was a false sense of contentment.

The week's grand rounds lecture was given by a female professor from Harvard, Professor Miriam Soletsky. Her topic was the psychological aftermath of adoption. She had researched over 700 adoptees. Many of her population had experienced clinical depression requiring treatment.

"We have assumed for years that the early transition from biological mother to foster mother was relatively seamless, save for a time during young adulthood when many adoptees start to question their adoption. Some even physically search for their real mothers. Now we know that there exists more pathology than we had thought. Many adopted children miss their real mothers even if they have never consciously known them. Is this, then, a biological memory? We will have to do more research." The speaker asked for questions and Ziggy's hand flew up. I hadn't noticed him in the back section of the seating.

"What about the women who give up their children later in life? Is there information on their depressions?"

"Are you speaking of mothers who abandon their children?"

"I am."

"An interesting question. Yes, I would think so but the actual data is missing."

"They should become depressed," Ziggy stated.

"Do you mean that anyone who gives up a child deserves depression," Professor Soletsky jested, "or do you mean that clinically, such a person is at risk for depression?" The audience tittered. "I'm sure that a percentage of women who relinquish a child suffer a loss."

"What about the child?"

"I don't know."

Ziggy persisted. "What percent of women actively hunt the children that they've given away for adoption?"

"Also, no data available," the professor answered.

"Wouldn't you expect some effort to find the child?" Ziggy persisted.

"Some do. Some are guilt ridden and don't. Probably the child makes a greater attempt to find the mother than vice versa."

"Do you think it's ethical to give up a child?" Ziggy asked. The audience began to mumble.

"You're getting into foreign territory," the professor warily said. "Let me get some questions from over here," she sought refuge in another part of the audience. Afterwards, I sought out Ziggy. We decided to go for coffee at a local donut shop off campus.

Ziggy held forth. "No child should ever be given away," he announced.

"Be reasonable, Ziggy. Some parents can't manage."

"Nor should any parent ever abandon his or her child."

"That's your conclusion? No one should ever leave anyone. Is that it? Every union between human beings is sacred. Immutable," I quipped.

"Adults are OK to separate."

"I see."

"Because by then, they're competent to make choices. A child can't make choices."

"All adults are perfectly competent?" I found myself getting irritated.

"That's right."

"And you really believe that, Ziggy?" I questioned.

"That's right."

"So, let's take an example of a delusional man. If a delusional man wants to hang himself, it's OK?"

"It can be."

"How's that?"

"It just can be."

"What the hell kind of answer is that?" I demanded. We were crossing the large meadow that sloped down from the front of the hospital. I stopped and let him walk ahead of me, now quite angry at his obstinacy.

"You coming?" he called back at me from down the hill.

I stepped up my pace and joined him at the bottom. Cars and trucks zoomed by, their fumes visible in the cool air.

"Cheer up," Ziggy said as he regarded me. "You're too serious."

"Answer my question, Ziggy. How is it OK for a delusional man to kill himself?"

Ziggy pulled a joint out of his jacket pocket and lit it. "He could decide to end his life if the quality of his life was abysmal. Like a cancer patient, for example, someone who's riddled with cancer. I don't suppose you'd like a drag?" he said offering the lit joint to me.

"You make no sense," I said to him. "Skip the donuts. I'm not walking on the street with you getting high."

"Sure thing," Ziggy quipped, and crossed the street away from me. "I just bought some fantastic weed to celebrate," Ziggy boasted. "They've renewed my grant. Great news," he yelled over the traffic from the other side.

"Christ," I muttered. "Congratulations," I shouted back at him half heartedly

"Thank you!"

I retraced my steps back up the path to the meadow. Turning around, I saw Ziggy lying on his back on a park bench. He was furiously puffing away, a human smokestack.

* * *

On morning rounds, I found Grace in her room, picking at her breakfast. She had finished one piece of toast. An untouched poached egg was on her plate. She'd not drunk her apple juice. A nurse came in and took away her tray.

"You don't have treatment today," I remarked to her. "A day off. You must be relieved."

She gazed at me, wordless.

"Close your eyes," I instructed, "and tell me what you just had for breakfast." I wanted to assess the effect of ECT on her memory. She had undergone four treatments.

"Just now?"

"Yes."

"Apple juice."

"And what else?"

"I'm not sure. Coffee, I imagine."

"Yes?"

"That's all. I wasn't very hungry."

"You ate some toast."

"I did? Can I open my eyes?"

"Sure."

"Oh. Toast and eggs. I forgot."

"Your memory will improve," I told her. I reported her progress to Vanderpol.

"You have to be careful as she improves," he said. "When depressed patients start to get better, there's a risk period for suicide. No one knows why, exactly, but it's possibly related to the fact that they have more energy to carry out the deed, or they realize how sick they've been and how far they have to go to reconstruct their lives. Keep an eye out," he paused and contemplated. "There's something else I need to talk to you about. Your friend Ziggy. He's in a bit of trouble."

"Yes, he mentioned he might be."

"What did he tell you?"

"That he was accused of meeting a patient off campus. But the ward had told me that no one was missing."

"However, it turns out that there was someone missing," Vanderpol declared. "They actually checked the rooms again. All the patients looked to be asleep but in one room there were pillows propped up under the sheets and no one was in the bed. Her name was Melody."

Melody. It was the young patient I had seen when I was on call. She had scratched her wrist and in the course of our conversation, she had asked about Ziggy. And, she was the girl I had seen with Ziggy in the coffee shop.

"The girl hasn't positively identified Ziggy. She's denying that she even left the hospital. They'll be an investigation."

"Are you on a committee that's investigating him?" I asked.

"No. But listen, Ben. You're a good man and you don't want to be tarred by the same brush," Vanderpol was very serious. "Keep a distance between yourself and Ziggy," he warned.

"Will he be kicked out?"

"I don't know. If he turns out to be the person who took the patient out of the hospital, he'll surely be evicted from the program."

"What horrible judgment," I said.

"Indeed. You're going to find that very eminent men, distinguished men of letters, politics, science, whatever, make awful judgments involving love and sex. It's disillusioning, but it's a fact. Ziggy may have badly strayed."

"He needs therapy," I declared, "but he'll never get it. He told me so."

"We've had errant doctors before who gladly practice therapy on others, but refuse treatment for themselves. They've ended up resigning in protest. With Ziggy, who knows what'll happen. If he gets treatment, maybe he'll improve. It all depends upon the alignment of the stars or who wins the world series or the amount of snowfall this year or how hot the coffee is in the morning." Vanderpol philosophized.

"It can't be that random," I protested.

"Who benefits from therapy often seems utterly random, yes." he declared. "You get a Harvard Ph.D. and he's a lump of coal in treatment while the local janitor starts yakking and makes a switch-board full of connections during sessions. Yeah, you need intellect and all that, but in the end, the world is full of surprises. Forgive my cynicism," Vanderpol explained. He leaned against his desk. "I'm due to race down in Virginia but the carburetor in my car is giving me grief. The soul of a race car is its carburetor. Very annoying."

"You'll get it fixed in time?" I inquired.

"I think so. You can fix carburetors. Souls are a little harder to repair as I'm sure you're learning, right?"

* * *

As Grace improved, Ted got even worse. He stayed in his room all day with the audio cranked up to ear-splitting volume. I managed to click off the radio and talk with him.

"The voices are bad," I said.

"A little."

"Sounds like a lot."

"Sometimes."

Ted had been lying on the bed, and he hurled himself off and strode to the window.

"And what do they say now?" I asked.

"Stuff," he replied, his back to me.

"They laugh at you?"

He didn't answer me but shrugged.

"Do they tell you things?"

More shrugging.

"Like what?"

"Things."

"They tell you to harm yourself?"

"Not today."

"Yesterday, then."

"I don't remember."

It was then that I noticed a line of abrasions around his neck. "What are those?" I pointed to them.

"What are what?" he answered, pulling up the collar of his shirt.

"Those burn marks. Around your neck. What did you do, Ted?"

"Scratches."

"You tried to hang yourself?" I was getting apprehensive.

"No."

"Ted. Ted. It's obvious. Tell me what you did." I scanned the room for a rope. I went to his dresser and abruptly opened the drawers.

"You can't do that!" he yelled at me.

In the bottom drawer was a length of electrical wiring. I took out the wire and held it up to him while I noticed that a floor lamp was missing a cord.

"Jesus, Ted," I exclaimed. He had split the wiring lengthwise in two and tied the ends together.

"The knot stretched," he explained. "It came undone. It didn't work."

"But you wanted it to work," I calmly stated, but I was horrified by what I was seeing.

Ted stared at me.

"Because?"

"To get rid of the voices."

"Where did you loop the wire?"

"The edge of the door," he pointed.

"And then?"

"Then I changed my mind. By then the wire knot had come apart." Ted ran fingers through his hair. He sat down and slumped forward.

"But what made you change your mind, Ted?"

Ted shrugged. Just then the nurse came in bearing Ted's medication. I held up the wire for her and motioned to his neck. She blanched at the sight and then moved towards Ted and put her arm around his shoulders.

"I was asking Ted what made him change his mind," I said to her.

"I guess I wanted to live," he murmured.

"As quickly as you thought of dying, you thought of living." I stated.

"I guess."

Ted was now a much more dangerous entity. There was a mortal battle going on inside him and he was not strong enough to control the forces of his mind.

"Suicide watch? the nurse asked.

"The highest. Someone always with him," I directed, yet feeling defeated. I again increased the dose of medication and went to the telephone to reach his parents.

"Is he any better?" his mother immediately asked me.

"No, Mrs. Henderson. He's worse. He tried to hang himself but changed his mind. He's on continuous observation. Someone needs to be with him all the time. He hears voices telling him to harm himself."

"Oh my God," she began to weep.

"What's wrong?" I heard her husband in the background.

"Ted tried to hang himself."

"Give me the phone," he said and came on the line. "Is this true, Doctor?" he demanded.

"It is."

"Aren't you supposed to prevent that kind of thing? Isn't that why he's in the hospital? Isn't the medication you're giving him doing anything? I mean, why on earth---"

"He's not been taking the medication," I interrupted.

"You stopped the medication?"

"No. We had brought him the pills and he hid them in his shoes."

"How is that possible, Doctor?"

"We gave Ted his daily dose in a cup and assumed he took it."

"You watched him take it, of course."

"No. We generally assume patients take their medication. We had no reason to think otherwise with Ted. But even if we had, patients can pretend to swallow the medication and spit it out later."

"Is your work with Ted supervised?" Mr. Henderson now asked indignantly.

"There's an attending on the hall, yes. Dr. Vanderpol is his name."

"I will need to speak with him, Doctor. My wife and I are not pleased with our son's progress at your hospital. Perhaps we ought to move him. What are you doing now about his medication? Is it being given by injection?"

"Liquid." I said, thinking that he could put a wad of tissue or cotton in his cheek to absorb the liquid and then spit it out when no one was watching. I'd seen this done when I was at Norwich State Hospital.

"I don't understand why you wouldn't routinely use a needle," Henderson said gruffly, "for someone as disturbed as my son."

I could visualize Ted not wanting an injection and then being held down against his will on a stretcher with a nurse jabbing a syringe needle into his squirming body. Is that what Henderson pictured? I wanted to say that we avoided regular injections in the service of dignity, but that type of response had an accusatory ring and would just make Henderson angrier.

"Most displeased," Henderson repeated. "I must leave for an urgent meeting." He put his wife on the phone.

"Ted doesn't call us," she said. "Do you prevent phone calls?"

"No, no," I replied. "I'll have him call you."

"This depression that he has, will he get over it?"

"I certainly hope he does, Mrs. Henderson."

"I've read about shock treatments," she said. "Do you use them? In cases like Ted?"

"We're starting to use ECT here," I said cautiously. I recalled what Ted had revealed about his mother's depression and treatment with ECT. I decided to take the plunge.

"I wanted to talk with you about your own experience with depression," I began. "Ted tells me that----"

"I've no wish to discuss this matter," she shrilly interrupted. "Ted should never have mentioned it. I've told him repeatedly that this is my personal and confidential business. It's in the past and I wish to keep it in the past. It has nothing to do with Ted whatsoever."

Her sudden vehemence floored me. She had seemed so gentle with Ted, so comforting. I was at a loss for words.

"How can what I suffered possibly relate to my son's condition, Doctor? Tell me that," she attacked.

"We like to get a family history of illnesses," I explained.

"Are you implying that I passed on a disease to Ted?"

It was surely possible, I thought, but of course I said otherwise. "I know you didn't willfully pass on a disease to anyone," I told her. "You're aware that Ted has used drugs in the past?" I probably shouldn't have volunteered this fact, but I felt defensive after the husband's allegations about my failure to cure his son.

"Drugs? What kinds of drugs?

"Hallucinogens."

"We have no knowledge of that," she challenged. "Who told you that? Did Ted tell you that?"

"He did."

"We would know if he had taken drugs, doctor. I find that very hard to believe. Ted's always behaved himself. It is imperative, Doctor, that this matter of my illness be strictly confidential," Mrs. Henderson told me. "I do not wish anything in the hospital records mentioning my condition. I hope that is understood," she said curtly and hung up.

I was rattled by the phone call. Mrs. Henderson's metamorphosis was shocking. There were land mines everywhere, mothers and fathers and sisters and brothers were all waiting in the wings, ready to pounce. Even Mueller. It was daunting.

I headed for my own therapy session.

Dr. Templeton appeared to have lost weight. Her face was pale. I immediately thought that she might have cancer. The idea was upsetting.

"Your thoughts?" she pushed as I sat without speaking.

I was too anxious to tell her what was on my mind and worried about how to reply.

"Holding your thoughts back does not help us," she said.

"I was worrying that you might be ill," I managed to relate.

"Yes, you seemed upset to see me."

"You could tell?"

"You looked momentarily stricken."

"I was concerned."

"About?"

"Whether you might have cancer."

"And if I did?"

I was embarrassed by my selfish reaction. If she did have cancer and died, I bemoaned to myself, I would have to start over with someone new, assuming I had the energy to find another therapist. I would have to build trust all over again. It would be overwhelming.

"Yes?" she urged.

"Please don't get cancer," was all I could say.

"I will try not to. But if I did get cancer, it would be from my own disease."

"I don't understand."

"Your mother died of a malady. It was uniquely hers. You had nothing to do with it. Did you ever wonder about the origins of her inability to love you? Do you know anything about your mother's background?"

"Adopted. She was adopted."

"And do you know anything about her parents? Her mother?"

"No."

"Have you wondered about her biological mother?"

"Not really, no."

"Because?"

I writhed in the chair. This was a moment like the one I had experienced during the evaluation of Sunshine when Dr. McAllister had asked whether I'd interviewed Sunshine's mother.

"Where do you think your mother's inability to love you comes from?" Templeton asked more forcefully. "What could have happened to your mother to account for her distant behavior?"

"Are you asking me if I thought my mother suffered from a depression?"

"It's possible, no?"

"I suppose it's possible," I said, softly. "But she was so animated at the diner."

"The inconsistency of some forms of depression. On stage, actors wow the audience. Off stage, they drink and take drugs to deal with their agonies."

I thought of the patients I had encountered, actress Sofia Barbarosa and musician Sanchez Remo. They had a limited ability to deal with themselves.

But depressed mothers still care for their children," I rebutted. "Even schizophrenic mothers can love."

"Certainly."

"My mother didn't seem so ill that she couldn't love me."

"We don't know how ill she was, do we." Templeton asserted. "You were seven years old when she died. You knew her for only seven years, as a young child. Some mothers cannot love. Particularly if they themselves haven't been loved. Her own mother evidently rejected her."

I closed my eyes, contemplating what Templeton was saying. It was surprisingly profound.

"You have taken everything upon yourself. A part of you decided that her behavior was your fault."

"I know better."

"Part of you knows better," Templeton said. "It's a question of fault. Guilt."

"Fault," I echoed.

"It's difficult for you to let this go," Templeton said. "We've talked about this before but you still cling to the notion of culpability."

I paused and considered her comment. "What if I no longer have a sense of responsibility, or guilt, or whatever I have about her, then what?"

"Ah." Templeton exhaled a gust of cigarette smoke, "Then the intensity of the relationship you have with your mother will recede. She will become an ordinary, flawed mother who tried and failed."

"Dr. Templeton," I sputtered. It started to rain outside. Droplets formed on the window of the office.

"Guilt binds you to her," Templeton said.

"I'm trying to grasp all this."

"Pay attention now," Templeton instructed. "This is crucial. You have been found to be guilty in your mind's court of law. Now the appeals court has reversed the decision. You are innocent. You are free. But," she held up her hand like a traffic cop, "but you will now be on your own. Alone."

"I already feel alone."

"It will be a different aloneness. Your mother won't be such a huge psychic burden. You will mourn her and forgive her and move on in your life." Templeton held out her hands, palms up, and moved them up and down, as if she were estimating the relative weights of being free versus being alone. "A loss. You'll experience a loss.

Guilt has bound you to your mother. Giving up guilt will evoke a sense of loss."

What Templeton was saying was almost incomprehensible, though I felt strangely relieved by her explanation. I put my face in my hands and then looked up. I was silent, watching the water cascade down the window panes.

"Dr. Soloway."

"What?"

"Where are you?"

"At the diner," I heard myself answer, forlornly. "Looking for my mother."

"This diner that she worked in. Does it still exist?"

"Yes. I would imagine so. I could check."

"Well, then," Templeton nodded. "You might wish to visit it. And the gravesite as well."

"They're in Massachusetts," I protested.

"And?"

"It's a long trip," I said.

"No, it's not," Templeton gave me a slight smile. "It's huge in your mind. Much, much less on the highway."

The session ended. Outside her office, I stood under a nearby store awning and pondered my mother's death as she lay on her bed in the locked bedroom. Would she have drifted into a peaceful sleep? Would she have thought about me? Obviously not. I was superfluous at that moment in time, irrelevant, inconsequential, a large nothing. Acute resentment now crept into the picture. How could she have discarded me to flop helplessly like a fish hooked on the end of a line. I made a run for my car. Once inside, I punched the dashboard repeatedly. Templeton hadn't mentioned rage, yet here I was feeling what Ziggy was feeling. I drove back to the hospital very slowly and carefully, as if an accident would crush the fragile insights zooming around in my mind. At home that night, I hauled out a map of the east coast and studied a route to Boston.

The next morning, I sought out Vanderpol. We discussed Ted's attempt to hang himself.

"The room he's in isn't safe," I said. "There are plenty of places he could hang himself. It's too tempting."

"It's Ted who isn't safe," Vanderpol clarified. "The room is just a room. There are some measures in place to suicide-proof it. We don't put coat hooks on the walls and the windows are screened, but in the end, if you want to off yourself, you can do it on a closet door, a shower head, even a door knob. We can't put him in solitary confinement like they do in jails. His case is a malignant one. You've increased his Thorazine?"

"To the limit," I confirmed.

"Try another drug," Vanderpol suggested. "In this glorious business of ours, drug response is a crap shoot. Nobody knows why one drug works and another doesn't. I wish it was like an infectious disease. You could take a throat swab from a patient, put it on agar, let the germs grow, and apply the antibiotics to see which one kills the germs. You can then actually choose the right drug. Compared to that, our field is in the stone age."

"But that'll mean, I'll be starting over with a new drug." I complained.

"Uh huh, you will. It'll take time. Symptoms resolve slowly. It's not like removing an appendix. Listen, Ben, you need some diversion. I'm going racing this afternoon. Why not join me?"

"Sure," I said, with lackluster.

"You may like it," Vanderpol grinned.

That afternoon, he took me to a racing event at Oyster Bay Speedway.

There was a large crowd. Men brought regular and souped-up automobiles to compete against each other. I was amazed at the variety of cars. Gathered were 40's hot rods and home-built contraptions with slick tires and hoods bulging with the tops of chromed engine blocks and carburetors. Multiple tail pipes protruded from their rear ends. Barbecue smoke mingled with the odor of gasoline. Blasting loud rock music blared from multiple speakers at the top of high poles. Two wide asphalt strips, flanked by complex traffic lights, stretched into the distance.

"What do you think?" Vanderpol yelled over the din.

I cupped my ears with my hands and shook my head. He grinned.

The spectators in the stands were eating and drinking. They watched as the racers lined up to take their turn. The contestants revved their engines impatiently. A pair of cars came to the starting line, waited for the multicolored light countdown, and erupted in a mighty screech down the track, leaving the acrid smell of scorched tires lingering in the air behind them. The crowd roared. Then it was Vanderpol's turn. I climbed into the passenger seat and cinched my lap belt. Next to us was a yellow Camaro trembling with power. The driver was wearing sunglasses and signaled thumbs-up to Vanderpol who returned the salute. The light sequenced down to green and we were off, hurtling down the track at a speed I had never experienced. The Camaro was right alongside and as we neared the finish, Vanderpol took a slight edge and whisked by at an even 90 miles per hour. I was paralyzed with fear and choking from fumes and dust.

"Different from psychotherapy," Vanderpol quipped as we drove at reasonable speed back to the starting line. He bought two hotdogs from the concession stand and handed me one.

"Another lap?"

"I think I'll take a cab home," I said, and Vanderpol burst out laughing.

"Let's watch the next one," Vanderpol pointed to a white Oldsmobile with its rear tires jacked up. "I know the driver." The car was matched with a black Nova. Both cars bristled with energy like horses at the starting gate.

The light turned green and the vehicles screeched to a start and sped down the track. Near the end, the Oldsmobile blew a tire and suddenly veered to the right and ended up with its front wheel up on the guard rail. From the distance, we saw the driver exit the car, give a thumbs-up, and walk back towards us. Vanderpol sprinted down to meet him. As they came closer, I could hear them talking and laughing.

"Ben, this is Jimmy Breckenridge," he introduced us. "Jimmy's an attorney and he likes to race. We've raced together many times."

"Risking our lives," Breckenridge joked.

"Indeed," Vanderpol said. "Jimmy likes risk. He's an aggressive skier and he likes to play hockey."

"Sky diving also?" I ventured.

"Not yet. Soon," Breckenridge chuckled.

We said our goodbyes and headed for the car.

"Are there accidents here?" I asked.

"It's pretty safe. Last year, we had a car that went out of control and overturned and the driver sustained a broken arm. But generally, it's a safe sport the way we do it, with one track for each car. Racing at high speed around a track is more precarious."

"I guess your friend who likes risk has to prove himself," I said as we drove away. "But what is he compensating for?"

"Who knows?" Vanderpol replied as we exited the racecourse. He drove more slowly as we made our way back to the hospital. "Not everything is explainable. And you have to be careful, Ben, not to overanalyze everybody. Otherwise, you'll miss out on the good things man is able to achieves. It's easy to lose sight of healthy people. We work in a hospital. We see the sickest. Some of our patients have the equivalent of lung cancer."

Lung cancer. I pictured Templeton's chest film brimming with opaque clumps.

"End stage illness," Vanderpol was saying. "You have to get used to it."

The conversation had rambled around to death. There was a question I had been hesitant to ask Vanderpol and now was my chance.

"You've had suicides?"

"A couple," he replied. "One hanging, one carbon monoxide."

I had never dared ask this question of any psychiatrist and Vanderpol's response unnerved me. I had the fantasy that no patient under his care would ever succumb to a self-imposed death. They would be safe under his watch

"You're surprised?" he looked over at me.

"A little."

"You know any psychiatrists who didn't have deaths in his practice? You probably never asked."

"Were they a surprise to you, the suicides?" I delved deeper.

"Yes and no. The first one had tried suicide before but he still took me by surprise. He hung himself, his second try. I thought he was recovering but obviously he wasn't. I was fooled. I thought his marriage was on the mend but it wasn't, and his wife had decided to leave him for good."

"Knowing he was suicidal?"

"Well," Vanderpol drove cautiously around a rotary. "It was more complicated than that. The wife put him in the hospital so he could get well and then she could leave him. But the tactic didn't succeed."

"She left him knowing he would kill himself?"

"She had no way of knowing. But she wanted out. His death ended up being her freedom. Picture yourself being hooked up with a suicidal person," Vanderpol was saying. "His or her suicidality controls your life. Of course, there are some people who can't live without the other. You read about it in the papers. A man kills the woman who leaves him, and then sometimes himself as well, sort of like the case of Buzzy at the jail, except his wife didn't physically leave him, just emotionally left him. Buzzy formed a death bond with her."

Vanderpol pulled into a gas station and halted at the pump. A young attendant sauntered over to the window and admired the Charger.

"Fast machine," he exclaimed, and he and Vanderpol promptly became engaged in a discussion about suspensions, tires, and the sizes of engines. I stayed seated, pondering what we had just talked about.

All of us in training harbored the continual fear that we might fail to keep a patient alive. If a patient had liver disease or a bad heart, then death would seem a fully natural outcome. Yet the death of a psychiatric patient loomed as a colossal failure to be fully dreaded.

Vanderpol got back into the car.

"The second?"

"What second?"

"Suicide."

"Ah, you see, I forgot. We don't want to dwell on things that went wrong. Anyway, the second suicide was a man who entered retirement with nothing to do, nothing to look forward to, no hobbies, no outside interests. A most barren man who continuously told me he was not suicidal. I should have disbelieved him. But let me tell you something," he said, burning rubber as he accelerated out of the gas station. "Some very suicidal patients don't reveal their suicidality. Suicide is configured early in life and the patients learn to live with it. I had a patient who carried a vial of lethal pills with her, just like spies carry cyanide. The urge to die is always loitering in a dark corner of the mind. Always ask patients about suicide, Ben. Don't necessarily accept a negative reply."

We entered the main drive of the hospital. It was springtime. Robins were digging up worms from the ground to sustain themselves, just as the patients, me included, were ever searching for affection.

Jolene called me that evening from New York where she was taking her course. She was completely blotted and could barely articulate her words. She told me that she missed me and hated me, that she had slept with three men, that the work was boring, and that she thought she loved me. Then, in the middle of a sentence about sex, she hung up. I hadn't said a word throughout her tirade. I was just left holding the receiver with an empty dial tone. Of course, her call made no sense and despite her madness, I found myself aroused, and simultaneously upset with myself for being aroused.

The next morning, I told Vanderpol I needed to make a trip north.

He nodded. "Unfinished business?"

"Yes. I'll just be gone a day, maybe part of a second day. I've arranged for coverage. Don't worry, it's not Ziggy."

"Good."

"I'll phone in twice a day," I said.

"We can survive in your absence, Ben. Have a productive trip."

My old Plymouth hadn't taken a trip in a while. I topped off the oil and filled the tank. Rain was forecast. I found an umbrella way back in the trunk of the car. It had a floral pattern and several of the struts were broken. It was my mother's umbrella. What had possessed me to keep it all these years?

I started out at dawn. On the drive, I listened to the radio. There was a broadcast of a lecture from Cape Canaveral. The head of NASA was confidently proclaiming that we would have rockets travelling to Mars within the next ten years.

"Man needs to explore the outer limits of our solar system," he said.

"How will the men get back?" someone in the audience asked.

"We're working on that. Mars is a lot further than the moon, of course, so much more fuel will be needed. The rockets will need to be bigger and store more fuel. We're researching new and more efficient propulsion systems. It's our top priority."

"What have you discovered so far?" another person asked.

"I'm not at liberty to say," the director replied. "As you know, we are in a bit of a race with the Russians so we have to guard our findings."

The moon, I though. Mars. There was so much out there and here I was, utterly earthbound, my tiny world a hospital ward full of unhappy souls and I was laboring among them for clarity and stability. Maybe there were little green men on Mars who were carefree and content. Who knew?

The cemetery was located in the little town of Canton, a suburb about 45 minutes from Boston via route 28. Traffic crept in the dense fog. I was apprehensive. I had to stop several times at gas stations to ask for directions. I reached the cemetery just as the custodian was opening the gates for the day. I parked in the reception area and went inside the guest building to look at the site map to locate my mother's grave. An attendant, dressed in a bright yellow slicker, asked if I wanted him to lead me to the site but I declined. I soon realized my mistake because I promptly got lost amidst the circular maze of lanes and plots of land. After a long while, all the landscape began to look the same, no matter where I drove. I ended up retracing my steps back to the entranceway.

"I do need your help," I said to him.

He led me to a section and pointed to graves located alongside a small stream swollen with the rain. The ground was sodden with the downpour. I'd forgotten to take the umbrella out of the car and I plodded along, looking for markers under branches of trees dripping with moisture. Then I suddenly found them. There were two adjoining stones, one for my mother and one for my father. Compared to my mother, I had barely talked about my father with Templeton. Now, standing above the marker bearing a simple inscription of his name and dates, I realized how much I missed him. But I was here to deal with my mother's death. I tried to focus on my mission and instead, I recalled the image of my father concocting a special fluid in a laboratory in the basement of our home. The fluid could deflect the rain off the windshields of cars.

"I can make windshield wipers obsolete," he boasted to me. "Watch carefully." He sprayed fluid on half a plate of glass that he had divided in two with masking tape. He rubbed the fluid evenly onto the half surface with a cloth. Next, he took the glass over to the sink and let the water flow onto the entire sheet. On the treated half, water coalesced into little rivulets and ran off, leaving the surface clear. Blotchy drops and puddles remained on the untreated half.

"Astonishing, isn't it?" I was standing in front of him and he pressed my shoulders with enthusiasm in a rare gesture of physical warmth. I was nine years old and his hands were large and strong. "Now, I have to make it last. Eventually the water solubilizes my mixture and it wears off. But we've got something here. I know it," he said enthusiastically. "Think how many automobile windshields there are in the world! What do you say we celebrate for lunch? Where would you like to go?"

"Howard Johnson's," I said.

"As you wish," he replied.

Of course, it never occurred to either of us to go to my mother's old diner where I could just as easily have ordered a hot dog and he could just as easily have had his chicken salad sandwich. Or, if it did occur to us, we were both careful not to verbalize the thought. We never talked about my mother, not even years later, when he became ill with dementia. I regularly visited him in the nursing home. I would sit by his bed and talk with him or read the paper. His dementia worsened to the point that he barely knew who I was. And then, following a short bout of pneumonia, he died at the age of 62.

Surprisingly, a large number of people came to his funeral. He had clients galore, many devoted by his representation of them. For a while, he had taught patent law at the local college so there were college professors and some students as well. I gave a eulogy which I had spent hours and hours perfecting. I described his wisdom and candor, his inventive genius and his capacity to help and encourage others. But what I didn't talk about was my relationship with him, constricted as it was. Still, I felt sorrow at the time.

Every part of me now was wet. I was so lost in thought that I had been oblivious to the downpour. I began to feel cold and sought refuge in the car with the engine running and the heater turned up full blast, much as I had with Jolene. I peeled off my outer layers and gazed through the window at my mother's tombstone. Though my parents were buried next to each other, each one was a separate entity, barely bound to one another in life and never joined in their care of me. I had felt like an orphan growing up. Or maybe a half orphan? Who mattered more, a father or a mother? I mulled over this question sitting in damp clothes, hot air filling the car, the rain pelting on the roof and hood. Did I believe in an afterlife where my mother and father were united in love? I pictured them wandering in some meadow in the sky, walking in opposite directions, wordlessly, not hand-in-hand.

I left the cemetery, wondering what had I expected in coming here? Why had Templeton sent me? Obviously to dredge up the memories of my past, as if I needed prompting to make my work with her flow along. Men and women, and even children, visited gravesites all the time to show respect, it was a common act of remembrance. Why was I feeling so resentful? Of course, my reminiscences were hardly happy ones but shouldn't I feel something? I was glad to drive back through the wrought iron gates and gave a large sigh of relief as I left the burial grounds behind.

Watertown was 45 minutes away. I found the diner. It was still chromed and shiny after all these years, with a somewhat larger parking lot than I had remembered. Inside was a row of red vinyl stools in front of a long stainless steel counter. The place was busy but after a few minutes a stool opened up and I took it. I gazed around, looking for reference points that I would remember about this place that was so important to my mother. Most of the waitresses were middle aged. Had they devoted their existence to this diner as well? When was I last here? Decades ago. I was hungry before I pulled into the parking lot, but sitting in this place now made my appetite vanish and I ordered black coffee only. The diner was noisy with conversation. Steam rose from the back kitchen and the clatter of dishes and silverware filled the air. Men and women laughed and ate. The waitresses gaily took orders from customers they knew and slid porcelain plates laden with food in front of them. I felt swallowed up by forces of vague familiarity, a déjà-vu of sounds and sights.

One much older waitress was among those behind the counter. I changed seats so that I could be opposite from where she was working. Her name tag said 'Helen.'

"Have you worked here a long time?" I asked her.

"Forever," she answered me. "Or that's what it seems like." Her face was wrinkled and worn.

"Did you know a waitress who used to work here for many years? Delores was her name."

"Delores?" Her wizened eyes bore into mine.

"Between fifteen and twenty years ago. A long time."

Attempts at recognition flitted across her face. "Delores?" she frowned.

"Yes. It was a long time ago," I repeated.

"Delores? That one over there?" With a knife she was holding, she pointed to a gallery of photographs displayed on the wall behind the cashier. They were black and white images behind aged celluloid. I got off the stool and went over to the wall. Sure enough, there was my mother surrounded by other waitresses, all wearing white aprons. I stared at her. Her hair was black and tied in a bun. She was grinning openly at whoever held the camera. Despair swept over me. "I think she killed herself, the poor thing. We all heard about it," Helen said.

"Yes, she did."

"You knew Delores?" Helen asked looking at me more closely.

"I'm her son."

"You're her son?" she proclaimed with true wonder. "That's amazing. Delores' son. I remember her talking about you."

"Me?"

"Oh, I remember her now Hmm," She paused. "She would talk about the things you did at school. Oh yes." She smiled.

"You remember that?" It was my turn to be surprised.

"I do, yes. Where are you from? You live near here?"

"Hartford, Connecticut."

"Ahh, And, what kind of work do you do?"

"A physician."

"Isn't that amazing," Helen exclaimed. "Just amazing. I remember her saying that she hoped you would grow up and become a doctor. I remember that, yes I do, it was so long ago but I still remember it. We were like a family here."

"My mother actually said that?" It seemed unbelievable.

"Oh yes. She was proud of you. Very proud. She said you were a good student. I remember that too."

"Proud?"

"Oh yes. We all talked about our children."

It was incomprehensible, this dialogue. Did my mother actually profess pride in my existence, or was she just keeping up with the conversation among the other waitresses? I was utterly confused. New customers entered the diner and Helen became busy taking orders. I waved goodbye to her, retreated to my car and sat there, stunned by what has just transpired. My mother, the woman who had barely shown affection to me, boasted about me to others? How was that possible? I found myself becoming incensed. What on earth prevented her from displaying her pride about me, to me? And her suicide, an act that seemed to come out of nowhere, how could she have shown such gaiety at the diner and then just kill herself? Was Templeton correct in hypothesizing that my mother may have been depressed? Was she a case of a smiling depression? Later in my training, I saw many cases in which a despairing man or woman made a big show of looking dazzling. They would cultivate an appearance of success to obscure a crippling mood. I also learned that how they looked and dressed had nothing to do with how precarious they felt inside. An elaborately planned dinner party gone astray might lead a hostess to overdose after the guests left, or a rigidly ambitious man might consider death if he had been overlooked for a promotion. Years later, I made a small study of how depressed patients smiled. I concluded that there were smiles that were hollow, and just involved the working of the muscles of the mouth. But the most malignant smiles were the broad-based beaming folks who needed to convince the world of their achievements via an expansive display of fine white teeth.

I drove through the night back to Sandstone.

Chapter 19

It had been several weeks since Grace had begun ECT and her memory seemed intact. Her mood had improved. Ted had his music playing a little more softly. He wasn't wearing earphones which I took to be a good sign. Feeling a little more hopeful, I went to morning rounds.

Mueller began by announcing that someone on the faculty had won an award.

"Before we begin this morning, I want to report that one of our residents has won this year's Cunningham Draper Award for excellence in research," he proclaimed. "As you know, we pride ourselves on the fact that many of our researchers, and our clinicians as well, have received acknowledgement for their contributions to mental health." Mueller reached into the inner pocket of his suit jacket and hauled out a sheet of paper which he unfolded. He scanned the document and continued his speech. "In the past five years, staff have received the Abelson Prize, the McPaulson Award for excellence in biology, two major grants from the National Institutes of Mental Health relating to advancements in schizophrenia, the Stafford Award for excellence in psychiatry, and now the Draper Prize from the Pullman Foundation. This year, the total major publications emanating from Sandstone have been 18 in number. It is gratifying to know that Sandstone continues on a path of noteworthiness and

I want to thank each and every one of you who contributes to this effort of superiority and distinction."

"Who's the resident?" someone called out, irritably. "Who won the prize?"

Mueller looked up, perturbed. "Did I not mention his name?"

"No," scattered voices from the audience replied.

"Dr. Harrington. Are you here, Dr. Harrington?"

Ziggy, in his usual back row seat, raised his hand. The audience applauded. I was flabbergasted. Ziggy had never mentioned any award to me. I stared at him but he looked away.

"Now then," Mueller eclipsed further dialog, "we have another matter. I will be assembling a task force to study the use of electroconvulsive treatments here at the hospital. Some of you have expressed an interest in this modality of treatment. As you all know, we have tended to favor a more traditional approach, based on sound psychotherapeutic principles. Our patients expect such methods and we are known for our conservatism. Electroconvulsive therapy, in my view, subverts the very bedrock of our treatment philosophies. However, it is perhaps time to revisit the matter and I have asked Dr. Wilhelm Roessinger to chair a task force on the subject. Wilhelm? A few words, perhaps?" Mueller stepped back.

Astonishing, I thought. What had brought this about? Was it my involvement with Grace? Had I actually propelled forward the use of ECT at Sandstone? I was thrilled at the thought.

Roessinger was a short statured man dressed in a handsome tweed suit with a bow tie. He had a marked German accent. He had trained abroad, and was the past president of the Boston Psychoanalytic Institute. I knew him to be as unlikely to endorse shock treatments as Freud himself would have been. Roessinger tossed out the names of the other members of the task force, all of whom were also practicing psychoanalysts. All of this made no sense to me. Psychoanalysis was almost a religion at Sandstone. The psychoanalysts positively worshiped the forces of the mind. They were as eager to endorse shock treatments as Mueller was to become benevolent.

We will approach the topic with an open mind," Roessinger concluded. "Electroconvulsive therapy is, as you all know, a very old modality of treatment with significant side effects that we must carefully consider, if we are to offer these treatments to our patients."

"Thank you, Wilhelm," Mueller gave him a tight smile and neatly cut him off.

Ziggy now arose, incensed.

"An open mind?" Ziggy said with some incredulity. "Forgive me, but I'm a little confused," he directed his remark to Roessinger. "Are there not going to be any people on the task force who believe in ECT? Or who can actually perform it? Dr. Buchanon conducts the procedures at our sister hospital downtown. There's even a neurosurgeon at University Hospital who's doing cingulotomy operations on patients with intractable anxiety and obsessive-compulsive conditions. He actually cuts some of the fibers deep in the brain," Ziggy challenged. "Shouldn't someone like him be on the committee? Someone who favors biologic treatments to balance out the talking therapies?"

I could see Mueller inhale sharply. Roessinger blanched.

"Our task force is in the formative stage," Roessinger stated.

"I'll bet it stays formative," Ziggy pounced. "You guys want nothing to do with ECT, isn't that so?"

"I would ask you to be civil, Dr. Harrington," Mueller said harshly.

"The issue isn't civility," Ziggy shot back. "The issue is scientific truthfulness."

"You may find, Dr. Harrington, that the reports of positive results from ECT, or even from the neurosurgery that you mention, are less than scientific and even less than truthful," Mueller retorted.

Hands started flying in the air, a free-for-all in the making.

"This is a hospital," someone called out. "We're acting like it's a political contest."

"Electroshock is a treatment which should be available in every hospital."

A dissenter spoke up. "A very convenient way of inducing amnesia. We're in the business of awakening memories, not destroying them!"

Mueller drew himself erect and pounded the lectern to restore order.

"This is clearly a polarizing topic," he said, with intensity. "I'm not sure that morning report is the proper forum for this matter. Dr. Roessinger and I will make absolutely certain to allow the input of anyone who wishes to comment on the subject. Perhaps we will present the findings at a Wednesday morning rounds in the near future, yes Wilhelm?"

"Most assuredly," Roessinger nodded briskly.

"Thank you," Mueller dismissed us.

I headed over to Ziggy. He was fending off a number of congratulations. I waited until the hall was almost empty.

"The man's evil. Evil. Treacherous," he said to me in a low tone as soon as I sat down next to him.

"Ziggy, Jesus, your confrontations with Mueller and Roessinger were over the top. Almost disrespectful," I chided.

"Richly deserved," he replied. "They both need challenging, that's for sure."

"This prize you won, Ziggy. You never mentioned it. You never mentioned that you had applied for it. What is it? What did you do to earn it?"

"Son of a bitch Mueller didn't even mention my name until someone asked," Ziggy exclaimed, "Son of a bitch."

"Tell me about the prize," I repeated.

"Gotta go. I've an experiment running." He stood up.

"You don't want to talk about this prize, Ziggy. Right?"

"I wrote a paper, it's that simple. On dopamine. How it regulates moods. Anybody could have written it."

"Must have been an important paper."

"I was going to tell you about the prize," Ziggy said. "Except it doesn't seem so important right now, given other issues. Anyway, I'm amazed that Mueller even condescended to mention the prize. Of course, he twisted the whole thing to highlight his hospital. Jesus. I hate the man, I really do."

"Ziggy. You and Mueller are on a collision course. You know that, right?"

He stiffened. "So?"

"Why are you doing this, Ziggy? You can't win."

"It's a battle worth fighting." He said vehemently.

"Because of this mother thing," I said.

"This mother thing!" he shot back at me, outraged. "Is that what you call it? This mother thing?"

"If this thing about your mother is true, Ziggy, I would think that you'd be angry at your mother and not Mueller."

"I have to go," he said contemptuously. "I'm late. The mice need injections." He whirled around and headed towards the lab. I watched him trudge up the hill but at the last moment, he turned down a small gravel path away from the building and towards the parking lot. For some reason, I continued to stand there and observe. Within a minute, I saw his green Volkswagen chug around the corner on its way down the main road.

I realized I hadn't raised the matter about the country club incident. There had been no time to ask about the accusations. I did think about his prize, however. It was unlike Ziggy not to boast about his work. His statement that 'anyone could have written it' aroused suspicion in my mind. Could he have paid someone to write the paper? Could he have fudged the results? These were disturbing thoughts.

Equally disturbing was the fact that I had reverted back to feeling that I was the cause of my mother's lack of affection. The notion seemed to stick in my brain, like hardened cement.

Chapter 20

Dr. Templeton had improved. She had some color in her face and there were no cigarettes visible on her desk, just the pervasive smell of tobacco mustiness in the room. I settled in the soft chair and began talking about the diner I had visited.

"Brave of you to seek it out," she remarked. "I assume it was upsetting."

"What did my mother get out of working in a diner?"

"Companionship, perhaps?"

"But to not be close to one's own child?" I protested.

"Some people can only be intimate with strangers," Templeton explained. "You will see this in your practice. Men and women can be friends to the world and to their patients and clients. They can relish the company of their colleagues and constituents, but not their families. It is not unusual for them to ignore their own families."

"I wish I hadn't gone to the damn diner." I said glumly.

Templeton reassured me, "On the contrary. You are facing reality. Perhaps not a pretty reality, but an important one."

"My mother killed herself after an argument with my father," I said. "Why would she have done that? What made her do it?"

Templeton leaned forward in her chair. "You must understand that we cannot account for everyone's actions on this planet. People do bizarre things. Some we can make sense out of and some we can't. We may never understand the actions of your mother."

"It all has to make sense," I insisted.

"Physics and mathematics make logical sense. Not the mind."

I pulled myself erect in the chair.

"You are struggling mightily to comprehend why your mother got joy from working at the diner but not at home. You would think it would be the other way around, that she hated her work and took refuge with her family. But that wasn't the case. So often people do not find nourishment in their own families. A family is supposed to be nurturing and comforting, but you know from your own work that this is not always the case," Templeton reminded me.

"My mind keeps returning to me as the culpable agent. When I leave this office, I relapse into blaming myself. I can't help it," I said.

"Yes, you can. Remember, the mind doesn't like change," Templeton said. "It's like moving into a new neighborhood. You have to adjust to it. It takes time for the brain to relinquish the old map and adopt the new."

"Sometimes I think of myself as cold and detached and distant," I trailed off.

"Self-recrimination," Templeton reacted. "Of course, you are none of those things. Your battle is with affection."

"Affection, affection, affection," I moaned out loud. "I wish I'd had a dog that would jump all over me when I came home."

"Did you want a dog growing up?"

"I had a hamster. My father said he didn't have time for a dog."

"Ah," Templeton nodded.

"I've always wanted affection," I said with longing. "I still do." I thought of Jolene, an affectionless character. In contrast, Vanderpol was a man who sustained me.

"Did your mother hug you when she came home from work?" Templeton now asked.

"Did she? I don't know. I don't remember."

"Would you have wanted her to?"

"Yes, of course."

"And your father?"

"Beyond what I told you, I can't recall."

"I'm sure you can."

"Not really."

"What does 'not really' mean?" she probed.

"I told you about the rocket incident."

"But not a real hug. I mean a hug of joy. Do you recall your mother showing affection to anyone?"

I closed my eyes tightly, trying to conjure up an image of my mother hugging anyone. Once, while I was in the car with my father, waiting for her to come out of the diner, I saw her inside the door hugging another waitress who was retiring. But no, I couldn't recall her hugging anyone, not even my father.

"What happened when you got sick?" Templeton asked me.

"What happened? You mean, did I stay home from school?"

"Did your mother care for you?"

I was perplexed by her question.

"Make you chicken soup. Sit with you. Play a game with you."

"I was usually left alone in my room."

"For the duration of your illness?"

"My father would come in and check on me when he came home, but not my mother."

"You must have felt quite alone."

"I listened to the radio."

"For company."

I nodded, thinking of the big yellow RCA radio that sat by my bedside. I listened to the Breakfast Club, The Shadow, Jack Benny, the Lone Ranger. I could still hear their voices.

"Did your mother ever listen to the programs with you?" Templeton inquired.

"Not that I can recall."

Templeton regarded the clock on her desk. "This is a difficult time for us to stop," she announced with a small sigh. "It would be useful for you to continue pondering this false proposition that you were the cause of your mother's lack of affection. You very much seem to cling to this notion, which is a child's point of view, and not that of you as an adult. We also haven't talked about your visit to the cemetery. We must talk about this next time, yes?"

I stood up and nodded, shaken as usual. I took the elevator to street level and immediately ran into Ziggy. We stood facing one another wordlessly, bewildered by the sudden encounter. He had a camera bag over his shoulder.

"Seeing your shrink?" Ziggy gestured to the building which was known as the 'Psycho-Hilton' because many therapists had their offices there.

"And you, Ziggy?"

"I needed some film from the photo store." He pointed to a shop a few stores down.

"Right. Taking pictures?"

"Yes."

Ziggy's face was strained. Were those tears in his eyes? I couldn't be sure.

"A lot of pollen in the air," he said, trying to divert me. "See you on campus."

"On campus," I echoed. As we parted, I ran through a list of hypotheticals. Did he come to meet a girl? Another new woman? Or worse, a patient from his ward? Why did he have a camera with him? Whom was he taking pictures of?

That night, Jolene appeared at my apartment. She was dressed in a raincoat. Underneath, she was dressed in nothing at all.

"I'm flashing you," she said laughingly.

"Listen, Jolene," I began but faltered. She had on some new intoxicating perfume. She smiled temptingly. I was no match for her mission. I let her undress me and we engaged in sex for hours, first on the floor, then on the couch, and finally in the bedroom, after which I fell asleep. This time, I was the one who got up first, early in the morning before the sun came up. I dressed hastily, determined to leave before she awoke. I drove to the hospital and went straight to the canteen and ordered breakfast. That small gesture felt dimly victorious,

Later that morning, I saw Sunshine. She was hugely distressed. She had met a boy from another hall and told me that she loved him.

"So quickly?" I asked.

"Isn't love supposed to happen quickly? It does in the movies."

"It can, but you have to be careful, Sunshine," I warned.

"Of what?" she challenged me.

Of what indeed, I thought. Pregnancy, venereal disease, emotional betrayal, loss. Surely Sunshine had some awareness of these risks. "Getting hurt," I summarized.

Sunshine looked away, tearful.

"He used me," she blurted out. "Roger. I let him use me. It's my fault. The other girls warned me about him and I didn't listen. I really liked him. He's involved with someone else now."

"Used you how?"

Sunshine bowed her head.

"Sex," I answered for her. "Where?"

"In the meadow," she said. She began weeping. "I was used. He used me just for sex. Just to screw."

"Was it protected sex, Sunshine? He used a condom, yes?"

She shook her head, wordlessly.

A surge of anger and disappointment flashed through me. I thought she had been doing so well, and now there was this complexity, as if she had introduced it just to spite me. What had Vanderpol told me? Recovery was a mighty zig-zag mess and not a straight-line. I should have probed the matter of sex earlier in my work with her. How could I have overlooked this, given her age? I made a mental note to tell the attending psychiatrist on Roger's hall what had occurred.

"If I'm pregnant, I might as well kill myself," Sunshine was now declaring.

Fear now entered the amalgam of emotions I was feeling. My perverse medical specialty seemed brimming with people wanting to throw their lives away, so little did they cherish their existence. Their brains sputtered with malfunctions.

"We don't know that you're pregnant," I said to Sunshine.

"But if I am?"

"If you are, we'll deal with it."

Sunshine shrugged. "You're right," she said without any conviction whatsoever. "Why did this have to happen to me?"

'Why did this have to happen to me?' was a common expression of victimization. 'I never saw it coming,' patients would lament after they had ignored some palpable warning sign. But who was I to talk? Hadn't I just spent a dissolute night with a predatory creature who was clearly no good for me? Where was my own common sense when Jolene showed up last night? Suddenly, my triumph over leaving Jolene that morning was puny and meaningless. More important, I realized that I had made a serious omission by not talking about sex with Sunshine. Clearly, I hadn't seen her at all as sexual. It was another blind spot. I turned away from her, irritated with myself.

"You're annoyed with me," Sunshine began openly crying.

"No. More with myself for never discussing sex with you."

"I wouldn't have wanted to talk about it anyway," she said. "I would have refused."

"Maybe so, but you allowed yourself to be exploited. It makes me upset to see you taken advantage of."

"What do you want me to do?" she asked meekly.

"No, no, no, Sunshine," I countered. "It's not what I want you to do, it's what you think you ought to do. You," I emphasized.

"Get myself tested," Sunshine finally concluded. I nodded encouragement while at the same time feeling dismayed. How had Vanderpol put it? 'Good judgment is the premier function of the mind. Without it, we limp through life like a drooping flag awaiting a wind.' Some kind of compass was lacking in Sunshine's mind, a sense of direction or purpose, an inability to shape her destiny.

Outside in the corridor I ran into Vanderpol.

"I just saw your Ziggy," he said to me. "He looked distressed. He was carrying a camera with a telephoto lens. Anyway, I hear Ziggy confronted Mueller big time at rounds. You were there?"

"I was. He did. It was about ECT. Mueller said he was forming a committee to study ECT and a Dr. Roessinger would be in charge of the task force. Roessinger said he would approach the subject with an open mind and Ziggy challenged the idea of the hospital ever having an open mind about ECT."

Vanderpol shook his head. "We should put Mueller and your friend Ziggy in a boxing ring. It would be more direct and effective, eh? Have you seen Grace and Ted today? Grace is a touch better, and Ted also seems better. Oh, by the way, we're getting a new patient," Vanderpol consulted a file card. "Bertram Rinehardt. Bertram W. Rinehardt, III. He's a neurosurgeon. A distinguished man, about 75-years old. The good doctor is said to have exposed himself on a bus. They say he may be in the early stages of dementia, but you'll determine it for yourself."

"On a bus? A crowded bus? An empty bus?"

"You'll have to ask him, though I doubt he'll tell you," Vanderpol answered. "These exhibitionists don't just go to school yards, you know. They flash anywhere for attention, office building windows, front porches, airports, bowling alleys, we even had a guy expose himself at the zoo, right next to the elephants with their big trunks."

"We're admitting a man just because he exposed himself?"

"Yeah, well, the VIP perverts need to get out of the line of fire from the media and public eye so their attorneys hustle them into the Sandstones of the world. You'll find the doctor a challenge, I'm certain. They all use righteous denial, it never happened, it's all a big mistake. But you relish a challenge, Ben," Vanderpol smirked at me.

Dr. Rinehardt had an M.D. and a Ph.D. He had written papers on the chemistry of the brain, trained as a neurosurgeon and was the Distinguished Donald and Maude Jenson Professor of Neurobiology at the University of Pennsylvania School of Medicine. And he acted like it. Even in his lowly pajamas and shuffling around in his slippers, he swept my face with majestic disdain, a replica of Sanchez Remo Esposito the composer who wanted to phone all the symphony orchestra conductors.

"A first-year resident, I imagine?' he quipped trying to maintain his authority. "Where is your attending?"

"I'm here to do the admission intake," I replied.

"No need. I'll wait for your boss."

By now I had learned a little about managing narcissists and I sat down opposite him to make myself less easy to dismiss. I opened my notebook and took out a pen.

"I prefer to give my history to a more senior clinician," Dr. Rinehardt haughtily declared.

"Yes," I nodded. "I understand. Just some basics, It won't take long."

"Please make a note that the food here is atrocious," he said. "The toast was soggy. So were the eggs. So was the bacon."

"I'm sorry," I said earnestly. "I expect lunch will be better. In the meantime, may I ask you your birthdate?"

"It should be in the admission packet," he scowled, trying to intimidate me.

"I am sure you're right," I agreed. "Can you help me out and give it to me nonetheless?"

"I shall wait, if you don't mind," he replied, stubbornly holding his ground.

I tried another tact. "It's a privilege to meet you," I said. "All of us in medicine know of your work with the brain blood barrier."

"Thank you," he replied gruffly, but the statement did manage to crack open his door a fraction of a millimeter and he actually revealed his birthdate.

"I know you to be an eminent man, but if you could fill me in on some early years, it would be helpful. Where you were born, your schooling, your family background." I probed more.

"My wife is coming shortly," he barked at me. "We've no time for all this nonsense."

I was told that his wife was in Arizona, visiting grandchildren. She hadn't been informed yet of her husband's behavior and hospitalization.

"Your wife's away," I said to him.

"In New York."

"Yes? I understood she was in Arizona."

"Of course, That's what I meant," he quickly corrected.

When he finally allowed me to assess his cognition, he proved to be deficient in his short-term memory. He could barely recite back the three numbers I had presented to him only moments before.

"I've slept poorly the last few nights," he said in exculpation.

As to his exhibitionism, my inquiry was hopeless. I confronted him with the fact that three schoolgirls sitting opposite him on the bus had seen him unzip his fly and take out his penis. This statement provoked an outburst of absolute denial, the gist of it being that the alleged behavior had never occurred and whoever observed it was deranged. He would file a report against the arresting officer to the Commissioner of Police, whose brain blood clot he had recently removed. He was emphatic that he would get to the bottom of all this and would get it all straightened out.

I made arrangements for him to be seen by the consultant neurologist and left his room. I felt drained. I went for a walk by the lake, thinking about how I could successfully rid myself of Jolene. Ziggy had seemed to accomplish it effortlessly. Suddenly, several honking geese descended from the sky and skidded to a landing on the surface of the water. I was startled by their intrusion, as if they were the embodiments of Jolene coming to wreak havoc with me. I hastily retraced my steps back to the hospital. Vanderpol was reading the morning paper.

"Dr. Rinehardt is quite a handful. Surely, exposing oneself so blatantly in a public place seems very childlike."

"The more organic the case, the less discerning the exposer is. If you have a lot of brain damage, you jerk off in the middle of a concert performance."

"What do we do with him? What happens next?" I asked.

"His fancy lawyer will get the charges reduced or dismissed on the basis of brain damage. After that, the family can hire a baby sitter so he's never left alone."

"He's a prominent man and he still practices surgery," I said. "It's sad."

"You want an exhibitionist taking out your brain tumor?" Vanderpol countered.

"One has nothing to do with the other," I tried to support my argument.

"Are you sure?" Vanderpol challenged.

Was I sure? No, on reflection, I didn't want an exhibitionist taking out my brain tumor. I wanted a surgeon with excellent executive skills, uncontaminated by any sexual preoccupation.

"Very wise. Wisdom," Vanderpol added. "That's the problem with your friend Ziggy," Vanderpol suddenly turned around the subject. "He may be correct in what he says, but his choice of delivery is faulty. The trick is knowing what to say and when to say it. Or, in some cases, knowing when not to say anything at all."

"Is there any more known about the investigation of Ziggy"

"Not that I've heard," Vanderpol replied. "How about you? Has he confided anything to you?"

"I haven't asked him."

"He probably wouldn't admit to anything anyway," Vanderpol ventured.

That night, I visited Ziggy. His apartment was unkempt. Dirty dishes towered in the sink. Clothes were strewn around on chairs and door knobs. A plant he had by the window drooped with thirst.

"The experiments are taking up all my time," he told me. "Plus, my grant renewal is due." Lines etched his face, and he looked as if he hadn't shaved in a few days. On the dining table were piles of papers. They covered the chairs as well, and there were mounds of them on the floor.

"You've not slept, Ziggy," I observed.

"Sleep's a luxury," he quipped.

"How about I take you out for a meal," I offered.

"No time."

"You have to eat," I insisted.

"I take out food."

"Ziggy," I began. "I have to talk to you about the rumor that you took a girl off campus."

Ziggy glowered at me. "We've discussed this."

"Did it happen?"

"Preposterous. It's another attempt by Mueller to discredit me."

"It didn't happen?" I asked hopefully.

"That girl is ill and in the midst of her delusion and she makes up a story about a man kidnapping her."

"But she was missing from the unit."

"So? Patients elope from here all the time," Ziggy grunted.

"It wasn't you she was with?" I was determined to get a straight answer. "Was it?"

"You're as bad as Mueller, you are. Do you really think I'm capable of abducting a female patient from this crazy madhouse? Do you consider me deranged? Do I seem that stupid to you?" He turned and faced me threateningly.

"Easy, Ziggy. Easy."

"Easy what? Christ!" Ziggy picked up a pile of books and rearranged them.

At that moment I saw a photograph propped up against a flower vase on the shelf above the sink. It was a blurred image of a woman standing outside the entrance to a building. I could make out the letters 'SWAN.' As I studied the letters, I realized that it was the delicatessen where Ziggy and I ate. 'The Black Swan.' Ziggy saw me studying the picture.

"My new telephoto lens," he said. "Needs adjustment, it's out of focus."

"Who's the woman?"

"Mueller's wife. Mueller's still inside the restaurant."

"This is the woman you think could be your mother?"

Ziggy turned away from me, silent.

"But how could you have known she was at the restaurant, Ziggy?" I interrogated.

"I just knew."

"Knew how?"

"Never mind," he said rearranging papers and files to avoid any more questions.

"Ziggy, you had information about the luncheon. How did you get that information?"

"Why did you come here? To interrogate me?"

A thought occurred to me. "Mueller's calendar. His daily calendar. How would you have had access to Mueller's daily calendar?"

"Guess."

"You looked at it? No, you couldn't have---"

"I didn't need to," he said.

"Ziggy."

"Someone told me."

"Who?" Then, almost as quickly, I thought about Mueller's secretary. She was an attractive young woman. Undoubtedly, she kept all of Mueller's appointments.

"His secretary? You made friends with his secretary? You dated her?"

"Bravo! Bravo, Dr. Soloway. You figured it out," Ziggy growled.

I was nonplussed and hurled myself down on the couch.

"Time for one of your little rebukes, isn't it?" he said sarcastically. "My inappropriate dating of the boss's secretary?"

I ignored his comment. "And you think that Mueller's wife is your mother. You're still fixated on this belief?"

"Yes, I'm delusional, lock me up." He put his hands together in a grand gesture signaling for me to put handcuffs on him.

"Ok Ziggy, let's be real. Suppose she actually is your mother? Then what?"

"I haven't decided," Ziggy barked at me. "I'm still considering the options!" There was ominousness in his voice. I thought about Buzzy, the murderer Vanderpol and I had interviewed. "Why the hell don't you confront her?" I asked. "I mean, she'll either deny or confirm it. I don't understand."

"I'm not sure," Ziggy answered, more subdued.

"You're afraid," I realized. "If she actually is your mother, you'll have a mess on your hands and she'll have to explain a lot. And if she isn't who you think she might be, your theory goes up in smoke and you're still without a mother. Either way, you get hurt."

"I'm already left without a mother," he said softly. "I was left without a mother long ago."

The words echoed in my head. We both lapsed into silence.

* * *

I hadn't heard from Jolene for a while. It was a relief, though I knew that I was still vulnerable to her.

On rounds the next day, I found Grace a touch high. She wore a bright yellow blouse with a red skirt and her face had an abundance of makeup. Her speech was more rapid than usual.

"I have an interior decorator coming to the apartment today," she said gaily. "Actually, I have two of them coming. I need to fill all that empty space."

A nurse entered the room to tell me there was an urgent phone call for me. My heart started thumping as I imagined it was Jolene.

"Have you ever had your damn sperm checked?" Jolene screamed at me.

"What on earth—"

"Your sperm checked! It's where you jerk off into a jar and they count the damn sperm and watch them wiggle around, Jesus Christ!"

"Are you drunk, Jolene?"

"No, I may be pregnant! Christ!"

Panic descended on me as I grasped the receiver. I didn't know what to say.

"You didn't use a condom last time," she accused.

"I did!"

"You didn't. You ran out of them and we screwed anyway. I warned you. Now I'm missing my damn period. I've never missed a period, ever." She was getting hysterical.

"Jolene, I can't be the only one you've had sex with," I whispered into the phone.

"I've been screwing for years and never gotten pregnant. It has to be you and your goddamn sperm. You've got some kind of hyperactive sperm."

"Jesus, Jolene, what the hell kind of accusation…"

"The clinic opens in an hour. I'll be the first one there," she said and hung up.

I was openly perspiring and my hands were sweating. My mind was in a whirl of confusion and shame. Hadn't I just had a similar conversation with Sunshine? Here I was, the therapist, just as bad as the patient I was treating. Worse. Irresponsible. I tore out of the nursing station. I needed to finish rounds but I was in no shape to listen to anyone. From a private phone in Vanderpol's office, I called Templeton.

"Could I see you for a session?" I asked straightaway.

"Of course," she said. "You sound upset. I have time today, at 3."

Her availability calmed me down immensely and I was somewhat able to finish my time with Grace. A nurse in the hallway told me that Ted was asleep on the bed and there was no music playing which I took to be a good sign. The new medication was working.

I went for a walk and aimlessly wandered around the streets, killing time before my therapy session. Jolene pregnant. It was hard to fathom all the implications, assuming it was true, assuming I was actually the father, assuming that there existed even the remotest desire on either of our parts to have a child.

I nervously flipped through magazines in Templeton's waiting room until she opened the door and ushered me in. Within moments, my story came tumbling out.

"So," she summarized, breathing out through pursed lips. "You've gotten yourself into an unpleasant situation which we have to wonder about, no? Against your better judgement, you've continued this relationship with Jolene, knowing she is unstable and irrational." Templeton revisited the facts out loud. "Is this an infatuation? It doesn't sound like love. The risk you are taking is worrisome. I understand the pregnancy news is only hours old, but I am sure you've been reflecting on it. What does Jolene represent to you? Surely you've been considering this question?"

"Sex. A sexual object," I heard myself say, immediately realizing that it was a poor answer. "Also," I said more embarrassed, "I am treating this young patient who thinks she may be pregnant and I never thought of asking her about sex and birth control." I fell back in my chair, defeated by my confessions.

"Two issues of pregnancy," Templeton frowned. "Oh my. Let us start with your own."

I talked about Jolene again, emphasizing the sexuality of the relationship.

"I don't really think the issue is sex," Templeton reached for a sealed pack of cigarettes, then thought better of it and slid them into the drawer, banging it shut. "I imagine it's a bit more complicated that just sex," she said with irritation in her voice.

"Sex. Sex with Jolene. I don't love her, you're right," I admitted. I felt like I was disappointing Templeton.

"But there's a compelling force, no?"

"Besides the physical? How do I feel when I'm with her?" I asked out loud. "There's a feeling of closeness when we are having sex but it doesn't last. It just doesn't last," I wavered, "I hoped... I hoped for something more," I waved my hands in the air in frustration.

"I ask you again. You feel she is an asset to your life? A fulfilling force?"

"God, no." I made a face.

"Someone you want to spend your life with," Templeton pushed. "Someone you fantasize being by your side as you get older?"

"She could be having my child!" I exclaimed, frustrated with the distracting questions.

"I imagine she will get herself tested, no? We will have to wait a bit. But about Jolene, is she someone you yearn to be with?"

"Without sex?"

"With or without sex, it makes no difference," Templeton declared. "You called me up today to meet. At that moment, you can agree that you yearned to talk with me. I imagine you occasionally yearn to talk with your attending, Dr. Vanderpol. Even this friend of yours."

"Ziggy."

"These are people who mean something to you, do they not? What does this Jolene person mean to you?" she paused and instructed me to take more time to think about the last question.

"I guess I hoped she'd become my companion," I answered. Wretchedness enveloped me.

"Is she?"

I shook my head back and forth.

"And yet?"

"I keep hoping."

"And you're aware of the subject we've been tracking here in these sessions."

"My mother." I again pictured the diner. "How she could be so animated with strangers and even talk about me with them but never translate any of this onto me, her son." The question was a repeating one in my mind. I was asking the same question over and over.

"As I said earlier, men and women can love the world and ignore their own children. They are incapable of close, intimate relationships. Often, they themselves are the product of such an upbringing and have been disregarded in childhood or as they got older. Not every mother loves her child. These are facts. Some mothers give them away and there are some mothers who destroy their child or abort them before they even enter the world. But you know all this."

I sat there, absorbing her comment.

"And once again, your mother's defective mothering had nothing to do with you."

"Nothing to do with me," I declared, as if reciting catechism.

"You've not been ready to fully accept this proposition," Templeton said. "We talk about it here repeatedly and then you go home and self-blame creeps back into your brain. Tell me about visiting the cemetery."

"There isn't much to tell," I said.

"Of course there is," Templeton argued. "I realize that you are presently beset with pregnancies but try and concentrate. The cemetery."

It was an effort to speak. "Why did you send me up there?"

"Dr. Soloway, I'm sure you know the answer to that, no?"

"It was raining and everything was wet and I got soaked in the rain—"

"And?" Templeton said impatiently.

"And," I repeated, "and, and—" I precipitously burst into tears and sobbed and sobbed for what seemed to be minutes. Templeton quietly pushed a box of tissues my way. I stopped, looked at her, and then wept some more. Mucus flowed from my nose.

"Why am I crying?" I blurted out.

"You are overloaded, Dr. Soloway. Mother, father, and now a threatening pregnancy to cope with. You are finally letting go," she said. "Your grief has been in cold storage. You will learn in your work that guilt and anger often cover over the sensation of loss. Loss is profound. We are not necessarily good at experiencing it. Jolene is a powerful diversion from loss."

I was exhausted.

"We've some time left," Templeton said.

"About my possibly pregnant patient," I began, and talked about Sunshine's treatment.

"A difficult case. Anorectics usually are. Are you now blaming yourself for not asking her about sex? We don't always ask all the questions we should. She is quite young and times are changing and you will have to consider sexuality more in the patients you see. But you are very hard on yourself. Perhaps you can forgive your over- sight? In the meantime, she will also get herself tested. But lest we lose sight of the matter, you must rid yourself of this Jolene."

I was surprised that Templeton would be so directive. I was supposed to reach such a conclusion on my own, but clearly, I wasn't able to. I felt a bit chastised and told Templeton so. But she bypassed my comment and continued with her advice.

"And, do you think it would be a good idea to be more cautious around your friend Ziggy? He seems as unstable as your Jolene. You have to wonder why you pick persons like these to befriend. Perhaps, as you feel better about yourself, you will make healthier choices. Yes?"

"Yes." I looked at my wristwatch.

"Are you glad the time is up?" Templeton asked.

"Sort of. Part of me likes coming and part of me dreads it."

"Sounds about right," she said. "You may find, as the secrets inside you empty out, that the proportions may change. We'll see. Let us hope that the women in your romantic and professional life turn out not be pregnant."

I rubbed my eyes and nodded. In a daze, I left Templeton's office and steered the car back up to Manning House to see Dr. Rinehardt. He was dictating into a transcriber by his bed.

"Lecture notes?" I asked him.

"A keynote address at the IOM."

"IOM?"

"In Washington. The Institute of Medicine," Rinehardt said conceitedly.

"An honor," I acknowledged.

"Indeed, it is. What do you wish to ask me? I'm sure you have questions in mind."

"Have you had any more thoughts about what happened on the bus."

"I've told you. Nothing happened."

"But there are witnesses," I reminded him.

"Yes, Dr. Vanderpol has informed me also."

"Their stories all agree," I added. "Is it possible your memory is not correct?"

"Infuriating," Rinehardt snarled at me. "Your allegations are infuriating!"

"The police have charged you with exhibitionism, Dr. Rinehardt."

"They will have to speak with my attorney," he snapped back.

"But you can't so easily dismiss the charge."

"I can and I will. I wish to leave this forsaken institution. Tomorrow. I've informed Dr. Vanderschmidt."

"Vanderpol." I corrected.

"Whatever he's called."

Vanderpol saw me coming out of Rinehardt's room and raised his eyebrows in consternation.

"You may have to let him go," he said when we got to the nursing station. "Try and first make contact with the attorney. He might insist that Rinehardt stay longer so it looks as though he is sicker and needs more treatment. Unfortunately, there are no grounds to commit him. He's surely not dangerous."

"How can he pretend nothing happened?"

"He's not pretending," he explained. "He's constructed his own reality. It's air tight. We all have the capacity to exaggerate the size of the fish we caught, and, as you know, after a while, we believe our own story."

A phone rang in a nearby office. For an instant, I thought it might be Jolene with news that I wasn't ready to hear. I was startled. We both let it ring.

"His reality is no more shakable than any of the other patients we have," Vanderpol was saying. "Ted is positive he hears voices. For all we know, Grace still clings to the notion that her husband will take her back in his arms, even though she wants to divorce him. That's probably why she doesn't furnish her place. She sees it only as temporary."

I hadn't considered such a dynamic to explain Grace's behavior.

"You get better at guessing people's obscure reasoning," he encouraged, sensing my dismay. "Don't despair."

"We should try and work up Dr. Rinehardt's dementia before he leaves," I said.

"That is becoming your specialty. Brain disease. And yes, we should."

"If he lets us," I qualified.

"Uh huh. So much revolves around these patients' willingness to be helped," Vanderpol commented.

That night, I toyed repeatedly with the phone. I wanted to call Jolene to get information about her possible pregnancy. I knew I should wait for her to call me but my anxiety was awful. As far as I was concerned, the only answer to a pregnancy was abortion, and I would be responsible for it. Or would I? Would I become entangled in an ugly paternity test of some kind? Suppose Jolene, crazed as she was, wanted to keep the baby? What would I possibly do? My worries began to ebb into terror.

I started pacing my apartment, trying to alleviate the panic arising in me. After about an hour, I remembered I had some Seconal capsules in the bathroom cabinet. The tablets were very, very old.

They were, in fact, a gift from my father, many years ago, from a supply he had been prescribed for insomnia. Back then, his physician had prescribed refillable quantities of 100 tablets. We were both insomniacs, actually, and when I was in high school, we would stay up half the night watching television and waiting for fatigue to overcome us. He usually capitulated to taking a capsule. There was a ritual to this. He would tap out the powder from the capsule into Seltzer water, claiming that gastric absorption was enhanced by the frothy mixture. He even tried to patent the process, but without success.

On one of my brief visits home from medical school, he gave me an envelope of these pills.

"Use them sparingly," he instructed. "The night before an exam, maybe. Don't use them as frequently as I use them." I knew him to use them almost nightly. My mother, on the other hand, was a person who could lie on any horizontal surface and fall into a sound slumber within moments. It was ironic, the fact that she could sleep on command, so to speak, and then end up in a self-induced fatal sleep, aided by what I presumed to have been sleeping capsules.

The Seconal, old as it was, worked its magic and I became drowsy. Jolene, mercifully, faded from my mind.

Chapter 21

"Ben," Vanderpol called me on the phone. "I'm stuck here in New Haven with a busted radiator. I'm supposed to see a patient. Can you see him for me? He's an alcoholic and untreatable. Harold Dempsey is his name."

"Are you sure?"

"You'll do fine. I'll be there in a few hours."

I felt flattered by Vanderpol's request, but nervous. Harold Dempsey was a half hour late. He came in wearing sneakers and carrying a tennis racquet. His white polo shirt and shorts highlighted the redness of his face.

"Got caught up in a game," he offered as he pumped my hand. "Harold's my name. Vanderpol told me he'd be running late. Expected an older man as a substitute," Harold declared. "I guess you'll do. Well, let's get this over with. My older brother made me come. He's the executor of the family trust. Or, to put the matter more concisely, he doles out my money. You probably think I'm ungrateful and you'd be right. As siblings, we're not exceptionally close. In fact, we're pretty distant. Frankly, I can't stand the bastard. Forgive my candor, Doctor, but it's best to lay out the truth, is it not?" Harold extracted a flask from inside his tennis racquet cover and unscrewed the top. I immediately smelled liquor and realized he was drunk.

"Now, you'll want to zero in on this little flask of mine here because that's what drives my brother, the executor, crazy. Drives him bat-shit, to be more precise. You see this top? It's a nipple. A rubber nipple. What d'you say to that? Are you gonna be as disgusted as my executor brother?"

"Unusual," I inspected the rubber membrane. "I assume there's a reason."

"Sure. Smooths out the drink," he explained. "Makes you imbibe more slowly. Plus, you have to work your lips and mouth so it's more pleasurable, sort of like chewing gum. More sensations. You ought to try it. So. Any questions for me?"

Questions for Mr. Dempsey? How would I begin? I asked him how he could play tennis while intoxicated.

"Play better. It loosens me up."

"Do you consider yourself an alcoholic?"

"No more than the next guy at the bar. No DUIs. No DWIs. I'm quite functional," he said proudly and stood a little straighter for effect.

"Your work?"

This question evoked an abrupt outburst of laughter. "I'm retired, Doctor. I've been retired all my life. So has my brother. We live off our trust fund."

"And the source of this trust fund?"

"My father, to the extent he could be a father to us, dealt in futures. Do you know what futures are, doctor? It would be like going to the race track and betting on a losing horse. He was very good on predicting loss. I mean, he made money on stocks gaining as well, but losing was his specialty. So, doctor, I imagine you think

I'm alcoholic. My brother is convinced of it, of course. He thrives on any misfortune I have."

"Yes, Mr. Dempsey, I imagine you are alcoholic," I said.

"And you'll tell my brother and advise a course of treatment, I'm sure."

"When was the last time you were abstinent?"

"Ah, abstinent, the word you doctors love to throw around. I was semi-abstinent about five years ago. For a week, I think. My liver acted up." He chuckled.

I gaped at this man before me, implacable, most likely harboring a bad liver and every other alcohol related disease. How long could he last? What role could I possibly serve for such a defiant man? None, I decided. We bid each other farewell and he sauntered out of the office, lighting up a cigarette in the hallway.

Vanderpol appeared within the hour, his hands black with grease. As he washed up, I related the story of Dempsey. Vanderpol shook his head as he brushed his fingernails.

"He's been unwell for so long," he said. "The black sheep of the family."

"A flask with a nipple," I said.

"It's rare to see nipples," he said. "An extremely rare fixation. Were you shocked?"

"I found it more pitiful."

"The mouth," Vanderpol dried his hands. "We live by our mouths. It's the first act of a newborn, probably the first instinct a child has. There are many variants of suckling. Eating, drinking, smoking, kissing, oral sex. It's surprising, isn't it, that more alcoholics don't use nipples. I've often wondered whether there's a difference between alcoholics who use the bottle versus those who use a drinking glass to imbibe. But who knows? You have a prognosis for Mr. Dempsey?"

"Poor."

"Your recommendations for treatment?" Vanderpol quizzed me.

"No recommendations."

"Truly? The man has a serious disease, does he not?"

"End stage," I agreed, "but he'll never agree to any therapy."

"And if we could hospitalize him?"

"He would dry out and relapse the moment he hit the street."

"Excellent prognostication," Vanderpol said. "A tragedy, Harold is." Vanderpol extracted another aluminum tube from his coat pocket. "My comments about regression involving the mouth obviously do not apply in any way to cigar smokers," he sighed and grinned at the same time.

I felt a gush of gratefulness towards Vanderpol. He had become a benevolent figure in my life, an affectionate and paternalistic man.

Alcoholism, it seemed to me, was what Ziggy was also suffering from. By chance, he phoned me early in the morning.

"Can you cover my patients?" he asked me. "For a few days? I have to go out of town."

"Research?"

"Sort of. Some personal research."

"As opposed to biochemical research."

"So, can you cover or not?" he pressed.

"You don't want to talk about it."

"I'm in a hurry to get to the airport," he said brusquely and rang off.

Rinehardt's lawyer had left a message for me to call him.

"I'm given to understand that you intend to discharge my client," he declared without any preamble.

"He's discharging himself," I replied.

"That's how it's done at your hospital, doctor? Patients come in and out at will? Surely you'll be wanting to retain him longer?" he said haughtily.

"There are no grounds to retain him."

"Doctor, are you aware of what he is alleged to have done?"

"I've read the reports. Dr. Rinehardt admits to nothing. Nothing happened."

"He's under extreme stress, of course. You are aware, Doctor, that he is an esteemed surgeon, with an international reputation, and that he has engaged in an extremely destructive and disturbing behavior? You are aware of that? His reputation stands to be demolished. Destroyed, doctor. Utterly destroyed."

"What do you suggest I do?"

"Commit him."

"On what grounds?"

"He stands to lose everything."

"He's not suicidal, Mr. Fitzpatrick."

"He is highly self-destructive."

"To his reputation, not his life."

"A man's reputation is his life, Doctor. It's that simple. Now I am requesting that you initiate these hearings you have there and keep this man under lock and key. The next person I will call is Dr. Mueller. Are we clear on this?"

"We are not at all clear on this," I heard myself saying. "I dislike intimidation."

"You will most assuredly hear further from my office," he warned and hung up. His call aggravated me, as did the call I anticipated getting from Mueller. I was getting a little more confident about reacting to the outside forces that impinged upon my treatment of patients.

I went to see Grace who was still high, scrambling through pages in the Sears Roebuck catalogue and hastily making notes.

"Furniture," she retorted.

"Truly? What are you buying?"

"Three sofas. Leather ones, two green and one red. And a dining table to seat ten. And some lamps--"

"Grace," I interrupted.

"The lamps are beautiful. Oh, and some end tables and two leather recliners."

"Grace, you're getting high."

"Oh no, no, no."

"Have you paid for all these things?"

"Not yet. Why?"

"Have they delivered them to you yet?"

"No."

"I want you to cancel the orders, Grace."

"Why?" Her face was crestfallen.

"I doubt you need a table for ten dinner guests, Grace. Or three sofas. The apartment's not that large. You're not thinking straight. You're getting manic."

"No, I'm not."

I had the thought that the mania on this occasion might be propelled by an underlying fear of a life without her husband. So I gambled on a confrontation. "Grace," I said, "Listen. You've started a new phase in your life. You're going to be on your own. No longer married. Your husband isn't returning."

Grace stepped back from me, aghast, her body almost crumpling from the force of the statement. Then, almost miraculously, she recovered and continued her grandiosity.

"I may buy a piano," she said. "I've always wished I could play the piano."

"No piano," I said, though my injunctions had little effect.

Eventually I left her, somewhat defeated. I went over to Ziggy's hall to see if any of his patients needed attention.

"You should look in on Louisa," the nurse said. "She hasn't come out of her room for days."

I read over her chart. This was Louisa's second admission to Sandstone. Louisa suffered from severe obsessive-compulsive illness. She was fearful of germs and washed her hands repeatedly and was afraid to touch door handles and coat hangers, sinks, faucets and light switches, and silverware and drinking glasses. She would continually use her bathroom where she scrubbed her skin raw. The world was an agony, her room the only sanctuary from bacteria.

"She's sequestering herself," the nurse told me. "We have trouble getting her out."

I knocked on her door and announced my presence.

"Who are you?" came a muffled reply.

"I'm covering for Dr. Harrington," I shouted.

"You can't come in," she answered.

"Can I at least open the door?"

"A little. But you can't come into my room."

I turned the knob and pushed open the door. She stood at the far corner of the room, wearing white cotton gloves. She was an attractive and tall girl in her 20's, her hair pulled back into a bun. Her face was stern.

"Don't touch anything," she ordered.

I put my hands in my pockets. "I just want to see how you're doing," I said.

"Fine. Don't touch anything. Please leave," she said.

"How upset are you?"

"The usual."

"Meaning?"

"Everyone here asks me if I want to kill myself and I keep telling them I don't. I just want to stay healthy and not get sick. This place is full of germs, loaded with them."

"Dr. Harrington is helping you?"

"I wouldn't know. I don't see him much," she said.

"Why is that? You won't let him come into your room? Germs?"

"He's loaded with them."

"What do you mean?"

"He just is."

"How?" I asked her.

"He always wants to shake hands with me and I don't shake hands with anyone, even with these gloves I'm wearing. He wants me to take my gloves off."

I stood there, momentarily puzzled. Assuming what she said was true, could Ziggy's request be interpreted by Louisa as a disrobing? No, it was my unconscious thinking about Jolene stripping off her clothes. I asked Louisa if she thought she was otherwise making any progress in her fear of germs,

"I took a shower yesterday," she said very seriously. "That isn't easy for me to do. But I did it. I touched the water faucets and even adjusted the shower head but I cleaned it first with alcohol. Last time I was here, I did pretty well."

"Good," I said encouragingly. Obsessive-compulsives were difficult to treat. If they could harness their various phobias, they could find careers where cleanliness and order were occupational priorities. I knew a dental hygienist who talked openly about her early struggles with bacteria. She had channeled her neurosis into a profession.

Back at Manning House, two messages awaited me in the nursing station, one from Jolene and the other from Ziggy who had returned from his trip. I called Jolene first.

"You'll be relieved to hear that I got my period," Jolene told me. "We can resume sex."

It was certainly welcome news, yet I was dumbfounded that she would be so cavalier about the matter.

"We're not resuming anything," I said. "Nothing. I need a break, Jolene."

"A break from what? A break from sex? You like sex. Part of you can't resist me. You'll be phoning me within a week, you'll see."

"A break," I reiterated. "No, not a break," I corrected. "An end. I want to end our relationship, Jolene."

"Just like that? End our relationship, just like that? What, you're afraid of me?"

"Jolene, I need to be alone at this point in my life," I said.

"There's someone else," she asserted angrily.

"No. No one."

"Jesus," she exclaimed, "what kind of a person are you? And you're going to be a shrink? You need a shrink yourself. You have no sensitivity at all. A weakling is what you are, a loser. You'll miss me, you'll see. You'll be sorry, you'll regret what you're doing, you'll never amount to anything—"

I slammed down the receiver and stared at the phone, numb. I had never hung up on anyone. Then I contemplated what I'd just done. I was free, but I didn't feel free. No, I would miss the passion, her desperation, her devouring of me. I would miss being wanted. But I wasn't wanted for me, I was wanted for my body and my penis. I shook my head as a dog shakes off rainwater. I phoned Ziggy.

He was gushing with the strangest enthusiasm about Dr. Rinehardt whom he had wanted to meet for the longest time. The fact that he was admitted for exhibitionism had not the slightest effect on him.

"He's a genius," he said to me. "Rinehardt is a giant. He's done some of the work I'm now doing. I want to come over and meet him. Did you know he won the Mercury Award? He's famous."

"He's a narcissist," I said to Ziggy. "And a pervert."

"When can I come over and see him?" Ziggy asked.

"You can't," I said.

"What?"

"It's inappropriate."

"What? What are you talking about? Have you become a policeman while I was gone?"

"He's a newly admitted patient and you can't fraternize with him. He has to be treated as an ill patient, not a celebrity."

Ziggy totally disregarded what I had just said. "I'll come now," he said. And within minutes he appeared at Manning House.

"Where is he?" Ziggy asked.

"Ziggy, leave him alone."

Ziggy strode through the corridors looking at nametags on the doors. "Here," he said.

My instinct was to block the entrance to Rinehardt's room, but then I realized that all this could escalate into a loud quarrel. I acquiesced.

"I've a grant from the French Academy of Science for work similar to what you have done, Dr. Rinehardt," I heard him say as I shut the door on the two of them.

I went to see Ted. He was napping. The stereo was silent. I thought he had a smile on his lips. On his nightstand were two books on preparing and applying to an automobile trade school, both very hopeful signs. I was delighted.

Ziggy emerged from Rinehardt's room two hours later.

"He wants to see my research," he said enthusiastically. "Tomorrow morning he's coming over to my lab. Can you imagine? A man of his stature coming to look at my experimental set up? Fantastic!"

"He vowed to leave tomorrow morning," I said.

"And he's asked me to look at a paper he's preparing. He wants my input."

"Ziggy, he's a patient here!" I exclaimed. "He's not your mentor or your colleague."

"He agrees that the catecholamines are the basis of affective disorders."

"Ziggy, you ought not to be involved with this man. Are you aware of why he's here?"

"Some kind of peeping Tom business. Is this another one of your boundary obsessions? I'm not involved in sex with the guy, I'm just talking with him. You know, you really piss me off sometimes, you really do, like you're some kind of goddamn virtuous saint."

"Just go back to your hall, Ziggy. Leave the doctor alone," I said firmly.

"Let me tell you something. The research he and I are doing is going to advance this profession a hell of a lot more than all your freaking concern about what's proper and what's not proper. You seem to forget that there's something wrong with the brain to account for all the illnesses we have in this God forsaken hospital. If it were up to you, you'd be trying to talk patients out of polio or rheumatic fever or syphilis. You guys need your own heads examined, all of you." Ziggy was gasping with fury. "I'm meeting him tomorrow whether you like it or not."

"You won't. He'll be gone tomorrow, thank God."

Once again, our raised voices summoned Vanderpol, who now appeared in the doorway.

"Gentlemen," he said. "We can hear you down the hall."

"We're discussing Dr. Rinehardt," I explained quietly.

"Let's move down into the library," he instructed.

Just as we entered the room, the phone rang and Vanderpol picked it up.

"I doubt we can do that," he said after listening for a moment. "The man's not harmful to himself or to anyone else."

I could hear the ranting of Dr. Mueller's voice over the phone.

"No," Vanderpol was arguing. "We can't lock people up for bad judgment. No, I don't feel comfortable doing that and besides, what's to be achieved by committing him? Yes, Dr. Mueller, you can do that, of course." Vanderpol hung up, shaking his head.

"He's getting another opinion. He's sending over Dr. Roessinger. Mueller may come himself. What are you two disagreeing about?"

"Roessinger and Mueller," Ziggy snorted. "Laurel and Hardy."

"Ziggy is doing the same kind of research that Dr. Rinehardt is doing," I explained. "He wants to consult with him. My view is that there shouldn't be any kind of fraternizing between the two."

"We're scientific colleagues," Ziggy said. "That's the reality. Should I pretend otherwise?"

"Let's all of us stay away from Rinehardt until our Wise Men finish their deliberations," Vanderpol ordered. "They may well decide he needs commitment. We'll see."

Ziggy huffed off, leaving me with Vanderpol.

"What's Ziggy doing here on this hall?" Vanderpol asked me critically.

"He invited himself. I tried to stop him."

"Correct, he shouldn't be here. Ben, the man is most likely on his way out. I know you're fond of him but I doubt he'll be staying here long. He belongs in a lab."

"What's been decided about him?" I asked with alarm.

"Nothing definitive yet. It's only my prediction."

Vanderpol's statement that Ziggy was on his way out was not a complete surprise, but it was still a blow to me. Our entanglement was something I would profoundly miss.

"Who will make the final decision about him?" I inquired.

"I'm sure Mueller will have the ultimate say."

"They can't just throw him out."

"Ben. Listen. They can. We've had residents dismissed from the program before."

"There's nothing that can be done?" I asked.

"Such as?" Vanderpol challenged.

I plopped into a chair. Of course, there was nothing that could be done. What was I thinking? A miraculous transformation of character, perhaps? Vanderpol and Templeton both had expressed reservations about my friendship with Ziggy. I shouldn't be surprised about his fate. I had blind spots, especially when it came to Jolene and Ziggy. These were people whom I should have broken away from long ago. I had some kind of sick proclivity to befriend the highly afflicted, like the description of the Lone Ranger: 'A friend to those who have no friend.'

"Ben," Vanderpol said. "You've been working very hard. You need to take some time off. You need a vacation."

"A vacation," I repeated. "These problems aren't going to go away."

"Of course not. But rest sometimes allows us to gain a better perspective and confront problems better."

I shook my head.

"You haven't taken much time off since you started here. There's no accumulation of vacation time in this place. Use it or lose it," he said. "You need a break. These folks will burn you out."

"There's too much going on." I argued.

"There always will be. It never stops."

"I've no place to go," I said rather sadly.

"You'll think of something."

"Who will cover my patients?"

"You're looking at him," Vanderpol raised his hand in the air.

"Where would I go?"

"A nice white sandy beach. Or a sparkling mountain top. A lush green meadow. Someplace clean and pure and refreshing. Without any Ziggies and without any girlfriend. How's it going with your girlfriend?"

"It's gone," I said.

"A good gone or a bad gone?"

"A thank goodness gone," I answered, though I sounded tentative.

* * *

"About the cemetery," I said to Templeton. I was back in her office.

"The cemetery, yes. You have further thoughts on the matter."

I talked about the realization that I missed my father more than I had realized. More, actually, than my mother.

"Grief has strange vectors," Templeton said. "And it keeps its own time. It makes its appearance when the host organism is ready. You can't force a person to grieve."

"You made me go to the cemetery," I said accusingly.

"I suggested you go," Templeton nodded.

"A strong suggestion."

"It was, yes. Sounds like you're blaming me."

"A little. I don't know why."

"Perhaps the anger's misplaced? Isn't the real issue the anger at your father and mother?"

"I'm not angry at my father," I declared defensively.

"He left you," Templeton said softly.

"He died."

"An abandonment of sorts. No?"

"God," I lamented. "It's so complicated. I'll never resolve it." I said woefully.

"You are resolving it."

"I didn't tell you," I suddenly announced, "that Jolene isn't pregnant."

Templeton leaned her elbows on the desk. "Tell me," she said intently, "what you will do with this woman?"

"I told her it was over. Our relationship was over. I hope she doesn't call me," I added.

"You hope?"

"If I can resist her."

"If you can? This implies some inability to control yourself."

"It isn't easy." I admitted.

Templeton's eyes narrowed with intensity. "You're going to find in your profession that patients won't easily give up alcohol or drugs or pathological attachments. And in all these cases, they know full well that whatever they're victimized by, it's bad for them. They're waiting for a magic event that will help them let go. Divine intervention, so to speak. This magic push could also be a nugget of insight, or an epiphany of some kind, or a revelation, something to make it easy for them to break free of the shackles of bondage. But the inspiration never comes. In the end, they have to marshal their own resources and quit." Templeton paused for effect to make sure I was listening. "We're talking about altering one's own fate. Granted, it all has to do with self-esteem, but in the end, Dr. Soloway, the patient has to gather up his own strength to say "no more." And, of course, there is pain involved. Abstinence and withdrawal. If you fully push Jolene out of your life, there will be an emptiness to contend with. It is all part of the process. Two people out of your life, your mother and Jolene."

She took a sip from her coffee and looked at me. "You haven't talked much about emptiness and loneliness. You may fill your world with Jolenes, and with people like that fellow resident you've talked about, this Ziggy. Correct me if I'm wrong, but he doesn't seem capable of a sustaining relationship with you either. But this Jolene is dangerous. She specializes in chaos and she can wreck your life. Only last week you had a scare, which had you bouncing off the walls."

I gazed up at Templeton, her face hardened. "I feel chastened again," I complained.

"You see? Now you are taking a victim's role. You are blaming me for chastising you when, in fact, you fully realize the need to bring this chapter with Jolene to an irrevocable close."

What time was it? I unabashedly pulled up my sleeve to regard my watch. I was surprised to find that we were over time. I told Dr. Templeton that I was considering a vacation.

"Useful," she said. "We psychiatrists are often poor at planning pleasurable activities." Templeton smiled broadly, "How long will you be away?"

"A week."

"A short time," she said. "It often takes a week to wash out the mind."

Chapter 22

My father had a cousin, Milton, who lived in a gated community in Boca Raton, Florida. I would occasionally spend either Christmas or Thanksgiving with him but I hadn't seen him for years. He was a retired attorney who had worked for the government. He had been a widower for ten years. His wife, Cathy, had died from the complications of multiple sclerosis. They had no children. I thought about visiting him. That night I called.

"Absolutely you can come down," Milton said in his gravelly voice. "We lead the good life down here. Eighty degrees, early-bird specials, spirited shuffleboard competitions. It's nirvana, except for the old people who talk incessantly about their ingrown toenails. When can I pick you up? I still drive, can you believe it?"

I made flight plans.

Drs. Mueller and Roessinger decided to emphasize that Dr. Rinehardt might lose his job and reputation and then commit suicide. Rinehardt ranted and raved with protest.

"And I was the one who called Mueller," Rinehardt grumbled. "And that other misshapen German fellow, I forgot his name, he spent, at the most, five minutes with me. I will write to the Board of Physicians and make a formal complaint, I will. Thirty days here is an eternity. It's utterly punitive. Their actions are an abuse of power.

Malpractice. Now this Dr. Vander of yours. I didn't hear him say anything about retaining me here."

"Vanderpol. Neither he nor I felt that was necessary."

"So, I will have you both testify on my behalf. My attorney is coming this afternoon."

I left Dr. Rinehardt fuming at his injustice and went to tell Grace I would be taking a short vacation. She was a good deal more subdued.

"We used to go to Ft. Lauderdale during the winter," she said, remembering her married life. "How long will you be gone?"

"Just a week."

"That's nice. Will you go alone? Oh!" she exclaimed. "I shouldn't be asking you such a personal question. I'm sorry."

"It's OK. How are you feeling, Grace?"

"I cancelled all the furniture," she told me.

"Are you annoyed with me about that? "

"Oh no, doctor. Who will take care of me while you're away?"

"Dr. Vanderpol, Grace."

"Oh. That's good. I like him."

Grace gave me a smile composed of politeness and desolation. There was no mirth in it at all. I reluctantly left her room.

I told Sunshine about my upcoming vacation. I had inquired earlier about her pregnancy test but the results had not come in yet.

"A vacation," she said. "Where are you going?

"South," I said.

"South where?"

"Why are you asking, Sunshine?"

"Just curious." Sunshine unbuttoned the top of the polo shirt she was wearing.

"What do you feel, Sunshine?"

"About your vacation? Or now?"

"Both."

"A little excited," she grinned at me, reaching for the next button.

"Stop," I said, pointing to her shirt.

Sunshine's hands halted in mid-air.

"This won't work, it shouldn't work. It won't work here or outside the hospital."

Her smile ceased and her eyes became misty.

"Your feelings, Sunshine. The feelings inside of you." I pointed to my chest.

"I don't have any."

"Of course you do."

"Why does everything have to relate to our feelings?"

"That's all we are, Sunshine. A whole collection of feelings covered by our skin and bones. We're hollow and stuffed with feelings. They spill out of us, ooze out, pour out."

"I don't want you to go away," she said softly.

"Because?"

"I don't want anyone to go away."

"Who's left you?"

"No one."

"Not true. That's not true, Sunshine. You've been alone a good deal in your life."

"Why can't I get over it," she said morosely, buttoning up her shirt. "It haunts me all the time. I thought if I stopped eating, my parents would worry about me and stay home and not travel and—," she crumpled onto the bed.

"And?"

"Take care of me. Love me." I watched her curl herself up into a fetal position.

"Lost love."

"Lost love means you had it and you lost it. I never had it," she wailed.

"You had some, I imagine. I'm sure you did."

"Why couldn't my parents stay home more, tell me that," She sat up on the bed, suddenly defiant.

"Have you ever asked them, Sunshine?"

Sunshine hesitated and nodded.

"And?"

"They told me they were busy with their work."

"And I imagine that answer wasn't very satisfying."

"How would you react?" she accused.

"Not well," I conceded, thinking of my own odyssey.

"So, Sunshine," I began. "This love business gets people in a hell of a lot of trouble. You've already fallen in love with the wrong guy. You have to be careful with whom you fall in love because a part of you is so very needy," I said as gently as possible. "You'll have to learn to avoid men who just want to have sex, nothing more. You are a fine person. You have to appreciate that you are worthy of a healthy body and a healthy mind and that a responsible man can genuinely love you. A real love, not an exploitive love."

"You're telling me not to have sex?"

313

"With the right person," I said. "With someone who respects you."

"I wish you could hug me," Sunshine said.

I paused. A part of me did want to hug her. Ziggy, wherever he was, would probably hug her. "Yes," I said. "But I'm the wrong person to do that. You'll find someone you can hug and he will want to be with you and hug you back."

Sunshine's dismay left her face as she nodded and my statement seemed to take on some traction.

Chapter 23

The next morning, with some ambivalence, I packed a few changes of clothes and drove to the airport. I was able to find a quiet corner to sit and wait for the boarding announcement. Then I realized that I had forgotten to say goodbye to Ted. Why had that happened, I asked myself? Was I afraid of his getting worse again or his reacting to my absence? I called the hospital but by the time they roused him to come to the phone, my plane had started boarding.

"Ted, I said, "listen, I'm at the airport about to take a flight to Florida for a week. I will call you in a few hours."

"Cool," he said, quite reasonably.

As the plane taxied down the runway and gained altitude, I scanned the ground below looking in vain for Sandstone. Soon the landscape below became insignificant and as the plane levelled off above the clouds, my worries about patients slowly ebbed. After downing a lunch cocktail, I fell asleep, awakening just as the aircraft was about to land.

My uncle was easy to spot outside the terminal, waiting in his gray Mercedes-Benz diesel sedan. He was not a man given to the intimacies of hugging and he shook my hand firmly in greeting.

"Hardly recognized you, you've lost weight," he said, scrutinizing me sideways. "Those mental patients do that to you?" The car started up with a clatter of pistons.

"They can get you down." I commented.

"Never understood why you chose psychiatry. Full of misery. Isn't that so?" Milton's world as a lawyer with the IRS had been to make sure that recalcitrant citizens paid their income taxes. I imagined that there would have been just as much frustration in that choice of career.

"You fix any of your folks?" he continued. "I read most of them stay sick for years." He carefully pulled out of the parking lot and drove slowly in the right- hand lane as other cars whizzed by us. A hot wind sifted through the car windows. Outside, palm trees dotted the road. Intense sunlight blinded me.

"Occasionally one or two get better, Uncle Milton," I shouted over the traffic.

"Glad to hear it. You mind stopping at a big flea market near Boca? Started going to flea markets after Cathy died. Got myself hooked on 'em. You got a cure for that kind of addiction?" he joked.

"I imagine it's incurable, Uncle Milton,"

"Right, that's right." Milton took a series of turns through back streets and came to a parking lot brimming with cars. Adjoining it were rows and rows of tables laden with tools, kitchen wares, art objects, paper goods, and antiques. Vendors, perched on stools and chairs, shaded themselves with umbrellas and canopies of all shapes and colors. Milton promptly disappeared amidst the tumult of hawkers and buyers and I wandered across the street down to the beach and the water. Sitting down under the shade of a tree and watching the boats, I found myself worrying about my patients. I looked around but couldn't see a phone booth to call Ted as I had promised.

I thought about Grace. What was I doing here on the hot sand of this foreign place when she might need me?

I returned to the market and located Uncle Milton, vociferously haggling over a keyhole saw. The man wanted four dollars and Milton was offering one dollar. They were three dollars and miles apart. I handed Milton some single dollar bills and he pushed them away.

"You're spoiling the process," he grumbled. "Go away."

I again looked for a phone booth. A gaggle of voluptuous girls in tight two-piece bathing suits drifted by, chattering. One of them could easily have been Jolene. As I watched them, I spotted a payphone and headed across the street to call Ted.

"Is it hot down there in Florida?" he asked, not commenting on the fact that I had left without telling him.

"Yes." I asked about the voices.

"Hardly any," he said.

"Excellent." I was again relieved. With Vanderpol's encouragement, I had landed on the drug which melted away his inner voices through a biochemical mechanism no one fathomed. Would Ted appreciate the value of the drug and take it once he was discharged? That would be another battle.

Uncle Milton was still buried somewhere in the throng of merchants. I was standing there all alone. Despite Dr. Templeton's caution, I called Ziggy.

"I always hated Florida," he told me. "Full of old people. I saw Rinehardt yesterday and showed him my research and he made a bunch of suggestions. He's done some interesting stuff, We're going to collaborate."

"He came over to your lab?" I shouted into the phone, incredulous. "Vanderpol gave permission to let him visit your lab, Ziggy?"

"What permission? I just came over to Manning House and walked him over to the lab."

"Jesus, Ziggy, does Vanderpol know this?"

"What difference does it make?" he said nonchalantly.

"Ziggy, I told you. You just can't come over and merrily take a patient who isn't yours for a walk off a ward. What the hell! Is there any protocol that you don't defy?"

"This is why you called me all the way from Florida? To castigate me? More of your sanctimonious crap? I'm hanging up now," and with that, he did.

I emerged from the phone booth bathed in sweat and exasperation. I paced and took a few deep breaths on the hot sidewalk. I decided Ziggy had left me with no choice. I reentered the booth and called Vanderpol.

"More Ziggyness," Vanderpol said. "Go back to your vacation," he said. "No more phone calls from you. No more calling patients. Understood?"

"Yes," I answered meekly and exited the booth.

"Hey!" Milton came towards me. "You disappeared! Look at you! Have you been jogging?"

"Calling the hospital from an overheated phone booth."

"Time for the early bird dinner. Hungry?"

I wasn't at all hungry. My mind was whirling with Ziggy's disobedience.

"We're going to a fancy Chinese restaurant for that early bird. Old people get hungry early. Great martinis at half price," Uncle Milton told me gleefully, rubbing his palms at yet another bargain.

Martinis were what Jolene drank and I didn't want any. Milton drove into Boca Raton. Banks and drug stores lined Dixie and Federal Highways, and interspersed with them were open air restaurants crowded with mostly elderly people. Milton maneuvered the car into one of the few remaining parking spots next to a pair of stern-looking concrete dragons. and we made our way into the dark interior of Chopstick Gardens. Without consulting me, he ordered two gin martinis on the rocks. I sipped mine. Food eventually arrived. I was disinterested and picked at it.

"Gonna' take you a while to decompress," Milton predicted.

Milton got tipsy and I ended up driving to his condominium. It was located within a white stucco apartment building with yet another gurgling fountain in front, flanked by white stone mermaids. His place was on the top floor and from the window, you could look out upon other condos and some tennis courts. My room was unadorned, with a chest of drawers, a double bed, and one large artificial palm plant in the corner. Milton and I watched the news, then a quiz show and I ended up retiring early.

I dreamed of Jolene. We were naked and making love and saying tender things to one another. I awoke with a feeling of acute desolation. I hurled myself out of bed and after a shower, felt a little better and headed outside for a walk to the nearby beach.

I had only gone a few blocks when a vehicle approached and honked. It was Milton.

"A round of golf?" he called from inside the car.

"Golf?"

"You hit a little white ball with expensive metal clubs. It'll do you good. You look glum."

"Uncle Milton, I'm not good company right now."

"That's the utter beauty of golf. You don't have to talk. C'mon. Get in."

I submitted. Milton headed for the highway and branched off at an exit for Dunes Resort. We drove along the perimeter of a pond and through elaborate iron gates onto a gravel parking area. Extracting a set of clubs from the trunk, he handed me a spare pair of shoes and a white baseball cap. Milton himself was garishly dressed in a pink jersey with green pants.

"The shoes fit OK? Good, you look perfect. When's the last time you played?"

The last time I'd played golf was with my ex-wife in Tempe, Arizona. We'd argued about something during the course of the game and ended up not speaking to one another. I told Milton.

"Never liked your wife," he said. "You got someone in your life now?"

I shook my head.

"Have to introduce you to Linda. She's the office manager at the condo."

"Please," I pleaded, "I am not interested in a new relationship right now."

"It's that bad? OK, we'll see. Let's tee off." Milton handed me some balls.

I hit the first ball far off into a distant sand trap. It took many embarrassing strokes to rectify the error and make it onto the green. My putting was no better and I consistently missed the hole. Milton was amused by my clumsiness.

"I hope you're a better doctor," he quipped.

We played the next day and I was much improved and so was my mood. I found myself enjoying the challenge of the match. I was beginning to loosen up. Our playing was becoming more intense. On the third day, at the end of the 18th hole, my score was better than Milton's. For some reason, I felt almost euphoric by my small triumph.

"Winner pays for lunch," Milton said, and led me to the club house where we each had a beer.

"So," Milton settled back in his chair, "I need to ask your opinion about something. A professional question."

I raised my glass and reminded him that I was supposed to be on vacation.

"It's been bugging me all along. You remember meeting a friend of mine named Jeff?"

"No, I don't."

"A stock broker guy from Wisconsin. Well to do. A nice guy, we got on well with each other. Anyway, he lost his wife about a year ago and got depressed. He never saw a shrink and he got worse and worse. Finally, he got drunk one day and jumped into the canal at the back of his house, right here in Boca. He said he wanted to drown but more likely he would've been gobbled up by the alligators or crocodiles, I always forget which you find in fresh and which you find in salt water."

Milton took a large gulp from his beer. "Anyway, as soon as he jumped into the canal, he decided he wanted to live so he starts screaming for help and they drag him out of the water and he's saved. And that's the end of his depression. I mean, the depression leaves him. It's like the jump in the canal cured him of his illness. So, my question to you is, how is that possible? I mean, can any of us jump into a canal full of alligators or crocodiles and be cured of depression? Is that treatment in any of your textbooks? Canal therapy," Milton chuckled but was obvious serious about his question.

"Canal therapy," I sighed. "Something shocked him back to life. Sometimes this happens. We don't know why. If they try to kill themselves and they live, they figure it's a sign from the Almighty, something like that. I read about the few people who jumped off the San Francisco Golden Gate Bridge and survived. The moment they jumped, in mid-air, they changed their minds about wanting to die. They never again tried suicide."

"I have to tell you that when Cathy died, I was plenty depressed. I got over Cathy's death by playing golf," he stated. "Played 18 holes every day, rain or shine. Golf therapy. Got pretty good at it. Didn't need any psychiatrist," Milton said proudly. He summoned the waiter and asked for another beer. I deferred. After lunch, we drove home. Inside the condo lobby and behind the desk was the girl that Milton had mentioned earlier. She was young, blond, and pretty. She smiled at me and asked where I was from, how long was I staying, and other idle conversation. In my mind, I compared her to Jolene who was obviously still embedded in my psyche.

"See?" Milton said in the elevator. "I told you, pretty and nice."

"Uncle Milton, I'm just coming off a bad relationship. I can't form a new one just yet."

"Really that awful?"

"Bad."

"OK, OK, I'll leave you alone. But you need to find someone someday," he chirped.

I had not the least idea of how I would ever find the someone Uncle Milton was talking about. My mind seemed fully cluttered by my patients and my own personal struggles.

Golf, naps, and swimming consumed the next few days and I felt refreshed. On the sixth day, Milton complained of a backache so I headed to the golf course alone. I was on the green of the tenth hole when I saw a golf cart trundling in my direction. It was Milton, and he cruised alongside the green.

"A Doctor Vanderpol called you," he shouted over to me. "Wants you to call him right away. Wouldn't say what it's about. I'll drive you to a telephone."

In the brief time it took us to crest the hill to the club house, I went through all the possible catastrophic disasters. Sunshine had discovered she was pregnant and overdosed. Ted had succumbed to the voices and bled out from the jugular vein in his neck. Grace had crashed and cut herself badly. I telephoned the unit and Vanderpol answered on the first ring.

"Ben. Listen. It's Grace."

I instantly knew what had happened. "She's killed herself," I finished for him.

"That's right. She was high as a kite and then her mood plummeted and she hanged herself."

"She's dead," I said, exactly as my father had uttered the same words upon seeing my mother's body lying on the bed.

"In her apartment. Her sister discovered her," Vanderpol cut into my thoughts.

Guilt kicked in immediately. I had overlooked something. I shouldn't have tried to push her to be independent. I was the one that encouraged her to seek out her own apartment to live alone I was misguided.

"I worked so hard with her," I heard myself say as my throat tightened.

"You did," Vanderpol said. "And you lost her."

"I liked the woman, I felt sorry for her."

"Me too," Vanderpol sighed deeply. "She was likeable.

I should have realized deep down that she was doomed and suicide was always there.

"Damn her," I uttered

"Ben."

"What?"

"Ben, listen, she's gone. There is nothing we can do now. We've a death to contend with. I have to meet with the other patients. Call me when you get back in town and we'll plan to attend the funeral or at least see the family. The husband lives in New Hampshire, outside of Concord. The sister is already at the house. We can drive up to Concord together."

"God almighty, the funeral. The husband will blame us."

"We'll talk. I'm about to meet with the other patients. Call me back."

Milton saw the look on my face. "Something bad?"

"A patient of mine just killed herself."

"Oh, Jesus," Milton put his arm on my shoulder. "This just happened?"

"Hanged herself."

"In the hospital?"

"In her apartment. Milton, I've got to get to the airport."

"Don't you want to call ahead for a reservation?"

"I'll fly standby."

"Sure. We'll go back to my place and pick up your stuff and then be on our way."

Milton drove with agonizing slowness. "Imagine you get close to these folks you treat," he said understandingly. "This patient of yours, was she very sick?"

"She was."

"These people who kill themselves. You figure they've been kicking around the idea of suicide for a while? Does it just happen? I mean, do they just wake up one day and decide to commit suicide? My friend who jumped in the canal, I never heard him talk suicide Your mother, Ben, she had tried once before, right?"

"She did. For some people suicide's been on their mind for years." I answered.

"Childhood? Back to childhood?"

"Sometimes."

"Never thought of suicide in my life. You ever think about suicide?"

"Yes," I answered Milton. Had Templeton ever asked me about suicide? Did I ever reveal my thoughts about it to her?

"Can't say I ever considered doing myself in," Milton said again as we entered the single lane entrance to the airport. "Guess you need to be careful with the work you do," he said. "You think suicide is like a virus? Infectious? Don't envy your profession," Milton concluded as he shook my hand at the terminal. "Come back again, you hear?"

Luckily, there was space on the next plane. Once airborne, I considered what I would say to Grace's relatives. I got home in the late afternoon and immediately drove to the hospital to see Vanderpol. We talked about Grace. I told him that I couldn't tell whether I wanted to cure Grace for her sake, or to help me so I didn't have to endure her suffering.

"Well," he said, "it's both, isn't it? We try and help patients out of their misery so we ourselves don't have to suffer it. There's always some selfishness to the healing maneuvers. It's not all altruism."

Chapter 24

Vanderpol drove with his characteristic speediness. We were both preoccupied with our thoughts. During the second hour of the drive, I began to regret that I had taken a vacation. Perhaps I should have used a higher dose of antidepressant, maybe more ECT, I should have more deeply explored her isolation, or gotten her into a more intensive group therapy. I had stopped Grace from buying a piano. What harm would it have done to let her have the thing? She had enough money. She could afford it. I was too focused on her manic disease. I related my doubts to Vanderpol.

"There are a million intervention points with any patient," he said. "When a suicide occurs, you think of all of them at once."

"I didn't let her buy a piano."

"Manic people tend to spend all their money and go broke. You have to protect them."

"So, what would you have done differently?" I asked.

"I. Really. Don't. Know," Vanderpol spoke each word slowly, with the tone of defeat.

"How come I can think of a lot of things and you can't?" I asked him.

"I've been doing this a lot longer than you," he looked over at me. "After a while, you conclude that you can only do so much. We see these patients for what? A few minutes or an hour a day? The rest of the time they're on their own."

"You've spoken with the husband?"

"Former husband," Vanderpol corrected me. "No."

"He must be upset."

"Maybe he's relieved that her illness is over."

I fell silent again. Was my father relieved by my mother's death? I had no idea.

"Almost there," Vanderpol said. We came to our freeway exit and Vanderpol maneuvered the car onto the road toward our destination. We saw the church as soon as we entered the town. It was on the main thoroughfare, an ancient clapboard structure with a spire and belfry, built at the turn of the century. Inside were velvet cushioned pews with an elevated pulpit. Many people had already gathered and were sitting quietly waiting for the service to begin. We headed for the front row where a solitary figure sat. Vanderpol introduced us.

"Please call me Killian. It's so good of you to come," he jumped up and pumped our hands. He was thin and short and wore a rumpled navy suit. "I know, you both tried to help Gracie. I know you did. Poor Gracie, that's what I called her, Gracie. She spoke fondly of you. She was so very difficult to help, though. So ill, so very ill," he said morosely. His distress was disconcerting. I had actually never met him and expected to find a powerfully statured man with a countenance of disdain. I had anticipated finding a husband who would embody the torture of which Grace had for so long complained.

"Do you think she suffered very much in the end?" he wrung his hands. "I wish I could have done more. She called me several times before she took her life. She always wanted to know if I'd found another woman. There was no other woman in my life," he began weeping and collapsed onto his seat. "I didn't divorce Gracie because of another woman or anything like that. I divorced her because I couldn't bear her illness any longer. I could no longer stand by her. I failed her. I just couldn't cope with her illness anymore." He blew his nose and cried pitifully.

Vanderpol and I regarded one another, perplexed and suspicious. Part of our therapy with Grace had been predicated upon the belief that she needed to be rescued from a malevolent entrepreneur who was insensitive to her mental illness. Was this so, and was the man simply putting on an act? Had we been utterly mistaken in our belief? It was unnerving. At that moment, the minister appeared. Simultaneously, an organ in the back sounded forth. The organist began playing a hymn I didn't recognized.

"We have come to cherish the life of our dearly departed Grace Cardigan," the minister began. "She has passed on to a higher place of love and adoration, a place that removes us from the daily toils and hardships of our existence. God in His highest place embraces us with peace and well-being, and soothes our spirits and souls." After almost 30 minutes of biblical chatter and dreary hymns, during which not a word was said either about Grace, her suicide, or her surviving husband, the minister concluded.

"Thank God," Killian murmured as he leaned over to us. "The only good part about coming to church here is reaching the end of the service. I hope you'll both come to my house for the wake. Please, it would be an honor. My home is about five miles away. I imagine there'll be a small cavalcade of cars you can join."

We were the last car at the end of the line which wove through the town and out into the country on a small two-lane road. At length, we turned into a smaller lane which led through a grove of stately trees that opened up onto a set of white fenced pasture where horses grazed. In the distance was a stable and a riding track. Even further away in a clearing, I could see the windsock of an airstrip fluttering in the breeze. The road continued on past a pond and culminated at a sprawling estate. Two manservants approached our car and opened the doors for us.

"Grace's cozy little home," Vanderpol remarked as we walked toward the main entrance.

"Which she's not been to in a long time," I replied.

Inside was a small ensemble with fiddles playing Irish jigs. The dining room table was laden with abundant foods, trays of smoked salmon, shepherd's pies, and corned beef and cabbage. There was a bar featuring Irish beers and whiskeys, and as people drifted in, they immediately headed for it and began drinking. Soon, the room was crowded with mourners laughing and eating. Killian clapped his hands together for silence.

"I'm glad you're all here to celebrate Gracie's life," he said. "I'll start our celebration of Gracie's life by telling you a few stories about her and I hope each of you will tell a story as well. I want to introduce, first, the musicians over here. They're called The Jiggers. Gentlemen?" The musicians bowed and the group clapped with enthusiasm.

"And, of course, we have other kinds of jiggers as well," Killian pointed to the bar, and the mourners again clapped and hooted.

"We also have distinguished guests here today and I want to introduce them. They're Gracie's psychiatrists. Over here," he extended his arm in our direction.

The crowd clapped. Again, I was dumbfounded with embarrassment. Vanderpol waved back halfheartedly.

"Please introduce yourselves to them. They worked hard to keep Gracie alive. And doctors, we're here to tell you that the best medicine is still a good Irish whiskey taken as prescribed." People cheered.

Killian again asked for order and began talking rather poignantly about his former wife, their courtship, their marriage, their relationship.

"A fine, fine woman," he said as he began to tear up.

"To Grace," a man raised his glass and others followed.

We stood silently and listened to a flow of vignettes told by various friends and relatives of Grace as the eating and drinking continued. I was astonished by the details of their recollections. I had felt some intimacy with Grace, but what I knew and felt about her was trivial in comparison with what was being revealed. The musicians started up again. People started singing. Grace's sister, Lilly, came over to where I was standing and introduced herself. For a moment, I was startled by how much she resembled Grace with her sunken cheeks, gray hair, and thick eyeglasses. She wore a polished gold pendant over a black sweater. Grace had barely ever mentioned her sister, yet I wondered if they were twins. I asked her.

"Oh no, Doctor. We always looked alike but that's the extent of it."

"Your mother died some years ago," I said.

"That's right. It's been about ten years now. Mother and Grace never really got along, but I'm sure she talked about this with you. Grace tried so hard to please Mother but she never succeeded. All of her music, the violin, it was all to please Mother, but she never could. Grace barely pleased herself. Pleasing someone else is so terribly difficult, don't you think? I never tried. I think I escaped my Mother's critical nature. It wasn't easy but I married a man who is very understanding and shielded me from her. Mother probably never should have had children. Of course," the sister lowered her voice, "Killian's intention to divorce her didn't help. He tried to be patient with Grace but in the end, he gave up and wanted to move on with his life. I think deep down he really always loved her."

I was flabbergasted. What Lilly was saying didn't jive at all with the picture Grace had painted of her husband. Could I have been that naïve as to not see through her distortions? Did Grace need to see her husband as evil? Was his divorcing her so painful that Grace inverted the act so that she was divorcing him, not the other way around? Did she still love him and was she unable to admit it to herself or to us? I looked at Vanderpol and he furrowed his brow.

"Anyway," Lilly continued, "I should be offering you sympathies. I know you were very fond of Grace and she liked you too. It must be hard to lose a patient."

"You lost your sister," I managed to reply.

"I just had come to the east coast to visit her in her new apartment. I was the one who found her. She had climbed up on a chair and was hanging. It was an awful, awful sight." She looked down shaking her head. "Hanging. Just dangling from a light fixture in the ceiling, just like a rag doll--" She broke off and turned away from me, distraught. When she turned back around, her face was ashen and she dabbed her eyes with a handkerchief.

"I'm so very sorry," I said. "Had she ever made any reference to hanging?"

"Oh no, Doctor, never," she blew her nose quietly "Wait. I just thought of something. I take it back. A long time ago, Grace owned a toy poodle. Owen was his name. She really loved that dog, but one day the dog's collar somehow got caught on a small metal fence in the back yard and he strangled himself. Grace was heartbroken. Absolutely heartbroken. She mourned that dog for months, Grace did. Oh dear, what a memory. Do you think that means anything?"

Lilly's eyes started to tear up again. "Is it true, Doctor, that men and women choose different ways of ending their lives? I recently read this."

"It's true, but no one knows why," I offered.

"I would never think of hanging myself," Lilly said. "I would take pills if I had to die."

This macabre conversation was interrupted by Killian making his way over to us with a glass of whiskey in hand. He was somewhat red faced.

"Are there some folks who get cured of this illness that Gracie had?" he asked.

"It's a tough disease," Vanderpol replied.

"Someday they'll find a cure, though?"

"Let's hope so." Vanderpol commented.

"Up and down, up and down, up and down," Killian said morosely. "Did I do wrong, do you think, by divorcing her? It was a difficult thing to do."

"You didn't," I said, though I wished that he would have stood by his wife rather than discard her as he apparently did. But I knew at that moment this man needed comfort.

"Did I do her in?" Killian now turned to Vanderpol.

"You did not," Vanderpol said.

"I can't help thinking otherwise."

"Survivors always blame themselves. Her illness was severe, and what you did or didn't do hardly affected its course."

"She had a lethal illness," I added.

"Still," Killian trailed off, drinking from his glass.

"You may want to talk to someone about this," Vanderpol suggested.

"Yes, you're quite right." Killian nodded and switched gears as quickly as he had revealed his guilt. "Have you tried the smoked fish? I get it sent to me from Seattle. Three kinds. I like the Sockeye the best. Wonderful stuff. Excuse me," Killian broke off and went across the room to embrace another man who had just entered the house.

"Ready?" Vanderpol dangled his car keys. "But you may have to drive, assuming you've had less to drink than I have." We waved goodbye to Killian who came over and escorted us to the front door.

"Thank you, both of you," he said quite earnestly.

Once inside the car with the noise of the party abruptly excluded, both of us stared straight ahead through the windshield, humbled by what we had just experienced.

"I'm utterly confused," I blurted out.

"Indeed. Who knows the real truth about Grace and Killian? It's quite bewildering."

"I guess men leave ill women," I said. Of course, I thought of Jolene.

"Sure. It seems heartless, but would you have stayed married to Grace?"

"I don't know. Probably not. Not as ill as she was. But there's the marriage oath."

"The marriage oath is generally uttered in a moment of bliss," Vanderpol said. "Reality sets in later and creates many doubts. The marriage vow recedes in significance. Still. Still, one person can do another in as surely as if he had a gun. Mental anguish. It has a morbidity and a mortality. It can kill you."

I thought of my parents. What Vanderpol said was true.

On the return trip, Vanderpol began talking about himself. He'd never spoken of his upbringing in the time since I'd met him and now, he suddenly felt the need to tell me about his father.

"A businessman. Very successful. Killian's house reminded me of our house in Shrewsbury, but without the horses. My father sold scrap metal. Junk. Golden junk. He had the first car crusher in Massachusetts. I used to go down to his place in Dorchester and watch it work. An enormous hydraulic ram pressed two slabs together with a car in the middle and the metal and glass would slowly crumble like a cookie in your fist. My father loved the noise, boasted about it to all his friends. He badly wanted me to go into the business. He saw my choice of medicine as a sort of betrayal. My mother was delighted that I was getting away from the ragged salvage business. She was my main support. A lovely woman," Vanderpol said wistfully.

"And racing cars? How did you get into that?"

"I saved cars from his crusher. Then I fixed them up and raced them."

"He knew you raced?"

"Sure. You can't keep that kind of thing secret."

"Are your parents alive?"

"Alive and well. Yours?"

"Dementia for my father, as I told you. And," I took a deep breath, "my mother committed suicide. I never mentioned this to you. It's haunted me for decades and I'm in therapy for it. I don't know, I wanted to keep my relationship with you a professional one. Perhaps I should have said something sooner."

"My God, Ben," Vanderpol regarded me. "And here we've just emerged from a suicide. It must have really shaken you."

"When I heard, yes."

"How did she die?"

I hesitated for a moment, somehow thinking that if I told Vanderpol, it would dilute the intensity of what I revealed to Templeton.

"It's OK if it's between you and your therapist, Ben."

"I can talk about it," I decided. And it took me the whole ride home to relate my story. Vanderpol was silent a lot of the time except when we neared Sandstone. He reached over and rubbed my shoulder.

"I'm truly sorry, Ben," he said to me. "I had no idea."

"Actually, I had no idea about the complexity of it all. I'm only just working through it now."

"You like your therapist?"

"I do."

"Good," he said. "You have to like your therapist, or at least respect him or her. You don't have to like your surgeon but you have to like your therapist." Vanderpol didn't inquire as to who my therapist was and I admired his sense of privacy.

Sandstone swept into view. I was calmed. I think Vanderpol felt the same.

* * *

I drove straight home to my apartment. A note was stuck in my front door frame. It was handwritten and from Jolene.

'Came to visit, hopefully to have sex with you. Do you miss me? Have you had enough of a vacation from me?' I crushed the note. What would it take, I thought, for her to let go of me? What level of rejection did she require? I was only now beginning to understand and appreciate her pathology, her drinking, her insatiability, her inability to form a comforting union.

There was also a phone message from Ziggy. I hit the 'play' button.

"I've been trying to reach you," he said. "Jesus, I'm really sorry to hear about your patient, I really am. I guess it's obvious she couldn't stand her life anymore. Jesus, you must be really upset, knowing you. Give me a ring."

I returned the call.

"What a horrible event," Ziggy said. "Actually, I've been thinking about suicide. You know, when the results of my research reach fruition, we'll be able to save all these people. It's a question of the right chemistry."

"I know that's what you believe, Ziggy."

"Absolutely. Suicide won't be able to occur. Drugs will block it. We'll wipe out suicide like it was diphtheria. They'll be a vaccine against suicide." I could tell he had been drinking.

"Of course." I didn't have any energy to argue with him this evening. I was too drained.

"I have to meet with Mueller," Ziggy changed the subject. "And they're sending me for a consult with a Dr. Brickman. He's a high mucky-muck, sees troubled doctors. Do you think I'm a troubled doctor, doctor?"

I hesitated.

"You obviously must think so," he challenged me.

"At times," I had to admit.

"Because of my subversive values. My radical views on mental health. My challenge of authority. Am I right?"

"While you were away, Ziggy, I saw one of your patients. Louisa. The poor girl. A tormented soul."

"She'll get over her obsessive nonsense," Ziggy said.

"Ziggy, the girl is tortured. She'll very ill."

"She'll recover."

"It's not so easy," I said. What I really wanted to tell Ziggy was that he didn't seem to care much about his patients. Even though he was fixated on curing mental illness, he seemed lacking in compassion for their suffering, A test tube doctor is what he was. Could I ever say this to him? No, I couldn't, I had to admit to myself.

"This accusation from Melody has really screwed me," he said.

"Ziggy, it's a serious thing."

"I'm not sure I'll agree to see this Dr. Brickman. They can't force me."

"Ziggy, they can force you. We're all here on probation. We're entirely at the mercy of the staff, Mueller, everyone. You know this, Ziggy."

"I can file a lawsuit."

"Claiming what, exactly?"

"Prejudice."

"Huh?"

"I'll have to think it through. Something about my research. They're against me because I prefer research over clinical work." His statement had the flavor of the distortion Grace had felt about her husband.

"Oh boy, Ziggy. This is getting very strange. You're losing it."

"My mice," he now said, "I have to go to the lab. Goodbye."

I lay on the bed and tried to tie together the loose ends of my experience at the funeral, the errors I might have made with Grace, Jolene's fixation on me, and Ziggy's deteriorating course. Would they force him to leave Sandstone? It seemed fated. Would he ever shoot himself with that gun of his? No, he was too absorbed on his experiments. He was too vain a man. Thank God for vanity.

Chapter 25

I saw Sunshine and she somberly announced that she wasn't pregnant. A sense of liberation reverberated within me. Sunshine was a very attractive young girl but she was becoming a woman and I needed to keep this in mind as I treated her burgeoning sensuality.

Ted was smiling. The voices were in abeyance. He looked calmer. I felt triumphant, yet when I asked him to open his mouth, I saw some very slight tongue twitching and knew this could be a side effect of his latest drug. In time, such movements could progress and involve other parts of the body. I therefore, would have to keep him on the lowest possible dose of the drug or change it again, something I was loathe to do in light of his improvement. It wasn't simple, this medication business. The royal road to recovery wasn't very royal.

Dr. Rinehardt had been involuntarily detained by the hearing officer. I was initially aghast at their actions and the mention of suicide. Rinehardt had never said a word about suicide and it seemed to me that his grandiosity almost precluded such an event. Vanderpol was critical of the hearing as well, but qualified the issue of suicide.

"Mueller and Roessinger should have stuck to the facts and not speculated as they did," he said to me. "But you may not be correct about men like Rinehardt being invulnerable to suicide. Very rigidly egocentric folks, like him, can't tolerate any dishonor or disgrace. It can be cataclysmic for them. They can spiral downhill rapidly and shatter. Speaking of grandiosity, you think there's a similarity between Rinehardt and Mueller?"

"Mueller hasn't yet exhibited himself," I joked.

Vanderpol burst into peals of laughter. "Very, very good," he said.

* * *

Jolene called me to say she was coming over.

"No," I replied. "We're done. I don't want to see you again."

"Of course you do!" she insisted.

"Jolene, I don't feel anything for you anymore. I'm sorry."

"Sorry? What are you sorry for? You're sorry we're not having sex?"

I was sitting in a chair and I stood up. "Listen, Jolene, I'm not in love with you and I don't want to have sex with you anymore. It accomplishes nothing."

"It satisfies you," Jolene said. "Tell me it doesn't."

"No. I don't want to be satisfied by you."

"You can't exist without me. Without my body. My luscious body. Admit it." She whispered in a seductive voice.

"I'm going to hang up, Jolene. I hope you have a good life."

"You never cared for anyone except yourself," she yelled at me.

"Goodbye, Jolene. Don't call me again. Goodbye."

"You sick bastard," I heard her call out as I put the phone on the cradle. My heart pounded. What was I scared of? Leaving her? Letting go? Being alone, I decided.

"Man doesn't do well by himself," Vanderpol had once told me. "He needs the presence of another, even if that other is 10,000 miles away, as long as he believes that there is another."

Another. I had no another. My patients didn't count. Ziggy? Vanderpol was another but not an equal another. Would I ever find another? Feeling quite wretched, I showered and dressed and headed to Sandstone. I parked the car and crossed the street to the lakefront. Surprisingly, Ziggy was there, sitting on one of the benches.

"I have something to tell you," Ziggy said as soon as he saw me. He stood up. "Let's walk. But first, I need a joint to get through what I want to tell you."

"Now? Right here?" Alarmed, I watched him extract a freshly rolled cigarette from his chest pocket. "In a public place?"

"Yeah. It's in the fresh air. No one will notice."

"Listen, Ziggy, I don't want to be caught with you smoking pot. The cops regularly park here at this entrance. Why the hell are you doing this?" Christ, I thought, Jolene, and now Ziggy. I was surrounded by rebellious and manipulative beings.

"Just listen," he inhaled deeply.

"No. I will not listen to you. I'll see you later, Ziggy."

"My father was not in real estate," Ziggy spat at me. "He was into pornography. He was a well-known pornographer in Washington, DC. He sold porn. He made films. He was friends with Hugh Heffner, the guy who started 'Playboy' but my father made much more explicit movies. 'Nimble films' was the name of his studio. The government tried to shut him down repeatedly but he hired big time first amendment lawyers and they saved his neck again and again. He had a store on Dupont Circle for a short time but it was repeatedly vandalized, so he closed it down. He didn't need it. He travelled all over the world selling his products. He was peddling porn in Denmark when he croaked," Ziggy paused, "Of a heart attack. I bet my mother was pleased. Anyway," Ziggy exhaled smoke away from me, "the reason I'm telling you this is—"

"Put your cigarette away," I warned. "There's a group of people ahead."

"To hell with them."

"I can't believe what you're telling me, Ziggy."

We walked past mothers and baby carriages. Tag football was being played on a small expanse of lawn near our path. Ziggy resumed smoking.

"What you're saying is incredible, Ziggy."

"Now you can understand why my mother left my father. Who would want to be married to a porn king? A purveyor of smut. My father made it into a big deal with all his freedom of speech crap. It was like he was a saint of civil rights but in the end, he was just a porn king. I think the thing that got to my mother most were the films. The movies. He hired women and men to make porn films. He got friendly with some of them and he would invite them to the house for breakfast or for dinner. Can you imagine having porn stars for dinner? My mother would refuse to cook for them and she would leave the house. Mind you, for some reason, he never had sex with the women. He had this weird sense of fidelity to my mother but he never saw that porn was a massive infidelity in itself. I was a kid all this time. I didn't really understand what was going on, and only later did I figure it out. If you can ever really figure it out."

I was appalled at what I was hearing. Was all this true or was this another fabricated story? I didn't know what to say.

Ziggy went over to the path by the lake and stared into the distance at a motorboat. He ground out the stump of his smoke with his heel and extracted another from his pocket.

"Oh no, Ziggy," I said. "No more. No more weed. I'm going. Goodbye." I headed up the embankment surrounding the path and plowed through the thick pine trees growing on the side. The needles were slippery and at one point, above street level, I lost my footing and began sliding down the hill. I grabbed a branch to stop myself.

"She married Mueller," Ziggy shouted up at me. "She found Mueller and married the bastard."

I brushed pine needles away as I got up. "Ziggy, you've no proof. All you have is a picture and your photograph and a fleeting glimpse of her at a party. That's not proof."

"I've done more research."

"What kind of research?"

"I'll tell you."

"Put down the freaking cigarette," I shouted at him.

"I won't. If you don't want to listen to what I have to say, then leave, Just leave. I don't need your damn righteousness."

A man and woman walked by and regarded us silently as they continued on their way.

"I went to the courthouse in Washington DC and paid to get a copy of Mueller's marriage certificate. Mueller was working at the National Institute of Mental Health then. He's been married twice. His second wife's last name was Harrington before it became Mueller. My last name is Harrington. Don't you see it? I know who she is."

"Ziggy," I grabbed his arm. "Listen to me. I do not want to hear a marijuana inspired story of the hunt for your mother or anyone else. You're getting blotto. If you're so sure of this woman's identity, why don't you confront her in person, for God's sake. I've asked you this before."

Ziggy stared at me for a long time.

"Because," he said.

"Because what?" I demanded.

"I'm afraid," he murmured.

"Of what, Ziggy?"

"She'll reject me."

"Jesus, Ziggy," I grabbed him by the shoulders. "You're a grown man!"

"Or she'll turn out not to be my mother."

"Mother, mother, mother, mother, mother," I hollered at him, then realized it could just as well have been my mother I was yelling about. I started jogging away from him, back down through a line of trees.

"Wait!" Ziggy bellowed.

I ignored him and ran on, up the crest of the walkway towards the parking lot. Looking back, Ziggy was nowhere in sight. I hastened to my car fumbling with the keys and jumped in. As I was backing out of my parking space, Ziggy suddenly appeared by my window, gasping. He knocked forcefully on the driver's pane.

"Open up," he commanded, oblivious to people nearby.

I slowly backed out but he moved to the rear of the car and stood there, his hands on his hips.

"Son of a bitch!" I sprang out of the car.

"I'm sure Mueller's wife is my mother."

"You're crazy, Ziggy. This is an utterly incredible tale. You're ill, Ziggy. You've smoked too much pot. You need help. Get help!"

I was blocking traffic and cars began honking. "I'll find you someone to talk to," I said to him and got back into the car and resumed backing out. "Someone to help you," I called back to him, and sped away.

From my apartment, I called Vanderpol.

"You think he's on drugs?" Vanderpol asked after hearing me out.

"Besides marijuana? No."

"Cocaine?"

"I don't know. He's not high. He's still got this thing with his mother."

"That may be so, but I have to tell you, Ben, that Ziggy saw Dr. Brickman. It doesn't look good,"

"No. I'm not surprised."

"Brickman found a lot of what he called 'unsettling pathology.'"

"What the hell does that mean, 'unsettling pathology'?"

"Personality stuff."

"Like we all have," I said defensively.

"Ben, the man is not cut out to work with patients. You know this. I know you know this," he said solemnly.

"Will they let him resign?"

"I don't know, Ben."

"Dear God," I said. "Dear God, this can't end well, it just can't end well." Misgivings about Grace flashed through my head.

"He's meeting with Mueller this afternoon," Vanderpol said.

"It'll be the end of him."

* * *

Early the next morning, I called Ziggy.

"I'm finished," Ziggy said to me with slurred speech. "I'm finished. Finished. Finished, completely. The man has finished me

344

off. He's killed me. He can't do this to me, Jesus, he'll pay, I have no future left, I'm finished. I'm dead. I'm dead."

"Ziggy, what the hell—"

"Mueller has finished me off," Ziggy screeched. "I have no future left. Do you know what he did? Do you know, son of a bitch, do you know? I'm finished. I'm removed from the program. And my grant is nullified, the bastard called my foundation and told them I was being evicted and they cancelled future funds. He told me to leave, son of a bitch, he told me to get out. I'm finished! Do you know why he's doing this? Do you! It's my mother. He knows that his wife is my mother and the motherfucker wants me far away, as far as he can throw me. He's destroyed me." I heard glass tinkling, then smashing.

"Ziggy, for God's sake!"

"You don't believe me either, I know you don't. No one does. No one does. No one believes me. He told me to take my stuff and get out. You understand, I'm finished," Ziggy shrieked. Something else shattered on the floor. I heard him kick something over.

"Told me I'm not fit to practice, didn't even give me a chance to resign. I'm finished. Do you know what this means for me? Do you? Do you know what it means? The man has killed my career. I'll never get a grant. I'm finished. The man has finished me. But you know what? Do you? Do you know what? I may be finished with my life but his life is over also. Over. He's finished like I'm finished. He's done. Finished. I've made up my mind. A life for a life. He's taken my life so he will have to pay with his."

"Ziggy, don't say these things. Ziggy, please." I was becoming terrified by his dark and sinister ramblings. I knew he was drunk but his anger and revengeful thoughts were frightening.

"It's finished."

"I'm coming over," I said.

"I won't be here," Ziggy vowed.

"Please, Ziggy."

"Mueller told me that I took a patient to a dance. Told me I sinned. Mueller told me that I was no good. No boundaries. I told him to screw himself and he told me to get out. I should have punched him in the face. Wish I had. Wish to hell I had. But it's not over. I have to go now."

"Wait!" I yelled at him as he hung up the phone.

I ran out to my car and headed down Trabian Road. There was construction going on and the route took forever. Traffic crept at a snail's pace and automobiles were backed up for blocks and blocks, horns honking. When I got to Ziggy's street, I double parked, ran up the stairs to his apartment and pounded on the door. There was no answer. I doubled my efforts, calling out to him but there was still no reply. I sat on the floor, helpless.

Then, I realized I hadn't tried the doorknob. Thankfully, it was unlocked. I rushed in. Ziggy wasn't there. I stood in the middle of the room, trying to remember everything Ziggy had said, 'a life for a life.' Then I started looking to find where Ziggy stored his revolver. I yanked open all the cupboards, and then I looked on all his shelves and in his closet and under his bed. Then I finally opened the drawer of his bedside table and there was the plastic carrier box he had bought to the shooting range. It felt empty and I fumbled with the latch. The gun was missing.

I grabbed the phone and called Sandstone. I asked to be connected to Mueller.

"He's in session," his secretary told me.

"It's an emergency."

"Pertaining to a patient?" she asked.

"No. Pertaining to Dr. Mueller. It's life and death."

"Are you a security officer?"

"No! A doctor."

"Shouldn't you be calling security, then?"

"Listen to me," I tried to calm myself down. "Listen. I believe Dr. Mueller is in danger. A man is headed over to your office with a gun. He plans to kill Dr. Mueller. He may kill you in the process. Now put Mueller on the line."

"You seem very worked up," she said.

"Did you hear what I said!" I yelled into the phone. "Dr. Mueller may be shot by a man who is coming with a gun. He may shoot you too!"

"Oh?" was all she could say, and put me on hold. A moment later Mueller came on the line.

"Who exactly is this?" he demanded. "What are you calling about? Who is this?"

"Your life is in acute danger," I said. "This is Dr. Ben Soloway and I think Dr. Ziggy Harrington is headed your way with a gun."

"And why would he do that?" Mueller asked.

"Because you fired him. He thinks you married his mother."

"Poppycock. He is unfit to be a member of the profession," Mueller said.

"He has a gun, Dr. Mueller! You're in danger!"

"Hogwash! I have ordered him to leave this campus immediately."

"Leave your office," I pleaded.

"You are his friend, are you not? What makes you think I am in danger? I will alert security about this situation. If he comes here, they will take care of him."

I was dumbstruck by Mueller's obstinacy and denial. I rang off and jumped into my car and headed to the hospital. I was at a loss and didn't know what else to do. Once again, I found myself caught in the same road work traffic jam as before. I sat there fuming and pounding my hands on the steering wheel. My heart was pumping wildly "Come on!" I yelled out loud. Then I saw a traffic officer sitting in a police car idling by the construction site. I got out of my car and ran up to him and identified myself.

"I have an emergency," I gasped. "You have to help me, it's urgent. I think my friend is going to kill someone! He has a gun and he has been drinking," I shouted. "He said he was going to murder the man that fired him." I was talking as fast as I could to get his attention and to explain the situation at hand.

"Who are you," he asked.

"There's no time for this," I panted. "Please."

"Sir?"

"I'm a doctor at Sandstone Hospital. Another doctor is on his way to kill the director."

The policeman looked me over and grunted and shifted his car into gear. He picked up his radio and called in the details to his command.

I was beside myself with helplessness. I needed to be at the hospital. "Can you plow through this traffic?" I urged the policeman. "I'll be too late. I've got to get there, please help me. I have to do something!"

The policeman activated his siren to clear a path ahead. I jumped back into my car and followed behind him. Cars scattered to the side. We drove through every traffic light, the siren wailing. It seemed to take forever but eventually Sandstone came into view. We turned into the driveway and drove up to the entrance of the hospital. Everything looked normal. The officer turned off the siren. It was eerily quiet and there were no signs of any mayhem. I jumped out of my car and bounded up the grand stairway. There was no one around. I ran down the corridor towards Mueller's office. The door was open. I immediately saw Ziggy inside. He was standing on the other side of Mueller's desk and pointing his gun directly at Mueller's chest. The policeman, overweight as he was, came puffing up behind me, his gun drawn.

"You should stay away," Ziggy said to me with bloodshot eyes. "Leave." His revolver was still trained on Mueller.

"Ziggy, please, put that thing down."

"Sir, put down your weapon," the police officer said harshly.

"Dr. Harrington," Mueller said in a surprisingly calm voice, seemingly oblivious to his own risk. "I demand that you leave this hospital. You are not well."

Ziggy clicked back the hammer of the gun. "You are the sick one, Mueller."

"Give me the gun," the police officer commanded.

"Did you know that your wife is my mother? Did you, Mueller?" Ziggy now held the gun with both hands.

"You are a psychopathic misfit," Mueller growled. "You belong in jail. You are deranged."

"Sir," the officer again started, "drop your weapon. Give it to me now."

"Officer, remove this man," Mueller barked, escalating the situation.

"Sir, did you hear me? drop your weapon," the officer ordered and swiveled his gun at Ziggy.

Ziggy ignored him. "I want to see you suffer," Ziggy snarled. "I'm going to count to ten. When I reach ten, I will kill you," he said sinisterly "I will kill you slowly, though. I've six shots. One shot to each extremity. One to your heart and one to your head. Are you ready, Mueller?" he threatened, giving him a menacing smirk.

I was frozen with fear. "Please Ziggy, for God's sake," I managed to say. "Listen to the policeman. You don't have to do this. Let's talk about it."

"Too late, I'm done talking." Ziggy clenched the gun more tightly.

There was a bang. I jumped. The officer had fired at Ziggy's hand but he missed and the bullet went into the wall. Plaster tumbled down onto the carpet.

Mueller's demeanor abruptly altered as he realized he was in serious danger. He started to tremble. Ziggy began his count. "One."

"Wait!" Mueller said in the weakest voice.

"Ziggy!" I yelled at him.

"Two."

"You'll not get away with this," Mueller whispered.

"Three."

"You're diseased," Mueller hissed.

"Four."

"Let's talk. We can talk this through," Mueller now pleaded. "Perhaps I can talk to the committee to override their decision."

Ziggy leaned over the desk, closer to Mueller.

"Wait," Mueller begged, putting up his hands.

The policeman, who had been slowly making his way closer to Ziggy, now lunged at him. Ziggy abruptly pushed him away and the officer fell on the floor as his pistol flew out of his hand. He scrambled to retrieve it.

"Five."

I moved toward Ziggy who swiveled the gun at me. "Don't," he warned. I heard a noise in the hall and the secretary appeared at the door. She screamed and ran down the stairs. Ziggy and I locked eyes for an instant.

"Six."

The officer reclaimed his gun and stood up.

"I doubt that your research has any worth at all," Mueller said, reclaiming his bravado.

The policeman took a step forward. Ziggy fired at him and he crumpled to the floor. Bright red blood appeared at his shoulder, soaking through his uniform.

Mueller moved his chair away from the desk. "You really are insane," he said with incomprehensible provocation.

"Seven," Ziggy said. Mueller's face was drained of color.

"Eight, nine, ten," he counted in rapid succession. Then he pulled the trigger repeatedly and fired three rounds into Mueller's chest and one into his forehead. Blood and gristle exploded everywhere. A piece of his skull landed on the leg of my pants. Ziggy stood over Mueller, heaving.

"Fry in hell," Ziggy spat. His face was grotesquely twisted. He turned and regarded me.

"Good bye, mother," he said.

He raised the revolver to his open mouth, inserted the barrel, and fired the final shot. The back of his head blew out in an enormous spray as he collapsed into a heap. Blood pulsated out of his brain and started oozing onto the carpet.

Men came running up the stairs. We all stood and gaped at the carnage. For a whole moment, no one talked.

The policeman, on the floor, groaned with pain. I ripped off the buttons on his jacked to get to the wound and tore off my shirt to stem the flow of blood. I started shivering with fright. I'd been too late. We'd all been far too late.

Chapter 26

Bedlam ensued.

Within hours, the news media descended and focused on the disaster for days. Gawkers drove onto the campus of the hospital and were turned away by security. A reporter, wearing a badge pronouncing him to be a physician, tried to gain entry into the Administration Building. A helicopter hovered in the skies above the Sandstone campus and the image appeared on the news that evening. Men and women set up telephoto cameras from the sidewalks on adjacent streets. Journalists attempted to interview patients and staff as they left the hospital. The New York Times ran an article about death in mental hospitals.

Templeton phoned me.

"It is devastating," she said. "You must feel quite awful, I'm sure."

"Coping," I said. "I'm coping."

"You liked the man, I know, as difficult as he was. You'll have to tell me more when we meet, yes?" She rang off. I was touched by her call.

Eventually, the acute sensationalism subsided, but it was followed by a trickle of lurid interest which continued for weeks. There was a barrage of articles about screening for suicide, more gun control, the hazards lurking inside asylums and the potential dangers that the mentally ill posed to the public. Both the local and State police launched investigations during which many of us were interviewed.

To Vanderpol, I blubbered out recriminations. Should I have had a premonition about Ziggy's downhill course? As a psychiatrist, should I have deduced from our visit to the shooting range that Ziggy might have been considering suicide or murder. Ought I to have forced him to confront his mother?

"Ben," Vanderpol put his hand on my shoulder. "Ben, Ben."

"It's unimaginable," I gushed, "except it really isn't, given how much Ziggy hated Mueller and Mueller disliked Ziggy. What a tragic mess. And all over a phantom mother. A horrible catastrophe. What must the patients think? What must everyone think?"

Vanderpol inhaled and exhaled deeply. "Everyone will think it's a catastrophe," he said. "A huge jumble of human errors. Everybody botched it, not just you."

"How will we ever make it right?"

"We won't," Vanderpol said to me. "All we can do is talk it through."

"They'll blame us."

"Of course," Vanderpol threw his arms in the air in a gesture of futility. "Of course. Blame is the antidote for bad outcomes. There can be no random events. For every terrible outcome, there's a watchman at the railroad crossing who failed to prevent the train from hitting the oncoming car."

The patients all thought the worst. They wanted an explanation of how a murder could occur within their hospital. Was the facility that much out of control? Could a psychiatrist become so crazed as to kill another staff member? Should they remain at Sandstone, given the recent chaos? Should there have been more security? Could the deaths have been prevented? I fielded the queries I received as best I could

Sunshine urgently asked to meet with me.

"I'm scared," she told me.

"The whole thing is terrifying," I agreed.

"Is it like an infection?" she asked. "Can I catch the suicide illness?"

"Suicide isn't infectious, Sunshine."

"I read that after Marilyn Monroe committed suicide, a lot of people tried.to kill themselves"

"Yes, that's so, she was very notable. The publicity was enormous."

"What about the policeman?"

"He's OK."

"Could I murder someone someday?" Sunshine gravely asked.

Her question took me by surprise. That a patient might fear becoming murderous hadn't occurred to me. But I could see now that what occurred could make anybody question their own impulses.

"No," I said. "You won't. No."

Sunshine put her arms around herself.

"No," I repeated

"I've been so angry with my mother."

"I know. But not to the homicidal proportions we've just witnessed."

"But it could erupt into homicide."

I thought of Ziggy. Had he precipitously descended into homicide or were homicidal and suicidal instincts residing within his brain all along? And what about my own mother? How long had she wrestled with the notion of killing herself? Sunshine regarded me intently, waiting for my response.

"Sunshine, you're not a murderous person."

"But how do you know?"

Indeed, how did I know? If there was a police lineup to ascertain who would become a future murderer, how could I pick out the right person? What were the tell-tale signs? Sunshine wasn't a stranger to me. I knew a great deal about her. I also knew a great deal about Ziggy and I hadn't figured him as a murderer. I made a vow to be more insightful, more inquisitive, more prescient, more aware of the dark side of men and women. I would ask more questions and probe more deeply.

"I don't always know," I finally answered Sunshine. "We can't read minds and we can't predict all the behaviors of people. Sometimes I can guess. Sometimes I can miss cues," I shrugged, again thinking about Sunshine's sexuality which I had missed.

Sunshine nodded solemnly, somehow satisfied by my answer and the limits of my knowledge.

I asked Ted about his reaction to the calamity that had occurred.

"I guess this stuff happens," he said, without any further curiosity. I took his reply as indicative of his illness which left patients without much sense of social awareness.

Eventually, the days of crises passed. Several weeks after the shootings, a commemorative service was held in the auditorium. All the seats were filled and the overflow sat on extra seats that had been brought in, and even on the floor. Two surprises occurred. First, Jack Vanderpol got up and walked to the podium. He unfolded some notes, smoothed them out, and began to speak. The second surprise to me was that Vanderpol talked not only about Dr. Mueller, but included Ziggy in his remarks.

"A few of my colleagues have asked me to speak about this tragedy," Vanderpol began, "so I've cobbled together some notes and hope they make sense to you all. This tragedy has forever changed the face of Sandstone. It has forever altered whatever naive views we psychiatrists have clung to regarding our patients and our colleagues. We like to think that we can understand people if we try hard enough and spend enough time with them. We embrace the predictability that comes with intimacy. We begin to trust others and we repress any possibility that a patient, or a doctor, or anyone might have a propensity to harm us. And most of all, we see colleagues as largely immune from the ravages of disease that makes patients harm or hurt themselves. Or kill others, or destroy themselves. Who would have thought that Dr. Harrington would kill Dr. Mueller? Or kill Dr. Mueller and then himself? Who could have imagined such a cataclysmic event? Who among us would have envisioned such a violent day on our utterly serene campus? For a moment, we were no better than a war-torn battlefield. People now drive up the street by our hospital and point to it as a place of violent derangement." Vanderpol paused to take a breath. The audience murmured and shuffled about. Tension was high.

"That's where Dr. X killed Dr. Y, people will say smugly, proving to themselves that no place is safe, that psychiatry is as riddled with violence as the streets of the slums downtown. That famous hospital, Sandstone, could not properly safeguard those it agreed to protect. And, if a mental hospital cannot control its patients, who can?" Vanderpol cleared his throat. "We, as healers, are deeply defective, despite our white coats and our psychodynamic insights, our training, and our super special vocabularies and technical terms. In the end, a man, a psychiatrist, we knew, became a vicious murderer, a suicidal killer, a slayer, the man you read about in the papers.

Should we have better screened out the Dr. Harrington's among us? We knew Dr. Harrington was troubled, but perhaps we did not act decisively enough in forcing him to deal professionally with his troubles. Perhaps we should have been more aggressive. Perhaps. There are so many 'perhaps' events we can think about."

Vanderpol shuffled his papers and shifted his weight. He looked around at his audience.

"So now I will say a few words about Dr. Mueller and my comments will surely not sit well with everyone. Dr. Mueller's profile was large. He could be feared, and men who are feared often become victims of anger by others under their rule. The Dr. Muellers of the world are often insensitive to how others react to them."

Vanderpol took a long pause, as if he was deciding whether to continue with what he had planned to say. He was anxious. I had never seen him anxious. He took a large drink of water and glanced up at the clock.

"I come to the most delicate of matters, and that is the motive in this crime. Most of you are undoubtedly wondering what led Dr. Harrington to murder Dr. Mueller. There is a motive that I feel we need to know and learn from as soon as possible. So, I will talk about it, though, strictly speaking, it is privileged information. However, I feel that secrets fester and openness cleanses and heals. I trust what I say here will go no further. Dr. Harrington was erratic in his behavior. He had engaged in a serious boundary violation and he struggled with substance abuse. And he struggled with having lost his mother. It haunted him and he searched for her. Motherlessness can be a terrible disease, of course. What is awful here is that Dr. Harrington did not seek help for his illnesses and his behavior, and no one forced him into a position of being a patient. He was ignored. And he exiled himself as well.

Seeing and knowing about Dr. Harrington, we could have done better. Dr. Harrington was under review, but we may wonder whether that review process was handled correctly insofar as his award-winning research was taken away from him. Was Dr. Harrington given due process? Could his life's work have been salvaged? Was his termination too crushing?" Was it fatal?"

The room was drop-pin quiet.

"The greatest damage facing us now is the damage to our patients. We must take pains to address the terrors and uncertainties that have arisen from this awful event right here on our campus.

"I may have expressed my opinions too openly and possibly disclosed too much. I predict that this horror will be quickly suppressed by conscious and unconsciousness forces, just like our patients who bury their fears and traumas. I feel there should be an anniversary lecture of this tragedy. I suspect, however, that there will not be one because future administrations will want to promote the good name of Sandstone, and it will be upsetting and painful to relive. Bear in mind, however, that we observe other memorial events which pertain to other major losses, World War II being a good example. I recommend we strive to keep the memory of this catastrophe alive in some way, not as a punishment, but as a way of learning about the distressed men and women who come to our doors. And by men and women, I mean caretakers as well. Doctors and nurses. They deserve the same therapeutic interventions that we offer those we label as patients. We must try to mend them before we decide on a dire outcome."

Vanderpol paused, folded his notes and whispered "Thank you." As he looked up and around the room, I saw his eyes moist with tears.

A remarkable thing then happened. The audience stood up and applauded. I myself was swept up by Vanderpol's speech. He had spoken eloquently to be sure, but we were all moved by his candor and outspokenness. The clapping slowly subsided and people surrounded Vanderpol and then moved with him out of the hall. I stood there for a few moments by myself, reflecting on Vanderpol's speech. When I turned around to leave, I saw one person in the back row where Ziggy used to sit. It was a woman dressed in black, sobbing quietly. I threaded my way through the seats. As I got closer, I thought I recognized her from the banquet we had attended at Mueller's house

I sat down next to her. "I'm Dr. Soloway," I said.

"You work here?" she asked.

"I do."

"Did you know this man who killed my husband?" she asked.

"I did, yes."

"Did you know him well?" Her face was drawn and her eyes sunken and mascara stained. The fingers of her hands were tightly interlocked,

"Pretty well, yes."

"Well enough for him to tell you who I am? Who I was?"

At that instant, I was thunderstruck. For all the times that Ziggy had talked about his mother and for all the times that I discarded what he said, here, right before me, was the woman herself, in the flesh, the person who had plagued Ziggy for so long. It was difficult to behold her.

"He told me and I didn't believe him," I sat up in the seat. "I never believed him. You're Ziggy's mother."

Mrs. Mueller buried her face in her hands.

"You knew he was here?" At this hospital?"

360

"I saw a list of the incoming doctors along with their photographs."

"But you hadn't seen him in years. Decades."

"His name and picture were enough. A mother recognizes her son," she said, and wiped more tears from her face.

Her statement seemed so outrageous. A mother forsakes her son and then announces that she could identify him decades later, as if she had been searching for him all along. What popped into my mind was the bizarre question of whether my own mother, if she returned to earth, would recognize me.

"And, and," I fumbled for the words. "Did you want to make contact with him?"

"I was afraid. I was so afraid of him. I was afraid of what he might say to me. He'd blame me for leaving him and he'd hate me. I should have been the one who died." Tears restarted.

Afraid. Two people so afraid of each other that they trembled with loneliness. As least Ziggy did, I wasn't so sure of his mother whom I was meeting for the first time. "We don't need more death, Mrs. Mueller," I said.

"Ziggy," she started to say.

"You left him. There must have been a compelling reason, Mrs. Mueller. Ziggy told me about his father and what he did for a living."

"I wasn't thinking clearly. I was in a terrible state. I had to flee. I just fled."

"Over the years, did you try to reconnect?"

"No, no."

I propelled myself up from the seat and took some steps downward toward the podium. I needed to put some distance between us.

"How do I forgive myself?" she called down to me.

I hadn't the slightest idea. I bowed my head, powerless, thinking that Mrs. Mueller could have saved her son and saved her husband.

"Your husband knew about Ziggy?" I looked up at her.

"Not really."

"He never suspected? He must have known you had a son from your previous marriage."

"He knew that, but he never asked any details and it was a subject we never discussed."

"Never?"

"I kept if from him."

I gaped at her, speechless.

The door to the auditorium opened and Vanderpol looked in, saw us, and shut the door.

"I've repulsed you," Mrs. Mueller said to me.

"It's hard to understand."

"I had no choice," Mrs. Mueller claimed. "I really didn't think I had a choice."

Her assertion bowled me over and I did the thing I never should have done, I turned on her.

"No choice? You had no choice, is that what you're saying? No choice, did you say? In all these years, you could have reached out to Ziggy." I found myself hurling the words at her in a rage. "Found him, sought him out, reunited, something! Not nothing! Not just silence! What good did your stillness do? What did it accomplish? Two people are dead!" I barged out of the auditorium, my mind swirling with thoughts of how affectionless mothers played in my past and present life. Then I walked out of the building and into the meadow, away from everyone. I grabbed handfuls of flowers and shredded them as I walked. Vanderpol came down the meadow towards me.

"Ben," he began as he saw me. "Whom were you talking to? I could hear your voice from outside the door."

"That was Mrs. Mueller. Ziggy's mother."

"His mother? That was really his mother? What Ziggy suspected was true?" Vanderpol was shocked.

"True, yes."

Vanderpol stood stock still and closed his eyes. "It's beyond belief," he shook his head.

"I got very angry with her. I should have offered some solace. I should have kept my emotions in check."

"His mother? His real mother," Vanderpol repeated. "Mueller's wife. Did Mueller suspect his wife was Ziggy's mother?"

"She never admitted it."

"What do you mean?"

"She and Mueller never talked about the missing son."

"This is an impossible story," Vanderpol said.

"I lost control," I said to Vanderpol. "I shouted at her. I blamed her for what happened."

"What did you say?"

"That she could have saved her son and husband. I lost control."

Vanderpol nodded. "You've witnessed a violent homicide and a suicide, Ben. You've lost a friend. This may not be the best time to expect yourself to render sympathy".

"It's a bad dream," I rubbed my eyes. "What should I do? What is there to be done?"

"Ah, Ben. We've no choice except to let the emotions settle."

"And then?

"That's easy," Vanderpol said. "We go on with what we do."

"Just like that."

"Just so. Just so."

"How could she have done what she did?"

"Women desert their babies," Vanderpol stated. "You know that from all your studies but we generally don't get to see or interact with them. Social workers get to see the mothers We see the casualties of their desertion." I thought about the Rhesus monkeys and the wire cloth mother experiments.

"She left Ziggy." I said.

"There was still a father. She didn't place Ziggy in a dumpster. Do we know anything about the father?"

"He was a pornographer. But she was the one who destroyed her son," I said.

"You think so? As your Dr. Ziggy was fond of saying, does not the victim bear some responsibility? Dr. Ziggy sprang to life without his mother and became a doctor and—"

"He was not 'my Ziggy,'" I said defensively.

"You and he were friends," Vanderpol said with quiet conviction. "To the end. You were his Ben and he was your Ziggy. You can't disavow the relationship because he's dead. In any event, Ziggy thrived for a good deal of his life. Then he did some questionable things here at the hospital. He screwed up. And he sure picked a dreadful exit strategy."

"He killed Mueller and not his mother."

"Perhaps a symbolic matricide. Who knows why? Yes, you'd logically think Ziggy would do her in, not her husband. But Ziggy had an abundance of wrath and who knows whom he hated more, his mother or Mueller. And he had all those drugs and alcohol to warp his thinking. Yet, he was a brilliant researcher."

"Like our friend Grace who played a good fiddle when she felt at her worst. It's hopeless," I murmured. "Understanding all these vectors and the causalities is hopeless."

"That's why I race cars. No underlying issues. The fastest driver wins."

My immediate reaction here was that Vanderpol was trivializing the disaster and I felt annoyed with him. In fact, I found myself consumed with anger at everyone in my present and past world. Fortunately, I was due to see Templeton the next day.

"An incomprehensible calamity," she said to me as soon as I walked in.

I remained standing and spouted facts which I'd not told Templeton before.

"Ziggy mother left him when he was a child and he believed she was now married to Dr. Mueller. As it turned out, he was right. Ziggy's mother left the father because he made his living from pornography. She left him and left Ziggy. Ziggy never got over it. That's why he came to Sandstone."

"It would help us if you sat down," Templeton gestured to the chair. "I can only imagine how distraught you must be. What you're telling me is bewildering."

"There's more. Ziggy took a patient, a young girl, off hospital grounds. He smoked pot and drank. Mueller evicted him and reported him to the people who granted him his research funds. His funding was cancelled."

Templeton arched her eyebrows in exclamation.

"Ziggy's mother was at the memorial service. I spoke with her."

"Had he seen her earlier?"

"No. Not since childhood."

Templeton shook her head in dismay. "It's absolutely mystifying, beyond belief."

"I wasn't nice to Ziggy's mother," I said. "I berated her."

"How?" Templeton was frowning.

"I told her that she should have reached out to Ziggy and reunited with him. It might have saved lives."

Templeton heaved a sigh. "I gather that you believe that to be true?"

"I do," I moaned in dismay.

Templeton tipped her cigarette into the glass ashtray on her desk. She paused for quite a while.

"You know, Dr. Soloway, you can so easily turn this disaster into a self-reproaching prophecy which will alter your life. It is like the suicide of your mother for which you have falsely taken responsibility. Be very careful. We don't control the world, let alone many aspects of our own lives. This Ziggy cut his own destructive downhill path, did he not? Alcohol, women, no sense of boundaries. He was severely damaged before you ever met him. We meet these people in our practice and in our daily lives. Little can be done for them. You must absolutely learn this lesson."

"I didn't listen to Vanderpol when he told me to steer clear of Ziggy and I didn't listen to you either," I said to Templeton. "Also," I continued, "there's something I never told you. You never asked about it. At one point, many years ago, I was briefly suicidal. It was after I broke up with a girlfriend."

"And you are telling me this now? Why?"

"I didn't want you to think I was sick. Diseased."

366

Templeton smiled at me. "I have assumed all along that you struggled with suicidal thoughts. The intimate victims of a suicide always do. They think about suicide often, sometimes all the time. They wonder about it. It plagues them. When they're prescribed a bottle of pills, they think about what it would be like to overdose. When they walk over a high bridge and gaze down, jumping springs into their mind. Tall building, pictures of nooses, the exhaust from a car engine, all these things evoke thoughts of death. These things must be familiar to you."

"Some," I admitted.

"And let us not forget loss. Those who have lost heavily frequently think of death as a means of easing the pain. But the issue, lest we lose sight of it, is what you have learned from all this?"

My mind was jumbled. How could I possibly extract anything useful from the chaos I had witnessed?

"Be careful whom you choose to rescue," Templeton answered her own question.

"But I'm a psychiatrist," I said. "My job is to rescue the ill."

"Treat," Templeton corrected me. "Your job is to treat patients."

"Dr. Vanderpol gave the eulogy at the memorial service. He made the point that we should not deport troubled doctors, we should treat them"

"Indeed, treat," Templeton agreed. "Not rescue. Rescue is something different. You rescue a drowning man or someone trapped in a fire or you rescue someone from an automobile wreck. That's it, no more. You do not rework his mind. You do not attack his defenses or deal with his inner fantasies or repair his mood. These things are far beyond the scope of rescue. Your friendship with Ziggy had an ulterior motive. It had less to do with him and more to do with you. You wanted to reform him. You tried to become a parent to him, as you would have wished your mother to be a parent to you. But he seems to have been quite ill."

"I recognized his illnesses," I protested. "I saw him drink. I watched him smoke pot. I saw him take a patient to the country club."

"And, did you at any point distance yourself from him?"

No, I easily concluded.

"Remember, you are exquisitely sensitive to abandonment. The bigger issue," Templeton wheeled back from her desk, "is to learn to distance yourself. In your work, you will find that there are patients you cannot cure, no matter what you do. You must learn to step back from them lest you become entangled and exhaust yourself. The same holds for any relationship. You must discover how to pick people who are sturdy. They may need your help from time to time to share problems with, but they otherwise bring out the best in you." Templeton lit a cigarette.

"You shouldn't smoke," I suddenly reprimanded her.

"Quite so. I am trying to stop."

"Good. Smoking can kill you," I blurted out and just as abruptly found myself weeping.

"I see. And what are these tears saying?" she asked gently.

I was aware that Templeton represented a maternal figure to me. Now that it was almost out in the open, I felt a huge longing and an urge to be hugged.

"Please talk about your feelings," she urged. "They seem powerful."

"To be hugged," I said. "By you."

"Of course. But you will find someone else to hug you. All of this takes time. It takes time for you to mourn the loss of your mother. You've never given yourself permission to grieve, nor have you gone through the process."

I closed my eyes.

"Mourning is hard work," Templeton said. "You've actually picked a profession that specializes in many forms of mourning, while all the time you, yourself, have been tamping down your own sorrow. It's both simple and complicated at the same time, isn't it?"

Chapter 27

Vanderpol and I began taking long walks around the hospital campus and around the lake as part of our daily routine. One night, I'd experienced a dream in which both Grace and Ziggy appeared. They were arguing about the unlikely fact that they were mother and son. Grace was insisting that Ziggy was her son while Ziggy disavowed any such relationship. The argument escalated in intensity, and Grace pulled out a knife and plunged it into Ziggy. I was filled with terror as I woke up.

"Some nightmare," Vanderpol declared.

"Ziggy and Grace never ever knew each other," I said.

"Yet in your dream they obviously did. What did you do yesterday?" he asked.

"Yesterday? I admitted a woman with a post-partum depression."

"Anything unusual about the woman?"

"She had overdosed ten years earlier after her first husband left her," I replied. "Why do you ask?"

"Dreams involve what Freud said was the 'residue of the day.' The dream incorporates the events of the day into events of the past. If you don't mind my being your dream shrink for a moment, I'm guessing that this dream is about you more than it is about Grace and Ziggy. But I may be stepping on your therapist's toes."

"Go on," I urged. "I have plenty to talk about with her."

"So, in this dream of yours, the woman murders the son. Now your mind has to make sense of four distinct events. The first is the suicide of your mother, the second is the suicide of Ziggy, the third is the suicide of Grace, and the fourth is the homicide of Mueller. A lot of death. A lot of dead people, Ben."

I had not considered that my mind could be processing four deaths.

"So," Vanderpol continued, "tell me about the knife."

"A kitchen knife," I said. "An ordinary kitchen knife with a long blade."

"When did you last use such a knife, Ben?"

"I don't own such a knife," I answered.

"Did you ever?"

"Probably, once upon a time. Why?"

"Describe the knife."

"A knife. A regular knife with a black handle and a shiny blade," I said irritably.

"You're getting defensive," Vanderpol observed.

"I am?"

"Your mind is on alert," he said. "It's protecting itself from an attack."

"How can a mind protect itself," I countered. "You speak of it as a discrete entity, like an alien force. Some kind of science fiction monster."

"The mind is something we don't fully control," Vanderpol turned towards me. "It's got a consciousness of its own. It's a foreign power with its own set of rules and it stores feelings and sensations that aren't necessarily within our reach. Hate, love, lust. Forbidden stuff. In your dream, it's Grace who wields the knife, but most likely it's someone else—"

"Who? Who would it be," I cut him off, but in the same instant there flashed into my mind an image of a knife which the waitress at my mother's diner was holding as she talked with me during my visit.

"My mother," I deduced, aghast. 'Plunging a knife into me. It can't be," I protested out loud. "It can't be."

"It's a dream, Ben," Vanderpol quietly asserted.

"A dream," I echoed weakly.

"With disguises," Vanderpol added. "So you don't recognize the darker side of yourself."

"Why would she want to kill me?" I demanded. "Her own son."

"No, no, no, Ben. It's more abstract than that. More symbolic. Your mind interprets the event as symbolic to spare you anxiety. Abandonment becomes murder. Your mother's abandonment of you becomes your annihilation."

The impact of Vanderpol's interpretation made we sway on the path. I bumped into a tree.

"I've upset you," Vanderpol said.

I admitted that I was shaken.

"We're all a little crazy," Vanderpol declared. "And our craziness is reflected in our dreams. That's when our craziness comes out. At night. When we sleep."

We continued to walk. By now, we were on the return loop home. Dusk was settling. I saw the lights of Sandstone in the distance.

"These recent events have been very traumatic for you, Ben. Be prepared to feel lousy for a while." he cautioned as we parted for the evening.

And I did. My work seemed onerous. I took no pleasure in eating and slept poorly. But it all slowly ebbed. The intensity of the debacle faded and crises with other patients replaced my preoccupations. I was thankful.

Mueller was buried at a family plot and I never again saw his wife, Ziggy's mother. Ziggy, according to a scribbled will he had made, perhaps hours before he killed himself, wished to be cremated and buried at Sandstone. His request was obviously disallowed and I never learned where he was interred, nor did I understand his final wish, as he had spent so much of the time detesting the place. Clearly, there must have existed within him some warped attachment to Sandstone, reflective of the love and hate with which we all continually grappled.

* * *

Life slowly returned to normal at Sandstone and people stopped talking about Mueller and Ziggy. The psychiatric department at Yale New Haven Hospital eventually conducted its own inquiry into the tragedy, with the expected finding that there should be more intensive evaluations of incoming psychiatrists, to weed out "misfits" like Ziggy. The search for a new director of Sandstone took the better part of a year, and it turned out to be a biochemist from the University of California named Clancy Sloan. Dr. Sloan gave a lecture on the subject of novel medications which were being developed for the treatment of psychoses and mood disorders. Ziggy would have felt vindicated. Dr. Sloan was a short statured man with white hair and an open face. He smiled a good deal. He made himself a visible part of Sandstone and toured the various halls and expressed an interest in the patients, unlike Mueller, who had stayed isolated in his ivory tower office.

The doctors and staff developed an affinity for him, as we often viewed him walking around the grounds, eating in the cafeteria and browsing in the library. He invited each of the residents for a chat in his new office. It was smaller and had inviting chairs and a couch arranged near his desk. Open drapes ushered sunlight into the office. Pictures of former administrators were replaced by photographs of sailboats, mountain tops, snow covered forests, and family members.

"A pleasure to meet you Dr. Soloway," he said extending his hand. "As you can see, I changed offices. I thought I'd let Mueller's office air out for a few years." He beamed at me. "You have a very good reputation. You know you've entered an impossible profession," he said. "Do you like it?"

"I do."

"And you witnessed the most awful atrocity, which, of course, you never ever expected," he said wavering his hand for me to take a seat.

"It's fading," I said.

"To the extent these things can ever fade," he answered. "Anyway, I'm familiar with Dr. Mueller's reputation, his strong personality."

"He had that, yes."

"Your thoughts, Dr. Soloway, about this place. What this hospital should be?"

I was caught off guard by his candid question. "I think the institution needs to be less authoritarian and more, more---" I searched for the right word. "Gentler, perhaps."

"Less Mueller-like," he nodded.

"Less formal," I added.

"A useful comment, Dr. Soloway. Well, it's one thing to cure a patient and quite another to cure a hospital. We've been quite stuffy, I think. Thank you." He shook my hand firmly.

* * *

In my remaining time at Sandstone, I honed my skills as a therapist and came to see how the human mind could construct its own private and erroneous certainties. What patients believed could bear little relationship to reality. When depressed, a wealthy man would see himself on the brink of financial bankruptcy. An anorectic girl, with the appearance of a concentration camp prisoner, could believe with certainty that the image she saw in her mirror was that of a hideously obese circus freak.

Men and women equally considered themselves evil, exalted, persecuted, and worthy of self-destruction. I learned that the people I treated were incomprehensibly convoluted and that my probing of their thoughts and feelings were feeble and barely scratched the surface of their minds. Friends sometimes asked me what my occupation as a psychiatrist was all about. It was difficult to give them a coherent answer. They could understand a surgeon's work, or what a pathologist or radiologist did for a living. What I did was mumbo-jumbo in comparison. I usually ended up saying that I treated people who were depressed or anxious and tried to make them feel better. Since everyone had experienced a touch of both symptoms, they vaguely understood and accepted my explanation.

When the time finally arrived for me to leave Sandstone Hospital, I did consider whether or not to stay on as full-time staff, but decided that too much had happened to me and that I needed a fresh place to start. I had trouble deciding where to practice. I found fault with every facility I visited. One hospital was too rural, another too large, I didn't like the director of a third and then it occurred to me that the real issue was my leaving Sandstone. I felt like I was deserting the patients. But more painful a thought was that I would miss the place as a whole It had been my home. Finally, I picked a university teaching hospital in Boston, close to where I had grown up. Was I going back home? Templeton remarked that I was.

She was the first person to whom I said goodbye.

I was in her office harboring what are called "termination' feelings. It is said that one must learn to say goodbye in order to say hello, but at that instant I felt a void and blurted out something to the effect that I would miss her.

"Yes, we have done much good work together," she nodded. "So, the therapy is over. Or, should we be more precise, the therapy is interrupted for now. I feel that those who go into our profession should never stop self-examination. Without it, we can become overwhelmed by the illnesses of our patients. And," she continued, "I plan to be around if you ever need to talk. I've enjoyed our relationship. I wish you the best of luck." She rose out of her chair, walked behind me to the door of her office, and shook my hand, albeit stiffly. At the elevator, I looked down the hallway and was surprised to see her still standing there, watching me.

"Try to stop smoking," I called to her.

"I'm doing the best that I can, but it isn't easy," she called back in an uncharacteristic revelation of her humanity.

Next, I saw Sunshine. She had been at Sandstone for a very long time. She was much improved. She had become surer of herself, and less hostile towards her parents and the world. It was our final session and it was time for her to be discharged for good.

"It's been a long haul," I said to her.

"You've helped me. You're the one who has seen me through it. You put up with me."

"You'll miss this place?" I inquired.

"I suppose so, though right now I'm eager to leave."

"Still want to be a therapist?"

"I'm not sure. Maybe. I'm thinking about journalism." She grinned.

"Journalism. Wow. You'll be moving from private to public. What interests you about journalism?"

"My mother said that she thought of becoming a journalist before she went to medical school."

"Ah, you're seeing some good things about your mother. That's good," I encouraged her.

Sunshine gave me the biggest grin. I felt the urge to embrace her. "I'll miss our sessions," I said.

"Will you stay here at Sandstone after you finish the program?"

"No. I'm going to work in Boston."

"There's something I've always wanted to ask you. I never had the courage. Or, I thought it was inappropriate. Anyway, I wanted to ask you if you think you'll get married again."

"Tell me why you ask, Sunshine?

She blushed. "Curiosity."

"About what, Sunshine?"

"Just curious. I hope you find someone to marry again. I'd like to get married someday too."

I accepted her statement, though there was much more under-lying it. Most patients wondered about their doctors but did not stray into the intimacies of their lives. Indeed, when patients failed to show any interest in their therapists, it was often a sign of social detachment or extreme self-centeredness or even autism. Patients wished to ascertain that the doctors had successfully traversed the complex pathways of their lives and were thus qualified to serve as counselors. With Sunshine, there was a respectful attraction between us that made healing possible but I chose not to explore this aspect of intimacy as I was bringing her therapy to a close. She had recovered from her eating disorder and was no longer anorectic. In fact, in the time she was at Sandstone, she had matured, gained weight, and developed into an appealing young woman who would have no problem attracting men. For a moment, looking at her and kindled by the conversation, I felt an inside yearning for the touch of a woman. For months the sensation had been dormant as I struggled mightily with my own preoccupations.

I shook hands with Sunshine, cupping my left hand warmly over our clasped hands to demonstrate mutual appreciation and respect. A single tear made its way down her cheek.

Saying goodbye to Ted was more difficult. His hallucinations had vanished but his emotions were stunted, as one sees with patients who are ultimately diagnosed with schizophrenia. He told me, in a dispassionate way, lacking any enthusiasm, that he had enrolled in a technical school to become an auto mechanic. I asked Vanderpol about his future.

"There are no drugs to make people more animated," he said. "Ted will hopefully soldier on and maybe find a mate, assuming that he can fall in love. Some patients with schizophrenia can't love. That's their calamity."

Ted's father was not pleased. He had loftier goals for Ted and had great difficulty hearing about his son's limitations. Ted's mother was more accepting, but she sensed that the road ahead was going to be difficult for her son.

Leaving Vanderpol was the most difficult. We faced each other, tense with impending separation. He handed me a leather-bound copy of Freud's Introduction to Psychoanalysis. I choked up.

"Someone gave you good milk," he said to me. "I know about your mother. But we get our milk from several sources, so somewhere along the path it came your way. You have a gift of kindness and passion. And competence also. You're blessed with all three." He reached out to touch my shoulder, then fully clasped his arms around me, then hastily disengaged and backed away.

Of course, it had been Vanderpol who had furnished me what he called the "good milk." And Templeton.

"Keep us posted," he added, and then pivoted about and walked back to the nursing station. My stomach lurched with an emptiness that lasted the better part of the day.

Chapter 28

In my new job, as a young assistant professor, I began publishing papers about suicide. There was an enormous literature on the topic. I focused on the aftermath of suicide and how it affected survivors and complicated their lives. I researched more about the urge to die and how it is sometimes rooted in childhood, when the boy or girl sees little value in living and feels overwhelmingly irrelevant to anybody. But I also wrote about the fact that great things could come from great despair, including all things creative and life-changing. That had been Vanderpol's belief. Naturally, I had stayed in touch with him. It would have been impossible to cut the ties with someone who had been there for me during a crucial part of my development, as a person as well as a psychiatrist. We talked regularly, and I sought his indelible feedback for the ideas I was grappling with.

"Ben," he said. "I read your last paper. Good for you. We need as much light shed on this grim subject as possible. What did I read the other day? About 25,000 people off themselves each year. Pretty demoralizing, isn't it. Anyway, I still race cars, but not as well as I used to."

A month later, while vacationing in Maine I got a call from Vandepol's secretary who had tracked me down. Vanderpol had crashed his car while racing and he had not survived his injuries. I was in disbelief. "A lovely man," she was saying to me. "Well liked."

A 'well liked lovely man' was an inadequate description of Vanderpol. He was bigger-than-life and now he was gone. I was bereft. "When is the funeral?" I managed to ask.

"Yesterday," she answered. "A large one. Many people spoke. He's buried in the Meadow. I'm sorry I couldn't find you until today."

"Dear God," I exclaimed, I cut my vacation short and flew back to Sandstone. I hadn't been to the place in three years. A new outpatient clinic had been built, alongside an extension to the Administration Building. I walked down to the Meadow. Fresh dirt at the bottom of the hill came into sight and there was a gravesite marker with Vanderpol's initials on it. I stroked the granite. In that quiet moment, I reflected about the caring wisdom of Hugo, the elephant trainer from all those years ago. Vanderpol had been my caregiver and my brain had thrived in his presence. Or was it my mind that had thrived? Was it even possible to delineate the two?

Epilogue

Years went by and my career began to flourish. Sandstone became a collection of waning memories. As for my personal life, I met an artist whose husband had died of cancer. We dated for a long time and then cautiously, I moved in with her. We came to love one another and married. It took much courage for me to make that commitment, and in odd moments, I would catch myself fearful of desertion. Increasingly, I was able to dismiss such throwbacks to that earlier time in my life.

One evening while watching television, I happened to come upon Sunshine as an anchor woman for a nightly television news program. I was amazed to see her. She was polished and professional and I took pleasure in her obvious growth and success. In my profession, one did not always see such a positive outcome. I thought of calling her but it seemed unwise. She had made the separation from me and I surely needed to keep a separation from her.

A memorial lectureship was eventually established at Sandstone for Grace. It was funded by her husband. I was invited to be the first speaker and I talked about some psychological effects of suicide. I covered all the customary topics, such as what the risk factors were for suicide and how to handle the guilt that inevitably arose within the survivors. What I didn't quite know how to accurately describe was the almost telephathic powers one needed in order to predict